The Rift

Rachel Lynch grew up in Cumbria and the lakes and fells are never far away from her. London pulled her away to teach History and marry an Army Officer, whom she followed around the globe for thirteen years. A change of career after children led to personal training and sports therapy, but writing was always the overwhelming force driving the future. The human capacity for compassion as well as its descent into the brutal and murky world of crime are fundamental to her work.

Also by Rachel Lynch

The Rift

Detective Kelly Porter

RACHEL LYNCH

THE RIFT

CANELO CRIME

First published in the United Kingdom in 2021 by

Canelo
31 Helen Road
Oxford OX2 0DF
United Kingdom

A CIP catalogue record for this book is available from the British Library.

Print ISBN 978 1 80032 405 3
Ebook ISBN 978 1 80032 105 2

Look for more great books at www.canelo.co

Printed and bound in Great Britain by Clays Ltd, Elcograf S.p.A.

Chapter 1

Major Helen Scott made her way to the embassy on foot and took it slowly, not wanting to work up a sweat before she got there. The Paris summer was desperate to stick to her clothes, and she was grateful for the breeze that made her shirt billow and her hair waft. She wore large sunglasses and watched oblivious strangers from behind. She was fairly small of frame and, if asked, a passer-by would never guess her line of work. She dressed like all those who worked in any international police force: as Mr and Mrs Grey. Her wardrobe was made up of dark trousers and light shirts, as well as bland jackets, to conceal weapons when needed. Her hair was light brown from the summer sun, and she only tied it back when working in the field, which, thanks to her success, she hadn't done for a while. She wore little make-up: a little mascara and lip gloss, and a few sprays of her favourite Jean Paul Gaultier. At thirty-five, she felt at the height of her employability and walked with easy confidence.

The district was a smart area of the city, full of young, upwardly mobile couples, cool families determined not to leave their fancy apartments for the suburbs once children arrived, and diplomats. The tall white sandstone Haussmann buildings provided shade, and she peered up to the balconies above, typical in their style and reminiscent of the upmarket Palermo district of Buenos Aires, where she'd stayed when she'd worked in close protection for the Defence Attaché there. Most, if not all, of the ornate iron-barred platforms were decorated lavishly with lush greenery and summer flowers, and a heady scent wafted down to the street. She wondered what it might be like to live here and lead a sedentary life for a while as she ambled past the trees planted every couple of yards, offering further shelter and cooler air under their canopies.

Always alert, she absorbed the lay of the streets – their corners, doorways, places to lurk undetected – and the cars driving too slowly. Few people walked the pavements, not only because those with any sense left the city in these hot summer months, but also, this wasn't a tourist area and no one strolled about, taking pictures or seeking restaurants. It was a residential and business district. On streets such as this, Paris took herself seriously.

Upon arriving at the ambassador's residence, next door to the embassy, she checked both directions flanking the mighty doorway, and buzzed the intercom. She waited, clocking a car approaching down the street. It passed. The outer door opened, and she stepped inside, where she was greeted by a security guard, who allowed her to enter into the initial security checking area. She handed over her belongings and passed through the body-screening stand, which showed up any metal objects hidden under her clothes, as well as if she had a colostomy bag or prosthetics. It was standard. A quick body search followed and then signing in, scanning of passport and retina login. Once through, she was handed back her possessions and was escorted to a large hallway to sit on a Chesterfield sofa to wait to be called into the ambassador's private office. Officially he worked next door in the chancery, but in reality, he spent most of his time in here, at the Hôtel de Charost, surrounded by lavish rococo and baroque furniture and antiques.

Sir Conrad Temple-Cray was an officious man who kept time, and it wasn't long before she heard doors opening and the swish of air created by a man with intent. The diplomat had a long and illustrious career with the Home and Foreign Offices, and Helen had come across him several times in a professional capacity. His reputation was well earned and despite finding him eccentric, she respected his office.

'Major Scott,' he boomed, his voice echoing off the marble interior. He extended his hand, and she stood to take it, matching his strength. He looked her in the eye and nodded. His skin was tanned, and the wrinkles etched deeply into the sides of his eyes and cheeks gave him the air of a smart grandad. He wore tweed – despite the weather outside – and corduroy trousers, together with a crisp white shirt and bright tie, no doubt bought by his wife. It was every civil servant's nod to individuality: a few flowers and stripes here and there.

He led her into one of his no doubt numerous reception rooms, where there was a desk, filing cabinets and a vast bookcase covering one wall; she guessed this was where he worked. It was chilly inside the old chateau-style building but it was a welcome change to the temperature outdoors. She knew they'd take afternoon tea on the lawn, so she made the most of the cool air while she could.

'Great job,' he said.

'Thank you, sir.' She wasn't sure if he was referring to the report she'd submitted on his security set-up, or simply the fact that she'd turned up. One never knew with ambassadors: they didn't have to divulge anything. She'd been sent by the Ministry of Defence to conduct a security review for the upcoming NATO summit that was being held at the Palace of Versailles the following week. As an officer in the Royal Military Police, she'd found herself between permanent placements, which came up every two years. It was up to her desk officer in Glasgow, who managed all the careers of majors in the army, to find her ever more challenging posts to match her skill set, with one eye on what might make her next annual report stand out. Reporting to ever-changing chiefs, depending upon her secondment, was part of the allure.

She looked around his office, at the paintings adorning the walls, the leather furnishings and the silverware – probably stolen from India. It was the same with any ancient government institution grounded upon the great British Empire: the trappings followed the victories. She scolded herself for her cynicism, something that she was slipping into more frequently. Not for the first time did she wonder if her time in the military was finished. She'd thought that the Royal Military Police might be different, somehow less accountable for the misery suffered around the globe, but lately, she'd realised that they all worked for the same people.

'You're confident that we're back up to scratch?' he asked.

'Yes, sir. I was most concerned with the routines set by the drivers – they tend to stick to their favourite routes, and it's easy, here in Paris, to forget the threat level. Having said that, your personal bodyguard is excellent.'

'Sit down.' He motioned her towards a chair and he sat behind his desk.

She felt distinctly examined, and she shifted in her seat. Suddenly, the cool air brought no comfort. Her position at the MOD main building in Whitehall was liaising with MI5 and MI6 about intelligence received around the globe, most notably Five Eyes, a multilateral operation between the USA, UK, Canada, Australia and New Zealand. From there, they decided who to share information with. Recent intelligence had come out of Madrid and was on the radar of MI6; it detailed a potential threat from Morocco. It was a well-worn path: disgruntled nationals from the old French colony plotting the downfall of a Western power.

Sometimes she missed her role as a junior military police officer, investigating wayward soldiers who broke the law. But promotion brought desk jobs, and that's how it worked. It had taken all of her time at the MOD to shake the misconception among other regimental staff that the Military Police were only out to expose everybody for sleeping with their secretary or being thrown out of a nightclub. It was a lonely world.

Trust was relative.

But Sir Conrad only wanted her expert opinion, and her time in Paris had at least, in that capacity, been a breath of fresh air. In many ways, she was forlorn at the prospect of returning to the UK. She was more comfortable when her unique abilities, learned through a wealth of courses offered to the Military Police, were exploited. That's when she felt useful and worthy, if a little embarrassed, of her nickname, Wrench.

'This intelligence from Five Eyes – it's a good source. Did you discover any breach on our part? I believe that the focus was on drivers in Madrid, no?' he asked.

Sir Conrad seemed jumpy. Perhaps it was the summit. It was a huge moment in his career. He was to personally host the group from Afghanistan. The summit itself would be attended by heads of state, but after the main event, Sir

Conrad was to chair talks with the Afghans about their ongoing security needs.

'No, sir. I don't believe you have a problem with your locally employed staff here in Paris,' she reassured him. 'There's an elevated threat level across the whole of Europe, and we've had no specific intelligence on Paris, just, I believe, an increase in activity across the sea border between Spain and Morocco. Traffic between the two continents is always on high alert, especially at that particular border point between Spain and Portugal because of the amount of cash and drugs that change hands. I believe it's Interpol's role to deal with drugs and trafficking?' It was prudent for an ambassador of his calibre to take a wider interest in intelligence, but she wanted to know why he seemed so unnerved.

He waved his hand around and got to the point. 'It's more specifically the fact that one of the main players in arms and narcotics dealing from North Africa has been on the move lately, and it's making the Americans nervous,' he said.

Ahh, so this was the source of his concern.

'Yes, Fawaz bin Nabil,' she said. The CEO of Nabil Tradings Incorporated had been flying in and out of Madrid recently, raising more than a few eyebrows. Nabil was under surveillance by the Americans, but so far nothing had linked him personally to illegal arms dealing, which was, after all, made completely legitimate once one signed off the correct paperwork. The problem was that he was also suspected of being responsible for Morocco's most lucrative export: the finest hashish in the world. Toing and froing between continents was an audacious move, but it was the job of Five Eyes to get to the bottom of why such a prominent player would risk travelling between Africa and Europe so brazenly.

Fawaz bin Nabil was the kind of player who kept his own hands clean and had several layers of foot soldiers carrying out his work on pretty much every continent. The guy was a billionaire oil and gas magnate and would go to bed with whatever countries offered him the best trade deal, no matter their track record. He also dealt in stocks, bonds, textiles, electrical goods, fertilisers and fruit. He was a slippery sucker who touched nothing personally that an international authority could do much about. Of course, the US wanted to wade in there regardless, getting rid of anyone who was worth more than they were and seemed to have more sway over the big boys of the Middle East, but they also knew that it could potentially spark a costly and highly damaging war. So, they kept him under close scrutiny. Fawaz upping his activity in Europe was something that made heads in London and Washington turn. Was he up to something? Not directly associated with terrorist links himself, the chance that he was at least arming them was something that Counter Terrorism was also aware of. Perhaps Sir Conrad was privy to information that she hadn't seen. In her briefing the previous day with the Military Attaché here in Paris, Colonel Palmer, he hadn't mentioned the ambassador's heightened unease. But then her history with Palmer was messy and their relationship tense.

The ambassador was clearly angling for her ear, and Helen just wished he'd come out and say what he wanted. The rumble of the air-conditioning unit caught her attention, and she watched as Sir Conrad clasped his hands together in a bridge and glanced at the window deep in thought.

She was thirsty and wondered when she'd be offered a drink. His prevarication distracted her and her mind turned to her parents and the last time they'd seen each other. Things hadn't been the same since she'd told them the news about Luke.

Of course they'd been sympathetic – she still remembered her mother's cries – but it was more the fact that Helen couldn't face them for weeks afterwards. It had driven her away again as she looked for roles as far away from the UK as she could, to avoid the constant barrage of questions about her health and state of mind. In their opinion, the best thing for her to have done was leave the military and seek a more 'domestic situation' as her mother put it. After all, what sane, healthy woman chooses to join regiments of soldiers around the globe, putting herself in harm's way, just because every regiment on active service needs a Military Police attachment that any qualified man could fulfil? In fact, her career was the only thing keeping her going. Perhaps she was hiding behind it. The air-conditioning whirred, and she waited. She became aware of the pulse in her wrist; the blue bulbous snake throbbed and she realised that she was anxious. Any thought of that period in her life, when everything had stopped and settled for a while, resulted in the same flow of adrenalin. It was a glaring irony that she'd rather face hostiles than her past.

She knew one thing: ambassadors were political beasts, and Sir Conrad's motives would always be driven by self-preservation. The door opened behind them and she turned her head to see Colonel Palmer enter.

Here we go, she thought. 'Sir,' she greeted him and stood up. Her anxiety raged anew; she figured that she'd made some terrible mistake in her reporting and she'd missed a huge security breach, somehow related to Fawaz bin Nabil. She tried to conceal her elevated breathing.

Palmer nodded to her, and the ambassador beckoned him to take the seat beside Helen. They all sat and Helen crossed her legs, wishing for her own desk in the MOD, rueing the day she'd decided to throw herself into all that the Military Police offered a career-minded officer. Her head craved something simple, like investigating an infantry squaddie stealing Yorkshire stone from graves: a straightforward case attracting the wrath of a platoon of simple soldiers. The worse that could happen was you'd be called a 'monkey': a slur that might be confused as racist, but it wasn't, it was because the RMP were always on your back.

It was no secret to those who knew both of them that she and Palmer held each other in utter disdain, but the ambassador didn't know that. However, it was the colonel who had the ambassador's ear here in Paris, and while she was here, it was Palmer who she reported to, as her military senior. She braced herself for a brushing down. She was convinced that she'd missed something. Her eye had been off the ball since Luke. She cursed herself and resettled her sights on early retirement.

It was the ambassador who spoke. His stance more relaxed, she noticed. He had a fellow dick-swinger here, that's why.

'Everyone knows what you did for Ashraf Ghani, Helen.' He let that gem sink in.

Helen swallowed. This wasn't what she was expecting.

'Let me explain,' he carried on. She no longer heard the whir of the air-conditioning, just the blood rushing past her carotid artery in her neck.

'One of the objectives of the NATO summit is inviting members of the Afghan government to attend to discuss the Resolute Support Mission.'

'Yes, sir.'

'At the summit, Ghani and four senior figures in the Afghan government are meeting with NATO and the American special envoy at the Palace of Versailles for three days to discuss further US funding of the RSM in Afghanistan. As you know, the mission aims to transfer Afghanistan's national security back into its own hands. The UK, NATO, and of course, the hosts, France, will all be represented. Yours truly is the chosen candidate for the UK. After the cameras have stopped flashing and the prime minister and the US president have gone home, I'm in charge of these sensitive negotiations. The poppy harvest has been increasing steadily for years, despite the best efforts of the United States to curtail it, and Fawaz bin Nabil benefits immensely from instability in the region. His recent increased activity at the Spanish–Moroccan crossing could be linked to making sure the talks run the way he wants them to.'

'In other words, derail the Afghan government's efforts to curtail Taliban profits?' she asked.

'Exactly,' Palmer spoke, taking her by surprise. Was he on her side?

She gathered her thoughts. 'With respect, sir, the Americans have been at Versailles for the last six months. Security around the summit is second to none. Have they shared any intelligence relating to Fawaz? Has he any historical links with anyone attending the talks? Is MI6 sending a team, sir? Or the Foreign Office?'

'Yes, yes, of course, we know that. But I want my own reassurances. The Americans have their eye on their president – rightly so – and we commend that. There was no intel when you led Ghani away from his vehicle along with the UK's ambassador. How did you know?' he asked her.

Helen looked at the ambassador and to Palmer. She didn't know what to say. How did she know that a bomber was about to blow up Ghani's car and target the British ambassador? Instinct. But that was an insubstantial quantity and couldn't be reported on or measured. She felt foolish.

'Sir, I can only tell you that I'd been working with the ambassador in Kabul for some time. It was my sixth year in close observation and close protection. I'd made the usual connections on the ground with US personnel, embedded informers and the like. I noticed that the day Ghani was hit, his head of personal security went on holiday, which was highly irregular because he was due to attend the NATO talks in Kabul. She later turned up dead with her interpreter. My security brief for the day itself was rejected last minute by a Northern Alliance minister, who I knew had links with Pakistan in the past.'

She paused.

'You mean, you worked it out and nobody else did?' Sir Conrad concluded.

She was aware of Palmer shifting in his seat. It dawned on her why she might be here: Palmer had been overruled.

'I was still too late, sir. Ghani nearly died of his wounds.'

'But he didn't. I want you to stay in Paris,' the ambassador announced. 'You'll take over security for the summit, liaising with the US ambassador's office here in Paris to check what they've done at Versailles. Meanwhile, it's been arranged for you to have access to everything they share with Five Eyes directly. I don't want anything missed. You did a good job here, Major Scott, and I've read about your background. It's all agreed with the MOD, you're to stay here until the summit is over.'

'Clear, Major?' Palmer asked.

Helen stood up. 'Sir,' she replied to her senior officer before turning to the ambassador. 'I'm happy to fulfil any role you see fit, sir.' She nodded to Sir Conrad.

'Superb. Now, let's have tea in the garden.'

Chapter 2

Khalil drove in through the double iron gates to his home, which opened majestically onto a long driveway adorned with palm trees and exotic bushes and plants that were all quenched by a modern irrigation system, designed to keep them watered and voluptuous to the eye. The canopy provided shade and cooler air, and Khalil lowered his windows now he was in the safety of his own estate. He loved driving with the windows down but knew that out and about in the city of Algiers, it was inviting folly. Once stopped at traffic lights or waiting in a bottleneck, it took seconds for a gun to come through the window and demand watches and other saleable booty. It happened all the time, and with the cars Khalil drove, he was a four-wheeled advertisement for wealth.

He loosened his shirt and smiled as he completed his journey and pulled up outside the main house. Its façade was bright white, with windows framed in a sandstone brick. The huge front door was made from mahogany, but Khalil didn't go through it, but walked round the back instead to where he could slip in through one of the many rear entrances. His wife was likely out with her friends, either shopping or taking tea, and he thought he might jump in the pool before starting work. It was a joy to have it all to himself, and with the boys at school, and his eldest son, Hakim, safely back at university in Paris, Khalil was finally able to relax. He'd even sent his personal bodyguard to accompany Hakim for added peace of mind. He threw his jacket onto a chair and headed to the pool house, where he had a wardrobe full of swimming attire. He stripped off and folded his clothes neatly. He was aware of two or three of his household staff going about their daily business of tidying, washing, cleaning and laundering, but he had no cause to speak to them directly. If they crossed paths, he'd greet them politely and perhaps enquire after their families and their wellbeing, but that was it.

He dived into the deep end and came up like a great sleek dolphin, resplendent upon resurfacing for air. The water was a tonic and he swam lengths underwater. His dark skin glistened as he moved effortlessly through the water. His breath was regular and strong, and he paused after five lengths, hanging on to the side and catching his breath. He leant on the stone, dangling his legs beneath him, and looked over the city below, beyond the magnificent infinity pool. The breeze up here was balmy, and he felt at peace as he stared over the Bay of Algiers.

His thoughts turned again to his eldest son, and how he looked when he'd been told that he was returning to Paris early. Khalil's men liaised with senior members of the Parisian police, who had their wages topped up solely for the purpose of looking out for his son. Khalil was confident that it was the right decision to send him back. Here in Algiers, one expected threats, bribery and corruption. In Europe, things were different, apart from the odd backhander. Most of the people he worked with over the other side of the Mediterranean had never seen bloodshed. They were like porcelain dolls: unsullied by pain. Here in Africa, history was pain. Struggle was blood. Progress was unjust. He didn't want for Hakim what he, or more so his father, had endured as a young man. And he was in the fortunate position to make sure that was the case.

The War of Independence, almost sixty years ago, had provided many Algerians with new opportunities, and his father had been a shrewd man. A chance meeting with an old friend informed him of a vast swathe of abandoned land – uninhabited for a decade since the French family who owned it had disappeared in the 1950s – and suggested a business deal. Khalil's father, being a risk taker and a man of his curiosity, said yes.

They literally struck oil. By the time his father had died, he'd left Khalil an empire worth billions of US dollars.

Khalil pictured his father's face: deep wrinkles pitting his face, dark brown skin under a traditional brightly coloured turban. He rarely saw his father out of his ancient Berber dress, even though he'd once been beaten in the street for it by a French soldier – a story his father never mentioned but his mother told him. He wore it till his dying day. Inside the house, a portrait hung, an oil of huge dimensions, depicting the great man sat underneath a palm, surrounded by indications of wealth and status. It was positioned so that anyone visiting or working inside the house had to walk past it and admire its power.

Khalil swam for the ladder. He had an office in town, but worked mainly from his study in the house. It was as large as the main reception room overlooking the pool. The huge barbeque area dominated the outdoor space, and that's where they ate mostly as a family, with their cook preparing various meats (except pork) marinated in spices and tomatoes and skewered on to metal spikes over charcoal, eaten with flatbread, the juices dripping onto vegetable couscous and cooled with yoghurt.

He took his towel and dried off, wrapping it around his body, which was hard from training sessions with his personal trainer who came to his private gym every morning at six a.m. Taking care of his body had become more of a priority after a stroke stole his father away, as well as turning fifty this year. He took his clothes and walked towards the house, his head full of the meetings and phone calls he had to attend to today. He took his pile of clothes to the laundry room – he was the only member of the family who did this – and left them there, making his way to his private bedroom suite. After his shower, he changed into another pair of suit trousers, with a crisp white shirt, and finished his attire with cufflinks and expensive cologne. He didn't wear a tie.

His office was situated next door to his private rooms and was accessed by an adjoining door. One wall was entirely constructed of glass, enabling him to overlook the sea when he lacked inspiration or needed to take a deep breath. He had everything he needed to conduct his affairs, venturing into the sweltering city only when he had to. Not that climbing from an air-conditioned car out into a shaded parking lot underneath his headquarters was onerous or taxing, it was simply that he preferred the comfort of home. Meetings in the city were usually over a luxurious meal or a hospitality evening at the racecourse.

The house was hushed – he preferred the maids not to talk – and he went to the vast kitchen to make a coffee in the machine. He'd only begun to drink it when his business took him to the United States and Europe decades ago, tasting the bitter liquid for the first time. He was attracted to the sophistication of the ritual and the way that Europeans spent time savouring the frothy milk, sugar and small biscuits that accompanied the dainty cups. He always took water with his, like the Italians. He looked at his watch: the drive to the airport had meant a late start and his stomach rumbled as he realised that it was gone lunchtime. He'd lingered at the airport, not to see off his eldest son but to check details for the shipping of some of his containers bound for the French port of Marseilles. The border police headquarters was at the port of Algiers, but they had offices at the airport as well. He met with customs officials and had been offered light morning snacks with tea.

Ordinarily, he would have tasked the job to some-body else but recent developments spurred him to take control of the arrangements himself. A former associate had made contact with him recently, expecting him to offer his services for old times' sake. He'd been wrong. Khalil's operations might have dabbled in the grey world between international law at various points over the last few decades, but he'd found that adhering to multinational boundaries and agreements was better for the future of his company, than other, less transparent methods. This is where he broke the mould in African commercial circles: he had moved his company away from the shackles of warlords and corrupt politicians trying to shape him into something they could use and play with as a puppet. And that is why he actively encouraged Hakim to spread his wings, even if it was in the capital of the country that had tortured his father. Success was constructed not grabbed. He hadn't come this far, securing deals with Europe and the United States, to lose it all because he was found to be in bed with the last straggling factions of revenge politics.

This is precisely what made him vigilant and nervous at the same time.

Putting his coffee on the counter, he went to nose about in the fridge. Each one of their maids was also trained as a splendid cook and they prepared all meals, leaving in the fridge a veritable gold mine of carefully wrapped leftovers. He tucked in to crispy spring rolls and a chilli dip.

One of the maids entered the room and apologised. 'Sir, you are hungry? Why didn't you say? I'll make you some tortilla.'

The problem with good cooks was that they wanted you to eat their food. It was why he needed a personal trainer to keep him in shape, otherwise he'd roll about his office, eating all day long if he allowed them to indulge him. The problem with trained cooks is that they want to feed you every minute of every day. His wife, Taziri, was on the hefty side, but Khalil liked it that way: he had no desire for skinny European women who played with their food rather than ate it. And, of course, the boys burned off every calorie they consumed playing sport at school, frolicking in the pool or cycling with their friends (closely observed by security teams, of course).

He thanked the maid and went back to his office, but he'd only been in there for a few minutes before he heard voices and looked up. A different maid walked towards him with a member of security behind her. They both looked perturbed and Khalil wondered what might be upsetting them. Perhaps a beggar had tried to breach the wall again.

'Is there a problem?' Khalil wasn't one to mess around or circumvent news that might not be to his taste. He dealt with problems every day of his life. Khalil read the guard's face: it was grave. Khalil faced him squarely and waited. The man fiddled with his earpiece and avoided direct eye contact.

'What is it? Tell me now.' Khalil was commanding and didn't like to waste time. If someone had something to say, they'd better just come out and say it.

'Sir, it's your son, Hakim. He's been taken. He disappeared from the airport, shortly after landing in Paris.'

Khalil's legs went weak and his heart began to race. He felt sweat above his eyes, but the room was cool. His head became a giant, heavy bubble and the security guard's voice sounded as if he was underwater. Khalil tried to speak but found opening his mouth and moving his lips difficult. The sensation of hot searing fear lasted mere seconds and all the details of the room and what the guard was saying assaulted him like some awesome awakening. He stood in front of his desk, his hands shaking, trying to take in what he was being told.

'Jean-Luc?' He gasped.

'Jean-Luc is nowhere to be found.'

Chapter 3

Ten miles outside the city of Marrakech, away from the crazy souks, the peddlers shouting in the street, the sweltering heat, exacerbated by the endless huddle of bodies pressing against one another as shopkeepers tried to steer tourists to spend their dirhams, life was more peaceful. The isolated little oasis in the desert offered succour to those who visited, in the form of grand empty spaces, luxurious pools, lavish decor and warm hospitality – if one was invited, of course. Armed guards patrolled the walls and roofs of the property, and below, specially selected officers vetted anyone hoping to get an invitation to stay. As the sun gave her last rays of the day, the temperature began to fall and an orange glow was cast across the estate. Everybody present was there upon request, though perhaps some of them might not have wanted it that way.

Fawaz bin Nabil was not in a good mood.

He sat on a low sofa next to one of the pools, leaning forward, with his elbows on his knees and his hands supporting his chin. It was a contemplative stance, but also one of displeasure. Those present had seen it before. The cleverly engineered walls and gaps afforded freedom to the breeze, but didn't serve to soften the ambience, and the orange glow of the setting sun reflecting off pillars hand decorated with pieces of coloured glass, twinkling cheekily, did nothing to soothe him. They all waited.

Fawaz was an unassuming man by sight, shy even. He spoke quietly. Every move was deliberate. And yet he commanded the respect of those far senior in age who accompanied him, and in that capacity, he left his mark on anyone who met him. He also had a generous smile, when it suited him. At the moment, it did not.

A maid brought freshly squeezed juices, bowls of sweets, breads, dips made from aubergine and spiced with cumin, aromatic tea and pomegranate sorbet. The liquor was already out on the glass table by the pool, and the guests had been partaking now for four hours. Despite the heat of the day and the proximity of the Sahara, the shade afforded by the huge canopies alongside the gentle music wafting from the speakers – designed to calm one's guests – was not working on Fawaz himself. The northern edge of the Sahara burned into the white walls, and during the day, the incessant heat was enough to drive a man crazy. But not here in the riad. Curtains made of silk and muslin bellowed gently, adding to the illusion of the coming night being refreshingly breezy. It wasn't, but in surroundings such as these, one might dare to believe. Repose was easier when surrounded by luxury.

Not that Fawaz noticed it anymore. He'd grown used to the profits of his business. There was only so many houses, cars, women and gold one could buy before one became anaesthetised to its allure. For most of the time, unless there was a party and guests attending from neighbouring Marrakech, the empty pools didn't ripple, the kitchens didn't grill, the outside ovens stood cold, the petals in the fountains rotted and the incense in the lamps went rancid. He'd become a vessel, travelling for the sake of the movement rather than the journey. He'd always found it hard to sit still, and he stood up suddenly, compelled to move about, bringing confusion and even fear to his guests. They were all men. Sometimes, Fawaz provided girls from town, or willing tourists picked up in bars – and there were plenty of them eager to see the inside of a rich man's palace and partake of free hospitality and drugs all night.

He visited his children elsewhere. Fawaz had got rid of his wives years ago. He'd had seven. They all lived with his various children in decent enough apartments of their choosing across Marrakech, and that was where he arranged his visits with them. Here was his own space; private and away from the prying eyes of those who wished to ensnare him. Here, he could hide away, safe in the knowledge that his nightmares went unheard, and his escape into the world of regret and revenge remained a secret. It was also where he conducted his business. But in recent years, his focus had taken a different turn, and he would never again embroil one of his children in the true nature of his commerce.

So apart from the staff, and the odd stream of girls looking for a good time, paid or not, the residence was a man's world. They spoke in turn, discussing the problems they faced moving their products around Europe. It was an intricate process, but one that had developed over years of staying one step ahead of Interpol, who'd taken it upon themselves to wage full scale war on drug trafficking since 2013. The mission was called Operation Lionfish, and it was clear to see on the Interpol website. Their aim was ceaselessly seeking out traffickers on land, air and sea. Staying ahead of Lionfish was a major concern for anyone using the porosity of international borders to grow, manu-facture, courier, supply and deal anything deemed illegal in the eyes of international authorities.

'Why is the Tangier route so hot right now?' one guest asked.

'So is Algiers to Marseilles off the table?' another added. They were serious questions and Fawaz acknowledged them by gesturing his hand, indicating that everything was under control.

'Brothers, you all worry too much,' he said.

Crossing the Mediterranean was a fundamental part of supplying into Europe, and they had to come up with more and more ingenious ways to evade the authorities. Fawaz had started out in cannabis, as it was the preferred drug of choice in Europe, but later, as he found routes out of Pakistan and Afghanistan, he was able to tap into the larger heroin market in the US. He also discovered new trading partners. Logistically, as soon as they found one reliable method of transportation, they were caught up fairly quickly by their pursuers, and so they found another, and another way around, and so it went, never quite slowing enough to be caught by the international authorities so keen to see his empire fall.

But the noose was tightening, and that's why he'd approached his old friend for help. Not to transport drugs, he would never ask Khalil to do that, but on another matter entirely. Everybody visiting Fawaz tonight knew that it wasn't so much that Khalil Dalmani had said no, but it was more the way he'd done it. He'd been condescending to Fawaz and his pride was ruptured by it. Fawaz had never seen it coming.

Fawaz looked at them and they waited. He stood and walked to a maid holding a tray, taking a fruit juice from it.

'Nothing is off the table,' Fawaz added. The men looked at one another and Fawaz smiled. 'It's very much on.'

'But how?'

'I have something that Khalil Dalmani wants,' Fawaz said. 'It's very precious to him. In fact, it's more precious than any of his trading deals, his tankers, his oil or his pipeline with the Americans.'

Smiles spread across the faces of those present as they learned their plans could go ahead.

'So we could be up and running again as normal by when?' The man who asked was a patriarch who supplied his boys to Fawaz as anything from couriers, to guards, or speedboat drivers. It was a family affair and everybody got involved. That was everybody apart from Fawaz's children, because he'd made that mistake once before. And now Rafik was dead.

As such, unlike Khalil Dalmani, Fawaz did not have an Achilles heel. He couldn't be bribed and he couldn't be threatened, and that was his ace card. He had nothing left to lose. He'd made sure of it.

'How did Madrid go?' another associate asked.

'Better than expected. The software is tricky but there are plenty of computer experts willing to work for the right price – all we need to do is supply the components on time. And now we can use the Algiers to Marseilles route.'

'Come on, Fawaz, what have you done?'

For once, Fawaz actually smiled, and those in his company noted it as a very good sign indeed. It meant they could relax a little and perhaps enjoy some of the services on offer, courtesy of their host. But, though his smile was genuine, nobody knew the true reason behind his victory grin. Fawaz held the loyalty of those surrounding him but he hadn't been totally transparent with them. It wasn't a matter of trust, or indeed nor was he trying to double deal his closest associates. He simply hadn't shared his true motive for his interest in a smoother passage to Europe. He continued to smile, and as if on cue, the noise of a vehicle approaching in the still night air aroused everyone's attention.

'It's a bus from Marrakech.' Fawaz promised them. 'It should be full. I wanted to celebrate, so I splashed out a little. Turn up the music!' he bellowed.

The sound of laughter and heels click–clicking on the beautifully tiled floor distracted everybody, and the men looked towards the huge oak double doors that led to the courtyard at the front. It opened slowly and the noise grew louder. Perhaps twenty girls walked in and continued to gossip and giggle. They were the usual mixture of local and European women, eager to take advantage of a free party. Fawaz greeted them and showed them where they could get drinks and drugs on tap. Silver platters were on hand topped up with piles of cocaine, ready-rolled zoots, mini pipes full of meth, gold dishes full of pills and plain old American cigarettes. Maids appeared carrying trays full of flutes of champagne topped with strawberries.

The music turned from sedate melodies to American rock, and lights flashed across the white walls. It was fully dark now. Some girls began to dance. Fawaz sat back to watch as his associates, one by one, took a fancy to a girl or two, or three.

It was a good reason to celebrate.

Chapter 4

Helen looked at the plans of the Palace of Versailles spread out before her on the table. She was inside the British Embassy building, preparing for her visit to the historical site. A series of arrows, labels and markers denoted where it was most vulnerable. The biggest challenge regarding Versailles was its sheer vastness. The building itself had a footprint of 67,000 square metres. The surrounding estate covered over eight hundred hectares, with eight miles of paths. The perimeter would be tricky, but the dignitaries were scheduled to arrive only for the talks and then leave for their various accommodations around the city. There was nothing she, or anyone, could do by then, except brief each member state, because outside of the palace, each country represented at the summit would arrange their own security. They were to meet over three days. The good thing was that the gardens, parks, Grand Canal and the Trianon Estate (itself nearly one hundred hectares), which were all situated within the remit of Versailles, would all be closed.

She was due to meet with Special Agent Roy White, from the US president's Secret Service, at the palace at midday. The Americans had taken over the site and assumed primary control over summit security, which was standard. No other country boasted the resources available to the United States when it came to policing events on foreign soil.

The logistics of VIPs coming in and out of meeting rooms, taking tea and lunches on the Imperial lawns, being given courtesy tours of the Hall of Mirrors and such, was all a logistical nightmare, but Helen was confident that once Special Agent White ran through the arrangements with her, she could report back to Sir Conrad, and then pack up and perhaps return to the MOD. All thoughts of resigning her commission had vanished. The new assignment reminded her why she joined the RMP in the first place: to be attached to varied and multilateral operations in her capacity as an expert in certain fields; a free agent of sorts, assigned a new role every couple of years. The type of life that fitted around such transience suited her, especially now, but it wasn't for everyone. All her professional career, she'd missed birthdays, funerals, christenings and holidays because of her job. But she couldn't blame her miserable personal life on her professional choices. That was squarely her own fault. She'd tried to settle down, even attracting derision from former colleagues, who could never envisage the Wrench at home, feeding babies and mopping floors. But no one had known she was pregnant. Being fit and slim meant that she didn't show that much under loose clothing. After, everyone just assumed that she'd left a failed relationship behind because she was mis-wired and detached from her feminine instincts: an anomaly of Mother Nature. A female career soldier.

Fresh out of university, she'd told no one she was applying to the Royal Military Academy, Sandhurst, to become a commissioned officer of Her Majesty's armed forces. She wanted to prove that she could do it before informing anyone, including her parents. When she finally did tell them, the week before the passing-out parade, before the grandeur of Old College, with her at the head of her female-only platoon, the only one out of nine, they were speechless. They actually cried. Some of her counterparts never told their loved ones for fear of being labelled as either lesbians or nymphomaniacs desperate to fraternise with their male counterparts: an unfair stereotype but one nonetheless. For Helen, an only child, her parents' pride continued long after.

Years later, when she'd told them about her pregnancy, she sensed their relief that she was finally going to be, in their eyes, true to her sex and settle down. She didn't blame them, nor did it offend her: it was their generation. And they certainly hadn't been the only ones to raise eyebrows. Helen Scott in a serious relationship attracted derision, but for the opposite reasons. '*You're throwing your career away*,' a senior male officer had told her. '*It'll affect your report*,' another warned her. Of course, in the real world, one's relationships were nobody else's business, but the army was different.

Once she boarded the train to Versailles, at just before eleven, she busied herself with staring out of the window and watched the countryside fly past, as they left the depressed suburbs of the city; graffiti and concrete gave way to flat fields and the promise of cleaner air. Every journey seemed another milestone in separating herself from what had gone before. As she notched up the mileage, from city to city, she hoped that memories of Luke, her dead son, would fade, but they never did.

A Chevrolet Suburban met her at the station and she was driven to the back of the sprawling Versailles estate. The rear was underwhelming compared to the tourist entrance. She could still see the magnificent gardens as they sped towards the staff buildings, where the beating heart of the palace operated. Visitors stared at them, thinking the occupants of the car either famous or otherwise important enough to be chauffeured into the grounds. The darkened windows gave solace and the air-conditioning kept them cool. Apart from greeting her as 'Ma'am,' the driver said nothing and concentrated on being vigilant. He wore an earpiece and occasionally he acknowledged an instruction or observation. Helen took in the scale of the place. It must give any event organisers the jitters. The palace had played host to concerts and grand picnics in the past, but nowhere was safe from terrorism now, and a lone knifeman, missed by the scanners at the entrance, could cause havoc and instil fear: something that hadn't been expected pre-9/11.

The US operation was being run from the Petit Trianon palace, and they drove through the busy Place d'Armes, around the back of the main palace, then along the Avenue de Trianon, flanked by linden and chestnut trees. The signature character of the Petit Trianon was its English gardens, and Helen smiled to herself at the irony. The spectre of home was never very far away. Her father, a keen gardener himself, would love it. A great oak sat majestically in the middle of an open space, and Helen knew that some of them planted here dated back to the seventeenth century. The grounds were quieter away from the main house and few people noticed her leave the car and slip into a back entrance of the chateau.

She was taken to a conference suite and guessed that the guy in the black suit, pointing at interactive maps of the gardens and house, speaking in an authoritative and knowledgeable voice was Special Agent White. After he finished addressing the gathered team, he strode towards

Helen and held out his hand. She tried to take the measure of him, which was difficult to do with a special agent from any country. Their bread and butter was sinking into any background as the ultimate Mr or Mrs Grey. He was of medium height and build, slightly balding, tanned, pleasant and disarming: perfectly forgettable. He looked in his forties, had a kind unreadable face, and sported a large scar running down the side of his face.

'Call me Roy.'

The US security personnel filed out and, after asking if she wanted coffee, Special Agent White got straight to business, running through what they'd achieved so far regarding their final risk assessment. He took her over to the giant electronic map of the site.

'Snipers will be on the roof here, here and here,' he explained. 'We're creating a multinational team pulled mainly from the US and NATO, but it's my operation, so if you want anything adding, now's your chance.'

'I'll be with the British ambassador. Are there photos on the lawn?' she asked.

'Of course. They will take place on the first and last days, in front of the palace.' He pointed to the gravel balcony overlooking the Parc du Chateau, and she remembered the iconic view over the Grand Canal. He showed her where the world's press would be positioned behind cordons – all previously vetted and cleared by multinational agencies, of course.

'Should we take a look around?' he asked. It was a welcome suggestion and one that suggested his transparency was complete. He guided her back outside and into the waiting vehicle which had brought her from the station. The driver got out and saluted Roy. They drove slowly up the Allée St Antoine and Roy pointed out certain points of security interest. Once further up, he explained the logistics of the summit. Tourists pointed to the car.

Since the Second World War, there'd been thirty NATO summits. They were opportunities for member states to discuss matters of policy, unlike the regular ministerial meetings, which were more frequent and attended by senior civil servants. One of the purposes of this round of meetings was to discuss the new initiative in Afghanistan and how to reduce the amount of heroin being farmed and exported, despite the existing eighteen-year campaign. The problem was that drug money underpinned the Afghan economy. The car turned the corner and the palace sat in front of them, pristine and resplendent. The photographs of the world's leaders here would be spectacular.

'Journalistic gold,' Helen said.

Roy White looked puzzled.

'I mean the backdrop and the history. You know, the Treaty of Versailles, signed here, in the Hall of Mirrors,' she said.

'Woodrow Wilson, right?' he said.

She nodded. 'Though your senate never ratified it.'

'And twenty years later, we all paid the price,' he said.

'I didn't mean that,' she said.

'It's all right, Ma'am – we've got your back,' he said.

She smiled. Fair enough.

The sun shone gloriously on the estate, and the white stone was immaculately clean, adding to its splendour. It was tempting to get out of the car and Helen wished she were here as a VIP tourist for the day.

'Current intelligence?' she asked as they drove on.

'Very low threat. Recent terror cells have been swept up in Germany, Spain and here in France over recent weeks, thanks to a joint operation between your European governments. Your borders here are at best porous and…'

'At worst, leaking like an old Victorian toilet?' she finished for him, and this time he smiled at her.

'We'll have snipers on the roof over there.' He pointed and Helen looked up through the darkened window.

'All roads, canals and pathways are to be blockaded from zero-one hundred hours on Sunday, to zero-five hundred hours on Thursday.'

VIPs were scheduled to begin arriving from lunchtime onwards on Sunday, including the US president and the UK prime minister.

'Da'esh is on the back foot.' He was referring to the Islamic State of Iraq and Syria (ISIS). It was true they were damaged by recent wars in the region, but there were thousands of cells still active or sleeping across Europe, and the threat was always present. Home-grown grooming was rife, and Helen knew that around two hundred planned attacks were discovered and foiled every year in Europe.

'So no transport in or out, apart from the obvious catering vehicles and security services?' she asked.

'None.'

'What about air traffic?'

'Covered. The area over Versailles will be closed for forty-eight hours. It's a relatively quiet space, as you can see today. Look at that sky. It reminds me of Montana. French air traffic control have been planning for it for a month,' Roy said.

'I'll report back to our ambassador – he'll be encouraged. Thank you for giving up your time, Agent White— Roy,' she said. 'When do you pack up? Our ambassador is due to chair the meetings with the Afghanistan delegates after the traditional summit is over,' she told him.

'We stay on a week after the president leaves, Ma'am.'

'Good,' she said.

'There is one development, here in France, which I was only told about an hour ago. It's not mission specific, but it's turned heads.'

'What's that?' she asked. They were almost back at the control room. She hadn't been given any intel before leaving the embassy and she wondered what it could be.

'Hakim ibn Khalil Said Dalmani, son of Khalil—'

'I know who he is.'

'He was abducted from Le Bourget airport yesterday, shortly after landing from Tangier.'

Chapter 5

Grant Tennyson watched the electronic iron gates open slowly and steadily as the driver waited patiently. They both looked about the vicinity for opportunists with bad intent. Many people in Algiers knew that this was the home of the richest man in the city. Grant didn't like not being in control and he was as unhappy being driven as he was being flown. Helicopters were the worst, with their clunky blades threatening to spin off at any moment, leaving the bird to drop like a stone.

But it was a relief from the relentless heat to be sat in the air-conditioned car, and Grant leaned back in his seat and pushed his floppy sandy hair off his face with his hand. He'd allowed it to grow since leaving the military. He also remained unshaven for several days at a time. He was tanned by the sun, fresh from his visit to the Sahara, where he'd spent three weeks touring the AlGaz site, identifying vulnerabilities and vetting staff. It was a pleasure to be dust and sand free and in clean clothes again.

He travelled to the house of Khalil ibn Dalmani, the owner of AlGaz. The disappearance of Grant's boss's son yesterday, along with his head of security, was no secret, and in all probability the reason why he'd been summoned. The city air was clearer up here on the hillside and Grant felt the pace of life slow down, compared to the hectic chaos downtown, where he stayed at the Marriott

Hotel in between visits to Dalmani's oil and gas facilities all over the country. His job was to make sure that the company's perimeter was watertight.

The engine purred. Khalil made sure that the manufacturers of all of his vehicles disabled the eco-friendly system that cut out the engine when static, designed to save on fuel and bail out the environment. It was too risky. A trained driver's foot was quicker than any system made by an engineer in a factory, sat in front of a computer. The vehicle nudged forward when the width between the gates allowed, and they waited on the other side as they closed behind them. The driver clicked his key fob to open the inner set of gates only once the outer ones closed.

The grounds were immaculate, and they drove past water features, garages – no doubt housing Khalil's collection of classics and one-off editions – as well as elegant palm trees, pruned to look identical, and bushes full of brightly coloured flowers. The approach to the main house was long, and Grant peered ahead with curiosity. He'd never been here before. His final interviews for the post had taken place either on the phone, or downtown in the Marriott. AlGaz's headquarters occupied a whole block not far from the hotel district and rocketed skyward over fifty-two floors of metal and glass, and that's where he'd met the man just that one time and secured the job.

The car stopped outside the mansion and the driver got out, opening Grant's door for him. He climbed from his seat and the heat hit him like the inside of an oven. The main door of the house opened and Grant was received by a chunky male in a dark suit. When he'd first been employed, Grant had been given a tour of the company by Jean-Luc Bisset, the family's personal security head. Grant, an Englishman, had found the Frenchman decidedly aloof, and their relationship got off to an awkward start. Khalil's family security was made up of 90 per cent locally employed staff and the rest were, like him, Europeans who'd served in the military for their country. Grant questioned what experience Jean-Luc had, if any, and settled on the fact, found out later, that he'd been under the wing of Khalil forever: a hanger-on with no formal training. But his boss had affection for him, and Grant was the newcomer.

Jean-Luc was a man of few words, which no doubt complimented his hard-man image to those ignorant of what personal security actually involved. Grant had seen plenty of the type before. He'd winced at many of the routines and procedures he'd witnessed since starting with AlGaz, but he couldn't simply barge in and trash the system: he had to get Khalil's ear first. Perhaps that time had come.

He was ushered quickly through the house, and he took in the decor and opulence afforded to a residence of this quality. It was a style that one saw only in magazines, with crystal fireplaces, animal-skin rugs, vast polished tables, panes of glass the size of his whole room at the Marriott and stunning works of art. A huge portrait of a dignified gentleman in traditional Berber dress caught his eye.

They walked past a laundry room and two maids were busy sorting and folding, in silence. They didn't make eye contact. Finally, he was shown into a massive office suite facing the ocean, framed by the biggest single windowpane Grant had ever seen. The first voice he'd heard in an hour spoke quietly in English on the telephone. It was Khalil himself.

Grant waited. The man who'd escorted him left the room and closed the door gently. He'd noticed that the first time he'd met Khalil; that he liked hush, and Grant enjoyed the respite from the cacophony of noise that accompanied his usual work. Compared to repeating himself in English and French, with a little Arabic, in an attempt to make himself understood in a sandstorm, this place was a haven of peace and tranquillity, and Grant understood why Khalil preferred it to his office down-town. But the serenity emanated from the man, not the other way around. There was something about Khalil Dalmani that commanded equilibrium.

'Mr Tennyson,' Khalil said, finishing his phone call and standing up to greet him. 'Welcome to my home.'

Grant took the offered hand and tried to work out the mettle of the man before him. His son, along with a trusted member of the household, was missing, but here was a man who appeared cool, collected and in charge. He waited.

'Please sit down.'

'Sir,' Grant said. 'I was sorry to hear about your son.'

Khalil grimaced and nodded sternly. 'Thank you, Mr Tennyson. May I call you Grant?'

'Sure, you pay my wages,' Grant said.

'Good. I accept your sympathy, but what I want is your experience.'

Grant sat down on the sofa offered to him, and Khalil sat next to him in an armchair with a laptop in hand. The arrangement felt casual, but Grant knew better than that. He watched his boss; he wore casual trousers and a crisp white shirt, which looked expensive, and his dark skin contrasted in a way that white men could only wish for: the guy looked minted. But then, he was.

'I've brought you here because I want you to find my son.'

Grant waited.

'I've got everything you need in these files. They've been compiled by the National Central Bureau of Interpol, here in Algiers.'

Khalil handed over the laptop as he spoke. Grant wondered if the kidnap of a regular civilian would attract the attention of Interpol so quickly. He knew enough about the organisation, with their HQ in Lyon, France, to know that international kidnappings were taken seriously; however, he was also under no illusion that Khalil had them on board quicker than most, through the local arm based in Algiers.

'Is Interpol handling the investigation, sir?' he asked.

'Yes. My son has been placed on a yellow notice, and bureaus all over the world have been notified.'

Grant appreciated the political gravitas of Hakim's disappearance. After all, his father was one of the wealthiest men in the world and had important trade links with Europe.

'You're booked on a jet to Paris in an hour. Your accommodation is arranged and your budget details are all in there. I've many contacts in France and I'm trusting you to use them as you see fit. I read your CV carefully before I employed you, and I should have made you head of my personal security when I had the chance. I'm now paying for that mistake.'

'You don't trust Jean-Luc?'

'You're direct, and I like that about you. Continue to ask all the questions you need to. I do trust him. Both our fathers fought on the same side in the revolution. His passed away last year and Jean-Luc took it badly. His cancer, some said, was a result of working in mining all his adult life.'

'Your mines?' Grant asked.

Khalil nodded.

'So it's plausible that he blames AlGaz for that?'

'That's your new job, to find out,' Khalil replied.

'He's a Frenchman?' Grant asked.

'His father was Algerian, he has a French mother.'

'She's still alive?'

'Yes, and living in Lyon. The address is in there,' Khalil said, pointing to the laptop.

'Do you trust your son?'

'Yes. But if you prove me wrong during your inquiries, I'll accept it. Hakim is a studious boy. No businessman, but he's possessed with an academic intelligence I never had, and he applies himself. If he was planning to betray me, he could have easily done so without the drama.'

'Good point. Enemies?'

'You must know the answer to that, Grant. I sent him back to Paris early because I thought he'd be safer there. It was a last-minute change of plan. How wrong I was.'

It was the first sign of emotion that Khalil had shown. He got up and faced the glass wall. Grant followed his gaze to the ocean.

'Did you suspect some kind of threat?' Grant asked.

'It was Jean-Luc who informed me that his men talked much about offers of bribes they received for information about the whereabouts of my family at specific times,' Khalil said.

'And? Were they investigated?'

'Jean-Luc took care of it,' Khalil said. His head bowed a little and Grant recognised the gesture as one of a man who has made a terrible mistake and bears that weight on his shoulders. He blamed himself, like any parent would.

'So no details of actual plans or any names to work with?' Grant wanted to be clear about the extent of Jean-Luc's incompetence.

'No. I did have a request from an old associate, but it's nothing, really.'

Grant found the statement vague.

'When?'

'Around three weeks ago.'

'Who?'

Khalil sighed. 'Fawaz bin Nabil. He's—'

'I know who he is. I've just spent three weeks on your perimeter. His name comes up a lot. He's your commercial equivalent in Morocco, though perhaps more interested in profit that doesn't have to be declared. How was he your associate?'

'Our fathers started out in business together, but Fawaz and I parted company over technical disagreements.' Khalil coughed.

'You mean the morality of dealing drugs and arms? You look surprised. It's no secret who Fawaz is. What did he want?'

'He wanted to use my ships between Algiers and Marseilles. I said no.'

Grant let this sink in. Khalil faced back towards the glass.

'I'd like to be coming with you, but my head is not clear and my heart burns with rage. I need to be here to protect my wife and my other two sons. Part of your job is reviewing my personal security arrangements to look for holes. It's clear that somebody betrayed me. My jet flies at very short notice, and Jean-Luc arranged everything – the pilots, the transport and the itinerary.'

'Even old loyalties can be broken. There are a couple of people I trust out in the field looking after your perimeter. They should be transferred here. You need a tight group around you, but if you're so sure that it was an inside job, then you should be coming to Paris with me. You're not safe here.'

'But if they were after the whole family, they'd have taken us together.'

'Not necessarily. With Hakim gone, you're vulnerable because you won't expect another hit. You're nervous now, so you'll make mistakes. More importantly, you said it yourself, you don't know who you can trust.'

'What about Taziri and the boys?'

'Bring them. I'll make sure you have a team in Paris.'

Khalil made a phone call, and, even in Arabic, Grant knew it was to his wife. The tone, the familiarity and the sighing made that clear. He hung up.

'Taziri is packing. I'll get the boys myself,' Khalil said.

'No you won't, sir – I will. Delay my plane, I'll be back in half an hour. Phone the school and send them my iris recognition.'

Khalil nodded.

'Where do you normally stay in Paris?' Grant asked.

'The Ritz.'

'Call them yourself. Keep all of your staff here on full pay and conditions. The house should run as normal.'

'Here.' Khalil passed Grant a key fob from his pocket. It felt heavy in Grant's hand and he recognised the wings of Bentley.

'It's in the second garage – I'll walk you there. The house fobs are in the glove compartment.'

As they left the office, Grant heard a woman's voice. She was arguing with someone. Khalil winced. Peace was something that the Dalmani family would not find again until their son was found.

Chapter 6

Just outside the Moroccan city of Fez, in a small village populated mainly by farmers, a man sat outside a two-storey stone building. One road dissected the settlement, and, under that, passed the river Fez. The city itself was the crossroads of Morocco and saw trade pass from south to north, east to west, in a never-ending criss-cross of goods coming and going, being sold and bought; the pulse by which the sprawling urbanisation had drawn air for thirteen centuries.

The roads in the city were tarmacadam of course, but here, in the suburbs, which was more like a rural waste-land, the paths were sandy and made of shifting dust, and the houses were simple and stone. Square, with a rooftop terrace, they kept residents cool in the summer and warm in the winter. The man, though, preferred to sit outside. It was the best position to be in to get paid every month. If he was nowhere to be seen, then how did they know he did his job? He sat on an old sofa pulled up to a metal table. On the table were all the things he needed to strip, clean, oil and reassemble the items laid before him. Nobody came to the village unless they came to pick up the goods produced in the factory inside the home he guarded. That was the same day he got paid. His job was to make sure that no one stole the commodities inside.

Not that anyone would. They'd be imbeciles to try.

He squinted in the afternoon sun, and a cigarette hung from his mouth as he worked. The array of objects before him was, to him, a vision of beauty, because only if one respected the equipment would it perform to the correct standard. Out here in the sand and heat, fine dust stuck to anything, like a whore to a prince's leg. He had to go easy on the oil else all his efforts would be for nothing.

Two 9mm Glock pistols sat side by side, next to three Sig Sauer semi-automatics. Next to that, laid neatly, was an AK-47, a newly acquired AK-74, an American M4 carbine, and – his pride and joy – a Heckler & Koch MP5. There was an old and trusty Russian Dragunov sniper rifle too, and it sat there like a loyal dog, having accompanied its master on many missions.

He began with the smaller weapons, taking one of the Sigs and pulling back the upper case to check that it was empty. Next, he removed the two pins holding the casing in place over the barrel, revealing the mechanism inside. He removed the barrel and inspected the firing pin. He blew a few times, but the sand was stuck to the carbon deposits, and he swept the surfaces with a small wire brush. Happy, he pulled a lightly oiled flannelette through the barrel. He oiled the railings and wiped the spring, pulling the trigger as he did so, to test how smooth the weapon would be in its action now it'd had someone take good care of it. He got these weapons in all the time and they were in all kinds of states of shit. Someone nicknamed him Dirty Harry years ago, and it had stuck. Though, sadly, he'd never managed to get his hands on a Smith and Wesson .44 Magnum.

The larger weapons took longer to clean and put back together because they had longer and thicker elements, and it was worth taking out the firing pin and the trigger.

That's why the AK-47 was so popular – in fact, the best-selling gun in history – because it was so basic. Put it in the hands of an eight-year-old and they'll figure it out, so that's what they did.

Cleaning guns was like listening to music to Dirty Harry. He worked methodically and smiled occasionally when he managed to get some carbon off a barrel without removing the matt paint, leaving a shine that would glint in the sun.

A car approached, and Dirty Harry looked up. A Toyota Land Cruiser. He stopped what he was doing and took his cigarette out of his mouth. He stood up and went to the front of the table, covering the weapons with a cloth, but taking a newly clean and loaded Sig and sticking it into his belt at the back of his tunic.

Then he relaxed. He knew both the driver and the passenger, who was his regular contact, Abdul. He waved a greeting but still registered the extraordinary nature of the visit. The vehicle stopped, and the men got out. They shook hands and exchanged pleasantries about the price of ammunition and the football season.

'Can I offer you some tea?' he asked the men. They accepted, and he went inside and barked some orders. He beckoned them to sit on the dilapidated sofa but they declined. He waited. Finally one of them spoke and told him that a shipment had been apprehended between Tangier and a beach near Gibraltar. Interpol had been conducting another of their operations and congratulated themselves on seizing ten kilos of heroin from a speedboat. It was a mere blip, but still, it was a loss.

'The goods are needed earlier than expected. We have a new route and expect the transfer to take place tomorrow,' Abdul said.

'What? Tomorrow? We don't have enough time!' complained Dirty Harry.

'Show me,' said Abdul.

Dirty Harry pointed to the driver and told him to wait by the table as usual. He took Abdul inside. The darkness assaulted their wits, and it took time to acclimatise, not only to the dark, but to the air-conditioning and lack of desert dust. The room was one of two, the other one being upstairs, and it housed various stations, comprising machinery, computer screens and laboratory-style equipment.

'What more needs doing? We can't wait,' Abdul said.

'There are many delicate procedures that need finalising. The propellers, the landing gear, the motor, the transmitter – they're all standard and easy to install once the software is downloaded, but that's the thing, my friend. It takes time to perfect each individual profile.'

'I know,' said Abdul, 'And you have until tomorrow at three o'clock. We need to drive them to Algiers.'

'Algiers?'

'Ah, here is the tea. Let's drink it outside and you can show me your new toys, Dirty Harry.'

Chapter 7

Hakim tossed and turned fitfully, drifting between the conscious and dreaming world. His journey so far had been logged deep inside his brain as a result of his father paying a lot of money to have him instructed in certain skills that he thought he'd never need. At the time, he'd thought his father overprotective, foolish even, but that had all changed as they landed at Paris–Le Bourget Airport yesterday.

The flight had gone without a hitch until they were somewhere over the Mediterranean and Jean-Luc looked jumpy. Hakim only noticed because he usually held the demeanour of a Hollywood bodyguard: slick and in control. He couldn't pinpoint exactly why now, but he'd sent a message to Amélie by text, as if to assuage his confusion over Jean-Luc's body language and the palpable shift in atmosphere inside the cabin. The fact that he was even aware of the bodyguard was unsettling to him, because usually he wasn't. He'd tried to call his girlfriend, but Amélie hadn't answered. He didn't know what made him ask her to come to the airport, until it was too late. A hunch, a suspicion, a gut feeling, a flight of fancy? Father always told him never to ignore them.

But, by the time two men had boarded the plane at Paris–Le Bourget – a favourite destination for those who could afford private air travel, all thoughts of Jean-Luc's odd behaviour had been forgotten once more. It was the busiest private jet terminal in the world, but Hakim had seen it a hundred times and didn't bother to check the view outside as he got up to leave his leather seat. He'd been working on a thesis due in the following week. His thoughts were of dining at Le Jules Verne, in the Eiffel Tower, with Amélie. He never tired of the view. It was a little kitsch, because of its sentimentality, as the English students said, but everyone knew the English to be snobs of the worst order. The cliché of dining overlooking the city from the monument, in his opinion, was never out of taste, and his father agreed. In fact, that's probably why he'd chosen it for last night: to remind him of the man who he knew he'd miss so much, as well as to celebrate being with Amélie again. Hakim loved summers in Algiers: the smell of the heat, the cicadas going crazy, the late sun disappearing into the sea, the freedom of his brothers jumping on him in the pool, his mother's cooking and his labradors. But he also loved Paris.

Until he'd had a gun pointed at him.

He tried to concentrate on those images now as he lapsed between dozing and sentience. He'd been brought to an apartment, up some stairs, and he'd been in this room, on the small sparse bed, ever since, trying to replay everything in his head, just as he'd been taught during capture-and-interrogation training, never thinking that it might ever be useful and cursing his paranoid and over-protective father.

It was the only thing that kept the fear at bay: the what-ifs, the doomsday scenarios and the possibility of his father never finding him. His father, the great Khalil Said al-Rashid ibn Dalmani. A man who, to Hakim, was forever in his study but still found time to fool around with his boys in the pool. Hakim's younger brothers, Farid and Samir, jumped into his semi-conscious in vivid colour: throwing a ball, bothering the dogs to tumble and catch, whining to their mother about bath time and laying across Hakim's outstretched body on a vast sofa watching movies in the basement cinema.

Yesterday morning, on their way to drop off his younger brothers at school, his father's demeanour was odd. After delivering his sons, his father remained silent and Hakim knew this meant that he was troubled. Usually, they would have talked about Paris, art or cars. But yesterday, Khalil was distracted. The journey to the airport had been tense, and Hakim reminded himself of his father's pinched cheeks, the slight scowl above his brow, and the way he kept peering around. At the time, it had seemed merely the actions of a rich man who was vigilant in an unpredictable city, but now, in his half-dream, his father had looked pained.

Earlier that morning, his father had called him to his study and presented to him information about Amélie: photographs, background checks, family history and notes about her occasional recreational drug use. He'd hung his head in shame, having disappointed his father, but he'd still fought his girlfriend's corner. But, as it turned out, his father wasn't angry, just saddened that his son hadn't shared the fact that he'd found love in Paris. He wanted to know more about Amélie Laurent. What could Hakim say? She was beautiful, smart, funny and brave. She laughed with the kind of freedom he only saw in films.

Hakim woke fully, startled by the vivid image of Amélie in danger, and he held his head in his hands. The room hadn't changed. The locked door still taunted him, and the bed was still hard. He smelled tobacco smoke drift underneath the gap and heard the faint voices of jokes told in French with a North African accent.

This wasn't about Amélie.

He started at the beginning. He was calm. He knew that his head was his best ally. The moment he allowed passion to surface, he was dead. He refused to accept emotion into his psyche. Only responding to each situation as it presented itself would give him the best chance of seeing his family again.

His stomach rumbled. Hunger was just one process in the road to dehumanising a prisoner, and he prepared himself mentally for the effects that a lack of food would have on his body. As long as he was given water... He drifted off again. Thoughts of who might have taken him, or who wanted him, but more importantly, why, invaded his mind, and he opened his eyes. At a guess, he reckoned everything usually boiled down to money. His father was rich beyond most people's imaginations and thus an unsurprising target. What Hakim couldn't figure out, though, was how whoever had taken him had pulled off getting through the ironclad security paid for by his father. Betrayal? Bribery?

And that led him back to Jean-Luc.

Jean-Luc would never betray his father. From the moment the jet hit the tarmac to the doors opening and the two men boarding, he never heard Jean-Luc speak. Was this significant? All he could surmise was that he'd been overpowered. The vision of the gun pointed at him evoked a physical response even now in sleep, and he tumbled off the bed. Startled, he continued his trawling of his memory. The gun. That had been the moment that time stopped.

He'd known then, with certainty, that he was to be taken. He sat next to the bed, head in hands, recollecting every detail.

The men had cable-tied his hands behind his back and hooded him, before ushering him down some steps and into a waiting vehicle, which had sped off as soon as the door was slammed. In the seconds before the head cover blanked his vision, he'd committed their faces to memory, and one of them he recognised. That's when he calmed himself and began tracking every sound, movement, smell, and any other sensory information he could grab. He'd felt around: there was no one in the back seat with him. He'd listened carefully to the engine. His father had introduced him to the world of motor vehicles when he was still a toddler and he could pinpoint most noises made by a wide variety of them. This one was a Range Rover. Thoughts of his father induced feelings of shame once more and he cursed himself for his trusting ways and the embarrassment he'd caused to his father and his good name. The appearance of a new bodyguard, about a month previous to him leaving Paris for the summer, was something that Hakim nonchalantly accepted, but now he knew that it was something that he should have questioned.

Stop. No emotion.

He'd counted time. They'd travelled in that first vehicle through busy Paris streets. He heard shouting, car horns, cyclists' bells and the driver cursing under his breath as they sat in traffic. Hakim memorised every detail.

Then they'd come to some kind of queuing system, and Hakim had known that they were waiting to get through a péage. The familiar nosing forward, then the electric window coming down and the machinery accepting the driver's cash and dispensing change told him this. Of course, his captors wouldn't have an Emovis Tag, which allowed them to pass through the tolls automatically, as that would have been traceable.

He knew he'd landed at two twenty in the afternoon, local time, having taken off from Algiers at eleven a.m. – Paris was an hour ahead – and he figured they'd travelled – allowing fifteen minutes to leave the airport – for forty minutes at an average Parisian inner-city speed, with stops and starts, of perhaps twenty kilometres per hour. That meant they hit a péage around ten kilometres away from Paris-Le Bourget. He believed they'd driven away from the city, and that was about the same distance to the Paris ring road, the A86. They'd left the city. Another ten minutes later, they hit another péage, and as the window rolled down, Hakim heard children's chatter from a nearby car. They were talking about Disneyland. They were east of the city. Hakim figured that the vehicle in which he sat must have excellent black-out windows, else he'd be forced to lie down.

His senses kicked in to full swing after the initial adrenalin rush, but he refused to feel the discomfort of sitting forward because his hands were bound, and he ignored the fear and the bumping around in the back seat, because he wasn't strapped into a seat belt. He'd honed in on the physical processes happening inside and outside his body by concentrating on tiny details. He heard every stone under the tyres, every gust of wind knocking the car, and smelled the driver's cologne. He was like a wolf on the plains tracking deer; moving stealthily and silently, outsmarting his enemy.

After some time, though, he could no longer ignore his hands, which were turning numb behind his back, so he tried to wriggle his fingers to keep the circulation going, trying to control his heartbeat so he didn't overheat. The last thing he needed was to lose a finger or two to lack of blood supply. The plastic binding was tight, but he could take it. He was hardly sweating and shifted in his seat from time to time to take his mind off the discomfort.

The driver fiddled with the radio and Hakim listened intently. A news channel came on but the driver flicked it off angrily and slapped the wheel. The man was clearly an amateur; Hakim could tell that much. He was too distracted and nervous. That might work to his advantage later, however it could also mean that he was erratic, and that was less promising. A music channel came on next but was interrupted by an advert. Hakim heard a click and smelled the familiar and homely smell of tobacco. It reminded him of his father, and the memory comforted him. The driver buzzed down the electric window, perhaps not wanting to stink the car out with cigarette smoke. It had been another opportunity for Hakim to listen to the outside world.

They pulled off the road soon after and Hakim had been aware that they were parking in a bay. The driver unclicked his seat belt and got out. The warm air settled in the car and Hakim tried to make out any noises outside. He heard the driver speaking to somebody else, still in French: another male, who was angry with the driver for stopping. So, there was an accomplice car behind too.

'I need a piss!' The other man's French was also accented by another continent familiar to Hakim because it was his homeland.

'I'll wait here – be quick!'

The regional dialect confirmed what he'd already suspected: that his capture was something to do with his father's enemies back home. Regret screamed into his brain as he admonished himself for not telling his father about the new bodyguard's position. He hadn't even asked Jean-Luc for the man's name. It had been Amélie who was perturbed by the man, and he'd dismissed her.

Hakim was aware of the second man standing by the open door, and cigarette smoke wafted into the vehicle as he too lit up. He heard different voices, and Hakim's ears prickled with alertness. He was acutely aware of a woman and a child approaching the vehicle and, without realising it, Hakim's pulse rate elevated again. He stiffened and the man standing at the door slammed it shut, forgetting that the driver's window was open. Hakim listened to their conversation.

'Marie! Come away from the car! I'm sorry, she's learning to walk and goes in all the wrong directions.' The woman babbled, but the man ignored her. There was an awkward silence as the woman probably worked out that the stranger wasn't interested in polite chatter. 'Marie, this way! Good girl!'

'Forêt!' Hakim heard the little girl announce the word as if it was the most important word of all time, and he remembered his brothers, when they learned to speak, choosing random words to pronounce, expecting praise of the highest order.

'Forêt! Yes, forest! Absolutely. Well done, Marie! We're going to the forest.'

The voices faded. If they had passed Disneyland, the only forest they could be driving towards was Forêt de Fontainebleau.

When they'd left Paris, the sun had not shone on his side of the car – the right – but since Disneyland, and still now, it shone fully onto his side of the car.

They were heading south.

Chapter 8

Helen strolled through the garden with Sir Conrad, at his private residence, overlooked by the embassy. The lines mowed into the immaculate lawn could have hosted a Wimbledon tournament. They walked away from the house, and a pleasant breeze wafted through the trees lining the trail down to the ornate fountain. From there, one could imagine the Duke of Wellington surveying his wealth and congratulating himself on his victory over Napoleon. It was one of those residences where one simply couldn't forget its history, and Sir Conrad was a perfect host. But they weren't here to talk about the Battle of Waterloo.

'I was satisfied with the plans shown to me by Special Agent White, Sir,' Helen told the ambassador.

She'd accepted tea and they'd taken it on the terrace before heading down towards the fountain at the opposite end of the enormous garden. 'What exactly did Special Agent White say about the abduction of Hakim Dalmani?' he asked.

He seemed fixated on the topic. 'Well, Sir, in fairness, he didn't know much about it. His focus is the summit right now. It was my understanding that Interpol Algiers was dealing with it,' she said.

'Of course, well, you know these types of people, Major Scott,' he replied. His hand waved about absentmindedly, as if to indicate that her experience with the Middle East somehow made her an expert on anyone with darker skin.

'Sir, are you suggesting that the abduction of Khalil Dalmani's son has something to do with security here in France, surrounding the summit?'

'And that's why you're the man for the job, Scott!'

She ignored the glaring misogyny behind his choice of noun.

'From what Agent White told me, I believe the Americans see the incident as non-mission specific, but the kidnapping is on their radar none the less,' she replied.

Sir Conrad put his hands in his trouser pockets. Helen had already noticed that each time Sir Conrad was less than transparent with her, his hands sank deep into his pockets, as if he were physically hiding some information away. She'd already read in him that much. He did it when Khalil Dalmani was mentioned, and the same was true with Fawaz Nabil. She'd spotted it first when they'd been speaking together with Colonel Palmer.

'Sir, do you think it strange that Fawaz Nabil's increased activity in Europe coincides with the abduction of Khalil Dalmani's son?' she asked. His hands, briefly by his sides, once again disappeared into his trouser pockets. She watched, waiting for his answer.

'Well, they are business rivals, and their families were connected for a long time. And they're both African,' he said. Helen forced herself to gloss over his final observation. Some of his more old-fashioned prejudices were grating. She trusted he was more subtle in public where his role as ambassador carried the reputation of the country with it. But he did have a point.

She knew that both Fawaz and Khalil had holdings in oil and gas, but there was plenty of room in North Africa for both of them. One was based in Morocco and the other in Algeria. Both, as far as she could work out, from what she'd simply heard about in the news, had enough profits, year on year, to be unaffected by the other.

'I don't like coincidences, Major Scott.'

'Neither do I, sir.'

They walked further towards the perimeter wall, and Helen was wondering how long it would take them to get back to the main house. It was a beautiful walk, but she wasn't there to enjoy the scenery.

'Why don't the Americans think there's something suspect about it?' he asked.

'Sir, isn't that a question for MI6?'

'Of course, of course. But what do you think? Like I said, you know these people.'

This time Helen couldn't help but become frustrated with his appalling racial stereotypes. *Why do dinosaurs like him still represent British interests abroad?* she asked herself.

'Sir, I worked extensively in Afghanistan, Pakistan, Saudi Arabia and India. I've never worked in Africa, only coming across attached regiments through NATO and the UN. I'm no expert.'

He stopped to face her.

'Khalil Dalmani's son has been abducted. Can you imagine how that feels?' he asked. His passion startled her.

She stared at him, and all the sounds of the birds, the wind in the trees, and the faint hum of traffic ceased, as she thought about Luke, and what she would do to get him back.

'Of course, sir, but... but my job is to make you safe at the summit, and there isn't—'

'Major Scott. Fawaz Nabil has never forgiven Khalil Dalmani for not joining forces with him in his filthy drugs trade. Their relationship has been acrimonious for years,' he said.

'Which is why he wouldn't think twice about abducting his rival's son,' she offered. It was barely a whisper.

'But for what benefit? Why now? And how will Khalil Dalmani retaliate? That's what I want to know,' he said. 'And that's why I'm sending you to Interpol,' he added.

'Excuse me, sir? You're taking me off the security for the summit?'

'Quite the contrary, actually. See it as part of the bigger picture. I've spoken to MI6 and they've recommended, along with the Americans and Five Eyes, that the security threat level surrounding the summit – given the timing of the abduction, along with Fawaz's recent activities – should be escalated. Now, you said yourself that you're satisfied that everything that can be done around Versailles is being done. I want no surprises.' He stopped, and she paused alongside him. Special Agent Roy White can't have been privy to the latest decisions regarding this, either that or she'd left Versailles before he'd been informed. Either way, things were moving fast, and the summit was next week. A tingle of excitement, combined with apprehension, washed over her.

'Am I to join their search for Hakim Dalmani, sir?'

'You got it. Get to the bottom of that, and we find out what his father and associates are up to,' he said.

'You think this might be a business deal gone wrong?' she asked.

Somewhere in the distance, beyond the garden wall topped with barbed wire and CCTV cameras, she heard a loud bang. Her body jumped with a startle reflex, but it was so quick that Sir Conrad didn't notice. The symptoms of PTSD she'd suffered after the incident in another garden, many years before, came back to her.

She was suddenly acutely aware of the birds twittering and cheeping, as they had been when she'd been twenty metres from a car bomb, the other side of a wall, in the middle of a garden in Riyadh. The principal had been a British military attaché working at the embassy, but the target that day was his wife. An extremist group took offence to her westernised dress and planted a bomb under her car. Wives no longer accompanied their husbands on postings to Riyadh.

She was brought abruptly back to the moment by Sir Conrad.

'Interpol have a team working on the abduction of Hakim Dalmani. They think a plot was hatched in North Africa and carried out in Paris. They requested a specialist in close protection because they think that a leak must have come from Khalil Dalmani's personal security. I suggested you to the head of Counter Terrorism at Interpol, an old friend of mine. You're to go down to Lyon and lend your expertise. Of course, while you're there, you can snoop about a bit inside their initiative to tackle the movement of drugs out of Afghanistan and into Europe. Despite what NATO likes to say on their website, we all know it's mainly the US pouring billions of dollars into the Afghan government. Yet every spring, the heroin trade refills the Taliban's coffers and they grow arrogant enough to give NATO the finger. This is the first year that the Afghan government has formally invited the Taliban to discuss terms, and the elephant in the room is a little pink flower. I don't want to be caught by surprise when

I come face to face with the first members of the Taliban ever to accept peace talks.'

They stopped before the magnificent fountain.

'It was commissioned by Napoleon's sister herself.' Sir Conrad gestured towards the water feature. Helen wondered, given the noblewoman's reputation, what kind of parties were held here by the socialite.

'Sir, just so I'm clear, on the face of it, I'm representing you in several capacities; mainly guaranteeing your safety at the summit. In reality, I'm tasked with joining Interpol's investigation into the disappearance of Hakim Dalmani, while at the same time, gathering intelligence on Fawaz Nabil, NATO and the Afghan government.'

He laughed. 'That's a bit strong, Major, but yes. I can't think of anyone better.'

They both gazed at the huge marble depiction of a carriage, pulled by five horses galloping through the water, driven by a noblewoman. No doubt Madame Borghese modelled it on herself.

'She's the epitome of a strong woman,' Helen said.

'Isn't she? And a looker, too. Have you been to Lyon before?' he asked as they slowly circled the fountain.

'Yes, sir, I was seconded once before to Interpol.'

'This isn't a secondment – you're offering expertise,' he said.

'Yes, sir.'

It was made clear that their meeting was now over and he escorted her back to the house. A quicker journey than their amble down. He stopped to face her when they reached the terrace.

'All the details of your trip are next door with Colonel Palmer,' he said, before disappearing inside.

She was taken next door to the chancery and led to Colonel Palmer's office. It was a rendezvous she could do without, but he was technically her boss when she was here. But if she was working for Interpol, then she would no longer have to report to him. Colonel Ben Palmer was sitting in a large green Chesterfield office chair and looked up and nodded as she came in. He handed her an envelope before looking back down again to his desk. She thanked him and stood waiting to either be questioned, exchange chit-chat or at least be dismissed. He tapped on a keyboard and Helen knew he was enjoying the moment, taking his time and making her wait. His balding head taunted her and she had to stop herself from rolling her eyes. She'd worked with some prize bellends in her time but Ben Palmer was up there with the least memorable. It was inevitable, she supposed. Being surrounded by alpha males was bound to cause conflict. Men who only worked with men were particularly off-putting beasts. They farted, spat and told appalling jokes. Feminism hadn't really reached the army yet, despite what the papers said. Finally he looked up.

'The ambassador rates you, Scott.'

'Thank you, sir.'

'It wasn't a compliment.'

'Sir.'

'You need to report directly back to me when you're in Lyon,' he announced.

'Sir, the ambassador just told...'

'I'm your line manager here and I want to know the military angle of what's going on. That's my job. Yours is to report to me. You are an officer in the armed forces, Scott, and you answer to me, is that clear?'

The ambassador hadn't mentioned this, and she faced going over the colonel's head should she query it. Frankly, her trip to Paris was turning into a nightmare, and she couldn't wait to escape the city for the cool of the mountains of Lyon.

She had little choice but to confirm she would follow orders.

'Yes, sir.'

Maybe he was just irritated by her sudden elevation to the echelons of power, like men such as him usually were. Fuck you, she thought, she'd be reporting to the ambassador. She returned his stare.

As long as she remained in Lyon, she could avoid Palmer. She'd deal with what happened when she came back for the summit. The problem was that her time in France would be reported on by him, but it would have to be signed off by the MOD in London. RMPs were never going to be best friends with the infantry. Everybody knew that. She was used to being unwelcome, abused even. None of it ever fazed her and Palmer was the last person she'd think of as she took the train to Lyon. It was the perfect time to be leaving, and she felt a sense of freedom.

She held his gaze.

'You're not as good as you think you are, Scott.'

'Sorry, sir?'

'Don't get out of your depth. The ambassador seems to think you're some kind of specialist because of what you did in Kabul. You got lucky. Never underestimate the experience of a real soldier.'

Helen said nothing for a moment. In other institutions this sort of bullying wouldn't be tolerated, but not here. Some would file an official complaint, but Helen knew from experience that holding her tongue and letting her work do all the talking was always more powerful. She'd experienced it her whole career: men thinking they were better soldiers. Add to that, RMP officers were responsible for putting infantry soldiers behind bars, and it was a recipe for historic resentment.

'Of course not, sir. The next time I see a real soldier, I'll be sure to ask his advice.'

Her pulse quickened. He could have her disciplined for such insolence to a senior officer, but with no witnesses, her remark was as impossible to reprimand as his own had been. Tiny beads of sweat glistened on his brow and his skin went pink.

'If that's all, sir, I better get ready to depart. The ambassador has told me I'm leaving within the hour.'

'So, why are you still here?'

She nodded and turned to go. She wasn't in uniform and so didn't have to salute. Fuck him. She left, and once out in the sunshine, gasped for air to relieve her anger. Seven years ago, the then Major Palmer had pinned her up against a wall, behind the officer's mess, expecting a fondle. She'd kneed him in the nuts and told him to go fuck himself. She hadn't reported him because he was drunk and a nuisance, and that was all.

He'd never forgiven her.

Chapter 9

Helen boarded the train for Lyon. She always found that travelling on a French train for a long journey was somewhat romantic; maybe it was the countryside. Trips on English trains were grubby by comparison and reminded her of late journeys home after a heavy night out in London: the smell of the takeaways being munched by inebriated commuters, the unclean toilets, the sticky air and the feeling that something unsavoury had been spilled on one's seat.

Departing Paris allowed her to breathe a sigh of relief. Her ticket was checked upon embarking and she sat back to relax into reading the file given to her by Colonel Palmer. She started with Dalmani's security. It was headed up by a Jean-Luc Bisset. The information collated so far had been handed over by the National Central Bureau of Interpol in Algiers to Interpol headquarters in Lyon. Jean-Luc's employer seemed to have been more than willing to give the guard's history in a fair amount of detail. The report was thorough.

Born to a French mother, Marie, and an Algerian father, Basem, Jean-Luc had grown up in Algeria, and the family had worked for the Dalmanis for the best part of fifty years. Basem Bisset was an anomalous name, Helen thought, and she dug a little deeper into his history. The

French name Bisset had come from a colonial family and it appeared that Basem was the bastard of a French soldier.

Marie was also the daughter of a French soldier and her marriage to Basem must have raised some eyebrows during such a time of uncertainty. Helen found herself caught prying into a love story spanning generations and she fancied them running off together, like Romeo and Juliet, treacherous in their passion. She pictured the tortuous conversations that tormented their parents (if they were still alive) as the product of warring factions fell in love.

But by the time Jean-Luc was born, the war was over and Algeria was a land of opportunity for some, and their union wouldn't have attracted questions at all. It was a country starting over, and Bisset found employment with the Dalmanis. Helen gave a slight nod of admiration at the thought of the young scrapper who'd ingratiated himself with an up-and-coming family at such a time of opportunity. Helen read with interest the positions held by Basem Bisset and grasped the pattern of his past: he never got beyond the rank of foreman in several Saharan mines owned by AlGaz. Which was curious because in Khalil's statement to Interpol, he said he'd played with Jean-Luc as a child. Why would the son of the mine owner be allowed to play with a mere miner's son?

She turned to Interpol's notes on Khalil Dalmani.

It seemed that he'd grown up in the shadow of his formidable father, who was a war hero. A lucky punt on some scrubland in the Sahara had literally struck black gold: oil. The family was wealthy beyond Helen's grasp. It wasn't that she couldn't picture the yachts, the penthouse suites and the private jets, it was just she had trouble understanding where so much wealth came from and how it was sustained. She shook her head. It would appear after all that, despite playing together as children, Khalil and Jean-Luc's paths were very different indeed. Perhaps, after the sacrifices made by his father, loyal to the family for decades, being a bodyguard wasn't enough for Jean-Luc.

Added to which, the fact that one might say that only Lady Luck decided who benefitted from the fallout of the war. Algiers in 1973, when Jean-Luc was born, was a place in flux. The French had fled having been resoundingly defeated. The country licked her wounds, and Helen knew that resentments ran high for families like Jean-Luc's, whose fathers fought bravely, risking torture, murder and ruin, leaving deep scars. Jean-Luc followed in his father's footsteps and entered the family firm from a young age. He'd worked for Khalil's father, and then Khalil: did this demean him? Helen knew from countless colleagues in the security forces that personal entourages provided to high-profile and wealthy clients around the world were not always run by those who were most skilled, but those who were most loyal, and sometimes this led to mistakes. Jean-Luc certainly didn't fulfil the high professional skill set required by, say, the British or American Special Forces. As far as she could tell, he'd been on no courses, attended no military-training establishments, and boasted no accolades thereof. He'd simply been promoted and assumed the top role some five years ago.

She turned to his job specification and his exact involvement in Khalil's household, and read that Jean-Luc personally oversaw the itinerary of every flight taken by Khalil's private fleet.

Then she came across a name that made her blood run cold.

Three years ago, a British man had been appointed head of Khalil's company security. AlGaz's oilfields and working perimeter boasted a footprint of thousands of square miles and Grant Tennyson was in charge of it all. All except the private security of the family, which was kept separate and headed up by Jean-Luc. The instant rush of adrenalin subsided and she calmed herself. She gazed out of the window at the blur of fields and electric cables whizzing past. Grant must have been royally pissed off about not getting to run the whole rig.

They'd met during Operation Herrick 11. Helen had been attached to an infantry battalion in Helmand, Grant was a company commander. It had been an instant attraction. She'd never figured out if her magnetic pull towards some military men was as a result of meeting no one else, or there was something about them she found genuinely alluring. Grant had personally shown her around the camp. It had been a shithole carved into rock and sand, but he made it feel like home for his men. He'd soothed her anxiety over being a female imposter in a man's world. The gravitational force between them, apparent from the first cup of hot tea shared across an upturned ammo box, set the bar for the rest of the tour, which they spent in denial of their feelings. It was only when they returned to the UK, free from the threat of court martial for fraternising on an operational tour, that they launched into a whirlwind romance.

She continued to stare out of the window and studied the French countryside. She could already see the Alps in the distance and she wished she was skiing. With him? Not any more. Skiing was the only activity she did that allowed her to forget everything in her life. There was something magical about being on top of a mountainside, covered in snow, with bright blue sky affording the sun front-row seats, facing a red run on a wide piste flanked by pines and ferns. The heady scent was just as strong in winter. She preferred to ski in France because it offered the widest pistes, and it was drivable from anywhere in Europe. She'd skied in Germany and Austria, and they were prettier, but the French knew how to build a resort. She loved the Alps and any time she got to go adventure training with the army, it had been to go skiing. One of her more memorable postings was to Cyprus, and her trips to the Troodos Mountains, where they had about three workable runs, but she mustn't be ungrateful. It was no Les Arcs, but it did mean they could drive to Larnaca afterwards, within an hour, and get shit-faced. She smiled at the memories, but a frown soon followed. The pattern never changed; she couldn't think about Grant now without feeling the intense pain that accompanied it.

She tore herself from the view and tried to concentrate on the information in the file but seeing Grant's name had affected her beyond expectation. It took several attempts for her to work out a timeline. Like a senior investigating officer in the civilian police, she applied her knowledge of crime scenes and created a chronology of Hakim's last known movements. She studied the casefiles for the two pilots, who'd been found inside the aircraft bound and gagged, showing signs of severe dehydration. They'd sat on the tarmac in over forty-degree heat, with the sun pelting through the cockpit windows, the engines and air-con off, for close to an hour. Interviewed by French gendarmerie soon afterwards, they'd given artist's impressions of the two men who bound them. She looked over them now and they were generic sketches of men with dark hair and darker glasses. Both pilots had stated when interviewed that they knew nothing of the impending plot. They also suspected nothing untoward between landing and taxiing until the men entered the cockpit.

In answer to the query over how the two men had been able to access the cockpit, they'd replied that they never locked the door on private flights for Mr Dalmani's family. It seemed likely only the Dalmani family and Jean-Luc would know this. By the time the alarm was raised, any car carrying Hakim might have left the city. He could be anywhere.

Next, she turned her attention to Fawaz bin Nabil. The file, compiled before she left Paris, was huge. There was no way she'd get it read by the time she reached Lyon, and so she skimmed, using her instinct, to search for keywords and dates. She could see that Fawaz and Khalil's fathers had gone into business together in the 1970s, around the same time Basem had begun working for the Dalmani family. Had Fawaz known the Bissets? It seemed to Helen an important, if not crucial, question, and she searched the file to see if there was a connection. Fawaz's company, Nabil Tradings, was a relatively new set-up – registered in the 1990s, after the death of Nabil senior. This is when the two companies parted ways. The Bisset family remained loyal to the Dalmanis. Why?

Was Fawaz pissed off? Sir Conrad had said it was Fawaz's 'filthy' drugs trade that put off the Dalmanis, and she needed to know if this was true.

Her detective nose was kicking in and she had to remind herself to take care when being drawn down potential rabbit holes. It had happened before. Sometimes family rifts provided red herrings that seemed perfectly suited to a particular motive: the traditional lusty greed for land, money and power. This case had it all. However, her job was to sort through the reeds and come up with solid evidence that would make the most of her time. One thing was for sure: she couldn't interview Jean-Luc, and she couldn't interview Fawaz Nabil. She could, however, interview Khalil Dalmani. But to do that, she was also acutely aware that she'd have to go through, or at least deal with in some capacity, Grant Tennyson.

She left Fawaz's file for a moment and went back to Jean-Luc's, searching for any connection between the families. She found a series of photos and flicked through them. A waiter pushing a trolley came towards her, and Helen ordered a coffee. Long train journeys made her too comfortable and thus weary; it was something to do with the gentle rhythm of the unwavering speed, as well as the hush. She stretched and yawned and stirred sugar into her drink.

She went back to the photos and one caught her attention. It was a group photo taken in the 1990s, and right at the centre was Nabil senior; he'd died later that year. She squinted and got close to the photograph. Next to his father, she recognised Fawaz. He was a striking young man, and unforgettable. His most recent photo supplied by US Intelligence was of him attending an arms deal in Saudi Arabia two years ago. He hadn't changed much, and his eyes jumped from the picture, despite its age. A small shiver ran through her when she noticed the man next to him, whom he had his arm around. They looked like brothers and beamed for the camera. The face was unmistakeable, though he'd aged like all of them. The man in Fawaz's hold was Khalil Dalmani.

Not far away, also smiling for the camera, but off centre and not as well turned out as the two men embracing, was a face she also recognised. It was Jean-Luc. It didn't take long for Helen to pick out his parents too. Basem looked older than his years and Marie looked proud but wary. It was a photo depicting a chilling hierarchy, and sure enough, the periphery was made up of household servants. But they too were smiling. And why wouldn't they be? They were given a good life by these two families. By the time this photograph had been taken, the Dalmanis and the Nabils would have been filthy rich, and Helen knew they were generous.

What happened? She stared at the faces of Fawaz and Khalil, searching for answers.

She sat back, finished her coffee and took another look at the file on Fawaz, paying particular attention to the information on Nabil Tradings. It was mainly dry and technical, exacerbating Helen's drowsiness, but she persevered. The pages covering pre-2013 detailed the investigations designed to ensnare Nabil Tradings in illegal goings-on, but never led to any indictments. However, the several cases filed by Interpol since 2013, when they'd begun Operation Lionfish, told a different story. To date, they'd seized over a billion dollars' worth of illegal substances being transported by air, land and sea, mainly in Europe and South America. But not one shred of intelligence had led back to the big man himself: Fawaz bin Nabil. He was a local hero in Morocco, due to donating funds to various humanitarian agencies, schools and universities, and no doubt government departments, though there was no evidence of this. For Interpol to catch him, they needed him with blood, explosives or weed on his hands, and, so far, they'd got nothing. They continued picking off couriers, dealers and producers, but Fawaz remained elusive. Then there were the files on his arms trading, but all of it was legitimate. The guy was as clean as a whistle. Helen pondered the possibility of a ruse. A very intricate and complex trick to make the authorities believe that Hakim had been abducted, thus throwing them off the scent of something else? But what? And that would assume that the Nabils and Dalmanis never fell out in the first place. Her head hurt, and she needed a break. She'd been drawn into a labyrinth of intrigue and the task before her seemed more daunting than ever. However, what she did appreciate was that she was away from Paris and the politics of her job. Away from Colonel Palmer and his military dick-swinging, and on her own. It excited her.

This was her bread and butter: a bona fide police investigation. This was why she'd joined the military police. The army wasn't cerebral enough for her and the civvie police wasn't broad enough. This way, she got to step into both worlds, internationally, and once again, all thoughts of her handing her notice in because of some wobble of faith, because of what had happened to Luke, disappeared. If anything, she should never give up because of Luke. Giving up would be like saying it was her fault.

And she had someone else's child to find.

She rarely looked inside her wallet at the tiny photograph of her son, but she did now. Fancies of Hakim's disappearance being down to some kind of ploy or tactic melted away. She looked at her baby boy, swaddled in a white blanket, evidently asleep, and swore she'd return Khalil Dalmani's son to him.

She was rudely awakened from her daydream by the announcement that they were an hour away from Lyon. She sat up, surprised that she'd been thinking about Luke for so long, and put away his photograph. A whiff of guilt settled on her: she was supposed to be at work, studying the files. Looking at her watch, she believed that she could get in a little more reading before she arrived in Lyon.

Fawaz was separated from seven wives and had fathered fifteen children, all of whom he supported financially. None of them worked in the family firm, which was unusual. One would think that he'd be grooming his sons to take over his empire, but he wasn't. So who did he see as his heir? She saw that he hung out mainly at a famous hacienda on the outskirts of Marrakech. The same intel applied: Interpol had to have the grace of the Moroccan authorities to storm in, and they simply didn't have the evidence. They didn't even have a money trail, and no one knew how Fawaz laundered the millions of dollars he allegedly made from drugs and arms.

Her eyes focused on a date five years ago and the name of Fawaz's eldest son: Rafik. He'd been apprehended in London on terror offences and deported back to Morocco by the Home Office. It wasn't that unusual in itself; foreign nationals causing more trouble than they're worth were regularly shipped back to their native states, quietly and without press coverage. It was well known that Morocco wanted to improve relations with Europe and be seen as a legitimate, modern state. She read on and saw that Rafik died shortly after returning home, in police custody.

So Fawaz had lost a child too.

Chapter 10

The Gulfstream G550 was cleared for take-off. Grant sipped pomegranate juice from a glass and peered out of the window. He looked around at the luxury and wondered how it might feel to travel like this all the time. The two little boys seemed nonplussed, clearly used to it. He'd driven them home from school and they'd asked the questions that any curious young boys might in their position: 'Do you work for my dad?' 'Do you have a gun?' Otherwise, they'd been unfazed by the European stranger trusted with their care. He was taken by their innocence and wondered if they'd been told that their brother was missing. Probably not.

The interior of the aircraft was upholstered in soft beige leather and the mahogany tables were polished so well that he could see the reflection of his hand every time he went to put his glass down. Khalil sat opposite him, busy as always, on his laptop. Taziri and the boys sat to the rear of the plane. All three of them were glued to their phones. It was a common sight; he rarely saw people off the damn things. Families on holiday at the Marriott, supposed to be enjoying the pool, having fun and messing around, often spent all their time gaping at the screens in front of them. He decided he'd make a terrible father; he'd be execrably dull in his approach, expecting them to play games outside and interact with each other. Or that's what he told himself.

He and Khalil were sat far enough away from Taziri and the boys so they could discuss business without being overheard. Khalil's theory was that Hakim had been taken in an act of revenge for Khalil turning down Fawaz Nabil. It was a fair enough assessment, but Grant wanted to get the measure of the man who'd once been held in high esteem by the Dalmani family.

'How close were you?' Grant asked.

'We were like brothers. Our fathers fought together in the streets for the National Liberation Front, against the French. They were forced into the shadows, when the French wouldn't tolerate our independence, and they became guerrillas. Isn't it ironic, don't you think, that only twenty years earlier, the French themselves were doing exactly the same thing against the Gestapo? But they didn't see it that way.'

'One man's guerrilla is another man's freedom fighter,' Grant said.

Khalil was a proud man, but some, in Europe, might call his family terrorists. Grant had seen enough during his many tours of duty to know that perspective is irrelevant in war: it was only the winners who got to write about it afterwards. If the Algerians had lost, then Khalil's father would have rotted in a French prison and Khalil would never have been born, but here he was: one of the wealthiest men in the world, flying his private jet into the city of love to stay at the Ritz. That was the thing with money: it always had a story.

'So what made you go your separate ways and not speak for, what? Thirty years?'

Khalil looked away and Grant noticed pain in his face. It was a sore point, but it had to be asked. Khalil sighed. 'After his father died, Fawaz followed the money, no matter what the cost, but my father wouldn't be a party to anything that challenged his ethical beliefs.'

'His *ethical* beliefs?' Grant didn't think ethics had much to do with money.

'He'd worked his way up in the business world through straight and honest commerce. He was old school – he didn't believe in the new opportunities that the drugs and arms trade offered.'

'But the arms trade is legitimate,' Grant said.

'Yes, it is, but, to my father that was another glaring irony, that a man can sell a bomb to a country who pays in dollars but doesn't take responsibility for where that bomb lands. Of course, the arms trade is legitimate, but what of the moral cost?'

'So, he refused to touch arms. Didn't he lose out on a lot of cash?'

'I'm sure he did, but he slept well at night knowing that his product wasn't vaporising women and children.'

'He sounds like a very noble man, your father,' Grant said.

'He was,' Khalil smiled.

'And same for the drugs trade?' Grant asked.

'Exactly. He cut the business away from the Nabil family, and that was the end of that.'

'But Jean-Luc's family remained loyal to you?'

'Yes.'

'You sure?' Grant asked.

'Well, that's what we're going to Paris to find out.'

Khalil looked away again and Grant studied him. He couldn't dismiss the glaring fact that Jean-Luc was one of the most incompetent heads of security he'd ever met. Losing a principal just didn't happen – unless it's meant to. Grant had yet to make up his mind.

'So, Fawaz made contact out of the blue by telephone? You must have been surprised after all this time,' Grant asked. 'Did he think that, with your father dead, you'd be more open to the business that your father found distasteful?'

'I doubt it. He knew me well enough. He said he missed our friendship, and that's when I knew he was lying,' Khalil said.

'Why?'

'Fawaz is the kind of man who never does anything without personal gain. Even as a child he would give you sweets, then days later expect to be repaid in some way. It's a character trait that defines him and his business.'

'So, he wanted your ships between Algiers and Marseilles – did he offer anything in return? It seems to me that this would be a favour from you to him, not the other way around,' Grant said.

'Like I said, he was offering friendship, reunion, a chance to forget the past, but Fawaz forgets nothing. This is the man he is. He once took a woman away from me. She meant everything to me,' Khalil said. He looked over his shoulder to check that Taziri wasn't listening. It was a touching gesture from such a powerful man who could sleep with who he wanted, whether Taziri liked it or not. He carried on. 'He used her for one night, making sure I knew, and then discarded her. He humiliated her. I asked him why he did it. Do you know what he said?'

Grant waited.

'He said that when we were five, or thereabouts, a girl in our kindergarten favoured me over him, and I'd never acknowledged how much it hurt him. Apparently I used to hold hands with this girl. I can't even remember her name. He said that he vowed to himself that he would take a girl from me, and he did.' Khalil smiled and spread his hands. 'I have harmed him, and this is his revenge, taking my son. I have thought long and hard over what I might have done to provoke such a response in him, but I can find none, though he did lose his eldest son five years ago.'

'What did that have to do with you?'

'Nothing. Everything, perhaps? I have thought about it. I was trading with the UK, like I do today, and they were the ones who sent Rafik back to Morocco to be tortured to death.'

Grant shook his head. They were dealing with a very damaged man, and a very powerful one.

'His son was running drugs into the UK and was found living with suspected terrorists. This is what happens to sons who work for their fathers: they follow their lead. That is the nature of business. I have three sons to raise and I won't have them exposed to that world. Sons of that realm are reared and groomed to become criminals. It's the nature of their work: it's not only the product that is illegal, but everything that goes with it. Your job is to ferry substances around the globe undetected, so your whole model is built upon mistrust and danger. It matters not if it is arms dealing, people trafficking, money laundering or drug dealing, the list goes on. All of it is muddled up together and you can't avoid one single part of it. Name me a drug lord's son who grew up clean?'

'I can't,' Grant said. 'Nor can I name one who survived past forty.'

Khalil sat back and turned his head, checking again that his wife wasn't listening. Grant respected the man sat opposite him and he'd learned much about what made him tick. He couldn't help thinking there was more to it though. What he wanted to know was why Fawaz wanted those shipping lanes.

'We chose different paths and we can never be friends,' Khalil said.

It was a resigned statement and full of tragedy. Grant knew that what he was really saying was that it wasn't what Fawaz was asking for that was the issue here, but the very fact that he'd asked for anything. Hakim was a pawn. Grant reckoned that even if Khalil acquiesced, he might never see his son again. But was that a gamble worth taking?

'What if you said yes?'

'It might be my only choice now,' Khalil acknowledged. 'It would be the end of me and everything my father worked for. My containers are frequently opened by coastguard police and international shipping regulators, and so on. If I don't stay clean, I'm finished.'

This was a change: a resignation almost. 'But you can't know what is in every container,' Grant stated.

'For sure, but I can know ninety per cent. Also, I can always chase the paperwork to see who owns the container, who packed it and who supplied the goods.'

'But Fawaz didn't want to do that?' Grant asked.

'Exactly. He refused to tell me what he wanted to transport, and he also refused to have it traceable and recorded.'

'Fawaz doesn't strike me as an unintelligent man, but surely he'd have known you'd say no?'

'I don't know. Fawaz was always arrogant. When I spoke to him over the phone, he was different to the man I knew. He was edgy, desperate – manic even.'

'So, what happened next?' Grant asked.

'Until today, nothing. I never heard from him again until Hakim was taken.'

'And you're convinced it's him who is behind it?' Grant asked.

'Yes. There is something else that I haven't told you.'

'Go on,' Grant said.

'I received a mobile phone by post, to my home, the day before Hakim was taken. That's why I rushed him back to Paris. I saw it as a warning.' Khalil pulled the phone out of his jacket and showed it to Grant.

'Has anybody tried to contact you?'

'Only today. I got a call telling me that I needed to authorise certain containers to be loaded at the Bay of Algiers, heading to Marseilles, otherwise I would never see my son again. It was while you were getting the boys from school.'

'What did you say?'

'I agreed to the authorisation.'

'Have you informed Interpol?' Grant asked.

'No. If I do that, I'll never see Hakim again. This is for you only.'

Chapter 11

Fawaz looked at the photo in his hand. In his other, he held a tumbler of American bourbon. The ice clinked around the glass when he held it to his mouth. His religion strictly banned alcoholic consumption, but he was not devout. For five years now, he'd renounced the Prophet and pursued his own agenda in the world and life therein. His cynicism had turned to bitterness, and that to hate and revenge.

He was alone, except for the usual servants keeping the place tended. Sometimes he dismissed them for days on end and that's when things lost their lustre. Even matters of business did not hold his attention. On occasions such as these darker moments, outside, the pools turned green with algae, detritus blew across the courtyards and food rotted. The staff would be recalled when he felt the fog lift from his haunted brain, they were kept on full pay anyway, and they'd begin the clear up. He hadn't dismissed them today though. They were to stay on for a few days to make sure the place was spotless for his return – if he returned.

His eyes burned with grief. The young man in the photo was only twenty years of age. He'd worked in the family firm; a move that Fawaz had seen as a natural progression for all of his sons. He'd shown him the business, from top to bottom, missing no detail. Out of all of his children, Rafik showed the most aptitude. He was the eldest son of his first wife, and he had her wit and resilience. Once he got into a task, he never gave up until it was completed to the highest standard. The mistake had been allowing him to travel to Britain. In Rafik's unique way, he'd assuaged his father's fears, always quick to point out his gift for avoiding trouble.

But not any more.

He lit a cigarette and inhaled deeply. He took another swig of the liquor and got up to leave the office and go to his private rooms, still clutching the photo. Outside in the courtyard, the traditional riad was decked with balconies, silk curtains, tapestries and tropical plants, and richly adorned with beautiful bright-coloured tiles and mosaics. Had it only been yesterday when the place was full of leering old men, lusting after young flesh? Many of his rooms had been used last night, but not by him. Instead, he'd come to his office and got blind drunk. He wasn't interested in women, or sex of any kind, any more.

He walked through the atrium, around the fountain, free from bothersome visitors. He answered to no one. It was time to be alone and lose oneself in a stupor, so the memories couldn't sting like the spines of a lionfish. If he stayed sober too long, when moods of melancholy caught him unprepared, the pain seared his blood and made his head spin. The helplessness and the injustice turned him murderous, and there was no telling what he might do.

He'd learned, over time, that the only safe thing to do was to retire to his chamber, get drunk and fall asleep. He had to be up early; tomorrow would be a new day, and he had plenty to keep him busy. Everything was almost in place, and it wouldn't be long before he wrought his revenge. The scent of flowers cheered him a little, and he smiled, at least secure in the knowledge that shortly

Rafik's memory would be avenged. He checked his several mobile phones before going to the drinks cabinet and pouring himself a fresh glass of booze. He lay on his bed and opened his shirt, revealing hot, sweaty skin. He was not fat and soft like some men of his age; his body was hard and tight. He lit another cigarette and clicked a switch by his bed, which turned on his music system. He always listened to the same music when he was in this mood: Moroccan soul. It fused the traditional instrumental sounds of the lute, other string instruments and flutes, with a modern, cool Ibiza-type twist that relaxed his body and soothed his overstimulated brain. It also reminded him of Rafik, as it was on one of his trips to Europe that he'd discovered it and brought it back for his father. Fawaz would do anything to get close to him.

He closed his eyes and images flooded his memory of Rafik playing in the pool as a boy. The way his chest moved up and down when Fawaz went to say goodnight to him and he was already asleep, covers kicked off because he was too hot. The curl of his hair and the softness of his skin when he hugged his father in thanks for a birthday present. The deep chestnut colour of his body and the contrast of his two huge new white adult teeth when they came through, unmissable when he smiled, which he did often. Images of another boy haunted him: a fit and free vision of male promise, with his life before him, the son of another, but not for much longer.

Then, just before Fawaz dozed off, the terror began, as it always did: Rafik's last phone call to him. The panic in his voice as he realised he was in serious danger; a peril that his father could not make go away. The gut-wrenching desperation gripped him, and he opened his eyes again, staggering off the bed for a refill. Would it never end? He'd have to get fully intoxicated if he stood any chance of making the images go away, but his ability to cope with alcohol was stronger than ever, and it took more to anaesthetise him every time. He gulped at the whisky.

He lit another cigarette and barely breathed in between drags. He sweated profusely, and he tripped and landed on the floor, the glass tumbling noisily across the tiles, his drink soaking through his shirt. His heart pounded with the toxins circulating in his blood. He closed his eyes tight shut and hoped that inebriation would overcome him soon. Rafik's face filled his vision, and then he saw him beaten, broken, begging for his life, and, finally, thrown into a grave somewhere unknown for all eternity, damned to agonising separation from his father forever. His body remained unclean, his soul committed to wander, rootless for all time, and no one was allowed to pray for him.

He'd had countless people assassinated: government officials who swore they knew nothing of the young man's identity beaten to a pulp in a Moroccan jail, and the police who were on duty that night, but still he never learned where Rafik was dumped. Somewhere in the desert, no doubt.

Was he still in pain?

It was yet another reason to turn his back on religion.

–

Three hours later, a gentle knock on his door turned into a rather loud one that jolted him back into the land of the conscious. His body was exhausted from processing alcohol and he felt mildly fuzzy. It took him a few seconds to work out where he was, but when he did, he knew that it was time to get going. He dragged his still-intoxicated body to his shower room and stripped off, turning the taps on.

'Give me ten minutes!' he shouted through the door. He stepped under the water in an attempt to revive himself, and it worked. In five minutes, rather than ten, he was refreshed, clean, dressed in pristine clothes and ready to go. He grabbed the photograph of his son and slipped it into his casual bag. He didn't want to draw any attention on his journey. He wore jeans and a white shirt, carried two sports bags, a jacket and wore brogues on his feet.

He stopped by the door and looked around. Out in the riad, he allowed the breeze of the early-morning Sahara to wash over him, and quietly he said goodbye.

Chapter 12

Dirty Harry watched as the trucks lined up outside the stone building he guarded.

The pre-dawn light cast an orange glow across the black sky and he was reminded how much he loved the desert at night. He made out the fading Milky Way, the Big Dipper, Cassiopeia and Jupiter. He wouldn't be accompanying the trucks on their onward journey; his job was simply to make sure no one poked their nose around as they loaded. The route to the Algerian border was simple enough. However, the problem was that it had been closed since 1994. So they had to take the ferry to Spain and then to Algiers. This was out of the question, given their cargo. Their only other option was driving south to Mauritania and crossing there. Besides, they had business in Mali. But it made their journey eighteen hundred rather than six hundred miles.

The Sahara was an unstable region at the best of times, but they had boot-loads of weapons should they run into any unwelcome attention. They were also authorised to hand over envelopes full of money to bribe their way across. A contact had communicated that the course was clear but that meant little until they were actually over the border and on their way.

Fawaz would take the riskier option of crossing the Mediterranean and travelling through Portugal, Spain and into France across the Pyrenees. Harry didn't know Fawaz personally but everyone knew him by reputation. Their ties were bound through years of loyalty, and no one would ever rat him out. It wasn't fear that would prevent them, but rather an undying allegiance to the legend and the man himself; he looked after his people. Only last year, Harry's son had needed vital hip surgery to stop the spread of aggressive cancer through his weak body, and Fawaz had paid for him to travel to Tangier to be treated in a private hospital. It doubled the chances of his son's survival and he was still alive today, God willing, thanks to Fawaz's generosity. One day he'd like to thank the man personally.

The noise of men carrying boxes full of random cargo echoed loudly. Their grunts and groans hinted that the boxes were heavy, and Harry wasn't too old to help. He did his bit, not knowing exactly what was in them, apart from weapons. Each truck would carry a different load, ostensibly being transported across North Africa with different destinations. Or at least that was the back-up should they be stopped. One truck was almost loaded and would depart first.

'What's weighing it down so much?' Harry asked.

'One hundred cartons of dried milk and medicines. Charity for remote villages.' A man smiled at him and he nodded.

There was truth in it. Almost lost entirely to civilisation, these tribes were cut off from the rest of the world and relied on charitable organisations, such as the one Fawaz had set up, to deliver the precious goods. Though, this one would get lost and end up over the border in Algeria. The same applied to the other trucks, loaded with basic foodstuffs, clothes, shoes, children's toys and clean water. Each would pretend to become disorientated in the desert, should they be apprehended, and the worst-case scenario was that they were escorted back across the borders. But in the middle of the Sahara, no-one cared about aid trucks.

Harry watched as the men laboured under the weight of the heavier goods. He'd done his bit and lit an American cigarette. Most of the cartons and pallets, labelled with the brand names of various fruits, electrical goods and textiles, needed two men to load them, and Harry saw the wheels of the trucks sink deeper into the sand as they became fully laden. It would take four days for them to arrive in the port of Algiers, but they'd know sooner than that if any of them made it into the country. By then, Fawaz should be in place. The fact that he was heading the mission himself bred even more respect from his wide network of adherents.

It wasn't political. It wasn't religious. It was merely right.

The first truck was fully loaded, and as it began to rumble away into the coming dawn, Harry prayed silently to himself that the plan was followed through. He knew little of what it involved, only that Fawaz would bring them glory and recognition on the world stage. He wouldn't feel it here, of course, in this tiny backwater surrounded by sand. But he would hear of it soon enough.

No matter the outcome, they had already won.

Chapter 13

The Place des Terreaux was busy, and Helen pushed her way through the crowds, peering up at the seventeenth-century Hôtel de Ville. It was only a thirty-minute walk to the river from her hotel, then over the Pont Morand, and it meant she could absorb a bit of the city at the same time. She could have taken the metro, but she wanted to breathe the air and gaze at the Alps in the distance disturbing the horizon. Her apartment was clean and basic: all she needed. After reading into the early hours, she'd had a comfortable, if short, night's sleep.

Helen knew the city well from a previous second-ment to a joint international mission to gather intelligence on terror suspects embedded in Europe, working closely alongside Europol, Interpol's European cousin. And it had yielded some good results. They'd averted seven major plots to attack civilian targets across Europe, and had contributed to Interpol's growing database on lone oper-ators, how they functioned and who they worked for. Terrorism inside Europe had taken a sharp upturn in the last eight years, and the internet had fast become the favoured way to communicate between cells and their sympathisers. New waves of organisations used social media platforms to reach increasingly large numbers of potential recruits, and it was getting worse.

The months she'd spent on the Europol collaboration gave her good knowledge of the geography and demography of France's third-largest city. It was an urban sprawling hive of hiding places for criminals, with its ancient buildings and tiny back streets. Since the Second World War, the Croix-Rousse, to the north, with its series of intersecting traboules posed a massive headache for law and order. The covered passages had originally been used by silk weavers to transport their precious work, undercover, away from adverse weather conditions. Today they were ideal rabbit warrens for criminals, where they could lose the most ardent pursuer. As a result, Interpol was working hard at closing them down and making them one-way routes. It was an ongoing and uphill task.

Her stroll over the Pont Morand was pleasant, and she could see the colossal cube-like structure of Interpol HQ. As she neared the main entrance, she took a few deep breaths and reminded herself of her new assignment. Essentially, Sir Conrad wanted one thing: reassurance that the summit would go ahead without event. How she came to offer him such assurance was down to her. One thing was certain though: so far she'd uncovered not one shred of evidence to link Fawaz to the Afghan poppy fields. She hoped that this would prove Sir Conrad overcautious. In her book, prudence was preferable to dead bodies any day of the week, and she was here to offer solid assurances to the ambassador in that regard.

She entered the vast air-conditioned foyer, which reached three storeys up, and was surrounded by escalators and more glass on all sides. A whole line of security scanners awaited her, and she approached, showing her ID and signing in to see Commander Peter Knowles, Head of Counter Terrorism. She'd looked him up before her visit;

Peter Knowles, whom Sir Conrad had said was a personal pal, had a respected and acclaimed career in police work, mainly at the Met. He had an excellent track record, and Interpol had arrested seventy-two criminals associated with terror plots across Europe since his appointment in Lyon as part of the international force. If anyone was to know about Fawaz Nabil and his connections – perhaps even the circumstances of his son's death – then it was him.

She was searched and allowed to proceed to the fourth floor, where Peter's office was. She was slightly apprehensive because she didn't know what to expect, but she generally found that the civilians working at the HQ were all after the same goal: to stop the shitheads hell bent on destroying the social and civil liberties of member states.

Peter Knowles was busy but his secretary made Helen a great coffee. Her accent was French. The language of Interpol was first and foremost English, closely followed by Spanish, French and Arabic. There was a lot to be ashamed of as a result of the British Empire, but people speaking your language in every corner of the globe was something that Helen was grateful for, though her French was excellent. She stood in front of the glass windows and watched Lyon below, unable to divert her mind from what might be going on down there in the streets. It was this instinctive pull towards rooting out criminality, and wanting to expose it, that had landed her in the RMP in the first place.

'He's ready for you now,' the secretary told her. Helen followed her into the spacious office.

A large man in a smart suit walked towards her, holding out his hand. He had a warm face and clean hands. She imagined him starting out as a police constable in

Hackney, thirty years ago, cutting his teeth on the street. It was difficult to imagine him as Sir Conrad's personal friend though. The two couldn't be more different, and she wondered how they'd met.

'Major Scott. It's a pleasure to meet you. Your CV makes for entertaining reading indeed,' he said. 'Peter Knowles.'

Peter's voice was the kind that demanded attention without shouting, and she met his stare. He was sizing her up.

'Hello, Peter – good to meet you.'

'Sit down, please. I trust you've been reading up on your homework from Sir Conrad?'

'Yes, I have.'

'A yellow notice has gone out to all member states about the abduction of Hakim Dalmani.'

'Not a red notice then?' So, he was being treated as a missing person and not a fugitive. It was an important distinction and one that told her they'd weighed up the options. A red notice was issued for an international fugitive, while a yellow one was released for an international missing person where any border had been crossed – in this case, Algeria–France.

'The investigation with our office in Algiers is not my department, of course, but I'll introduce you to the woman in charge in a minute – she can fill you in on the details. So, Sir Conrad is worried about the summit?'

'Yes. I've been working on his personal security for two weeks, and yesterday I met with Special Agent Roy White, who's heading up the US operation at Versailles. I'm happy with everything from that perspective.'

'But now, Fawaz bin Nabil poking his head above the parapet has everybody jumpy?'

'Exactly.'

'That *is* my department,' he said. 'I'll be taking a keen interest in his movements over the next week. It's poor timing, I grant you that, and we've got eyes on him – as you must know, we've been watching him for years – but in all honesty, the most likely attack on a summit like Paris would come from Da'esh. Fawaz isn't, and never has been, affiliated in any way. He chases the money, billions of it. He's not a political animal, and as far as we know, he's not a religious nut either.'

'Coincidences mean you're on the right path...' she said.

He looked at her. 'Quite,' he said. 'Your detective nose?'

'Actually I can't take the credit, it's from a short story by Simon Van Booy.'

'I like it. That's your police head talking,' he said. 'As long as you're here, you may as well use your time to satisfy yourself that all ducks are in their respective rows and report back to Sir Conrad.'

'That's the idea. Thank you for allowing me to get involved – it's a pleasure to be back in Lyon. I hope I can contribute. Great coffee, by the way,' Helen said.

'It is good, isn't it? I love this city. My wife is happy here and the kids are at university back in England. Mind you, I wish I wasn't quite so busy, the statistics on increasing terrorist cells and how sophisticated they have become don't make for happy reading.'

He escorted her out of his office, along the corridor to the elevator and up one floor to another office and another introduction. This time it was to the head of International Missing Persons. Helen had worked in this department before, and it was depressing as hell. At any given time, there were some seven thousand active yellow notices issued by Interpol, and a lot of them were minors. It revealed the staggering extent of the problem Interpol faced when people went missing across several borders. She'd found herself trawling through them, looking at the photos supplied by loving family members, alongside that of Hakim, and couldn't grasp the unimaginable pain felt by the parents of the children staring back. Most of them would never be seen again. At least her boy had died in her arms.

Sylvia Drogan was Irish. She had a lovely soft accent, and Helen felt instantly comfortable. The head of International Missing Persons was stick thin and wore a chic navy suit, and she could have passed as French. Helen smelled tobacco smoke and figured this was Sylvia's secret to her figure.

Peter Knowles excused himself, and Helen thanked him. Sylvia got straight to work.

'It's a pleasure to meet you. I'll take you straight to the incident room we're using for this. The Algerian authorities have been fantastically transparent and we have some good CCTV from the airport there. Here in France, we've been searching for vehicles seen leaving Le Bourget between two thirty p.m. and three p.m.,' Sylvia said. 'Can I get you a drink?'

'I've just had one, thanks – I'm ready to get going.'

Chapter 14

Hakim had never had dirty nails before. He studied them carefully and picked out the dirt. It was greasy, and he was able to roll up each piece of grit with his thumb and forefinger and make it into a little ball and flick it across the room. He'd witnessed two sunsets since his capture and knew, therefore, that it was Tuesday. Today was his third day in captivity and his body ached for water. The room was about three metres square. It was carpeted badly and there were stains on the beige patterns. There was a wardrobe, which he'd searched carefully, but found empty. There was also a window that had shutters locked closed across it. With little else to explore, he'd spent most of his time curled up on the only bed in the room, on which was laid an odorous mattress, a sheet, a blanket but no pillow. He stopped picking his nails and concentrated his mind once more on the timeline of the last few days, so the details could be of use when he was finally found. He dare not think of any other outcome.

On Sunday, they'd travelled for well over three hours before he asked for a toilet stop. His driver had made a phone call and had pulled into a deserted rest area on the side of the road. The hood over his face was lifted off and the restraints on his wrists cut. The sunshine hurt his eyes. It was made clear to him that a weapon was loaded and inside the driver's jacket. Hakim harboured no desire to run, he just needed to piss. That's when he noticed the car behind him, which he'd suspected had been following them from the airport: driven by a man who'd spoken to his driver when the little girl was talking about the forest. That seemed a lifetime ago now.

Should he have run then? Should he have shouted at the mother for help?

He'd overheard the two drivers arguing as he was told to relieve himself in a bush, they had no change for a cubicle. A loan car drove past at high speed on the AutoRoute. Hakim, for a second, considered running after it but knew it would be suicidal to do so. The men who were bickering about whether or not to transfer Hakim to the other car, looked as though they wouldn't hesitate to use lethal force.

That's when he'd been told to get into the boot of the blue Peugeot.

The dark, tiny space made Hakim's terror more acute and he remembered it now. But at least his hands were free and he wasn't hooded for a second time. He'd ridden like that, rubbing his wrists, listening to the noise of the car, trying to overhear the conversations of the driver on his phone, and see daylight. He knew they'd hit another metropolis by the way the car stopped and started. Also, the driver's annoyance with other motorists made him confident they'd arrived in another city. There were several options as to which city that could be: Grenoble, Lyon, Marseilles or even Nice. He knew they'd continued to drive south or even south-east, because he could see the sun's rays filter into the boot through cracks. He was pretty confident that they were still in France.

The car had stopped and the boot had opened. He'd realised they were in a garage, and he'd been helped out of the car, stiff, thirsty and hot. The Range Rover wasn't there and neither was its driver. He'd tried to keep his eyes from looking too hard at the driver of the Peugeot, but he couldn't help staring at the gun pointing at him. It was a pistol and the man holding it looked as though he wasn't afraid of using it. Hakim had seen plenty of amateurs holding guns, only for their hands to shake. This man's hand was steady.

On his first morning, the door had opened and an old man came in carrying a tray. On it was a bottle of water and some pitta bread with a bowl of brown mush. The man didn't speak, and he didn't look at Hakim as he retreated from the room. He shut the door and Hakim grabbed the bottle, rushing to open it and gulp the contents. He sank it down in one go and the ecstasy was like nothing he'd ever come close to. He smelled the brown mush and recognised it as aubergine. He ate and felt revived and alert after as he lay on the bed. Sometime later, the man came back with a chamber pot covered with a towel, and some tissues. He also brought more water and took away the tray. He still didn't speak or make eye contact. Hakim found it curious that this old man never once seemed to give the impression that he was wary of his position. At any moment, Hakim could have overpowered him, knocked him out and escaped.

And that's when Hakim knew that there were others, probably armed. They'd been quiet, but Hakim had been obsessing about water too much to pay attention. Now, whenever he strained his ears against the door, he heard them. He closed his eyes to get used to their voices. As well as the old man, he believed there to be two others. The old man who never spoke came in twice a day, to bring food and water and replace his chamber pot.

Hakim concentrated on remembering every detail he'd absorbed. As he grew used to his surroundings, his senses had sharpened, and he heard snatched noises from outside, as well as the voices of the guards, what they spoke about, and routine traffic outside. He still hadn't worked out where he was, but it was urban and busy. He visualised the map of France and all the towns and cities that lay to the south of Paris. He could be anywhere. The men talked about food a lot and he knew they played cards and smoked. They argued about winning and cheating, and even sometimes threatened one another with violence. Hakim willed them to begin a fight, then perhaps he could get out of here.

The door opened, and the old man came in bearing the same tray as yesterday. Hakim sat up on his bed and tried to look beyond the door, but it was on a spring and it closed. The man set the tray down and on it was a jug of juice and a bowl of some kind of stew.

'Merci,' Hakim said in perfect French. The man didn't look at him but nodded. It was something; it was a form of human acknowledgement and a reason to be positive.

'Do you know why I'm here?' Hakim continued in the language familiar to him since early childhood.

The man stopped. He turned back to Hakim and looked at him in the eye. There was kindness there, and Hakim tried to read him, but it was impossible. He shrugged.

'Is it to get money from my father?'

'We don't need money,' the man said. He was French.

'What is your name?'

He left and closed the door. Hakim sighed and sat on his bed. If they didn't want or need money, then what did they want?

99

Chapter 15

They gave Helen a desk near to Sylvia's and she settled in to her new environment. The Irish woman didn't seem at all put out at the intrusion. Helen knew that with her years of experience, Sylvia was more than capable of running a missing-person case herself, but her interest in Helen's expertise was genuine and welcome. It made her feel at ease. She'd unpacked her things, which were sparse: a pencil case, her personal laptop for notes, the files she'd been given in Paris and her own coffee cup. She stared at the computer screen, from which she could gain access to live updates on any current case investigated by the giant operation that made up Interpol. The first time she'd been here was terror related, and she'd been part of a vast incident team tracking CCTV across France. She'd soon made herself at home. Sylvia was a quiet work companion until she fancied a chat, which she did now.

'Family with you?' asked Sylvia.

It caught Helen unprepared. 'No, just me. I'm not married. You?' she replied.

'Hubby has been a stay-at-home dad for the past twenty years, following me around my postings. Now the kids are grown up, and he's likely off sipping coffee and planning his next bridge contest.'

Helen smiled. The vision of domesticity was comforting. That's what normal people do, she thought.

'Where have you been posted?' Helen asked.

'It's easier if you ask where we haven't. Here is our favourite though. I'll show you around when we get a chance. There's a great little strip of cafes and bars along the river close to here. But you've been here before though, right?'

'Yes. It's nice to be back. I finished an assignment in Paris, so they sent me to lend a hand, not that you need me, of course,' Helen added.

'If we didn't need you, you wouldn't be here. I've got thousands of cases like this ongoing. It's a help to me for you to take the lead on this one. It's a hot potato, right?'

Helen found the metaphor endearing; the Irish always brought stuff back to food or drink.

'That's what I'm here to find out. Fawaz Nabil's increased interest in mainland Europe is odd timing given the abduction of Hakim Dalmani and the forthcoming summit. The UK ambassador wants watertight assurance that it's not going to affect security.'

'Watertight is a bit ambitious,' Sylvia said.

Helen laughed. 'Yeah, I agree, but as close as I can get it. I was wondering if any red notices stuck in your head flagging Moroccan nationals? Nabil is Moroccan, and I thought I'd start there.'

'There are hundreds, and some with historical connections to Nabil Tradings. I'll pull up a list,' Sylvia said.

'Thanks,' Helen smiled.

'So where were you before Paris?' Sylvia asked.

Helen wanted to get on with her work but she also appreciated that the woman was trying to figure her out and size her up, which was only fair, given that she'd been given a slice of her office space. Helen turned away from her screen and swivelled her chair towards Sylvia.

She gave her a precis of her life, and as she did so, felt the familiar tug of surprise and doubt. Her life was punctuated with job after job, rising through the ranks of the RMP, gaining qualifications enabling her to be loaned out to battalions fighting all over the world, most notably in Iraq and Afghanistan, as well as the odd desk job, which she skirted over.

'You like the action, don't you?' Sylvia commented.

Helen shrugged. 'You got me there.' She couldn't help feeling that the synopsis of her career sounded like an incessant thrusting charge towards promotion, which she admitted it was.

Sylvia seemed satisfied for now and offered to make her a coffee.

Helen turned back to her computer and looked at the intelligence gathered so far on Jean-Luc Bisset. His mother had been put under surveillance and had also been interviewed, and Helen read the transcript. Marie Bisset swore she hadn't seen her son, but the local authorities had obtained a warrant to search her apartment anyway. Interpol, no matter where their operation was based, tried to use the local police where possible, and the French gendarmerie was up there with the best. Helen read the report of the search and noticed that DNA samples had been taken from the apartment and matched to Jean-Luc. They had his profile from an overnight bag found on the private jet on which he'd flown with Hakim. Curiously, the bag was packed with toiletries and a few T-shirts but contained no ID, documents, phone or sentimental items one might take away for a trip.

Like any organic matter, DNA degrades over time, depending upon the conditions and circumstances under which it's found. Exposed to oxygen inside Madame

Bisset's flat, any residual DNA would degrade in a matter of weeks, so to find a trace of Jean-Luc in there meant that it was recent.

From the notes of Khalil's interview with Interpol Algiers, there was no log of his bodyguard visiting his mother in Lyon in the last few months. Jean-Luc hadn't been to Paris since Hakim's final term before the summer break. It was solid evidence that Jean-Luc had been to Lyon without the knowledge of his boss.

She turned her attention to traffic at Le Bourget Airport. CCTV from the airport, of vehicles leaving Le Bourget between two thirty p.m. and three p.m. flagged up several of interest. One of the pilots of Khalil's private jet recalled that he'd seen a black four-by-four in the vicinity of their parking allocation as they taxied, but thought it irrelevant at the time. They had seven vehicles matching that description leaving the airport, but only one – a black Range Rover – had blacked-out windows, and they'd traced it to a company registered in Paris. Traffic alerts had caught the same vehicle travelling south towards Lyon and it had entered the city at seven thirty Sunday night. From the entry point, they'd lost it, until it was picked up again, leaving the city and heading back to Paris. However, it had carried on its journey north, heading for Calais, where it had been dumped near the Eurotunnel entry point. It was burned out.

Their best estimate was that Hakim was here in Lyon, right under their noses.

Next she searched through Khalil's security records, checking all of his staff against what intelligence they had internationally. Jean-Luc had a clean record, but two members of his household staff, one responsible for the maintenance of fences and the other a gardener, had family ties to Morocco. Both men had gone AWOL. Fawaz Nabil was Moroccan; it could be important. It was a question for Khalil Dalmani directly. Members of staff didn't disappear coincidentally during times of family tragedy. It was a red flag, and she made notes of their names. She checked for any discrepancies in the data regarding Khalil's movements, logged by his security tracking, as well as anomalies in files that noted the assigned weapons, body armour and listening devices to his personal bodyguards.

On the day that Hakim had disappeared, two weapons and three radios had been marked as in use, but she couldn't find any evidence of them being logged back in. The information, supplied willingly by Khalil himself, said one of two things: either tracking of weapons and radios under household security was slovenly, or they'd disappeared along with the staff. Helen was impressed that Khalil kept such tight records, and it didn't indicate a man who was careless. It was in his best interests to be transparent. After all, they were trying to find his son.

Next, she listened to the cockpit voice recorder from the flight to Paris, also provided by Khalil's people, and it was without incident. The pilots were relaxed. They followed procedure and switched it off after landing safely and taxiing to their designated spot, when it would be set up for the next flight. She questioned why Hakim had travelled with only one bodyguard and had been told that this was normal, but it was far from regular in her book, and she decided to find out how long this had been going on. The answer Interpol had been given was that Khalil trusted Jean-Luc and Hakim was happy with him, but, to her, it was a massive lapse in security. Which is why she ordered tracing the other vehicles leaving Le Bourget at around the same time as the black Range Rover.

A forensic arson team had been sent to examine the vehicle dumped at Calais, but it would take time to run tests on the blackened shell. The car had entered Lyon from Mâcon on the E15 and the A6, and had travelled all the way into the city, crossing the Saône into La Croix-Rousse, from where it disappeared into the notorious alleyways, not covered by CCTV. Whoever was driving was either very clever or very stupid. A Range Rover with blacked-out windows should be memorable in that area of the city, but who cared? Who might remember? Their only positive lead was that one other vehicle that left Le Bourget Airport around the same time was also traced to Lyon by the same route. It was a blue Peugeot 206, a larger version of the 205 French classic, and it had entered the city by the A6 and crossed into La Croix-Rousse. It too disappeared into thin air, but they had a trace on the number plate, which led them to an address in La Croix-Rousse, between the rivers, where a team was heading right now.

'Ready for the show?' Sylvia reappeared with coffee and referred to the planned raid that was now displayed on Helen's screen, courtesy of body-cam technology, and Helen felt a frisson of excitement. Sylvia handed her a steaming mug and Helen thanked her and sat back in her chair to watch.

This kind of technology was something that was a joy to work with. She'd been attached to countless police departments across the globe and knew first hand that an organisation's ability to achieve results was based purely on funding, and Interpol had plenty.

They watched via body cam as a team of French gendarmes approached a garage, deep in the heart of the ancient passages that criss-crossed over the modern roads, cutting the district in two. Helen tapped a pen against her teeth and Sylvia drew up her chair.

The team parked underneath a balcony, and two men guarded their escape route, should they run into trouble. Helen knew Le Croix-Rousse well. It was a popular tourist destination, but for anyone in authority, it was a detested maze. They were hemmed in by flats, shops, bars and parked cars, and their line of sight was minimal. The radio crackled and Helen's nerves jangled. She wished she could be there, and her foot tapped in time with her pen. They watched the screen. Their brief was to raid the address, looking for anyone inside to apprehend and arrest under suspicion of being involved in the abduction of Hakim.

The garage was broken in to first and they heard the splinter of wood as the doors were bashed in. The footage showed a Peugeot 206 parked inside, and Sylvia banged the desk. It was a significant find, and Helen ordered it to be impounded and taken to a secure location for a full forensic test. The residential part of the building was accessed by a small wooden door on a first-floor walkway, with no rear entry point. The roof was accessible, so one man was stationed up there. Another two took the door. It went unanswered, and the order came over the radio to enter.

Helen and Sylvia watched closely. These were the times that Helen wished she was still operational on the ground. There was nothing like the adrenalin hit of pounding a door in, not knowing what was on the other side.

'You want to be there yourself, don't you?' Sylvia noted. Helen nodded.

'It's driving me nuts, I haven't got used to sitting behind a desk yet,' she replied.

'Don't worry, it's early days, you'll get out there when it counts,' Sylvia said.

Helen turned to her. 'I hope you're right,' she said, appreciative of the fact that some missing people were never found, and that was the case all over the world, no matter your background.

'Come on, get in there,' Helen said out loud. They watched as, on cue, they bashed in the flimsy wood and entered the small apartment. Helen screwed her face up as she concentrated on each of the bodycam images being sent live back to them in the office. She searched round the rooms as if she were there herself. Reports came back from each officer as rooms were cleared.

There was no one home, but what they did find was plenty of detritus to suggest recent human occupancy, like scrunched up sheets, cups and saucers, a sink full of water and a wet towel. Helen sat back.

'Alright, not what we wanted but it's a start. Seal the building,' she ordered. They'd wait for a forensic team to get down there and bag and tag evidence to be analysed in a lab across the city. Meanwhile, a foot search by the gendarmes would take place among the neighbouring residents to see if anyone knew who lived there.

Helen watched as an old lady came out of her balcony door and began to scold the team in very loud and colourful French, strewn with expletives a fisher-woman on the banks of the Saône would be proud of. However, when they explained who they were and what information they were looking for, she became demur, helpful and almost flirtatious.

'Jesus, she's a firecracker,' said Sylvia. The old woman had knowledge of who stayed in the flat, and she made no mistake about telling of her distaste for them.

'Their drugs smelled,' she said. She agreed to be accompanied to a police station for an interview and she smiled as they said they'd get her a coffee and make sure she was looked after. Her gums were gappy but her eyes sparkled with mischief. She told them that she had plenty to tell about the two young men who occupied the flat.

'They moved in two weeks ago, caused chaos with my cats and then disappeared just like that.'

'They left their car,' the body-cam officer said. The woman could be seen peering over the officer's shoulder into the garage.

'They had a van too,' she said. The officer took the details.

'Can you describe the men?'

'Of course! They were both ugly with bad manners.'

'We can start with that.'

But it was what the old lady added to her story that caught the attention of Helen and Sylvia, listening from their air-conditioned office at Interpol.

'Les Beurs.'

Helen had heard the term hundreds of times before. It was the standard derogatory French saying for second-generation immigrants from North Africa.

Chapter 16

Grant sat in a ten-year-old Renault, bought in cash, on the corner of an intersection joining two tiny Parisian streets busy with gossip and coffee drinkers. Cigarette smoke lingered on the air. He watched an internet cafe and took photos of people coming and going. He had a photograph on his front passenger seat and waited for one face in particular to emerge. The man was of Moroccan descent and was in the city illegally, under-standably without the permission of the authorities. But Grant wasn't here to dob him in to immigration officers. The man had come to his attention, via a contact of his in the desert. There'd been a recent scuffle on one of AlGaz's perimeters involving Moroccan nationals. It was frequent enough not to attract major interest, but the man's brother worked for Khalil, as one of his gardeners, and hadn't been seen since Sunday.

Grant's camera was the size of his palm, but it could take detailed enlarged images from a kilometre away: the perks of working for a rich guy. The lead had come from a bad-tempered employee possibly looking for more cash, but there might be something in it. And here he was. Employees that worked the perimeters of AlGaz land were casually vetted and paid on zero-hour contracts: that made them difficult to trace. He'd last seen him fixing a generator, and when Grant had asked questions, he'd tutted arrogantly, giving him vague answers. Most of them had one thing on their minds, feeding their families, but others might be ripe for turning to the opposition, be it to hand over technical information, or perhaps something more sinister.

Khalil was a decent man, and he tended towards seeing the good in his employees – Jean-Luc was a perfect example. Random employees failing to turn up to jobs was a normal part of running any company which paid them in cash, but it was Grant's job to make sure they then didn't sell out to the competition – namely Nabil Tradings. The ex-employee had used his own passport to fly to France: his first mistake. Second: where did he get the airfare?

Being ex-military, Grant had a network of old pals willing to feed him handy information from time to time, such as passenger lists on aircraft; people will do significant favours for comrades who save their lives. His contact in Algiers was a retired major who'd been injured in Iraq. He'd side-stepped to the Foreign Office and now worked in the British Embassy there. He met Levi occasionally for the odd pint in the Marriot, in the twenty-fifth-floor members' lounge.

The man was here. Grant sat up in his seat and held up his camera. A figure in sports clothes, wearing a baseball cap and looking about vigilantly, sauntered towards the doorway. He was inconspicuous and fitted in with all the other mixed nationalities typical of any Parisian street. Grant had parked underneath the shade of a leafy tree and took the photos through his closed window. The man slipped in through the door, and Grant saw him pay for something at the counter and take a seat.

Grant got out of the car and slammed the door shut behind him, locking it with the key fob. He walked across the road, avoiding the traffic, which was light. He went into the cafe and paid five euros for half an hour's internet access; he also ordered a coffee. His French was good enough for the man behind the counter not to answer back in English. He took a seat close to the stranger and listened intently. The man was speaking into an earpiece and Grant strained his hearing. It was sophisticated equipment for a man scrimping and saving to feed his family in the desert. He could make out the odd word but nothing that made sense. He logged on and switched his phone to camera. It was linked to a tiny recorder fixed to his jacket, which he pointed towards the man, and plugged a mouse to it, which he used to take images. It was kit only dreamt about in the army. This was one reason he'd left. Rich guys like Khalil could afford the surveillance equipment necessary to make life easy for those who knew how to use it. In the army, they'd had to put up with outdated gadgetry, often frustrating their efforts to track targets.

Grant nonchalantly browsed a few sites to give the impression that he was regular punter surfing the internet on a day off, sipping coffee, until suddenly, the man got up and left. Grant waited a few seconds and followed him, ignoring the stares from the waiter about his unused time. He looked both ways and spotted the man disappearing around a corner, and he set off after him on foot. He followed him for six or seven blocks, watching as the man spoke on a mobile phone; when he'd finished his call, he threw it into a rubbish bin. Grant searched the bin and fished out the mobile. Sloppy work, he thought. He put it into his pocket. He continued to follow for a couple more blocks, and Grant noticed the street signs told him they were in the eighteenth arrondissement, heading towards Gare du Nord. Finally, the man turned in to a parking area, and Grant fell back a little, not wanting to raise suspicion. He watched as the man entered a Haussmann-style block of flats and disappeared. Grant waited until he thought it was prudent to proceed and went to the entrance himself. The door had no lock and, as Grant entered carefully, he heard a door bang just above him. Otherwise the place was deserted. He jogged up a flight of stairs to where he thought he heard the bang and peered along the landing. The building was a far cry from the fancy boulevards of the tourist spots. The concrete stair-wells smelled of piss and the walls were covered in graffiti. He tentatively progressed along the hallway, which had lots of residential doors leading off it, and stopped short of one, where he heard a single loud, unmistakeable voice, indicating that someone was on the phone. It was the man. Grant took a note of the address and disappeared the way he'd come.

He called Khalil and updated him as he retraced his route back to the car. 'I'll find an opportunity to get in there,' Grant said.

'Make one,' Khalil said and hung up.

Back at his hotel, a far cry from the Ritz, he removed the SIM from the mobile phone he'd rescued from the rubbish bin. It was fairly simple to remotely access the server from the SIM card. Stupidly the Moroccan man hadn't thought to dismantle the phone first: a rookie error, thought Grant. He attached the phone to his computer and watched as the data from the handset downloaded.

There wasn't much on it, but Grant wasn't surprised. Burner phones were designed for single use, else why would people use them to achieve anonymity? That was the whole point. But what he did have was two phone numbers. The man had called each number twice and Grant made a note of the times: all were from today. There was also a text exchange. It gave an address in Lyon.

Chapter 17

'I wish all of my missing persons got this much interest,' Sylvia said.

Helen looked up from her screen and gave her attention to her new colleague. She had a point, and it sat in the air between them. She couldn't imagine the pain being suffered every day across the globe by thousands of parents unable to reach loved ones, never knowing what had happened to them.

'I'm sure you do, Sylvia,' she replied. She got the impression that Sylvia wanted to chat. The office was large and Helen guessed that it was usually only occupied by the head of Missing Persons. The subject of the crimes made the loneliness of the task more unbearable. Helen knew that a sizeable portion of missing people, mainly children, were trafficked for the sex trade, and the database at Interpol HQ was enormous. The part of Sylvia's job that most repulsed Helen was the way in which some of those children were tracked down: by flicking through images on hardcore porn sites on the dark web. She wondered whether, as a parent, it would be worse being told that your child had appeared on the grainy images, or not. She'd come close enough to being a parent to appreciate the vulnerability of children, and the stats were brazenly shocking. Children went missing all the time; snatched from streets, play areas and babysitters, eventually ending up as exhibits among Interpol files.

Hakim Dalmani was twenty-one years old, fit, athletic and bright. He wasn't the kind of target for paedo porn: he was too clever, old and strong. He could fight back.

So where was he? And why?

'We had a case in the army, oh, years ago, when a group of Artillery soldiers was eventually found guilty of providing street kids to suppliers in Germany. This was before the British barracks over there were handed back to German authorities. It was kept out of the news, in case you were wondering – that's how long ago it was. Christ, it'd be online in minutes now. I'd just started in the RMP, a rookie officer – all hope and glory, but no idea what people were truly capable of. That's why I'm still doing it,' Helen said. She surprised herself with her openness, but Sylvia listened.

'That makes it all worthwhile, doesn't it?' Sylvia said. 'Catching the perverted feckers red-handed. It makes me sick to my stomach. But the good news is that Hakim isn't your likely candidate for selling on.'

'Exactly. It's something to do with the father, I've got no doubt,' Helen said. 'He's worth something, but there's been no communication between the captors and the father, or at least that's what he's told us so far. I haven't spoken to him myself yet. He's flown in to Paris – I know that much.'

'What would he gain from being less than transparent with us?' Sylvia asked.

'Either he's been asked to do something politically sensitive, or he doesn't trust us to do the job,' Helen replied.

'So why would he cooperate at all?'

'To hedge his bets while he pays his own team to investigate,' Helen replied.

'He'll be hard-pushed to do that with his chief of security missing,' Sylvia said.

Helen didn't reply. She knew very well that Grant Tennyson was perfectly capable of running such an operation, she just had to prove it, and find out what he was up to. But she wasn't ready to share this with Sylvia just yet.

She turned their attention back to the information supplied by the old woman and it was a priority to track down the two men, as well as the van from the address they'd raided. She went over the information they had, going back to Hakim's journey to Paris.

'We've got Jean-Luc's phone records here. Look, his phone goes dead somewhere between Algiers and Paris, and is never switched back on.'

'He turned it off over the Mediterranean somewhere,' Sylvia said.

Helen nodded.

'Why would he do that?' Sylvia asked. It was rhetorical. They were both thinking aloud.

'He was expecting to be able to communicate in another way once they landed. And he knew he wouldn't need his phone again,' Helen said.

'You think this is evidence he's involved?' Sylvia asked her.

Helen sighed and sat back in her seat. 'In my opinion, when you're tasked with the security of a principal, communication is vital. He should have been in touch with the chauffeur on the ground, his accommodation in Paris, traffic checks and his boss in Algiers to at least assure him after take-off and confirm timings, etc.' Helen paused

'Do we know why Hakim was returning to Paris early? He usually spends the whole summer with his family, but term doesn't start for another month or so. What was he coming back for?'

'I don't know the answer to that. Have you tried the Ritz yet?' Sylvia asked.

Helen shook her head. She knew that she was putting it off. Part of her didn't want to speak to anyone who employed Grant Tennyson. Part of her wanted nothing else.

A junior police officer came into the incident room and informed them that CCTV from the La Croix-Rousse neighbourhood had picked up a van, travelling east along a one-way street, away from the address they'd raided. Helen opened the link the officer has sent across, and they watched the footage together.

'Can we enlarge this?' Helen asked.

'It's been done,' the officer handed Helen an envelope. Inside were two photos of the occupants of the front seats of the van. Both men appeared to be of North African descent and both pictures were clear.

'Fantastic, well done. Thank you.'

'A notice has been handed to all borders in the Schengen area, ma'am. They won't have left the EU by now unless they flew. We're working on tracking the vehicle and mapping its progress now. I'll notify you as soon as we have a trace.'

The officer left.

'I was working on what else there was on Jean-Luc's phone before he switched it off. No close-protection officer allows his phone to run out of juice, so I'm working with the theory that it was switched off on purpose. Hakim called his mother mid-air around two p.m. before he landed. She said he called to remind her to take his brother Farid to his water-polo practice, because over the summer, he'd been doing it,' said Helen.

'And?' Sylvia asked.

'That was after Jean-Luc switched his phone off, so my deduction is that Hakim wasn't overpowered in the air. The pilots didn't report a ruckus either, and they're adamant that no one else was on the flight. They had no cabin crew. Besides, security is usually tight around passenger lists on aircraft coming into Europe. Private jets used to get away with all sorts before 9/11, but now they can't, and it needs to be logged in advance.'

'Ok, so we've got Jean-Luc switching his phone off without Hakim's knowledge, and then what?' Sylvia asked.

'I'm more interested in before that. Jean-Luc's phone was highly active in the period before going to the airport in Algiers, which is what you might expect when preparing to transport your principal. But there's a series of short exchanges to mobile phone numbers that pinged off towers in Paris, and none of them are the registered numbers for the security Khalil was using here in France for his son. None of them are registered to a person, only remote servers. Also, all the lines are now dead, indicating they were single-use burner phones, not something anybody working legitimately for Khalil would be using.'

It was Sylvia's turn to sigh. 'Good work. Any phone activity on those numbers after Hakim's plane landed on Sunday?'

'One, this one here.' Helen brought up the information on her screen. 'It pinged off several masts between Paris and Lyon and then went dead. Look at the times.'

Sylvia looked at the screen. 'Jesus,' said Sylvia. 'That's pretty concrete – the timing coincided perfectly with the transportation of Hakim out of Paris, right here to Lyon. How is the forensic search of Jean-Luc's mother's house going?'

'She's been moved to a hotel, and the gendarmerie are preparing a second interview with her,' Helen said.

'Keep it up, Scott. Good work. I heard they call you "the Wrench" in the army. I'm beginning to see why.'

She left the room and Helen stared after her. That bombshell was a bolt out of the blue and a sure sign to Helen that Sylvia Drogan had spent a bit of time on her record. She cringed. She hated the name, not because it was derogatory – the opposite was true – but because it gave the impression of some gung-ho soldier swaggering about, showing everybody else up, which simply was not true. In this game, you couldn't get anywhere alone; it had to be a team effort.

With that thought, she realised it was time to speak to Khalil Dalmani. She needed to ask him why he trusted one man alone to accompany Hakim back to college. It was crazy. She'd never come across a high-profile and wealthy family such as this one who'd ever considered taking such a risk. It wasn't a matter of trust, but one of logistics and prudence. Drills and skills were the number one weapons of choice for close protection. Stick to the procedures or pay for it. With close protection, one couldn't wing it and hope for the best. Jean-Luc was just a man; but he'd been treated like some kind of super-guard, immune to the pitfalls that the other mere mortals might encounter. He'd been given far too much credit.

She called the Ritz in Paris to see if she could speak with Khalil. Sylvia had tried a few times but was told that the man was always busy. She waited patiently. Over the last forty-eight hours, Sylvia had tried to set up a Zoom meeting with him three times already and it left them reliant upon what had been obtained by the team from Algiers. It wasn't ideal.

The voice came back on the phone and agreed a time for her to use a secure video call, encrypted by Interpol, to have a meeting with him in ten minutes.

As well as the information supplied by Khalil to Interpol Algiers, she'd received his classified file from MI6, who kept a log of all persons of interest. Khalil had qualified for British intelligence attention when he was born, but now it might come in handy. She'd familiarised herself with it over the last day or so and absorbed everything she could about Khalil and his family. Shortly she'd come face to face with him, albeit electronically, but she was still undecided about who she trusted. Sir Conrad wanted to know if Khalil's old associate was up to something, to put his mind at rest about the summit in Paris. They both knew that even if he did know something, Khalil wouldn't simply deliver it to Interpol. She had to find an angle, and she reckoned it was Hakim himself. She looked at her watch and realised that her time was up, and she logged into the call, half expecting to see Grant in the background.

'Major Scott, I expected a man. I do apologise for my assumption, though I expect it's happened before?'

'Not really, no,' Helen replied.

Their call began, and Helen took in the image of the man in front of her. She'd seen his photograph several times now, but the man in person was warm, charming and alluring somehow. His skin was mahogany brown and his face was immaculately groomed: she'd grown accustomed to such good looks when she worked in close protection in Afghanistan. In the Middle East, a man's skin was the sure-fire way of distinguishing class. His was pure silk. She could almost smell his success through the computer screen. He stank of it.

'Let me introduce myself properly,' she said. 'I'm a major in the British Royal Military Police and I've been asked to take on your son's case—'

'Why is the UK military investigating the disappearance of my son?' He interrupted before she could continue. His voice was tinged with suspicion.

'It's not. I was brought in by Interpol as a close-protection expert, sir. The RMP is merely my cap badge. I believe you're familiar with the battalions of the UK military?' Khalil had been sent to the Royal Military Academy at Sandhurst by his father thirty years ago, as was the tradition of wealthy families around the globe. He didn't distinguish himself but that wasn't the point.

He smiled. 'And your credentials?'

She groaned inwardly. *A damn sight better than Jean-Luc's*, she felt like saying, but didn't. She reeled off some of her finer achievements and watched as his brow raised and creased. Her experience had the same effect on men from any country, rich or not. It surprised them. She managed to maintain her smile, waiting for the usual exclamations of astonishment.

'Impressive… What would you like to ask me?' Khalil asked.

'Two things. I want to know why Hakim was travelling back to college early. He usually spends the whole summer with you. Secondly, why was Jean-Luc a one-man team?'

She waited. The room behind him was richly decorated, and she knew he was residing in the presidential suite at the Ritz in Paris. If only she'd visited him before she left, in person, to get a sneak peek.

'Hakim has developed an infatuation with a French girl. He was lovesick, and I allowed him to travel back early, on the promise that he came back again before term began.'

Bullshit, she thought.

'Name of the girl?'

'Amélie Laurent.' He gave her further details, such as her name and area of degree. It would be enough to trace her. If she existed.

'And why a one-man team? I've never come across it in my line of work.'

'Jean-Luc is a skilled professional, and I trusted him with my life.'

'What about your son's life?'

Khalil winced.

'I know that you and Jean-Luc Bisset go way back and I'm aware that he's worked for you for a long time, but we have reason to belief he intentionally switched his phone off somewhere between Algiers and Paris. It never went back on again, and there was no one else on the plane, except the pilots, and your son of course. There are a couple of calls he made at your place in Algiers before he left – we're trying to trace them, but none of the numbers are registered. I'm assuming that you keep track of all of your security staff?'

'Yes.' Khalil nodded, clearly uncomfortable.

'Have you appointed a replacement yet?'

'I have, thank you,' Khalil said.

'Well, could I get in touch with them?'

'Why?'

'I need to liaise with him, about your current arrangements, and, for example, why you chose to travel to Paris and not stay in Algiers.' She tried to remain balanced but what she wanted should be bloody obvious.

'What if I appointed a woman, Major Scott?'

Shit, she thought.

He became serious again. His penchant for teasing wasn't lost on her, something Grant was good at too. 'I told your people that I want to be as close to my son as I can possibly be. I know he is still alive.'

'I'm sure he is. Have you received any demands, or been approached in any way?' she asked.

'No.'

His response came quickly. Too quickly. She stared into his eyes, trying to read them, but she couldn't, and it frustrated her. He stared back and remained steadfast.

'Could I perhaps talk to your new head of security please?'

'Major Scott, I have a meeting to go to. I'll get back to you on that – I don't want him compromised, like Jean-Luc was.'

'So, it is a man. Wait a minute, what do you mean? You agree that Jean-Luc was compromised? How?' she asked.

The screen went dead, and she banged her hand on the desk.

That hadn't gone well.

Chapter 18

The journey had gone to plan, with only one major close call as they arrived in Portugal. The coastguard along the southern coast of Spain, from Gibraltar north to the Algarve, was always hot on movement in its waterways. Fawaz and his crew had anticipated it, but they'd still got lucky.

At one point, on the first night, they were approaching a small rocky cove near Praia da Rocha, the most westerly point in all of Europe. It jutted out into the Atlantic like the chin of a petulant child, though in reality it was a mere blip on the continent's flank.

Lights had flashed suddenly and taken them by surprise. They heard the rumble of a vessel larger than their own, and Fawaz prepared himself to dive over the side, should it come to it. After all, he could see the coast from the blacked-out rig. However, after a few tense moments, the lights had passed and the boat accelerated away. They heard the arguments of a Portuguese couple on board and realised that they were squabbling over a game of cards. It wasn't the coastguard after all.

They'd had to climb a ladder from the beach near Praia da Rocha, as the cliff was steep and tall, which is why it was the perfect beach to land. Fawaz gave silent thanks to the strength of his body as he pulled himself up onto each rung; despite the alcohol and cigarettes, for the most part, he kept himself physically powerful with boxing and weights. Finally, he reached the top and was hauled over the cliff edge by a man dressed in black. He didn't look back towards the people who'd helped him thus far: they'd been paid well enough. A vehicle waited, and he concealed himself by lying down across the back seat, even though it was still dark. He braced his body as the Toyota Hilux pickup lurched from side to side across scrubland and sand dunes. A couple of times he fell off and banged his head, but he never made a sound.

The driver – the man who'd pulled him over the cliff edge – said nothing, but listened to terrible Europop on the radio. They'd taken the coastal road across into Spain and on to Seville, where he was dropped off at a farm-house outside the city. For the first time since leaving his mansion in Marrakech, he was alone, but he had a bed, fresh water and a shower. He slept for two hours before the courier for the next leg of his journey arrived. Fortified with Spanish tortilla and sweet tea, he sat in the passenger seat of a one-litre Peugeot that whined all the way to Madrid, around the city and on to Pamplona, where he rested in a small hotel for a few hours.

Now, Fawaz held on to the ceiling handle of another truck. He was unshaven, sweaty, fatigued and bored. This leg of his journey was over the Pyrenees, and he stared out of the window at the panorama of the mountains and valleys. The scene took his breath away. He was used to the colour of heat; Saharan blasts that forced eyes closed, but not technicolour like this. Africa was a medley of golds, browns and beiges. Europe – or parts of it like this – were pockets and explosions of colour. If it weren't for his discomfort, he might have felt at peace taking in the vista.

It wouldn't be long before his beard took real shape, rather than the higgledy-piggledy shadow it was at that moment. He could pass as a Spaniard, rugged from the mountain air, skin dark from the clear altitude, and eyes darker still from perhaps Moorish heritage. They approached a shack selling cold drinks and offering tapas and tortilla. All the people who had helped his journey to this point had done their jobs silently and without question; that's what money bought. His current driver turned to him, but Fawaz shook his head. It was too risky. All it took was for an international notice to be put out for him and some farmer to make a phone call. It was treacherous enough travelling in the light.

Despite there being plenty of other easier ways on offer to him, he'd chosen this long and arduous entry route into Europe for just that reason: no one would look for him out here on the road. Not a man who had private jets, power boats and helicopters available to him. And not a man who surveillance showed was still at home in Morocco.

Back at the riad, he'd arranged for a body double to stand in for him. It wasn't uncommon for figures of such wealth to do so; even the Queen of England had one. He'd known for many years that the Americans used their drones to track those under surveillance when they could no longer follow the money trail. His dealings were water-tight, and his bankers all over the world stayed three steps ahead of any investigative institution wanting to get to the heart of Nabil Tradings. The money was the only way they could catch any criminal today. It was the only proof of illegal profit, but if it slipped away and disappeared, then nothing was left, and he stayed out of court. His father had taught him how to hide money. Movement. That's all it ever boiled down to.

They were almost at the French border and, thanks to the European Union, they should be across in minutes. At the San Sebastián border crossing, it was mainly wanderers and tourists who passed there. The truck passed several cyclists, and Fawaz marvelled at how that might be, to live with such freedom and abandon, and experience the world with only the sound of the rushing wind and the exhilaration of downhill speed. He watched as one particular athlete dressed in bright Lycra reached the top of the hill just ahead of them.

But something was wrong. The back wheel of the man's bike was off centre, and it began to wobble. They'd only just navigated the highest point on the route and were travelling down a narrow pass. It all happened so quickly, and Fawaz watched in horror as the cyclist lost control and hit a rocky outcrop jutting over the edge.

Fawaz couldn't help himself as instinct took over. 'Stop!' he shouted to his driver. The truck halted roughly and Fawaz jumped out. He rushed to the cliff edge and peered over. The man hung on with his bare hands and Fawaz reached down to grab him. He could see that the man's leg was mangled but the fear in his eyes was not to do with his leg: it was the prospect of falling two thousand feet to his death. Fawaz looked him in the eye and said in French: 'Hold on!'

He pulled with every fibre in his body and was thankful that cyclists were featherweights. Fawaz heaved the man's body over the edge, and they both collapsed on the road. By then, the other cyclists had stopped and surrounded them. A barrage of noise began: questions about the man's state, thanks for the stranger who saved him, debates about whom to call. Fawaz stood up, panting. He looked to where the truck was parked and the driver stared at him, expressionless. He gave his apologies, in French once more, and backed away.

Protestations followed. He couldn't leave. The emergency services would want to talk to him. The man's family would want to thank him. At least leave a contact number? Fawaz shouted a made-up number and said he was sorry but the last thing he wanted was to cause a fuss. He didn't need thanks.

'You saved his life – I saw the whole thing.' The man was American.

Fawaz turned and jumped into the truck, which sped off, hopefully creating enough dust to mask the number plate.

Chapter 19

Hakim heard squabbling, and he listened intently to what the men were saying. He was to be moved. The door opened suddenly, and it wasn't the old man who came in, but a much younger one and he carried an automatic weapon. Hakim tensed. He'd tried to prepare himself for this moment. His father had taught him how to use a gun from the age of thirteen, and he was familiar with most models. He eyed the deadly firearm and prayed the man knew how to handle it properly.

The man standing before him, insisting he hurry to put on his shoes and sweater, held a crude AK-47 – not a sophisticated model at all. It was a far cry from the weapons Hakim used. The man pointed it towards him, and Hakim cringed. He knew how sensitive they could be in the wrong hands, and he hoped the guy had some form of training, else he was dead. It wasn't like in the movies where one bullet to the chest signalled the end. It was an agonising death, unless it was a head shot. The damage done to flesh by one single round could rip apart vital organs but keep the host intact, living long enough to contemplate what had brought them to this end. Then there was the blood.

Hakim nervously did as he was told, all the while watching the man's trigger finger. He spoke now in French.

'Hurry up. We're leaving now.' He was emphatic and nervous.

Hakim didn't say a word; he wanted to cause as little fuss as possible when faced with a bullet. When he was ready, he walked in front of the man calmly, holding up his hands. Another waited in the next room. The old man was gone. He felt a twinge of sadness because the old man had been some kind of lifeline. Hakim had worked tirelessly on him, using all the techniques taught him, and he felt as though he was getting somewhere. The old man had smiled once or twice when Hakim said thank you for his water and lunch. He'd placed towels gently and lingered a little while, checking that Hakim was comfortable.

He took in the adjoining room, noticing as many details as he could and consigning them to memory. He did as he was told and walked quickly out of the scruffy apartment into the sunlight, down two flights of stairs, into a waiting battered Peugeot P4. The tarpaulin was up over the back and Hakim was told to climb under it, reserving the only two seats for his captors. He followed the instructions immediately and without question, loath to attract any unwanted attention from the piece of metal pointed at him. The weapon was held low, giving Hakim the perfect opportunity, should he wish to take it, to jump out of the vehicle and run. This time he wasn't hooded. They were in a heavily populated area where a man wearing a hood, being escorted by two North African-looking men, sweaty with nerves, clumsily hiding weapons, would raise suspicion. Hakim took this as a positive: they were panicked.

He'd been kept alive for a purpose. To run now – even though hitting a moving target with an AK-47 was virtually impossible – he could jeopardise everything and end up dead. It was too risky. There would be other chances.

The men climbed in and the vehicle wobbled with the momentum. The engine started and Hakim had enough energy and humour left in him to smirk; the antiquated French army utility vehicle sounded like an underpowered Land Rover; a beast without guts. He hid his face and imagined himself telling his father of this moment and the image gave him strength.

They set off, jerking and stuttering through the streets. He kept his head down and again memorised every turn, every noise and smell from the outside world. From the few seconds he'd been free in the open air, he'd looked around briefly, trying to find a clue: a landmark or poster, or street sign that would help him work out where he was.

Then, in a microsecond, before he'd jumped into the vehicle and lay down, he'd spotted it: a street sign, covered in graffiti. It was white with an arrow pointing in the direction of something important, something that a tourist might look for. A landmark. It was a sign showing the way to the Notre-Dame de Fourvière, and he knew for sure that he was in Lyon.

The men were still jumpy and Hakim believed that only one thing would make them so hurried: their hideout was compromised. He'd read of captives being moved from location to location for lots of different reasons, such as to confuse the victims, but the body language and urgency of these men told Hakim that they were scared and in a hurry. That was a good sign. Whoever his father was paying to search for him had come close. The vehicle lurched and turned sharply around corners, and he lost orientation in the back seat, lying down, unable to calculate left and right.

After ten minutes of erratic driving, the vehicle stopped and Hakim heard a heated exchange between his two captors about how best to get him upstairs. He daren't move. One of them turned to the back and spat a threat to him.

'Run and you die,' one said to him. Hakim nodded nervously. At close range, there was no way he'd outrun an automatic weapon, especially one with a short barrel. His plan was to comply. He replied in French.

The engine was cut. And he followed their instructions to get out of the vehicle. He did everything they asked of him. Up until just moments ago when they'd fled the apartment, the two men who'd held him had been anonymous to him. Now they weren't, and he stared into their faces. That was not a good sign. He looked down at his feet, in a gesture of compliance.

They were parked at the rear of an apartment block, and the land around it was built up with tenements and other blocks. He listened intently and gazed around as much as he could without making it obvious that he was assessing his surroundings. He stood still, demonstrating that he had no plans to run. The men were too busy arguing to notice. One took his arm suddenly, his weapon now concealed. He was led to a stairwell and marched up three flights of stairs. On the second, they passed a woman hanging out washing on her balcony. Hakim caught her eye and lingered the length of half a breath. She looked away. He must be being moved between the areas of the city most populated by immigrants. Areas like this had, in recent years, become lawless, and the Lyonnais Gendarmerie were stretched to keep check on them. Hakim read the Paris press. On the third floor, they came to a door, and it was unlocked. Hakim was shoved inside but they needn't have bothered: he still had no intentions of running. He didn't know the area; he had no idea which direction to run and, as far as he could make out, he was surrounded by a potentially hostile population. Hakim knew only too well the undercurrent of France's immigration troubles and it wasn't as if he drew attention to himself for looking like a European: his skin was the same as theirs. Some said revolution wasn't far off. Why should anyone give a damn about him?

He was in the bowels of Lyon and all he could do was pray that whoever had discovered their last hideout was hot on their trail.

Inside was much like the last flat, and he was escorted to a bare room, the door locked from the outside. He heard the men discussing what they should do and who they should call but they didn't use names, just codes like they had in the last apartment. Names were changed to animals like Crocodile, Leopard and Sand Cat. The latter coming up the most.

Hakim realised that he missed the old man. He'd been a point of human contact that kept him hopeful. Now, it hit him how much he'd come to rely on that spurious and flimsy connection. He felt bereft, and heaviness sat under his rib cage. It took him by surprise and he felt his spirit waning. It was all part of the dehumanisation and reliance process used by captors – well, the clever ones anyway. It unnerved him that he'd disintegrated so far so quickly. His brain whirred as he tried to grasp reality and concentrate on what meant something important: his father's face, his brothers' laughter, and his mother's embrace. Amélie's kiss. It didn't work. They appeared detached and cold in his mind, and he began to panic. He couldn't breathe. He paced up and down the room, but as he did so, the images of his family blurred even further. Their faces disappeared, smudged and empty. Amélie's face, bright with laughter, replaced the disappearing images and he snapped.

He banged on the door and shouted. 'Let me out! I have to get out!'

Suddenly, the door flew open and the two men barged in, restraining him and forcing him onto the bed. They cursed at him in Arabic and French. One punched him in the gut, but still Hakim struggled. He felt like an animal might, caught in a cage, unable to free itself. All logic deserted him. He managed to land a punch on one of the men's faces, but the reprisal was harsh. The man brought the butt of his automatic weapon down onto Hakim's skull with full force, and it made his temples sing. Vibrations tore through his head and his eyesight faded.

He slumped onto the bed, and he felt more punches to his ribs and gut. He curled into a ball and retched. Finally, the men left, still cursing about the noise he'd made. Within seconds, they were back. He was gagged tightly and slapped in the face a few more times.

Exhausted, with his paranoia spent, Hakim lay down and closed his eyes, one of which was swelling, and calmed his breathing.

Chapter 20

'Tracing two men of North African descent in Lyon is like finding a white Catholic in Dublin,' Sylvia said.

Helen nodded. They sat in Sylvia's office discussing the case. It was her second day in Lyon on the job, having arrived Monday night, and she felt settled in the office space. Sylvia was in and out, with other work taking her away from the office sporadically. For the most part, Helen was left alone, but she appreciated the interjections from a fresh pair of eyes. Helen didn't know if the older woman was checking on her or being supportive and decided that it was a combination of the two. After all, Sylvia had admitted herself that she'd been through Helen's work profile. It was slightly unnerving, as if she now had something to live up to.

'But we do have the artist's impressions from the old woman,' Helen said. The drawings were detailed and had been distributed to the press and posted on the Interpol website, as well as given to all police departments in the 194 member states. It was standard for a yellow notice, but Helen suspected there was nothing conventional about this case.

'We've got the full forensic report from Madame Bisset's flat,' Helen said.

Sylvia stood in front of the vast window, overlooking the Rhône. Sylvia turned to her.

'I think you'll want to see this,' Helen said after scanning the file. She knew what she was looking for; years of chewing over investigative materials had honed her skills to notice anything that stood out. This nugget did just that. 'We already have Jean-Luc's DNA there from a few weeks ago, but they found chewing gum in a waste paper, on top of a newspaper dated last week, yielding DNA matching Jean-Luc's. He's alive.'

'And he's visited his mother. When is she to be interviewed again? She lied to the gendarmerie,' Sylvia said.

Helen made a phone call to the control room, where squad cars were dispatched across the city, and it wouldn't be long until Madame Bisset was in custody answering some uncomfortable questions.

'I don't think it's expedient to share this with Khalil Dalmani just yet,' Helen said.

'I agree,' Sylvia replied.

'He needs to be kept at arm's length until we've got some answers about why his son is so valuable. He says he hasn't received a ransom demand, so the motive isn't money. There's something else, and my guess is that he knows what it is. He wouldn't tell me the name of the security expert who has replaced Jean-Luc, but I have my suspicions.'

Sylvia looked at her, waiting for an explanation.

'He employed Grant Tennyson, a Brit, last year, as his security head for AlGaz.'

'I thought Jean-Luc was his head of security?' Sylvia said.

'Only for the inner family circle. Tennyson is ex-military. I know him.'

'So Dalmani is non-compliant to your investigation. Fuck him, Helen, crack on with what you've got. Are you still in touch?' Sylvia asked.

Helen loved Sylvia's down-to-earth Irish expletive-laden frankness. It made things much easier if one could talk openly, and it saved time. She'd worked with investigators in the past who tiptoed around red tape and vagueness and Sylvia's approach was refreshing.

'No. He's an old contemporary of mine, I don't keep in touch with many army people – the RMP isn't very popular among infantry regiments,' she added.

Sylvia smirked. 'I wonder why. You guys are always on their cases, right?'

'Something like that.'

'Have you got anything on the Range Rover burned out at Calais yet?' Sylvia asked.

Helen bristled subtly. The head of International Missing Persons was a busy woman, and she had other cases to review today, but she was lingering, and Helen couldn't help wondering if she'd had her nose put out of joint because, again, the RMP were encroaching on somebody else's turf: this time, civilian. Helen decided that Sylvia was simply keen to help. Her gut told her that Sylvia was on her side, and that she was being trusted to use her judgement with Interpol's absolute backing. Solid police work spoke for itself, and Helen saw in Sylvia a communal desire to catch the perpetrators of a crime. There was no agenda. And they had no history.

'Yes,' Helen replied. She brought the fire report up on her laptop and scanned the most important sections, which she'd previously highlighted.

'The plates were fake – any dodgy garage in France would make them up for twenty euros. The original plates from which they were cloned belong to a farmer in Normandy – they're still on his almost identical Range Rover. Any serial number or tool markings on the burned-out car were lost in the fire. There was evidence of ammunition having been in the boot and glove compartment at some point, indicating the owners mean business, and that they're familiar with illegal arms acquisition – a worrying development. The most promising detail is that the accelerant cans were found nearby. It was bog-standard petrol, but the idiots left their receipt in a plastic bag, buried in a very crap and hasty shallow grave.'

'It's always easier to catch dumbasses,' Sylvia said.

'We've traced it to a garage just outside Lille, and the CCTV footage is being searched as we speak.'

'Well done – that's great work,' Sylvia said, still standing. She turned around from her vantage point at the window. 'I had a memo come in to me from the head of Counter Terrorism.'

'Peter Knowles?' Helen asked.

'Yes. He's been informed by the UK Home Office that activity around the property of Fawaz bin Nabil has stabilised and he's no longer travelling to Europe. In fact, he's up to very little. I thought you'd be interested to know.'

The penny dropped. Sylvia had her back. Working for multi-layered international organisations meant that information could get lost in translation. What was important to Counter Terrorism and Peter Knowles might not necessarily strike anyone as important to a new secondment delving into a very different angle on the floor above. A standardised computer network would help but with that came further headaches to do with clearance levels. So the fact that Sylvia was passing on this information meant she was considered part of the team.

'Thank you. I am. Nabil Tradings is a rabbit warren of trails and dead ends – I've barely begun on them yet. It's curious that the Americans have been trying to catch him out for years, but yet they can't come up with an explanation for his recent behaviour. What does "inactive" mean? How are they so sure he's settled at home in front of a cosy fire?'

'He's been under their surveillance for years. Even the Americans make mistakes,' Sylvia said.

They held each other's gaze for a second.

'Here are my login details, familiarise yourself with the software – it's easy.' Sylvia scribbled down her password on a piece of paper and went to her desk to show Helen how to access her files.

'Why are you doing this?' Helen asked, following her and peering at the screen.

'In my experience, missing kids often fall through the net because people like us don't talk. Here we have an opportunity to find someone's child, but we improve our chances if we work together. Nail Nabil Tradings and you get closer to Fawaz himself.'

'It's not my area of speciality,' Helen said.

'So why do they call you the Wrench then?' Sylvia asked.

Helen was careful with her answer.

'What I mean is, I'm better at chasing people rather than money. What we need is a nerd who loves digging around in the dark looking for invisible numbers,' Helen said.

'I've got just the person. Go and see Hilda in Fraud on the fourth floor. Give her everything, she'll find a nerd for you. The Americans have never asked for our help with pinning criminal activity on Fawaz so far.'

'They rarely would,' Helen said.

'So, why now?' Sylvia said.

'They have? Specifically?' Helen asked.

'Via the British ambassador to Paris.'

'Sir Conrad?' Helen asked.

Sylvia nodded.

Chapter 21

Grant watched as the man he'd followed left his Paris apartment. The plan had worked. He'd posted a pay-as-you-go mobile through the man's door in a brown envelope, a universal tactic to contact sources, and called it after a few hours. The man had fallen for it and agreed to go to an address at four p.m. Now, he watched as the man left the stairwell and Grant calculated that he had well over an hour. He slipped on a pair of latex gloves.

It wasn't difficult to get in – a simple credit card down the door frame and a bit of physical strength did the trick. Grant shook his head: it shouldn't be this easy – the man was an amateur. He clicked the door closed quietly behind him and left the lights switched off. Instead, he let his eyes become accustomed and began to get to know the layout of the flat. It was sparsely decorated, with nothing indicative of a personal life. It was like a sniper's pad, indicating that the occupant was ready to move at short notice. Grant had lived embedded with two professionals in Iraq for six months, so he knew the signs. But he saw no obvious weapons on display. The bathroom was clear of the man's objects, as was the bedroom. A single camp bed lay in there with one chest of drawers, which Grant searched. He found several mobile phones and connected each one to the device he'd brought with him, telling him of their recent usage, and storing any information from texts. He placed them back where they'd been. Next he searched the living area, which was darker than the rest of the flat because it only had a window facing the stairwell. There was one armchair, a radio, a small TV set and a coffee table.

On the coffee table, he found an A4 pad and flicked through it. It read like the erratic note taking of a busy mother: lists, dates, phone numbers and addresses. All in Arabic. Grant's proficiency in the language was patchy but he recognised a few characters. One thing did stand out, however, and that was a crudely drawn map of what looked like a dock. He turned it every which way and read the labels – this time in French, a language he was more comfortable with. It gave directions to a storage facility, with the docks numbered so it was easier to find. The drawing was angular and uniform, making Grant think that it was a modern dockyard. There were two main points that were highlighted: a landing point and a meeting point. The drawing wasn't to scale but it did say that it would take twenty minutes to get between the two, but was that driving or walking? Scribbled along the port side of one of the arrows was 'Q d.p. Wilson' and Grant knew that it was the name of a huge Quay in Marseilles.

He took photographs with his phone before he closed the pad, leaving it as it was before, and went to check the kitchen cupboards. In the first he found electrical equipment. In the second were circuit boards in various stages of completion. He found antennae in the third, and in the last were radios. The guy was a nerd, but who for? And what was he making?

Grant left the flat and hurried down the stairwell, walking all the way to the metro at Gare du Nord, where he'd left the trusty battered Renault he'd bought with Khalil's money. When he arrived in Lyon, he'd buy another cheap French banger. He called Khalil and told him of the map of Marseilles docks, and the stash of electronics.

'Bomb making?' Khalil asked.

'It seemed a lot more sophisticated than that,' Grant told him. 'To make a bomb all you need is a few cables and some explosive, plus a vessel. It's child's play. I don't think the plan is to blow up your ships, if that's what you're thinking. They don't need you to get bomb-making equipment out of Africa – it's something else.'

'You know a lot about it. Where are you?' Khalil asked.

'On my way to Lyon to find Madame Bisset,' he replied. He picked his way through the Paris traffic, itching to get to the southern city as fast as he could.

They hung up. Grant rubbed his eyes. He'd never struggled with sleep – learning to doze off over an army-issue Bergen backpack stuffed with a hundred pounds of kit in the middle of the Iraqi desert with two hours' notice to move did that for you. He could sleep anywhere, and he did. But he was weary tonight, although he couldn't afford to rest. He knew that the authorities would have contacted Madame Bisset already. In fact, one of the first things Khalil did was call the mother of his trusty guard and warn her, giving her a cover story should she need it. That did two things: it made her feel as though her son's boss was in the dark over the whereabouts of Jean-Luc (which they were), and it also gave her the impression that Khalil was looking out for her (which they weren't, quite). It had worked, and Marie Bisset had been charmed by a promise of a new life, funded by Khalil, regardless of if Jean-Luc had anything to do with Hakim's disappearance or not. She was assured that Khalil certainly did not believe that his guard had betrayed his trust, and Mme Bisset seemed to believe it.

So far, she'd reported back to Khalil via Grant whenever the police asked her for extra information. She'd also communicated her worry that they didn't believe her. Grant had calmed her and instructed her to go for a walk later this afternoon. It gave him time to get there, and it was an opportunity to assess her surveillance team, then guide her to a safe place, without being detected or traced. As far as he could tell, she wasn't under house arrest – yet.

It sounded simple, but it all depended on how savvy the French reconnaissance team watching her was. Should Grant be lucky, they'd be tired, bored and only 50 per cent eyes on the job because it would be late when he got there after a four-hour drive and because they wouldn't be aware of the value of the source. Or, they could have been briefed already, making them alert, prepared and potentially dangerous. Time would tell.

The traffic out of Paris was hell but, once out onto the autoroute, he was able to cruise all the way to Lyon. The summer sun was dipping behind the horizon when he arrived. There was a different pace here, he noticed, and an industrial flatness. The city's lights were trickling on and mingled with the orange beginnings of a sunset.

The vast sprawling city enveloped him and he fought through traffic to the Part-Dieu district. Smart offices, uniform boulevards and the giant spectre of the Tour du Crédit Lyonnais towered over the surrounding streets. Grant parked his Renault and went on foot to the block of flats where Marie Bisset was staying while an Interpol forensic team finished searching her home. It had taken a phone call to a gendarme on Khalil's payroll, who usually looked out for his son, to extract the information. Madame Bisset was right: Interpol were closing in and that left them little time.

It didn't take him long to spot the surveillance team. They sat directly outside the doorway leading to the apartments. There were two of them, and they were eating – as Frenchmen tended to do constantly – and drinking coffee. They seemed to be having an amusing conversation. Occasionally, they swept their gazes up the street and peered up at the building. Grant walked around the back and, to his amazement, he could see no evidence of a team there. He texted Madame Bisset's number from a new pay-as-you-go phone and got an instant reply. She was jumpy. She'd had two phone calls: one informing her that evidence had come to light that required her to attend a formal interview tonight, and a car was being sent to collect her, then a second apologising for a member of staff being sick and her interview was scheduled for tomorrow morning, first thing. Now, there was a man outside her door.

Grant ran his hand through his hair. This would be trickier than anticipated. He texted her:

> When I text you again, it means you need to leave. Let me worry about the man outside your door. When you leave, go directly down the back service stairs and out to the carpark. I'll be there waiting.

He followed with a further text telling her what he was wearing and said he'd scratch his head as she emerged. He hung up. He headed for the back entrance and slipped inside, taking the stairs easily. When he got to the correct floor, he did one walk past of the apartment and confirmed that there was a single male gendarme outside it. He was armed. At the other end of the corridor was another stairwell and Grant thanked his stars. He took out his phone and texted Madame Bisset, instructing her to turn left out of her apartment. Then he shouted as loudly as he could, as if he was being mortally attacked. He banged on a door, making sounds as if he was being winded, and pleaded for help.

'Aidez-moi! Aidez-moi!' he cried.

He heard footsteps and lay on the floor, pretending to be badly injured. The gendarme was simply doing his job: his instinct told him to protect, and he was doing just that. Grant garbled in his best French that he'd been attacked. He pointed to the stairwell. 'He had a gun,' he said. 'He ran down there with my bag – it has medicines in it and money. Lots of money.'

The gendarme checked that Grant was not too badly hurt and took off down the stairwell, speaking into a radio. Grant's window had just become smaller. He shot up, sprinting to the other stairs, past the apartment, praying that Madame Bisset had not been tardy. He came across an elderly woman on her way down the stairs.

'Madame Bisset?' he asked breathlessly. She nodded.

'*Vous êtes Grant?*' she affirmed.

'We need to hurry,' he said.

They reached a door and Grant looked outside. Emergencies in France were casual affairs at best. Responding vehicles got stuck behind drivers unwilling to move aside, asserting their right to keep in lane. He thanked that Gallic trait now. If he'd been in Britain, traffic would be parting for them like the Red Sea did for Moses, and the cops would be here in no time. He was, of course, assuming that the gendarme had called for backup, so he could return to his duties guarding the apartment.

He held on to Madame Bisset's elbow and ushered her away from the building, down a small alleyway that led onto a street three blocks away from his car. He'd memorised the streets around the apartment block and calculated a route.

'Do you have a headscarf in that bag?' he asked her.

She nodded and pulled one out, wrapping it around her head.

He took off his jacket, put it back on inside out so a different colour showed and pulled a baseball cap out of his back pocket, placing it on his head.

They were at his car in under five minutes.

Chapter 22

Helen walked across the bridge and entered the park. It was a beautiful day, but nothing could improve her mood after the royal fuck-up of last night. Somebody somewhere had failed to communicate the critical nature of the mission to secure the movements of Madame Bisset. This was her one regret when relying upon local police: they weren't military. It was the ultimate irony of her job when dealing with civilian authorities. Her mind cast back to working with entrenched police forces elsewhere in the world; the extreme discipline which was bread and butter to the British military wasn't always transferred when embedded in a provincial unit.

The officer guarding Madame Bisset had been tricked, that much was clear. But why had he been alone? And why wasn't there surveillance to the rear of the apartment building? The lame excuse had come back as two officers being taken ill last night and unable to report on duty. Their replacements had arrived too late. Helen recalled that this was why Marie Bisset's interview was rescheduled for this morning. It was monumentally frustrating but one thing was for certain: Marie Bisset was gone. Had Helen underestimated the woman's resourcefulness or had someone got to her first? The gendarme on duty said he'd been called away to another emergency: a man who'd been attacked in the stairwell, but who'd disappeared into thin air shortly after. It stank. But the worst part was when she'd read the description of the man: white, Caucasian, six foot, blonde hair and blue eyes, and well built.

It was no coincidence and confirmed that Khalil was running his own investigation orchestrated by Grant Tennyson.

She felt like kicking the cement beneath her feet every couple of steps, but that wouldn't help. It was the desire of a petulant child who'd lost her favourite toy.

Helen's phone rang, and it was her father. It was a surprisingly welcome distraction. Her father's voice was calm and reassuring.

'Hi, Dad.' She explained that she was on her way to work.

'Of course you are, darling. You always are.'

'That's why I'm here, Dad. You know that.'

'Busy?' he asked.

'Always. How's Mum?'

'She's having her hair coloured for the party. We were wondering if you might not make it?'

Her parents' ruby wedding-anniversary celebration was arranged for the weekend after next. Two hundred invites had gone out and Helen knew they desperately wanted her to attend. Her plan was to be there but the way things were shaping up here in France, it might not be possible. She felt the familiar pull of guilt.

'Of course I'm going to be there,' she said. The summit was next week. If that went without a hitch, she should make it back.

'Well, that's marvellous. How are you, darling?' he asked. She recognised the tone. Her parents had been concerned for her state of mind ever since she'd lost Luke, even though it was three years ago. She couldn't blame them, because their sorrow at losing their only grandchild was barely overshadowed by hers as a mother.

'I'm good, Dad. I'm on a new case and it's keeping me busy. I think...' The phone crackled, and the call cut out. She gazed around her, baffled that she'd lost a signal in the heart of a European city.

'Dad?'

'Helen?' he replied. 'What did you say?'

'Oh, nothing,' she said. She'd been about to tell him her suspicion that Grant was here in Lyon. But now, she decided against it. He'd only worry further.

'The weather's nice.' Helen fell back on an easy topic.

'It's raining here,' her father said.

She laughed. 'Of course it is! It's summer!' It buoyed her to hear his voice and to discuss mundane issues like the British weather. Next they'd be talking about tea.

'I finish up here soon and when I do I'll bring some Belgian chocolates back for you and Mum.'

He was pleased, and they chatted for a few minutes more about family and British politics. Chasing postings around the globe meant that Helen avoided current affairs, and that suited her. She kept up to date as much as she was expected, but she ignored the media in general.

'You'd love it here, Dad – the restaurants and the cafes, and the weather!'

They chatted for a minute or so longer, but she was preoccupied by thoughts of her father's face when he'd seen his grandson for the first time. It was only in a photograph. Luke had died in the hospital in her arms. She closed her eyes and cursed her body.

'Dad, I need to go. I'll call you later in the week. Give my love to Mum. I'll be at the party, I promise,' she said and hung up.

The hot summer sun beat down on her head and she turned her face up to it. She paused halfway over the bridge and let a slight breeze from the river refresh her. The water swirled beneath her and she peered into it, hoping to find what? Some kind of explanation? Luke's face?

She carried on walking and forced herself to focus on the day ahead. Maybe finding someone else's child might help her find peace.

She refocused and cleared her head, physically shaking it as if that would help. It did. The evidence found in Madame Bisset's permanent residence was their strongest lead yet that the head of Khalil's personal security, and the man charged with Hakim's safety, was still alive. Not only that, but the fact that he had visited his mother, thus presumably was free to roam and not held captive like his ward, seriously implicated him. That was her focus for today. It was looking more likely with each passing hour that Jean-Luc was at the centre of Hakim's disappearance. The forensic results would show if Jean-Luc had been in the flat where the blue Peugeot 206 had driven to, which the old woman had said was occupied by Les Beurs; that would be concrete evidence that he was in on Hakim's abduction, but for that she'd have to wait.

Sweeps of the residential areas surrounding the flat had yielded nothing of significance. No one had reported seeing a van, or at least one that was memorable. It seemed like the woman was the only resident in the neighbourhood willing to risk handing over details of the comings and goings surrounding the garage. It was a common stumbling block to investigations: human reticence. Helen had yet to go to the press with finer details than simply persons of interest but was considering making this suggestion. Khalil expressly communicated that he wanted the case kept low profile, lest it harm the chances of finding Hakim alive. It was a fair point and one that she was taking on board, and indeed, given what the man was worth, the chances of fake information bogging them down was high, but she doubted he was sharing everything. To her, a man who was spending every waking moment trying to find his son, travelling to Paris to do so, would be harassing them daily at Interpol HQ, waiting for every shred of news. Khalil Dalmani wasn't doing this and it raised her suspicions further. She couldn't ignore her niggling worry that he was conducting his own inquiry, with the help of Grant Tennyson, flexing private muscle and exploiting private contacts. It was true that the man had resources at his disposal that made Interpol look like an amateur racket. However, what these billionaires failed to appreciate was that legal channels took time, but that didn't mean they were less effective. If this was indeed the case, there was little she or anyone could do, unless he crossed the line of legality, for example by using strong-arm tactics of interrogation or carrying illegal weapons. It was a precarious balance and one that Helen didn't fancy facing, but she knew that she might have to.

It made her think even more that whoever had Hakim must have made contact with Khalil in some way. Why else would he be so cagey? Surely a man desperate to find his son, with the assistance of the biggest international law enforcement agency on Earth, would be virtually camping on their doorstep, demanding progress daily? It verged on arrogance. He was keeping something from them, of this she was sure. She'd memorised his face from their brief electronic meeting. It wasn't lost on her that he expected a man to head the inquiry, and that had put them on an unequal footing. Would he trust her?

She couldn't help feeling that whichever way this investigation twisted and turned, she'd have to face the fact that, at some point, sooner rather than later, she'd have to make contact with Grant.

Chapter 23

Khalil watched his boys charge around the suite, and he smiled. Never again would he take them for granted. He wanted to witness their every whine, crash, bang, fight and annoyance. He felt physical pain when he thought of his eldest son; it had been his most important job to protect him, and he felt as though he'd led him directly into danger. The policewoman from Britain was right: he should never have put his whole personal security programme into the hands of one man. It shamed him to think that he'd entrusted his flesh and blood to a man who essentially he knew little about. He'd thought he'd known Jean-Luc, but he realised that apart from paying him, gifting him bonuses and benefits, he hadn't really got under the skin of the employee he'd inherited off his father. Now, he remembered his face and his eyes narrowing when Khalil added another jet to his fleet, or took delivery of a new Bentley.

Did it all boil down to money? If Fawaz had lured Jean-Luc to his side with a simple promise of wealth, then Khalil had been a fool indeed.

Taziri felt cooped up like a prisoner, he could tell. It was in the way she sighed and her grimace that overtook her face where once a light smile resided. Grant Tennyson had pulled together a team of British ex-special forces to guard them, but Taziri wasn't intimidated by them and that warmed his heart. She was as tough as the first day he'd seen her, arguing in the street about the weight of a fish she'd been sold. She was all indignation and female strength. Khalil had offered to help, to which she'd replied, 'Why would I need your help?' That's why he was shocked – delighted – to see a woman in charge of his son's case. He hadn't quite communicated his joy, and he feared he'd got off on the wrong foot with Miss Scott. Strong women impressed him but they were few and far between in his world. He toyed with the idea of being transparent with Miss Scott, but he mistrusted large institutions that were constrained by certain laws he disagreed with. And she was a cog in their wheel, not his.

But she intrigued him. There was an earnestness in her face that he recognised in his wife. She too had fire behind her eyes, and Khalil knew when to concede. It had taken him three months of visiting the market and trying to speak to the young Taziri before she finally relented and allowed him to contact her family. Three months later they were married, and nine months after that he held his firstborn child. It was a moment he would never forget. 'Hakim' in Arabic meant 'learned and wise', or more specifically, 'ruler'; it was a hefty expectation to live up to, but Khalil never doubted that he'd be proud of his son, no matter what path he chose. Thinking about Hakim now caused a stone-weight of dread to settle in the pit of his stomach. It had been five days. He turned away from the boys and went into a separate room that had been set up as his office. Affairs in Algeria and the running of AlGaz didn't stop because he was out of the country.

Escaping to the private space allowed him to vent the well of anger that had threatened to explode since his son had been taken, and he beat the table with his fist until it pulsed with pain. He sat down heavily behind his desk and heard room service arrive next door. The boys quietened down as they looked forward to filling their bellies. They loved staying in hotels, even when they'd been given no reason as to why they weren't out and about in Paris or seeing their brother. They'd asked after him, but the answer, agreed between him and Taziri, was that Hakim was in the middle of important exams and they'd celebrate together when he was done. The ages of the boys enabled them to process the information simply: they accepted it. They were in heaven: Xbox on tap, an open room-service menu, a private rooftop pool for their exclusive use and European TV. Youth was simple.

He hoped to raise his children without ego and instead teach them humility. He hoped that Hakim had drawn on these resources to soften his captors. It is infinitely more difficult to be cruel to someone who is kind. A scared animal normally bites back, but the one which keeps coming, despite the blows, touches something basic in the most barbaric. He hoped he'd disarmed them with his generosity.

Khalil needed some air. The thoughts going round his head of Hakim in a bare room, possibly bound and even gagged, guarded by thugs for hire, potentially starved and already descending into the depths of the dehumanisation process, made his blood boil and his body sweat.

Taziri came in and handed him a package. Khalil was puzzled.

'The men that are keeping us prisoner have told me it's been scanned electronically. They opened it, so I took a look for myself. Why are you being delivered phones, Khalil?'

She stared at him with those piercing eyes of hers. She was difficult to lie to.

'You're not a prisoner, my love,' he said.

'Pfft. Whatever you say. I know why we have to stay cooped up, that is the least of my concerns. What are you up to?' She held his gaze steadfastly. He was the first to look away.

'I have to make sure that everything is being done and Grant is being careful not to be traced,' he said.

'Grant? And how do you know you can trust him? He turned up pretty quickly from the desert, didn't he? Why do you trust a white man?'

He overlooked her traditional views. They'd been raised, as children, to mistrust the infidel, but Khalil read and watched, making his own mind up about the value of warring indefinitely. He'd witnessed the Twin Towers fall, and he'd studied what came after: Bush's wrath on the Middle East and the millions of lives obliterated. War wasn't the answer to anything, but Khalil knew that Taziri wasn't open to this logic at the moment. Perhaps another day, but not now. She was angry and lusted for revenge. He let her rant.

'What are you hiding, my love? Who sent you this?' Taziri asked. She still wouldn't accept his explanation, and that's why he loved her.

'I'm not hiding anything. I need to communicate with Grant in secrecy – I can't have people listening to my business. I have to get some air – I'm going to the roof. Don't worry, I'll take one of the guards.'

Taziri eyed him as he walked past her clutching the phone, in case Fawaz called him. He'd done what was asked of him, and now it was time to make some demands of his own. The container ship was waiting, as instructed, at the port of Algiers, and would load tonight. He'd kept to his side of the agreement, and now he would insist that Hakim be returned. There was no longer any leverage to be had by keeping him. He felt Taziri's eyes burn into his back.

He took a burly six-foot Englishman to the rooftop, by a private lift, and he wondered at the life they led; these mercenaries out for hire with all the training of the British Army elite. He supposed that his father, as well as Fawaz's father, had been somewhat similar in the sense that they were cast into the wilderness and fought for a cause, willing to fight to the death. These ex-special forces men were hard and steely. They knew the risks, which is why they got paid so much. The key was to stay ahead of anything anybody else might offer them. Loyalty had a price, and Khalil wondered if he'd paid Jean-Luc too little. He had to find a way to shed some light on what his ex-head of security's motivation had been. He didn't know where to start.

But perhaps his mother, Madame Bisset, did.

Chapter 24

The trucks bumped and bounced along the rough, sandy track. Travelling at night gave them respite from the fierce Saharan sun that beat down on them like the blast of a furnace, the air-con whirring like a whining dog as they still gained valuable miles. But at night, the moon lit their way, and they made better progress. They were able to open the windows and allow the cigarette smoke, accumulated by day, to escape in clouds. It was the only thing that kept them sane: the rush of nicotine to while away the boredom.

The journey to the Mauritanian border had gone without a hitch, despite it being the junction of four major North African territories: Mauritania, Morocco, Western Sahara and Mali. The Mali officials were the trickiest but had been paid handsomely in advance with weapons and supplies for the Malian army fighting insurgents pushing south for domination of the region. They had been at times funded by the French, and so that helped. Foreign occupants were always easier to bribe than a man defending his children.

During the long war between the Mali government and those Malians fighting for independence, in what the insurgents called Azawad, the French had supplied the government with weapons and explosives – namely – C4, produced in the UK, but traded everywhere it was needed, for the right price. After the loss of thirteen French soldiers in a helicopter crash sustained while fighting the rebels, French resolve had become harder than ever, and the Mali government, sensing victory, was grateful for any funds poured into their cause. Fawaz bin Nabil had been generous. This was his payment by return.

It was the exchange of packages at the border that was the pivotal moment of the whole journey. No amount of bribery could reduce the stress factor inherent to doing a deal on an African border, in the middle of a desert, faced with automatic weapons and no exit plan. To their relief, the trade went off seamlessly and the soldiers even laughed when they pointed to a box full of American whisky. Now Fawaz's men knew what it was for. They'd been sorely tempted to drink it but Dirty Harry had warned them not to because it would smooth their passage at some point. Now was that time.

Once into Mauritania, the onward trek over the Algerian border and the two thousand kilometres to the capital loomed before them, but at least they could relax a little. Not too much, though, as the road system, though improved, was neglected at best and lethal at worst. They were more likely to die in a road traffic accident than be hijacked by bandits looking to make gains from passing trade. They drove past burned-out and abandoned vehicles in the desert, which no one wanted to claim. It told a story of destruction at the hands of the careless, responded to by those who cared even less.

Their hands were sweaty as they took turns to drive, and water was running low. They took on gallons more at Abadla, a thousand kilometres from Algiers. From there, the roads grew busier, and they passed small villages made of stone, but mostly of dried mud made into bricks by the searing sun. They shone orange in the day and looked like the surface of a faraway planet, with their domed roofs and tight pod-like formations. No one came out to look at them. They attracted little attention. At least they had the luxury of a proper road now they were closer to civilisation. Each of the men dreamt of a bath, and of a woman. They itched, spat, wiped sweat from their brows and burped after a meal in transit: it was a man's domain, the little cabins filled with detritus from long journeys, like that of any long-haul driver discarding last night's dinner packaging wherever it would fit. They stank.

Conversation had ebbed to a minimum and, as they neared the capital, they were almost overcome by exhaustion. They sensed the end of their epic trip and what it might mean for them in terms of reward. Their payment was in cash: half before they set off and half when they reached the port of Algiers. They could taste the dollar bills on the tips of their tongues and, once on the outskirts of the city, they perked up, wily and alert once more, ever vigilant to the prospect of being pulled over. They'd changed plates at each border, and the vehicles carried the familiar licence of the country they were in. Algerian plates were recognisable for their long numbers, denoting origin and manufacture, and were distinctly modelled on their French counterparts.

They fitted in.

It had only been at Abadla where all the vehicles had risked being simultaneously connected by radio, and it was exuberantly celebrated that everyone had made it through. Now, nearing the port, they drove to their prearranged meeting point and waited. It was a carpark hidden among the vastness and chaos of thousands of ships waiting assignment or perhaps docking and unloading. They merged into the cacophony and looked ordinary in their mission. As the last truck parked up, the men got out and stretched, congratulating one another and swapping stories from the desert: scorpions scuttling away from their piss, rocks the size of houses, ditches challenging the axle, close calls with death in hidden ravines and riverbanks, and what they would do to the first woman they saw in Algiers when they cleaned up and went looking. The atmosphere was one of pure relief.

They'd done it.

Now, they had to wait for their contact to arrive. It was the last tedious part of their arduous odyssey. They didn't know the name of their associate, only that the guy in charge had a phone, given to him by an even more important person. The phone would ring at some point and then they could all go and get a wash. The congratulations and celebrations waned as they waited and smoked cigarettes. Empty packs of red American Legend littered the cabins but boredom eventually got the better of a few of the men and they began tidying up. Abdul, the man with the phone, who'd met Dirty Harry seemingly a lifetime ago, got out a pack of cards. Somebody else found a makeshift table: an upside-down plastic pallet, and they crouched around to play Agram. It wasn't unusual to see groups of men doing the same, passing time at the port, waiting for work, filling gaps between ships and the like.

When Abdul's phone rang, the men had almost forgotten why they were here, and the sun was dipping towards the horizon. There was a brief conversation, and they watched as Abdul nodded and took instructions. He hung up and walked towards the dockside, between huge containers looking as though they were out of use or forgotten. He came back empty-handed and gave a brief résumé of how they would spend the next few hours. They were waiting for a blue pickup truck and a man who would deliver their cash. After that, they were free to go wherever they wanted. Accommodation had been organised around the city and transport back to their homes in Morocco would be arranged as soon as it was possible. The men nodded and seemed appreciative of the thought that had gone into their welfare. They split into groups and stood chatting and smoking.

Waiting was part of what they did. They listened to the sounds of the working port and watched the sun sink deeper towards the earth far to the west, where they knew the sea to be. None of them had been near the sea in their lifetimes – apart from Abdul, who regularly travelled to Tangier for the boss. The nearest the others had got was a swim in the dam back home. But they still imagined what the sea might look like: sparkling and vast like they saw on posters and tourist pamphlets.

Some time had passed when a blue truck arrived and parked near the vehicles. There were two men – one driver and his passenger – who got out of the cabin and walked towards Abdul. They shook hands and the man gave Abdul another phone, plus several envelopes. He also handed him some papers, which Abdul studied. It was the inventories of the vehicles and Abdul nodded as he looked over them. The man looked satisfied and made a joke about how Algiers women would take care of them tonight. As he and Abdul walked back to the blue truck, more information was given and they shook hands again. The truck drove away and Abdul returned to the men, distributing the envelopes, which contained cash and hotel details. The men were excited and talked about where they might stay and if they'd have a sea view. Abdul smiled. Fawaz bin Nabil was a generous man.

Abdul opened his envelope and saw that he was booked into the Marriott downtown. He retrieved his personal bag from the back of one of the trucks.

'Don't go telling long stories about yourself tonight!' he teased the men in advance. 'Until we meet again, my friends.' He walked away. He felt dirty and wondered how he would be seen arriving at the Marriott in such a state. He soon forged a plan and managed to catch a lift with an engineer leaving the port after a long shift. He asked to be dropped off at the nearest McDonald's. There, in the toilets, he'd wash, change and refresh himself. Enough to look like a weary traveller just off a long-haul flight perhaps, unshaven and tired.

He waved goodbye to the kind stranger who'd driven him downtown and went to do his ablutions in the world's most anonymous bathroom. After, he ordered a burger and chomped on it, relishing the salt and fat. Outside, he discarded his soiled clothes in a waste bin and hailed a cab.

Chapter 25

Helen stared out over the city far below her and wished she could open a window. Nowadays, upper-floor windows were securely closed due to health and safety regulations, and it stifled her.

Sylvia breezed in and Helen saw it as an opportunity to stretch and walk away from her desk. She'd taken the decision to release a Photofit of the two men who'd vacated the apartment where the Peugeot was impounded, courtesy of the memory of a very sharp old lady. It had gone out to all major European media outlets this morning.

'If I wanted surveillance equipment set up in Khalil Dalmani's personal penthouse at the Ritz, who would I speak to?' Helen asked.

It was the kind of decision not to be taken lightly, but France's anti-terror laws were laxer than the UK's. It was another reason she'd joined the RMP; the excitement of a foreign field, with different rules of engagement and higher risk indices, as well as a broader orbit of responsibility all converged on cases like this one, and she was grateful to Sir Conrad – if only for a moment – for sending her. Only one question lurked at the back of her head: why he would put so much emphasis on what was essentially Counter Terrorism's concern. In her brief moments of pause, she'd read the files – courtesy of Sylvia's computer – on Afghan drug lords and their poppy trade, but Helen had found nothing pointing to Fawaz, yet Sir Conrad was adamant that this element of the summit was vulnerable. But that was her brief, albeit temporarily. Furthermore, Hakim Dalmani's case had caused her to wander into the territory of other branches of Interpol, and she couldn't ignore her findings. To Helen, it was Khalil's behaviour that was suspect, and it was a matter of international interest to watch him.

She waited for Sylvia's response to her proposal to bug Khalil's suite at the Ritz, which wouldn't be cheap. Her reaction would be a good indicator of Helen's status here. She couldn't help feeling that Sir Conrad wanted her out of the way – why else send her to another city? Though perhaps that was Colonel Palmer's doing. But at the same time, the ambassador had been emphatic in his case to her that he was sure that her new mission was indeed an important one. Hadn't he himself said to her that she was to dig around Nabil Tradings, to figure out what Fawaz was up to in Europe, as well as keeping one eye on other criminal activities of consequence, such as any noises regarding drug trafficking out of Afghanistan leading up to the summit? But then he'd gone behind her back by briefing Peter Knowles about his concerns. Or was she paranoid? Surely the head of Counter Terrorism had a vested interest in Fawaz's movements too? What didn't fit into her mandate was the glaring anomaly that trafficking out of Afghanistan usually went through states such as India and Pakistan, and Sir Conrad was adamant that Fawaz's presence in Europe was a red flag. Was he being overcautious? A typical civil servant covering his back? He certainly hadn't displayed the poise she'd expect from a senior foreign office official. She sighed. All she could do was keep her head down and complete her own assignment, and part of that was finding Hakim. It wasn't that she was unused to being uninformed on some aspects of a case – working for multiple agencies at the same time was an art – but like a mushroom, fed shit and kept in the dark, she didn't feel like she was privy to the whole picture. She smiled at the irony. Maybe Khalil knew this to be the case, and that's why he was conducting his own inquiries, or so she suspected, because he knew that his son's welfare wasn't the number one priority in all of this: European security was.

Yes, that'd be it.

'You look like your head is going ten to the dozen – I can hear the steam puffing away like an old locomotive,' Sylvia pulled her out of her musings.

'Sorry, I can't help thinking that this isn't a straightfor-ward missing-persons case,' Helen said.

'Of course it isn't, otherwise you wouldn't be here, and Hakim's file wouldn't have landed on my desk and attracted Peter Knowles's nose. It's taken you two days to work that out?' Sylvia asked.

Helen was shocked but only for a second.

'So, it's unusual for you to be sent secondments?' Helen asked.

'Rare but not that unusual. Secondments turn up here all the time, just not in my department. Don't get me wrong, I'm thrilled you're here, but I reckon the engine's been lit by someone sat in a lofty office somewhere higher than you or I can reach, and we won't know the reasons unless we find them ourselves. Why do you think I showed you the memo from the UK Home Office to Peter?' Sylvia asked.

'That's what's pissing me off. If there's an ulterior motive to finding Hakim, then I should know about it,' Helen said.

'Sure you should. In the meantime, I'd speak to Ricard in Surveillance if you want to set something up at the Ritz – tell him I sent you. He'll give you all you need.' Sylvia gathered a few things from her desk and left; she was always on the move and carrying a look of grievance across her forehead.

A quick phone call to Ricard gave her the answers she needed. She didn't waste any time and set about arranging for surveillance kit to be ordered, and installed at the Hakim's suite at the Ritz. They'd need compliance from at least one member of staff, but they had plants in all of Paris's major hotels. They'd need uniforms, shift times, a timetable of the family's movements (the hardest part) and time. Ricard explained the logistics of such a task without seeming to flinch at all and suggested taking the kit into the suite as part of a routine security drive. After all, Khalil Said al-Rashid ibn Dalmani was an esteemed guest and his son had been abducted. The Paris press knew that much at least. Ricard was keen to make sure everything ran smoothly, including checking entry and exit points to the suite, window and roof access, as well as picking up drone activity in the area.

Helen's concentration on Ricard's plans was interrupted for a moment as an officer delivered an envelope to her desk. She nodded her thanks and opened it with her office phone still under her chin. She scanned the document quickly; it was a lab report. She put it to one side while she finished her conversation with Ricard, whose enthusiasm gave her the impression that he didn't have much on at the moment. Sylvia knew some handy people, and, once again, she was thankful they'd hit it off. She was beginning to feel comfortable in her new surroundings. Once she'd finished with the logistics regarding the Ritz, she hung up and turned her attention to the report.

DNA had been taken from Khalil and his wife, Taziri, as a matter of course before they left Algiers for Paris. Children share exactly 50 per cent of each of their parent's DNA and, as a result, it was quite simple to create a profile for the child without their own DNA being readily available. Very soon after Hakim's disappearance the local National Central Bureau of Interpol in Algeria had taken samples from various items left in Hakim's suite, such as tooth- and hairbrushes as well as pillowcases. The lab report in front of Helen showed a match between a sample from one of those items and the familial sample given by the parents. They now had a watertight benchmark to hand when they needed it, which Helen prayed would be soon. She hoped it would never be used to identify a body.

Her phone rang and it was the control room dealing with telephone reports from the general-public tip line. Data could come in from all over the world off the back of an Interpol yellow notice, but this had come from right here in Lyon. It was a sighting of the two men in the Photofit. The source – a female living close to the La Croix-Rousse area of the city – told them she'd seen the two men talking heatedly in a cafe close to her house. It was a credible lead, because it featured both of their persons of interest at the same time. She said that they had attended the cafe more than once, always over lunchtime. The address of the cafe had been noted and the phone call to Helen was a request for permission to set up reconnaissance on the premises immediately. Of course she approved.

She hung up and searched through her notes for the forensic report of the vehicle apprehended at the scene. It remained in an Interpol compound and had been thoroughly processed. Three separate DNA profiles had been lifted from hairs: two from the driver's seat, replicated in the front passenger seat; and a third from the back seat, also present inside the boot. She ran the profiles through her computer but came up with no matches. Then she returned to the lab report.

She entered Hakim's DNA into the Interpol database and waited.

It was a match to the DNA found on the back seat and inside the boot. It was their first major breakthrough. She could now say with absolute faith – backed up by indisputable forensic evidence – that the two men traced to the flat where the car had been found, had at least journeyed in the same car as Hakim.

The cafe mentioned by the tip was her number one priority; they couldn't let these men get away. Questioning them was imperative, and, with the concrete evidence of her discovery moments ago, finding the men who might have had contact with Hakim was a priority. Part of her couldn't help wondering if Grant was as close.

She gave the direct order for an operation to commence at the address, and it wasn't long before they were in place. She checked her connection to the body cams of the officers attending and switched her computer to live so she could monitor the footage beamed from the three separate vehicles onto her screen.

The officers made final checks to their equipment and an operation order was sent to Helen as she watched live.

Two of the teams were plain-clothes, while another was fully uniformed and kitted for rapid response. All wore body armour, and all were armed. Helen's pulse raced as she watched the streets of Lyon whizz by.

The small unit arrived on scene and Helen prepared herself for a long wait.

The two plain-clothes squads got out quickly and observed the area. The uniforms held back, awaiting instruction; they would take care of any potential break-ins or arrests. The Police Nationale was informed and put on standby to secure the area if necessary, and prepare for armed retaliation. Helen had to sit on her hands as she watched the street view of the plain-clothes officers making contact with the cafe entrance. Two others went round the back, and she was relieved to see that only one door led away from the premises. It was secured.

Another officer sat in his car opposite the cafe, watching through a powerful camera lens, and counting the bodies inside. There was a waitress serving tables, a man behind a counter reading a newspaper, and three customers. Helen agreed that one officer should go inside and book an internet slot, order a coffee and check the toilets. She watched as his camera, fixed to his tie, showed her everything. Soft music played inside, and the officer greeted the staff, before being shown to a table. He ordered a coffee and sat down. It was midday.

Helen's heart rate began to taper off as she realised that they could be watching the little business for some time, and she told herself that she must carry on working. She couldn't sit there all day hoping the two men would simply waltz in and make her life easy.

She turned away from the screen and busied herself with the CCTV footage from the garage in Lille, where the purchase of petrol had been traced, thanks to the idiots who failed to get rid of their till receipt properly when they torched the Range Rover near Calais. But she was grateful to them for it.

The footage was crystal clear, and she peered at the images as she paused the frames. Two men of North African descent were seen paying at the counter at the exact time on the receipt, but they didn't match the descriptions and Photofits of the ones identified as Les Beurs by the angry Frenchwoman. It made sense to her and confirmed that this was a widespread operation, and one of some considerable planning, involving multiple vehicles. The two men who'd occupied the flat in Lyon had stayed here, while the other two – whom she was staring at right now on her computer screen – busied themselves with getting rid of the initial transport vehicle, the Range Rover, thinking their leg of the journey was complete.

'You cocky bastards,' she said under her breath. She enhanced the images in the hope that she'd get a good face-on view to run through facial recognition technology. It was a lengthy process and after a while Sylvia appeared back in the office, asking what she was up to. Helen didn't respond at first and Sylvia peered over her shoulder, raising her eyebrows.

'You've been busy,' she said.

Helen nodded and said she'd be a couple more minutes. After she'd finished, Helen flicked expertly around her computer, showing Sylvia the lab report, the CCTV and the live reconnaissance of the internet cafe.

'You go for the jugular, don't you? I like that about you. You work as hard as me,' Sylvia winked and Helen smiled.

It was one o'clock. Helen's stomach rumbled. She was aware that Sylvia had tensed and looked up to her questioningly.

'I know one of those men,' Sylvia said, pointing at the CCTV still from the garage near Lille. The one of the men paying for petrol. 'He's been on our radar before and is currently logged as a person of interest in connection with several cases of drug production here in France, as well as not registering for work or asylum in the first place. Peter Knowles will be interested in this – they thought at one point that he was part of a terrorist sleeper cell in Marseilles. He dropped off the radar two years ago and we assumed he'd gone back to North Africa or gone to ground here in France. The last time we had anything on him, he was in Paris. It looks like he's been out of the action, awaiting instruction.'

'From who?' Helen was stunned.

'He's associated with Fawaz bin Nabil.'

It was a bombshell.

Helen listened intently as Sylvia logged on to the database for Interpol's red notices, of which there were thousands, and it wasn't long until she found what she was after. The mugshot stared back at her from the screen, and underneath, his name. Ahmad Azzine, Moroccan national. Known by several aliases and code names, most notably 'Sand Cat'. The photo was black-and-white and grainy, but there was no doubt of the match. Helen noticed the hauntingly familiar deadness behind his eyes, so prevalent in criminals.

'Do we have DNA?' Helen asked.

'Nope,' Sylvia replied. 'I'll reissue the original notice, marking it urgent, and release his photo to the French national press.'

'What about these two? Are they connected in any way as far as you know?' Helen brought up the artist's impressions, aware that things had happened so quickly that Sylvia wasn't a party to their release. Sylvia studied them.

'Nope, they're new to us.'

'You sure?' Helen asked.

'If there's one thing this job will forever burn into my skull, it's the ability to memorise faces, Helen.'

'So, they're new recruits – it happens all the time. But it's more evidence of a wider operation, and what will Peter Knowles have to say about the connection to Fawaz?' Helen asked rhetorically, knowing the answer.

It was a curveball that neither of them had expected. It wasn't proven, obviously, and criminals work for lots of different people, but it set alarm bells ringing. Sylvia stared back at her, tapping her teeth with a pen.

'He'll want to know this – he's in his office until four. Any news on the cafe?' Sylvia finally asked.

Helen flicked her screen to the live reconnaissance. 'Nothing yet,' she said, moments before the radio feed crackled to life.

'Suspects spotted approaching the cafe, ma'am,' one of the officers at the scene said over the airwaves.

Sylvia drew up a chair and sat alongside Helen.

'Observe suspects,' Helen ordered. 'We want to know where they're based – I do not want them apprehended here. Repeat: observe, monitor and follow.'

The team acknowledged her request. The ideal scenario would be that the two men would lead them to wherever they were hiding here in Lyon. Helen held her breath as she watched body-cam footage of the two men.

The likeness from the old woman's memory was startling. Helen worked quickly on her keyboard to capture still photos of them. They were chatting intensely, and Helen was struck by how relaxed they were in their body language.

'Is Azzine a pro?' Helen asked Sylvia after switching her mic to silent.

'Pristine and slippery, one of the best. We couldn't catch him,' Sylvia said.

'What's he doing working with these jerks?' Helen asked, watching the two suspects saunter to their table like old friends catching up after a fishing trip. The waitress brought them coffee, and they sat at separate internet ports and logged on. Everything was captured by the Interpol officer at a table close by. At no point did either of the men look around, check their surroundings or look less than supremely confident. They were amateurs.

Sylvia had the same reaction as Helen. 'Jesus, talk about holding your cock and not giving a damn.'

'Let's hope they're as stupid as they look and lead us to Hakim,' Helen said.

'Well, he was in that Peugeot with two other people, so the very least we want is their DNA to match it,' Sylvia said.

The vehicles outside of the cafe remained on standby. Three officers would follow on foot, should the men leave that way. If they used a vehicle, then that option was also covered. The uniformed squad would await instructions depending on where the men led them. If they were drawn into the heart of Le Croix-Rousse, for example, then more foot personnel would be needed.

It was a tense few minutes, and Helen and Sylvia continued to watch the men chat and swap information, seemingly amused by titbits from the internet.

'What the hell are they doing? Passing time? Contacting somebody? Watching cat videos?'

Sylvia's impatience was mirrored by Helen clenching her computer mouse.

'We'll have the premises closed and the computers they used searched as soon as they're clear of the area,' Helen said.

Suddenly, the two men got up and paid for their coffees, leaving through the front and walking east towards the Rhône. The officers on foot did what they did best and took it in turns crossing roads, stopping in doorways and reading newspapers, while the vehicles hung back and tried to predict the route planned by the two men. The suspects didn't even attempt to separate, and it was clear to both Helen and Sylvia, and all those watching, that these men had no idea that they were wanted.

'Don't they check the papers?' Helen asked.

They walked towards the church of St Bernard and Helen looked at Sylvia. 'If they disappear into the traboules…'

'I know,' replied Sylvia.

They continued to listen to the live commentary from the officers on the ground and the uniformed response team wasn't far away, ready to move when they were needed. Luckily for them, the two men entered an apartment block close to the church, and Helen instructed the team to secure the exit points, as well as sending two officers up the stairwell behind them to see which apartment they entered. Tense minutes passed as Helen and Sylvia waited patiently for news.

'Here we go,' said Sylvia.

They had an address. Now, the operation would take on new life: it was to become a raid on an active location and more squads were called in to seal off the area. The district was well known to police, and the action was swift. It took twenty minutes more before they were ready to move in. Helen and Sylvia watched as pairs of gendarmes advanced with weapons ready. A battering kit was deployed to smash the front door. They heard shouts and warnings as the flat was put into a stranglehold. Helen gave the order. Crashing and the splintering of wood could be heard, followed by boots on the concrete as two teams entered the flat. It didn't take long to declare that the two men were in police custody, on the floor of the lounge, cuffed and ready to be brought in for questioning. Meanwhile, Helen ordered an emergency forensic team to search the residence and obtain physical evidence.

The two women sat back and sighed. Sylvia clapped her hands and asked Helen if she'd like a coffee, or something stronger, opening her desk drawer and bringing out a half bottle of unidentified liquor. Helen accepted a small glass and necked it.

Chapter 26

Helen took the stairs down to the fourth floor to pay Hilda in Fraud another visit. Her step was light with the giddiness of apprehending their first suspects.

She'd already introduced herself to Hilda yesterday, after Sylvia's recommendation, and found her officious but more than cooperative. Two junior officers, one an intern, had been tasked with number-crunching information on Nabil Tradings, and Helen wanted to see how far they'd got and if anything stood out. The fact that Ahmad Azzine was associated in any way, no matter how spuriously, with Fawaz Nabil was at best ominous, and at worst, terrifying for Hakim.

She needed to find a motive that might potentially connect Fawaz and Khalil, but at the same time follow the evidence. She went over what she had in her head so far as she trotted down the empty staircase. Everyone took the lift, but she preferred the physical exercise, which kept her alert. Even going up and down one flight perhaps five times a day was better than nothing when she didn't have time to get out for a run.

Sir Conrad had asked her to look into anything that might compromise the security surrounding the NATO summit at Versailles next week. His motivating factor was intelligence that Fawaz had become more active between North Africa and Europe, so Helen rewound and started from the beginning. The intelligence on Nabil Tradings was extensive. Not only had Operation Lionfish investigated him, the CIA had kept an eye on his multibillion dollar corporation for the last ten years, and Fawaz himself hadn't tripped up once. The cost of the inquiry was huge, but it wasn't Interpol's budget, it was America's. With all this information at the disposal of multiple agencies, either Nabil was clean or mistakes had been made. It happened. Sometimes a fresh pair of eyes on any inquiry breathed life into it.

She reached the fourth floor and went through the door, walking along the corridor until she reached Hilda's office. Hilda herself wasn't at work today but one of the juniors tasked with searching through information and business dealings going back decades was, and he looked suitably caught up in mind-boggling detail. He was young, maybe in his twenties, and he had a mop of shaggy hair, which he ran his hand through frequently, and glasses perched on top of his nose. He was attractive, with looks suggesting some Italian heritage, and Helen thought that bumping into him on a hot summer morning was a happy interlude. She chided herself that he was probably ten years her junior. He recognised her name and held out his hand confidently. His handshake was strong and certain.

'Angelo,' he said.

'What have you got for me, Angelo?' she asked.

He beckoned her to follow him and he led her to an incident room, where a whole board was covered in bits of paper. She smiled; it was how she'd trained as an investigator on the Special Branch course: the old-fashioned way, where visuals were everything and people relied less on computers.

'Fawaz stepped back from a lot of his business involvements five years ago when his son died,' Angelo began. 'Which is why it's curious that his activity has increased again. Apparently he's taking more of an interest now. The corporation is made up of divisions and each one of those is headed by a trusted employee of Nabil Tradings, all of whom have been working with him for over ten years.'

'An inner circle? Nepotism at its finest,' she said.

'Exactly. That's the way he likes to work: he keeps people close. But I started with each division and went through them one by one, and I found this,' Angelo said, gesturing to his computer.

Helen peered towards the desktop screen where Angelo had been working. He tapped a few keys and worked the mouse. The figures and names on the screen meant nothing to her. It was something about canning and argan oil.

'A quarter of Nabil's exports go to Spain, and another quarter goes to France. His shipping lanes have been routinely and non-routinely searched for years. Operation Lionfish launched a major inquiry in 2015 but it was cancelled last year. They must have spent millions of dollars on it.'

'They don't normally screw up,' Helen said. It was true; when the joint services within Interpol were requested to come together on such a huge operation, it was usually for a good reason. This time, though, it had come to nothing.

'They concentrated on Nabil Tradings' exports of argan oil going into France, beginning in Tangier and landing in Marseilles, but I think they were looking at the wrong channels. Look, his canning industry exports to San Sebastián.'

'He sends ships all the way around Portugal to land there?' Helen asked.

'That's the thing, they show they do, but I checked the arrival logs and no ships delivering canned goods landed there.'

'What? How is that even possible?' Helen asked.

'Well, if you look at the logs of goods for export and you have paperwork suggesting that it was received, then it all looks legitimate, but if you go further and check Spanish purchases of those goods, then there are none.'

Helen screwed her face. It was as if he was talking in a foreign language. Her head was built for spotting immediate danger, not following paper halfway around the coastline of Portugal. These transactions were imaginary, unsubstantial and floating around in the world of global trade. She couldn't see the ships, or the goods, and she struggled to conceptualise why somebody would use such complicated tricks to conceal them. She knew, of course, that this was exactly how criminals operated; it was something that had been honed to perfection over the past few decades. A criminal activity is performed, be it arms deals or drugs; the goods need producing and selling; then that money needs to be rendered clean so that the person at the centre of the empire gets filthy rich, else what's the point? But her head hurt at the intricacy of it. Here, on paper, they had argan oil being produced by Nabil Tradings in Morocco, travelling from Tangier to Marseilles and traded thereafter. Legitimate. Tick. Now, she was being told that Nabil Tradings canned food in Morocco, which was taken by boat from Tangier to San Sebastián and landed there, but it was never traded in Spain.

So where did it go?

'Either no one in San Sebastián wanted it, or the ships turned back. Or it never existed in the first place,' Angelo said.

'Have you told anyone about this?' she asked.

'I've only just got this far. I didn't really want to say anything until I followed the transactions.'

'What transactions?'

'Nabil Tradings has to register accounts every quarter, for VAT, like every company in the world – legitimate company, that is. It's taken me a few goes, but I finally managed to match the landing dates in San Sebastián to transactions in the accounts. Every month, on the same day as the ships supposedly landed in San Sebastián, there are large deposits made into a bank in Madrid. It's all there in the accounts.'

Angelo tapped some more keys and brought up pages and pages of accounts for Nabil Tradings.

'Here. The money comes in on the same day as the canned goods supposedly dock – but go nowhere and aren't sold – and then goes directly to a company address registered in Berkeley Square, London. It's quite a common method, and I'm surprised it wasn't picked up,' Angelo said.

Helen stared at him. Interpol's Operation Lionfish called upon the skill set of thousands of operators world-wide and here in this tiny office, an intern barely out of college had perhaps found something so explosive that she didn't yet know what to do with or who to tell. Had he made a mistake?

'How on earth did Lionfish miss this?' she asked.

'It was well hidden. They weren't looking for it. Maybe they only concentrated on Africa to Spain?' he suggested. Helen wasn't privy to that sort of information and shrugged.

'What's the trading address of the company in London?' she asked. He showed her, and she googled it on her phone. She knew Berkeley Square fairly well, as she'd worked in close protection for a senior politician who regularly visited a club there. On the days when he spent hours inside, apparently in meetings but more likely catching up with old friends and eating lavish meals, she'd watched the comings and goings of the elite members of London society who either lived or worked there.

The address was a large Georgian townhouse nestled between Corpus Sand Ltd, which was a shipping company, and Mayfair Executive Chauffeurs. Helen brought up Google Earth and looked at the street view. There was no sign on the door, wall or windows of the address in question. It looked more like a residential property. The company name was Rafik Mining and Minerals. It was the name of Fawaz's eldest son who'd died in jail in Morocco. She googled it and came up with a page linking the small subsidiary to a pipeline being built in North Africa. So she googled that: the pipeline didn't exist.

'Angelo, why would large amounts of cash be sent to a company in London when they aren't trading anything?' she asked, already thinking she knew the answer, but seeking confirmation.

'Laundering,' he said.

She sighed. She found it hard to believe that Operation Lionfish hadn't picked this trail up. Indeed, that no one had, but she knew that criminals had become more and more bold and clever in their need to hide and clean money.

'Angelo, can you find out if any ships are landing in Marseilles this week listed under AlGaz?'

'From Algiers?' he asked. The company was well known and highly regarded. Khalil Dalmani's name was associated heavily with French–North African diplomacy and had become even more famous since the abduction of his son here in France. Angelo smiled and Helen could see that he was delighted to be asked to delve into the world of such high-profile cases.

'Have you found him yet?' Angelo asked her.

'Who?' Helen asked.

'His son? It's all anyone is talking about, and I know you are working in yellow notices,' he said. Angelo was clearly an astute young man and keen as a terrier.

'No. But his father, as you know, is highly regarded and extremely rich. I want to rule out any bribery possibilities within AlGaz,' she said.

'I can do it for you right now,' he said. He tapped a few keys and brought up the trade corridors between Algiers and Marseilles. There were hundreds of them, but most of them came under the umbrella of AlGaz, the richest company in North Africa, closely followed by Nabil Tradings. Her hairs stood on end as he pointed to a container ship expected to land in Marseilles tomorrow night.

'Find out every single product on the manifest for me, and find the entry summary declaration filled out in Algiers,' she said.

He nodded, charged with excitement at being included in something so important.

Helen thanked him and instructed him to carry on working on the data, contacting only her if he found something more substantive. She gave him her private mobile number.

'Call me if you find anything else – I don't care how irrelevant it might seem,' she said.

Chapter 27

Madame Bisset sat on a comfortable sofa, sipping coffee. Opposite her sat Grant Tennyson, hands folded across his chest. He smiled at her, but she didn't smile back.

'How do I know you're not with them?' She jutted her chin to the window, indicating 'them' to be the police, presumably.

There was a knock at the door, and Madame Bisset almost dropped her coffee. She was nervous, and that's the way Grant wanted it to be: they had to catch her off guard if they were going to garner any useful information from her. Grant already knew she was a tough nut; anyone who would follow the instructions he'd delivered to her hours earlier, when he'd extracted her from her safe house, had to have balls of steel.

'Relax. It's not the police.' Grant walked towards the door and opened it, letting in Khalil. Madame Bisset's face dropped. She got up and placed her coffee cup on the table. Grant noticed her hands shake.

'What is this all about?' she demanded.

Khalil had flown to Lyon by private jet from Paris, and they planned to make the onward journey together to Marseilles when they were done here. During one of his conversations with Khalil, his boss had happened to mention the name of the officer working on Hakim's disappearance. Before now, Grant had listened to the details of Interpol's progress (or lack of it) with nonchalance. That had now changed. His brief was to find Hakim, not get bogged down in an incompetent and slow official investigation. But the officer's name had sent him into a quiet contemplation that went unnoticed by his boss. Khalil was a businessman and, as such, tapped in to the noises of money and trade, not emotions. And Grant was careful.

Major Helen Scott, UK Royal Military Police. It was an odd secondment, but that wasn't the point. Whatever she was doing there, it was obvious that she'd got herself assigned to Hakim's case. Maybe she was no longer RMP? A transfer to the Foreign Office would explain it, but he could never see Helen giving up her field-operative status for a desk job.

Khalil was fresh, no doubt from a snack and hot shower at his suite in the InterContinental in downtown Lyon. Grant didn't need a place to stay. His business was in the Le Croix-Rousse district, and they were to fly to Marseilles tonight.

'Marie, it's lovely to see you after all these years. Please sit. We have some catching up to do.' Khalil tiptoed around the reason why she was here. Grant admired his poise. He was a good player.

Madame Bisset sat back down, folded her hands across her skirt and nodded tersely. She was acting as though she returned the sentiment of a happy reunion with the boss of her son but Grant could see she remained on her guard. Did she harbour the same resentment towards Khalil about the death of her husband?

But under the current circumstances, Marie Bisset had little choice but to comply with Khalil's wishes. Grant's assessment of the woman was that she was shrewd enough to know when she was out of alternatives. He saw that she was uncomfortable and desperately assessing her options. Grant knew exactly what Khalil wanted, and how far he'd go to get it. He watched as Khalil opened his jacket and sat down opposite Mme Bisset. There was no small talk, indicating that Madame Bisset had nothing to say to the man who'd been so generous to her family. Upon the death of Basem, Khalil had handed his widow two hundred thousand dollars in cash.

Khalil expected loyalty, and that's why he was here: to ask the woman to her face if she was indeed trustworthy or treacherous. Grant fetched tea, and Madame Bisset remained seated, as she was told.

She was a small woman, petite in every way, but with keen hawk-like eyes. She reminded him of an old Italian nonna: ready to throw a plate of spaghetti over her wayward sons at any moment. Grant had spent many happy summers with his mother's family in Naples, learning to cook pasta and rolling gnocchi with a fork to get the right curl and shape every time. He smiled and knew from the woman's reaction that Khalil's presence was getting under her skin. The air-conditioning unit whirred, and a fly landed on the coffee table. Grant poured a cup of hot tea for his boss, but Madame Bisset declined a top-up of coffee. He sat back in the easy chair to the left of Khalil, and they both stared at her.

'Where is your son?' Khalil asked her.

'Je ne sais pas – I have no idea. He's working for you, I thought.' Marie Bisset sounded innocent enough. Her French was harsh, but Grant surmised that this was more to do with her personality than her education or upbringing. Her lips pursed when she enunciated vowels, giving her the aura of the thoroughly peeved.

'Marie, have I not looked after your family all these years as I promised my father? To what grievance do I owe such disloyalty?' Khalil opened the first salvo of the scrap. It was a serious accusation.

'What disloyalty, enfant?' She used the affectionately scolding term for a defiant child.

Khalil wasn't moved. He sipped his tea, complimenting Grant on its level of sweetness. 'I have plenty of time to sit with you and discuss why and with whom you have learned these mistrusting ways, but unfortunately, I don't have the inclination.' Khalil no longer hid his suspicion.

They spoke in French, and Grant followed almost every word. The tone was enough to finish off the sentences he couldn't quite catch. He held his teacup, presenting himself as a mediator or friend.

'Marie, the last time I saw Jean-Luc, he was helping my son load his luggage into a private plane – my private plane – heading for Paris. Since then, Hakim has disappeared, and so too has Jean-Luc. But I know he's been to see you,' Khalil said. It was the same contact at the British embassy in Algiers who'd fed Grant the recent discovery that recent DNA matching Jean-Luc's was found in Madame Bisset's flat. He imagined Helen Scott's joy when she heard the news.

'He has not! The last time I spoke to him he was in Algiers, waiting to hear if you would keep him as head of your private security.'

Khalil narrowed his eyes.

'So, revenge? He colluded with and took money from Fawaz bin Nabil to hurt me? To teach me a lesson because I employed an Englishman?'

Grant not so much saw the anger bubbling up inside Khalil but felt it. It pervaded the small room and Grant could almost touch it. He'd never witnessed it before. Surely there was more to Jean-Luc's betrayal than his own appointment?

'I take it this is his replacement? An Englishman? Il parle comme une vache espagnole,' she said scathingly, jutting her pointy chin again, this time at Grant.

It was a fine insult indeed, and Grant wished they had similar sayings in English. He didn't think his French was as bad as a Spanish cow but she was entitled to her opinion. Her aspersions were simply designed to buy time.

Khalil smiled briefly, before his face set like stone again. Grant didn't reply. He just stared at her.

Realising she wasn't going to get a rise out of either of them, Mme Bisset sighed and changed tactics. 'You hurt him, Khalil,' she said.

'Why didn't he tell me?' Khalil asked.

'You lost his trust.'

'So, this is how he repays me? He hands over my son to that drug-dealing terrorist connard?'

'Be careful, young Khalil – be mindful of who you are speaking to. My family gave you their lives, literally, and it was you who single-handedly ordered us away from the Nabils, for what? We would be rich indeed by now had we had the courage to defy you and your obsession with correctness and impressing the French.'

'Is two hundred thousand dollars not rich enough for you, Marie?' Khalil asked. She didn't reply.

Grant saw great pain in the woman's eyes, but from what he'd heard about his employer, he couldn't help disbelieving the woman. Greed must have played a part, because he knew first-hand of Khalil's benevolence. He kept way more staff on than he needed, he paid benefits to families camping in stone desert huts in the Sahara and had built three schools so far in remote dust bowls in Algeria. In his book, money was earned, not gifted, and it certainly wasn't extorted.

'Thank you for your clarity, Marie,' Khalil said. He finished his tea and turned to Grant. The meeting was over.

'These friends of yours, make sure they impress on the madame the importance of finding her son, so that I might have a chance of finding my own,' Khalil said.

Grant opened his hands and nodded. 'It's already taken care of,' Grant said in perfect French.

Madame Bisset shot Grant a seething look of defiance.

Grant had concentrated on his verb conjugations in his reply and got them spot on. It was a small detail but one that had the desired effect on Madame Bisset. His clean Parisian accent had been picked up courtesy of a posting years ago. He stood up and tapped a number into his phone.

Suddenly reverting back to English, which, Grant guessed correctly, wasn't Marie Bisset's strong point, she spoke. 'Khalil, stop, don't. I don't know where he is, I swear. All I know is that he came to me terribly worried about something and I gave him money.'

Khalil didn't move. The balance of power in the room shifted. Grant turned on her.

'When?' he demanded.

'Last Sunday,' she replied. Grant looked at Khalil who gave nothing away. It was the day Hakim had landed in Paris and, from there, disappeared.

'What exactly did he want and why?' Grant asked in French. 'Think very carefully how you answer because you'll pray he took you with him if you don't.' Grant towered over her.

Her eyes widened. 'Khalil!' she appealed to the young man who'd saved her family, who she'd betrayed.

'This Englishman knows his security processes, Marie. Unlike Jean-Luc, who was stealing from me all his life. Thirty years ago, it was a fish, last week, it was my son. I cannot help the family to which I was born. I cannot help the fact that my father made something grow out of the shit left behind by the war. I cannot help that your husband became a servant not a master. He had as much opportunity as my own father. You want revenge? Take it and lie in your bed and wait for the roses to grow underneath you. But, be careful, their thorns might prick you and cause you to bleed.' Khalil got up to put on his jacket.

'Khalil!' she wailed.

Grant walked towards her and sat next to her, close by, almost touching, and stared into her eyes. They were the eyes of disappointment and regret. Grant hoped he was never the possessor of such wells of despair.

'What did he want?' Grant repeated his question quietly in French as Khalil walked to the door.

Madame Bisset wrung her hands. She was a tough old hag, no doubt hardened by what she saw on the streets of Algiers. But Grant had seen tougher.

'He said he was knocked clean out and driven to central Paris, where he was left to come round on a park bench in Jardin des Tuileries.' She fired the words out. Her hands were emphatic and pleading.

Grant didn't fall for it and he knew his boss wouldn't either.

'He made his way here, to my flat,' she continued, 'terrified that he would be seen as responsible for the disappearance of Hakim. He didn't know what to do. I gave him money and told him to lie low. I don't know where he went.'

'Your son turns up out of the blue, terrified because Hakim Dalmani is missing, and you tell him to "lie low"?' Grant's tone was sarcastic. Khalil shook his head.

'You're running out of time, Marie – these aren't the answers I want or need. Do you know what I might do should any harm come to Hakim?' Khalil asked, standing by the door.

Madame Bisset went to get up. Grant stopped her. 'Let me translate,' Grant added. 'He knows you're lying.'

'He's my son,' she said weakly.

'And Hakim is mine.' Khalil opened the door, nodding to Grant. 'She's all yours.' He left.

Grant had never hurt an old lady, and he wasn't about to start, but the point was that Madame Bisset thought him capable and that's all he needed. He carried on, turning to her. Now she was trembling.

'Maybe he went with the new security guard who AlGaz has no record of, and who was employed only a few months ago by your son?' Grant suggested. This was a clear blow to the woman. Before leaving Paris, Grant had paid Hakim's girlfriend, Amélie Laurent, a visit, and she'd told him about the new recruit who stood out to her because she didn't like him. It was normal for them to be followed around Paris nightclubs by rough-looking bodyguards, and for most of the time, Hakim ignored them and let them do their jobs, but Amélie noticed the new face. It had been easy for Grant to access the CCTV footage of the last nightclub where Amélie had said they'd gone together, showing the man clearly talking to Jean-Luc. When Grant checked, Khalil confirmed he didn't know him and certainly didn't employ him. 'This man,'

Grant said, showing Madame Bisset a photo from the CCTV reel. 'There's Jean-Luc, and who is this?' he asked.

Marie Bisset was up and across the room like a whippet. Grant was quicker and managed to block her way. She was light as a bird, but strong. They struggled and she put up a good fight as she tried to get away from him. He might have laughed but for the seriousness of the situation, and he blocked her by holding her arms to overpower her. She cried out, but he'd lost any shred of sympathy he'd had for the small old lady, and held her tight until he could manoeuvre her knitted jumper over her head to make her stop. He didn't hurt her. He picked her up off her feet as though she were a sack of potatoes and hauled her over his shoulder, carrying her to a bedroom, where he placed her on the bed. He'd already deposited a length of rope, as well as other kit handy for holding tricky witnesses, in the drawers and used them to bind her. She tried to speak the whole time he worked, but he ignored her. Next she spat at him and he wiped his face with the back of his sleeve. As he gagged her, her voice was cut off, and he stood to assess his work. It wouldn't take long to find an old contact willing to earn a few euros to keep an eye on a defenceless, but very spirited old lady.

He made the call. She listened to him and kept shaking her head and throwing expletives at him, no doubt condemning him to a purgatory of hell and damnation. He'd heard it all before.

'Name?' He held the photo close to her again. She shook her head.

Grant sighed. 'My friend, Winston, will be here soon, and he likes old ladies. And no one knows where you are. Not even Jean-Luc, because he left you, didn't he? He hasn't got plans for you, has he? You're sacrificing your own life for his, aren't you? But did you imagine it would be so painful? And long? Winston – named after Churchill, of course – is a tenacious old dog, just like his namesake. And he doesn't speak French. He did, however, serve with your countrymen in Bosnia, and he learned many unspeakable things. I think it changed him. You know what happened in Bosnia, don't you? Neighbour against neighbour, sister against brother, children tortured, old ladies beaten and left for dead…'

Her face was purple and spittle soaked her gag.

'All I need is a name,' Grant said.

Chapter 28

Abdul approached the reception desk at the Marriott Hotel in Algiers and peered upwards. The vast atrium overwhelmed him; he'd never been inside such a building before. The ceiling must have been three storeys above his head and the light spilling in around the golden bannisters, bouncing off glass and flower vases, made him heady with excitement, as if he were a child again. It reminded him of his mother's baking dishes, warm out of the stone oven, full of couscous and lamb. The sweat, which had accumulated under his armpits from days on the road, and at his temples caused by nervous energy and doubt over whether the booking was a reality, dried in the air-conditioned foyer. Guests of all ages, creeds and nationalities milled about leisurely in their effortlessness and chic.

He felt a fraud.

The young woman behind the desk was beautiful, like his sister: dark eyes and with a silken scarf tight around her throat. She smiled, and he relaxed a little. He gave his name, and she looked at her keyboard, tapping on the keys and reducing his world to her hair and perfume. He stared at her and she was obviously used to the attention, because she did not blush or turn away. She caught his eye and smiled again. Repulsion at her brazenness and awe at her courage engulfed him, and he swallowed hard, trying to concentrate on her face, and if it would give anything away. Was it all a joke? Had he made some monumental error and he was in fact booked into a tiny hovel alongside the city's vast slums?

'Mr Mansouri?' she asked.

He didn't reply straight away. Her demeanour captivated him still, and she repeated her question.

'Sorry, yes, that's me. Abdul Mansouri,' he said quickly, smiling nervously.

'Long journey?' she asked.

'What?'

'Is this your first time staying with us, sir?' She moved on.

'Yes, why?' His nerves got the better of him once more, and tiny beads of sweat defied the cool interior air.

'My apologies, sir. I was just wondering if you knew where you were going. If not, it's not a problem at all, I'll get the porter to take you.'

'I don't need that, thank you – I'll find my way. Do I have a room or not?' He was abrupt, but the situation was quickly threatening to force him to flee. He could feel adrenalin pouring into his abdomen and he thought his bowels might betray him. Four days without home cooked food, and his system was shutting down. They'd eaten pastries, tinned food and chocolate (the bitter type with a special ingredient to prevent it from melting).

The young woman frowned for the first time, and he felt a twinge of regret. She was only doing her job, but why did she continue to stare at him? He was weary and grimy and desperately needed a bath. His hold on his bag was becoming greasy, and he longed to find himself in a situation that was familiar to him, and one that he could control.

'Yes, Sir, here we are, Room 521. I'll set up your keys now.' She walked away to a machine behind her and came back with two credit cards. He looked baffled.

'You slip them in the door of your room and it works like a key.' Her voice dropped, and he was grateful. He took the cards and went to leave.

'Your luggage, sir?'

'It's mine,' he asserted.

'I know, sir, would you like it taken to your room?'

'No, thank you. I will carry it.'

'Of course, sir. The lift to the fifth floor is around the corner over there,' she said.

He thanked her and walked towards the direction she'd pointed. There were five lifts and all were empty. He stepped into the first and pressed the number five. The doors closed, and he gripped his key cards tightly. He peered into the long mirror covering the whole back panel of the lift and felt uncomfortable. He looked how he felt: unclean and inferior. The lines around his eyes were packed with tiny grains of sand, and he cursed himself for not cleaning his face to a better standard in the MacDonald's bathroom. He licked his hand and wiped away the worst of it. His dark brown eyes were unfathomable, as they had been since he was fifteen years old and the news of the death of his father, killed in a mine deep in the heart of the Saharan desert, where his body still lay. Nightmares about whether his father had remained alive for days if not weeks in the dark shaft, alone and terrified, slowly starving to death, had plagued him ever since.

The lift halted and the doors opened, and he stepped out into the cool corridor. He breathed deeply but still dared not believe that a room was waiting for him in this palace. He found the correct door and stared at the card in his hand. There was a small card-shaped receptacle attached to the door above the handle, and he slipped the card in, like it indicated: stripe to the left. The light above the handle turned green, and he heard a click. He turned the handle and went inside.

The room was vast and overlooked the sea. He approached the huge window and stared out beyond to where he imagined Europe. He dropped his bag and explored. An envelope sat on the colossal bed and he took it and tore it open, absorbing the luxury around him. Everything was white and clean. He wandered into the bathroom as he pulled out a mobile phone from the envelope, as well as a USB stick. His eyes darted about and he spotted a laptop set up on a table by the bed. He quickly peered around the bathroom door and stood mesmerised by the opulence. The shower was big enough for four men, the bath could hold ten children, and a tiny strange sink was positioned next to the toilet.

He was torn between filling the tub and smelling the range of products lined up neatly on the side, and plugging in the USB. He decided that he could do both: a bath that size would take an hour to fill, he thought. He placed the items back on his bed and went back to the bathroom to choose what to put in the warm running water. He poured everything under its stream and went back to the bedroom. Logging on to the computer was easy, and he soon opened the USB file and read further instructions left by Fawaz. He was to meet somebody at the port tonight and supervise the loading of the cargo. He was to take the phone with him, which was loaded with one number only. He was told which cab company to use and which route to take, how long to stay there, what to confirm as loading was underway and instructions on calling the number when he could see the ship depart.

He nodded to himself and was thankful for such simple instructions.

Leaving the phone on the bed and the laptop open, he checked the bath, which to his amazement, was nearly full. The water steamed, and he sat on the edge, circling his hands in the soapy mixture. It smelled like a type of heaven: the heaven where he imagined going to. He undressed quickly and checked the temperature, before stepping in and submerging his whole body beneath the water. He closed his eyes and allowed the soap to begin its work on the dust and muck clinging to his body. He moved about in the water and rubbed his skin, feeling the grainy desert sand wash off. Emerging from the water, he lay there, steaming. He stuck his foot out of the water and examined his toenails, picking out dirt and doing the same with his fingernails. Had the woman at reception noticed them?

After twenty minutes or so, he was ready to get out, and he pulled out the plug, reaching for the shower head to rinse the bath of grime; the bottom was now covered in brown sludge and he washed it down the plughole. He reached for a towel and pushed his face into the softness, rubbing his fatigued limbs. He realised that he was extremely tired, and he looked at his watch: he had time for a nap. He got into bed, dry, clean and thankful, and wrapped the covers over him. The bedside clock had an alarm setting, and he quickly worked out how to use it and closed his eyes, sinking his head into the soft pillow.

–

When he awoke to the piercing sound of the alarm, he took a minute to remember where he was. His body was rested, and he sat upright, stretching, wondering if he lived like this all the time, what it might be like. Would it make him lazy and godless? Suddenly, the awe with which he'd approached the grandeur of the place left him, and he realised that he was hungry, and ready to complete the final leg of his mission. One afternoon asleep in such surroundings was enough to make a man soft. Now, he was alert and wary of falling for the lure of the trappings of the rich. He dressed quickly into the only other outfit he had with him and stuffed the soiled clothes into the empty bag. He ignored the cologne on offer, but only after removing the cap and smelling it. Why had Fawaz given him this room? What was he trying to achieve? Fawaz left nothing to chance. Why show him this place when he was to return to his village tonight or tomorrow? Then, he realised that it was a small reward for his efforts. Fawaz was bestowing his gratitude, and inside his head, it made him feel better about accepting to stay in such a place.

He was ready quickly and called the cab number. They would be outside in five minutes. He took the elevator back downstairs and noticed that the woman on reception was still there; she smiled at him. He did not smile back.

The journey to the port was quick, and he was dropped off at Gate 302. The car sped away; he was to use a different company on his return to the hotel. He waited in the shadows, close to the huge metal entrance that was big enough to fit an aeroplane through. A car arrived, and its door opened. Abdul got in the back and, apart from the driver, there was only one other man inside. He spoke Darija, and Abdul conversed with him comfortably in his native vernacular. They were to oversee the loading of the consignment, and Abdul was given papers to give to the customs official who would inspect the transit bound for Marseilles.

'Don't worry, he's one of us – it's just a formality.'

Abdul nodded. They drove in silence and arrived at another gate, but this time, it was busy and bursting with activity. Forklift trucks whizzed around, men in over-alls lugged boxes and officials swanned around with clip-boards.

'There's ours,' the man said. The car stopped, and they got out. An official greeted them and Abdul handed over the paperwork, which the man in high-visibility clothing perused and signed. Abdul recognised the load from what had been separated between the vehicles that had been driven thousands of miles from Morocco. He also spotted the five boxes picked up in Mali.

'All good?' he asked. The official nodded, and they shook hands. The man then walked away after handing him a docket, containing the shipment number, block and sequence that were to be handed over at Marseilles, and Abdul watched, alongside the man who'd brought him, as a forklift picked up the load and drove it to the side of a quay. It was only now that Abdul realised that a container ship sat there in the water, serene and silent. He looked up, thinking that the metal wall was part of the quay. The ship was enormous and Abdul had never been so close to what he'd only seen on posters. He couldn't believe that a ship of such size could float.

'Now we wait,' the man said. They walked back to the car and sat in the back, watching as the ship was fully loaded. It was ready to depart in under an hour and activity on the quayside subsided as the doors were closed and ramps drawn up. At first, Abdul didn't think it was going to move, but slowly, it drifted away from the quayside and he saw three tugs ahead of it, swirling water as they worked their engines. The great thing moved forward and Abdul sat in awe.

'We go.'

The ship was about a hundred feet away from the quay, but Abdul still stared at it.

'We will drop you at another quay and you can call a cab from a payphone. Keep the docket safe; that's the number you need. Scan it in to this phone,' he said, pointing at the document and handing him a new Nokia. Abdul knew that this was the information he needed to pass on over to the number he'd been given to whoever was waiting in Marseilles to receive the goods.

His job was done. He was dropped off and saw a row of payphones, from which he called a cab.

Back at his hotel, the receptionist had gone home, replaced by a man. He strode confidently to the lift and returned to his room to make the call.

Chapter 29

Grant made his way across the city on foot. He was heading to the Lyon address he'd retrieved from the phone inside the flat in Paris. His pal Winston had prompted in Madame Bisset a speedy response, and she'd given him a name, but it meant nothing to either him or Khalil. He committed it to memory, hoping it would come up and provide answers. Meanwhile, Madame Bisset was still held at the flat, watched by his old pal, whose real name was Derek.

Grant slipped through the streets unnoticed and anonymous. He didn't know what to expect, only that he needed to be fully alert. Always expect the worst and hope for the best, he told himself. He wasn't familiar with Lyon, but it didn't matter, anonymity was an art performed anywhere if one knew the tricks. He remembered driving through the city with Helen a couple of times on their way to Les Alps, skiing, during happier times. He pushed her face out of his head. They'd meet soon enough. She must be on to him by now, he thought. The passenger list of Khalil's jet to Marseilles would give it away if she didn't already know.

The streets were busy and hot. The summer weather was particularly humid here further south, and even the breeze from the Alps overshadowing the metropolis was scant. The mood in Le Croix-Rousse was expectedly buoyant. The area, famous for its inclines, enjoyed much tourist trade, and the cobbled alleyways, old churches and ancient markets still selling silks saw a steady stream of trade at night as well as during the day. The old traboules were being slowly gentrified, and Grant found them charming as he wandered past smart pink, white and grey apartments, cute delis, patisseries and the odd street vendor touting for business on the steep slopes of the hill, shaded by century's old ostrya, serrata and elm trees that offered much-needed shelter during the day. Madame Bisset had kindly helped him choose a short route to the address, after she'd calmed down and he'd assured her that Derek wouldn't molest her unless it was under his strict say-so. She'd remain in his care until Khalil was satisfied that she'd told the truth.

Grant wasn't a fan of torture, but advanced inter-rogation techniques could be extremely effective. They weren't about to pull an old woman's fingernails out, or subject her to any kind of indecent assault, but she didn't need to know that. One thing that Grant did notice was that Madame Bisset took his threats seriously, which made him think Khalil capable of more than he'd let on. It got him thinking about what Khalil must have witnessed in his childhood; his family hadn't always been the lords of Algiers. Grant's thoughts turned to Hakim, and Grant hoped the lad hadn't been hurt. He'd seen countless tortured corpses in Bosnia and Sierra Leone, as well as Iraq and Afghanistan. He also knew that it needn't just be physical. But it shouldn't come to that, he reas-sured himself, because, so far, Khalil had been completely cooperative with Fawaz's demands.

He stopped outside an apartment block and looked around; it was the perfect spot to hide illegal activity, and that's exactly what the Police Nationale were trying to wage war against by closing off many of the tiny streets. Grant's training involved close-quarter combat and it was because of precisely these types of circumstances that one needed to be prepared: going into a snake pit might get you bitten. He climbed the stairs on the outside of the building and slipped onto a balcony level that was deserted. He could hear the hustle and bustle from the street below, and the light shining off the buildings was quite stunning. From the hill, he could see virtually the whole of Lyon and beyond to the Alps. Oh, what he would give to be skiing down the Aiguille Rouge at Les Arcs right now. He imagined the crisp blue sky beating down on fresh powder dumped the night before. Maybe when this was all over, he'd make his way up there and trek beneath Mont Blanc's shadow. Helen's face taunted him again: her smile when she rolled over in the morning, her laugh when he told her a bad joke, her hand, warm on his.

He found the flat number he was looking for and checked his phone. This was the one. There were no lights on. He peered through the tiny window at the front, but it afforded him no view decent enough to make an assessment of who might be inside. He checked both ways to see if there was any movement in front of the other flats on the balcony, and there was not. He tried the door: it was locked. He looked up and noticed that an upstairs window was open, and he checked the street below. It was clear. He held on to a metal ladder that led up towards other flats and hooked his leg over the wall adjacent to the open window. The opening was big enough for him, and he jettisoned himself across to a wide sill, still holding on to the metal rail, which shook. Once he was in front of the window, he checked the street again and peered inside. The room was empty. He swung his legs in and found himself standing in the middle of a hot and stuffy bedroom. It was sparse, with only a bed and cabinet beside it. He trod carefully and made his way out to the hallway. He heard nothing. He took the stone stairs slowly and edged down to the lower floor, where he opened the latch on the door, should he need a speedy alternative escape. There was no one home.

The rest of the flat was small, also sparsely furnished and bloody hot. He dare not open any lower-level windows, lest he attract attention, so he put the thought of fresh air from his mind and concentrated on searching the few drawers and cabinets. He put gloves on and held a tiny torch between his teeth. It was a mini LED Lenser that gave off minimal ambient light, perfect for searching confined spaces, or shining into someone's eyes during interrogation.

He found some evidence of human occupancy, such as crockery and cutlery, as well as cooking pans and the odd packet of food, but in the bedroom, like the flat in Paris, Grant was reminded of something like the hideout of a special observation officer: ready to move on little notice. In other cupboards, he found similar electrical equipment to what he'd found in the other flat. He took photos.

He prepared to leave and couldn't help feeling disappointed. A part of him hoped he might find some evidence of a hostage situation, or at least a real live witness to question. He slipped out of the front door and checked that there was no one around before disappearing back into the throng of the bars and restaurants of Le Croix-Rousse and all its squares and hidden corners had to offer. He took out his mobile and made a call to an old Signaller pal of his. They were the guys who made everything work, from radios to satphones, and who, for the most part, stayed in the shadows doing their jobs and getting little praise for it. The British Army couldn't function without them.

They caught up briefly about the usual topics: civvies and how much shit they didn't know. Then Grant listed the kit that he'd discovered, both in the flat in Paris and there in Lyon.

'What sort of shit does that make?' Grant asked.

'Anything. But my guess is drones.'

Chapter 30

Hakim lay on a concrete floor. Gone were the days of relative luxury in captivity when he was fed every day and the old man smiled at him. Gone were the longed-for moments of light through a window or the sweetness of cold water. He could taste his own blood, but at least that meant he was alive.

The past few days had been tense as he'd been moved from flat to flat. They almost got caught this morning, as they waited at a junction for the light to turn green, according to the men who were becoming more and more nervous,. Police Nationale and Gendarmerie had both screeched past them, in the direction from where they'd come. Hakim's captors had stopped hooding him, and that was a sure sign that they were either very stupid or very scared; either that or he was going to die very soon. He was disorientated, thirsty and losing hope. His resolve, given to him by the training paid for by his father, was waning. All he could do, to keep sanity from slipping away, was to count his breaths. His body ached from the beatings.

He heard the voices of men. Like before, they were of North African descent, mixed with French, and he prayed that his father was closing in on him. The Dalmani family had few enemies that he knew of, but then he didn't know his father's business, and he tried to piece together the possibilities for the reasons for his capture. He surmised that the interest in him must have come from outside of Algiers, where his father was considered one of the most significant and influential philanthropists of his time. He listed all the motives for hostage taking – greed, jealousy and family secrets – and went over each one methodically. It calmed him.

So did prayer.

Up until this moment, he hadn't scrutinised the words of the Quran or the meaning of his faith. That's why he'd chosen Paris as his preferred city of study: the bohemian hub of hedonistic culture. Atheistic by nature, rebellious in spirit and free at its core, the city of love offered him an outlet by which he could explore who he was, who he'd been and who he might become. But now, isolated and afraid, it was the Prophet he turned to. The word 'Islam' itself meant 'submission and surrender'; to ask God for approval that one's heart was ready to do both was the core of Islamic belief. He felt shame for his sins and asked for forgiveness. Lying down with French girls topped the list, and he damned his lust in self-condemnation. Only by such submission could one hope for acceptance from God and thus the path to peace. His God was compassionate and merciful and only by renouncing ego could access to Him be gained. He held no form, but Hakim had to conjure an image in his head to find any kind of strength to carry on. For reasons unknown, he'd formed an image of a lamb. Its fleece was pure white and its face was benevolent and innocent, but its stature was large and powerful. The irony wasn't something he dwelled on and the likeness grew in his mind until it took over every thought.

Hakim knew that the five daily prayers could be somewhat flexible under special circumstances, and he wasn't sure if he'd prayed five times already today. He figured that his predicament allowed him some latitude on geographic knowledge as well as times of the day. He had no idea which direction Mecca was, and he had no idea if God would forgive him for not using a mat. Would his bare knees do? Or would God be offended? He knew that his father contributed millions of dollars every year in zakat (charity) for the poor and needy, surely this covered Hakim too?

His mouth formed around the verses of the Quran: the supreme act of worship. Though he couldn't purify himself before each recital, he had to believe that God would forgive him.

'Glory be to You, O God, along with Your praise, and blessed is Your name, and high is Your majesty, and there is no God other than You.'

His body felt broken and cold, but his mind was pure, and grew in strength when he prayed. It was as if his soul was feeding off his body in preparation for something. As the hours slipped by, he felt himself giving all his fibres, organs, consciousness and ego over to a higher purpose. His purpose. He saw that all matters of the flesh were secondary to the spirit, and thus any pain was peripheral to the health of the inner self. If he closed his eyes as he prayed, he found that his four other senses became more honed: his hearing, taste, touch and smell all worked together to form a picture of the outside world beyond the four walls of his new prison. But that was the point. He slumbered only in prison if his mind allowed him, and it did not. He saw the lamb beyond the wall and knew that he was safe. For if his physical body was to be sacrificed to save his essence, then so be it.

He'd made peace with his family and his maker.

He was ready.

Chapter 31

Helen returned to the office she shared with Sylvia after learning that Khalil Dalmani had flown to Lyon by private jet. She instructed Ricard to set up the surveillance on his suite at the Ritz in Paris in his absence, as it'd make the whole installation a damn sight easier with him away.

The change of scenery visiting Fraud, and the stretch, had done her good. She was itching to get out on the streets of Lyon and follow leads, but it was still early days and she couldn't chase thin air. So, she resigned herself to sitting behind a computer screen for now. She still hadn't decided what to do with the information about Marseilles given to her by Angelo.

As requested, Amélie Laurent had presented herself at a police station near Sorbonne University, Paris, at just after dusk. She'd gone willingly and was to be interviewed by the local Police Nationale, watched via video link by Helen in Lyon. As Hakim's girlfriend, she might be able to shed some light on his state of mind leading up to the abduction, and if she'd noticed or commented on anything unusual in the lead-up to last Sunday. Though Hakim hadn't seen Amélie for four weeks, she could give context to his movements and routines when he was in Paris.

Helen watched as the young woman was led into an interview suite and asked if she'd like a drink, which she declined. She was of petite frame, and her manner was open, if a little wary, but Helen put that down to nerves. Given the seriousness of the situation, Helen judged from the girl's mature approach that Amélie was a confident individual. She looked forlorn as Helen studied her face on the screen, and she picked her slim hands. She was dressed in fine clothes that looked as though they were tailored, and Helen wondered if Hakim funded her wardrobe. A flick through the information they had on her confirmed that her parents were of minimal means and her education was funded by loans. The Versace bag hung on the back of the chair didn't look as though it came out of a meagre allowance.

The formal introductions were got out of the way and Helen continued to observe.

'Thank you for coming in today. We'd like to ask you some questions about Hakim and his usual schedules when in Paris, if that's all right?' The interviewing officer was gentle. He was a local gendarme, usual for any Interpol case.

'Do you know where he is?' Amélie asked. She was softly spoken and keen for news of her lover. Helen was struck by her soft beauty, typical of effortless French chic, and she was taken in by her innocent warmth.

'No, we don't.'

Amélie sniffed and produced a tissue with which to wipe her eyes.

'Is he a religious young man?' the officer asked.

Helen bristled. It was a stereotypical racial assumption, and it got her back up.

'No,' Amélie replied. Helen could see that the young woman wasn't impressed either.

'So he doesn't pray?'

Helen rolled her eyes. Where was he going with this? She interjected by pressing her mic and she watched him listen to his earpiece. 'Can we keep it to his movements in Paris? His Sunni family isn't relevant here,' Helen said. The interviewer wasn't personally approved by her but it was all they had.

'Did he show any signs of being afraid for his safety?' He did as he was asked.

'No. He said his father is very powerful in Algeria and well respected here in France. But Hakim also told me that he'd been sent on extensive training courses to deal with scenarios.'

'Scenarios?'

'Just in case. It was silly, and Hakim thought it a waste of time, but now… His father wanted him to be wary. He said they carried a great responsibility and that their wealth attracted trouble,' Amélie said, fidgeting with a ring on her right hand. Her answers were open and full. Somebody with something to hide generally spoke in monosyllables, this wasn't the case with Amélie; she appeared to want to be as helpful as possible.

'Did he say what kind of trouble?'

'He had a bodyguard, as do all of his family members. I thought that meant they were safer.' Amélie sniffed again. 'I'm sorry,' she added.

'Indeed. Do you know the names of his bodyguards? Would you recognise them?' Helen had traced all but two of them, including Jean-Luc, and it was found that they had no idea of Hakim's disappearance or whereabouts upon initial interview because they were on full paid summer leave. They also had solid alibis.

'They all looked the same with their scowls and suits. He said the man in charge was Jean-Luc and that

215

he arranged all cover here in Paris when Hakim was studying.'

'So the bodyguards changed frequently?' the officer asked.

'I don't know, I didn't really pay attention. Hakim taught me how to ignore them.'

'And did he ignore them?'

'Kind of. He said that we should act as if they weren't there, so I did.'

Helen felt as though Amélie had something to add and she pushed the officer to allow her to elaborate.

'You don't seem too sure about that? Was there one that stood out, perhaps?'

Amélie nodded. 'There was one I didn't feel comfortable with. He... looked at me.'

'What do you mean "looked at"?'

Amélie shifted uncomfortably in her chair. 'He didn't seem to be focused on his job. I don't think he approved of me, of Hakim having a girlfriend.'

'Right. I have here some photographs of the men in the employment of Hakim's father. Please take your time and let us know if you recognise any of them.'

The pictures were handed to Amélie one at a time, and she nodded her recognition of some of them.

'Is the one who "looked at you" among the photographs?'

'This one,' she said.

The officer noted the exhibit number and the positive identification of the witness.

It was Ahmad Azzine, or 'Sand Cat'. Helen scribbled frantically. 'My, you've been busy,' she said under her breath.

'Are you sure?' he asked.

216

'Positive, that's him,' she said.

'And how many times would you say you'd seen him?'

'Maybe four or five.'

'Over what period?'

'He was new, about four weeks before we broke for summer. I told Hakim I didn't like him, but he reminded me that they weren't there to be liked. But I didn't forget.'

'Did you meet Jean-Luc?' he asked.

'No, but I saw him a few times. We were never properly introduced but Hakim pointed him out.'

'Did you ever witness Jean-Luc talking to the man you have identified as "looking" at you?'

Amélie thought.

'Yes. Hakim took no notice of them but I watched occasionally. I suppose I found it fascinating. I've never lived like this before – every move being monitored and scrutinised – I don't like it.'

'You've said. When did you see them converse?' The officer asked.

'When I noticed him start on the job. I asked Hakim about him but he was annoyed, reminding me that new faces came and went and that I should ignore them. I wanted to fit in, but it didn't feel right.'

Amélie was proving to be a reliable and natural witness. She was open and helpful. The officer showed her more photos, this time of places where they'd traced Hakim's last movements in Paris before leaving after the summer term for his break in Algiers. He also spread a map across the desk, and she pointed to each place on it, confirming her knowledge of the locations, even if she hadn't been there with Hakim.

'Would you say that Hakim's routines were predict-able?'

Amélie laughed a little. 'Yes.' Her smile was engaging and came out of the blue. Helen watched as her face melted into adoration as she spoke of Hakim. 'He took me to the coolest bars and the most amazing restaurants. We always went straight to the front of the queue, even if people were waiting in line for a long time.'

She stopped speaking and fiddled with her hands again. Helen knew that this was painful for her. She loved him; that was plain to see.

'You attracted attention?'

'Yes.'

'And the bodyguards? Where were they?'

'Hakim always surprised me, but I guess not the guards – they were always ahead of him.'

'So his plans were always run past the guards first?'

'Of course.'

'Every time, without exception?' he asked.

'Every time. Like I told them.'

'Who?' The officer stopped writing and looked up. Helen sat forward in her chair. Had someone got to her first?

'The first time I was interviewed.' The woman was suddenly wary.

'Where and by whom?'

Amélie looked worried, as if she's made a blunder. 'I thought you were all working together, looking for Hakim. Have I made a mistake? A man came to see me at my flat on Tuesday – he showed ID.'

'Ask her for a name,' Helen said. She closed her eyes and put her head on a single finger in the middle of her forehead. She knew the answer.

'This man, do you have a name?' he asked her.

'Mr Tess... erm... Tessin...'

Helen watched as the woman struggled to remember.

'He was English and very nice. He knew Hakim's family well. I thought…'

Helen slammed the table. Amélie couldn't hear her outburst but she was still aware that somehow, there'd been a blunder.

'Has he got something to do with it? He said he worked for the family. Did I do something wrong?'

Helen saw panic rise up in Amélie's body.

'What did you talk about?' asked the officer.

'I think he said that he was Hakim's father's head of security.'

Amélie was no longer concentrating on the questions being asked of her.

'That would be Jean-Luc Bisset.'

'No, it wasn't him.'

'Of course it wasn't him, so who was it?'

'An Englishman,' she repeated.

'Grant, you have so many questions to answer,' Helen whispered. She pressed her mic.

'Tennyson,' she said.

The police officer repeated his name.

'Yes, that's it!' Amélie was clearly relieved to be helpful after her mistake.

'I'd like you to try to remember exactly what he asked you and what he found particularly interesting.'

'Interesting?' she asked.

'Let's say the focus of his attention.'

'Ah, I understand. So, he seemed to be really focused on the man you just showed to me.' She pointed to the photo of the same man she'd just identified; the officer made a note. Helen closed her eyes in disbelief.

'And did you tell him that this man conversed with Jean-Luc?'

'Yes.'

'Thank you. I've one more question. We have a telephone call from Hakim's mobile phone to yours, made mid-air, as he travelled back to Paris.'

'Yes, I couldn't take it. I hate myself for missing the call, but he left me a voice message,' she said. Tears came to her eyes and spilled down her cheeks.

'Good, do you still have it?'

'Yes, of course.' She took out her phone and played the message on speaker. The voice of Hakim rang out in the small room.

'*Amélie, I'm arriving soon. Can you come to the airport?*'

Amélie bowed her head and her shoulders shook.

'He's never asked me to meet him at the airport before.'

'Never?' asked the officer.

'I thought he was joking,' she said quietly.

'And now what do you think?'

Amélie's eyes widened as realisation took hold of her.

'He was trying to tell me something.' She blew her nose.

Whatever happened on that plane, it now seemed Hakim potentially knew what was going on halfway over the Mediterranean Sea.

Chapter 32

Grant watched as Khalil paced up and down his suite at the InterContinental with the burner phone in his hand.

'"Sand Cat" – it means nothing to you?' Grant asked.

'It's a small cat from the desert in North Africa,' Khalil replied. He waved his hands around. This much Grant knew. It wasn't so much the animal's ecology or habitat that Grant was after though. He considered his boss. During the week he'd spent with him in close company, he'd observed a cautious man but one given to eruptions of anxiety, brought on, no doubt, by his pampered upbringing. For all the bravado and poise, Khalil did not control all things, and his sudden outbursts of panic belied a man who was scared.

'It's obviously a code name for someone – we need to find out who he is,' Grant said.

'So, you think leaving here, where my son is, to spy on my own ships in Marseilles will deliver him to me? What if I miss a call to meet somewhere here in Lyon? For an exchange, perhaps? I only just arrived.'

Grant was seated by the window, overlooking the city. Khalil's pacing made him dizzy.

'No, I just think that you getting on with your important business in your offices in Marseilles will distract you, while I track down who is in charge of your shipment. My bet is it's Sand Cat, or at least it will lead me to him. And then I'll find out where Hakim is.'

'And what if it is a code name for an event, not a man?'

'Madame Bisset was pretty shaken up by my friend. She was adamant that this was a name, not a place or a plan,' Grant said. He was eager to get going. 'Why don't you stay here, if you're worried?' he suggested.

The flight for tonight was logged and the passenger list approved by the authorities. Every flight in the world had to hand one in. Grant had suggested driving but Khalil wouldn't hear of it.

'I have nothing to hide,' he'd said.

But that wasn't the point. Any investigator worth their salt would be monitoring Khalil's movements in France during the investigation into his son's disappearance. And he knew that Helen was a fine operator. She'd see the passenger list as soon as she was aware that Khalil had decamped to Marseilles, and that meant she'd see his name as well.

'I know her,' Grant said. At last, Khalil stopped pacing.

'Who?' Khalil asked.

'Major Helen Scott, the one you spoke to. The one who asked who your new head of security was.'

'You know her, how?'

'We worked together, back when I was in the forces still.'

'Is she good?' Khalil asked.

'Yes. The best.'

'Good, so now I have two excellent operators trying to find my son – this is a bonus. We still fly. When she finds out you are with me, then it will make her work harder, will it not? I presume you were on amicable terms?'

Grant hesitated momentarily. 'Yes, we had much respect for one another.'

'Excellent. Let's go,' Khalil ordered. Their bags were already downstairs. The suite here at the InterContinental in Lyon would be kept for Khalil, as he expected to return after a day or so, once he'd checked in on his head office at the port in Marseilles. It was one of the most important trading posts for AlGaz, and Grant figured a visit from the boss would be a distraction from what was really going on at the port, hence giving him an opportunity to check the shipments.

The phone in Khalil's hand rang, and he jumped, almost dropping it. Grant watched as he composed himself and answered. Grant knew straight away, from Khalil's body language, that the person on the other end of the phone was Fawaz Nabil. There was no doubt that his boss was talking to the man who held Hakim's life in the balance. Grant had to acknowledge that time was running out. Almost a week had passed and they'd made headway but were no closer to their target. He knew that Khalil was losing patience and clarity of thought. This conversation could prove pivotal; after all, Khalil's ships, and whatever was being transported inside them, were almost on European soil.

'I want to speak to my son,' Khalil's voice broke slightly, and Grant glimpsed into the heart of the man whose exterior was as cool as the arctic tundra. It was clear that Fawaz denied this request. Khalil closed his eyes.

'I have done what you asked. Now it is your turn, on your honour, to show me that you are true to your word and release my son,' Khalil said. It pained Grant to see him beg.

'What do you mean, it's more complicated now?' Khalil's question astonished Grant, and he stood up, motioning to Khalil to put the phone on speaker but it was an old Nokia without that function and Grant tutted. What the hell was going on? The goalposts were moving, and Grant didn't like the sound of it. Khalil beckoned him over and they shared the handset. They both listened to the voice on the other end, which was as smooth as honey and utterly in control.

'Somebody very important to me has gone missing, and I'd like you to find her for me, Khalil,' Fawaz said.

'Who? If I do this, my son will be returned to me?' Khalil asked.

Grant stopped him with gestures. Khalil was pleading and on the verge of compromising any leverage he had, and Grant wanted to know who they were talking about before making any rash promises.

He found a pen and paper and scribbled to him in English.

> *Take control of your voice. He knows you're the prey here – he can smell it.*

Khalil nodded.

'It depends on the woman being returned unharmed,' Fawaz said.

Grant could have kicked something to vent his frustration at the glaring contradiction of the man, but he was dealing with scum.

Khalil replied calmly. 'You've changed the rules, Fawaz. How do I know that you won't break your promise again? My son's life is not a game. Tell me who this woman is,' Khalil demanded.

Grant nodded to him. They still had bargaining chips – the shipment full of Fawaz's goods, for one, whatever that turned out to be – and Grant was going to make it his job to find out. It was all about leverage. The question was how far Khalil could push Fawaz before the reality of Hakim's life being in danger hit him, and all bets were called off. Khalil's nerve had held until now, but Grant could see that he had little left in the tank. He listened to Fawaz.

'Two of our men were arrested by Interpol today. I can't guarantee that our operation won't be compromised. There are certain elements inside the French authorities who use excessive force,' Fawaz said.

'You know that well, Fawaz – I was truly sorry for the loss of Rafik,' Khalil said. Grant heard genuine solicitude in Khalil's voice.

Fawaz wavered. Khalil had hit a nerve. 'If the operation is put at risk, then, I'm afraid that the life of your son, like that of my own was, will become collateral damage. There is only one way to make sure this doesn't happen: you must find a way to refocus the inquiry by Interpol.' Then he hung up.

Khalil stared at the phone. Grant took it off him.

'We need to keep this because a signal might still be traced from it. It could help locate Fawaz in the future if all else fails.'

'You mean if Hakim dies and I no longer play by his rules?' Khalil asked.

Grant looked him in the eye and nodded. Khalil looked broken.

'Do you think this is all about his son?' Grant asked.

'I don't know. Fawaz never took responsibility for Rafik's death: the fact that he was working for his own father when he died. The body was never returned. It is the highest insult when a father cannot give his son his burial rites. I cannot imagine his pain.'

'So, he takes your son to replace his? An eye for an eye? So why go to all the trouble of using your ships and creating a circus? There's something more.'

Grant's personal phone buzzed, and it was the concierge informing them that their car for the airport was here.

'I'm coming with you and I'll find out what's in my containers,' Khalil said.

Grant nodded and went to the door. Fawaz hadn't told them the name of the woman he was so concerned about, but that could wait. Khalil was close to giving up. 'Let's go,' he said.

'Perhaps it's time to tell your Interpol lady the truth,' Khalil said.

Chapter 33

The lights of Lyon burned brightly beyond the Interpol building. Helen was weary, but she had the two suspects still to interview. She went to see Peter Knowles, and found him also still at his desk. The identification of Ahmad Azzine and the connection to her case had created quite a flurry of excitement in the headquarters.

'He's been on a red notice for the best part of five years, since the arrest and detention of Rafik bin Nabil. It's a huge step forward, Helen – massive congratulations.'

'It was Sylvia who spotted him,' she said.

He nodded. 'So, about your two unknowns who were arrested today, where are they being interviewed? Please don't set up anything until you've got a secure connection to my office – I want to be involved.'

'Of course, Peter. Did you say Rafik bin Nabil? As in Fawaz bin Nabil's son?'

'Yes, he was arrested five years ago in London on terrorism charges. The Home Office deported him back to Morocco where he died in custody, sadly.'

'I did come across that in my research into Nabil Tradings. How did he die?'

'The Home Office wrote to the Moroccan authorities, who were vague. As soon as a suspect leaves our soil, they no longer come under our authority, and so I'm not sure we ever got an answer. I was working in London at the time. The thing is, with some countries, you can never be sure about the intelligence regarding penal affairs. There are accusations of torture going on all over Africa. You never know, he might be alive and well with his father.'

Helen was surprised at Peter's nonchalance. The file she'd read stated very clearly that Rafik was dead. Fawaz's son had now popped up more than circumstantially. Helen believed that it was enough to explain any man's hatred for a system that protected those responsible for his death, but Rafik had died in Morocco, not Europe. She cast her mind back to the then Home Secretary, the now current prime minister. She shelved the information.

'So, how is he linked to Ahmad Azzine?' Helen asked.

'He was the one who gave us Azzine's name under interrogation,' Peter said, leaning on the side of his desk. 'Before he was deported, of course.'

'Why was he deported if he was so valuable?' she asked.

Peter looked at her. 'I don't know.'

'Aren't terror suspects held and tried in the same country as their crimes? Isn't that the whole point? To serve as an example? I heard it was their worst nightmare to be incarcerated in the UK or the US. Surely sending him home must have been part of a deal?'

'Maybe it was,' Peter said.

'Peter…' she began. He busied himself with his computer screen and she approached his desk.

'Hmm?' he looked up.

'Could you access the Home Office file on his deportation?'

He sat back and crossed his fingers together like a bridge. Helen got the impression that he was studying her.

'Why?'

'Isn't it enough that we were responsible for sending Rafik to his death? And here we have an associate closely linked to those responsible for Hakim's abduction, as well as evidence that Azzine might have been – and still could be – working for Fawaz?'

'But what evidence do we have that any of this is linked to Fawaz?' Peter asked.

'Surely we should find out?' She was losing patience and it showed in her voice. She apologised. 'I'm hoping that I'll get a positive ID from the two suspects in custody for "Sand Cat". If he's at the centre of it and Fawaz's son gave up his name under duress, then we can't ignore it,' she said.

'Be careful, Great Britain signed the Geneva Convention. We don't torture.'

'Of course we don't,' she said. 'But anyone who loses a child like that – in any way – would want revenge, wouldn't he?' she added. She thought about the trading name of the company in Berkeley Square, London. Something made her hold off telling Peter. His area was counter terrorism not fraud. Perhaps she should run it by Sir Conrad?

She could tell that Peter was a man who needed tangible proof. Gone were the days when Counter Terrorism officers used strong-arm tactics to extract information. Everything had to be legitimate and legally watertight now. Presumably, that's why he held his post. He was careful. The buck stopped with him.

Seconds passed between them.

'Of course, I'll get it for you,' he said.

'Thank you,' she said, not daring to add anything else lest he change his mind. They turned their attention to the questioning of the two suspects in custody. They'd been taken to a local station in Lyon, and a secure preliminary interview was being set up via video link. 'I'll let you know when we're all set up for the interviews with the two suspects we have in custody,' she said, and left his office.

As she walked, she called Sir Conrad's private number and told him about what she'd learned about Nabil Tradings.

'Well, I'll be damned,' he said.

Helen thought it an old-fashioned statement which reminded her of her father, but acknowledged that Sir Conrad's vocab came directly from the twentieth century.

'Rafik, you say?' he asked.

'Yes, sir.'

'Well, well… I'll be damned.'

He hung up.

Chapter 34

As she neared her office, Helen's phone rang. She was still distracted by Sir Conrad's reaction to her findings on Nabil Tradings and didn't check the number.

'Major Scott?' The voice spoke in English.

'Yes, speaking.' It came from a forensic contact who was heading the emergency search at the property they'd raided today. They got introductions and small talk out of the way and went straight down to business. A frisson of excitement flickered inside her, and she hoped it was positive news: something she could work with.

'In the rear room of the property, extensive genetic matter was recovered and sent to the BioLab here in Lyon. I've requested as speedy a turnaround time as they can muster – after all, we're paying five thousand euros for the service.'

Helen nodded. 'Right, and?' she asked.

'They've identified workable DNA but haven't profiled it yet.'

'Describe the room to me.'

'A bedroom overlooking the street. The window was shuttered. There was a single chair, a cot bed, what looks like a vessel for ablutions and a toilet.'

'Where was the DNA extracted from?' Helen asked.

'The bed. And the vessel containing live excreta.'

'Good. When can we expect the results?'

'Sometime in the next twenty-four hours, I'm told.'

'Are they examining the specimen for diet too?' Helen asked. Any information they could gather about Hakim's wellbeing was crucial.

'Of course.'

Helen hung up.

Back in her office, she opened her computer and saw that she'd been sent a live link to the interview of the two suspects. They were ready. She emailed Peter the secure password to join the proceedings. He replied straight away and told her that he was joining now. She did the same.

Two cells came onto the screen. In them sat the two men arrested this morning. They looked nonchalant and bored. Lawyers sat next to both of them, paid for by Interpol.

Biographies of the suspects had been filed by the lawyers. Helen had already scanned them. Arrested and interviewed under caution, they each had to at least give their names, nationalities and dates of birth. They were both Moroccan and here in France illegally. She had scant details on their histories but knew where they'd been to school (for a couple of years), where they'd worked (legitimately only) and their passport details. There were gaping holes in travel histories, but it was a start.

The interviewing officers signalled to Helen that they were ready to commence, and the preliminaries were got out of the way. In each room, the men answered a simple yes or no, as appropriately nudged by their lawyers.

The details of all present were read out in English and French. It was made very clear that the men were under caution and as such anything they said would be recorded and given in evidence. Helen was used to this kind of interview procedure, which was becoming more and more common among investigating teams. The senior investigating officer's physical presence, it was surmised, during the initial stages of the proceedings, was best used remotely, as an observer. Sometimes, interviews in person caused vital signals to be lost, due to the officers in question zeroing in on faces and words, rather than the whole picture. It was only once watched back on tape, that certain nuances became clear. This way, both she and Peter could scrutinise body language patterns, and the overall picture. She'd already instructed the first few questions and she was glad to see that, unlike the police officer interviewing Amélie Laurent in Paris, the Lyon officers were sticking to her brief to the letter.

It was pretty standard stuff until Ahmad Azzine was mentioned.

'Sand Cat,' the officer emphasised.

Helen watched the faces of the two men in separate rooms. Their body language was simple to read.

Both lawyers leant over to their clients and whispered into the men's ears privately. Each man replied, 'No comment.'

Helen was reminded of her first interviews in training years ago, at Pirbright, Surrey. Since then, she'd come to appreciate it as an art. Listening to the proliferation of 'no comment' was a standard and tedious part of her job. However, what was indisputable was how a human being reacts to being shown photographs. She'd studied experiments where people were exposed to highly emotive images, like war zones, compared to familiar images, such as of somebody they knew and felt comfortable with. Both men displayed signals of the latter when they looked at Sand Cat, if only for a fraction of a second before they shut down. Helen spotted the subtle reactions because of experience: she'd been waiting for them. She made a note of the time, so she could rewind the recording later.

She watched as the first pieces of evidence, as handed to the lawyers before the interviews began, were presented. The two men were shown photos of the Peugeot driven from Paris to Lyon. They were also shown the witness statement from the old woman, the tip-off from the witness overhearing them argue, the surveillance of the cafe, as well as body-cam images of their arrests and initial forensic findings. The men's DNA had been taken and Helen prayed the lab got back to her soon.

'It looks like somebody was held here,' one officer stated. The same assertion was put to the other suspect.

'No comment.'

'Was it this man?' They were shown a photograph of Hakim Dalmani. Again, the body language of the two men changed dramatically when they looked at the evidence. But one of them in particular looked the more nervous of the two. Helen looked at his name. Farid. The same name as Hakim's little brother.

'No comment.'

'Ask if their reward includes money to look after their families,' she said into her mic. 'Say their names,' she added.

The officer did so, listing the various members of each man's family back home in Morocco. The demeanours of the men shifted, and they fidgeted, and Farid put his head in his hands. Now for the master stroke.

'DNA from Hakim Dalmani was in the car that was seized at the flat where you stayed. This woman identified you both as driving it. How do you explain this?'

'I reached inside to steal a wallet,' the cockier of the two replied, before his lawyer could stop him.

As Helen watched and listened, she scanned the files of the two men again, looking for a way in. She found it. She brought up another screen: it was Ahmad Azzine's file, and a thrill of excitement rushed through her. She spoke into her mic.

'Tell them we find it impossible that they don't know Ahmad Azzine because they grew up in the same village in Morocco, and all three worked at the same canning factory for two years between 2005 and 2007.'

Silence.

The men looked at their lawyers, who asked for a break.

Chapter 35

Mid-air between Lyon and Marseilles, Grant used the sat phone to speak to his contact in Algiers. Levi Drum informed him that he was sitting in the lounge of the Marriott Hotel, in Algiers, sipping a genuinely good Singapore sling.

'It's simply the best in the city, with just the right balance of grenadine, lime juice and Angostura bitters. It's not Raffles, but it'll do.'

'Thanks,' Grant said, staring at his orange juice.

He owed Grant a few favours, which had stacked up over the years they'd served together in the military. The old boys' network compromised no moral code; it was simply another layer of investigative usefulness. Over the years, Grant normally asked his old pal for details about potential employers or who might hold certain roles in local government.

They'd hooked up again when Grant got the Algeria job with Khalil Dalmani. Then, there'd been nothing to divulge about one of the richest men in Africa. He was unambiguously clean.

Levi had made it clear to Grant that all anyone was talking about at the embassy in Algiers, where Levi now worked as the deputy defence attaché, was the abduction of Khalil Dalmani's son in Paris. Grant had confided to his old friend that Dalmani had launched his own investigation to find his son.

'Anything for me, mate?' Grant asked now.

'I've heard from Paris that Sir Conrad Temple-Cray is getting twitchy. Is it true that Interpol's inquiries are focusing on the movements of Fawaz bin Nabil?' Levi asked.

Grant evaded the question.

'We're concentrating on the bodyguard. Were you aware that Helen Scott is helping Interpol with the inquiry, in fact, she's heading the team?' Grant asked.

'Yes, why?' Levi replied.

'And you didn't think to tell me?' Grant asked.

'I just assumed you'd know. Interpol usually aren't at all obstructive like that,' Levi said. 'You two haven't seen each other in years, anyway.'

'They haven't been obstructive, I was just not informed until recently. No, I haven't seen her in years,' Grant conceded.

'You still got a flame for her, mate?'

'No.' The answer came too quickly and Grant knew it.

'Right. You want me to call her?' Levi asked.

'That might look suspicious – she'll know we're still mates. I don't need to compromise her – I reckon I've got more than she has, anyway,' Grant said. 'Besides, she'll know soon enough because I flew here with Dalmani and she'll have his passenger lists examined every time he moves.'

'So, do you think she'll call you?' Levi asked.

'Not interested, mate,' Grant said. Again, the response was too speedy. 'What are you up to?' Grant asked, aware that his friend was shuffling about.

'I'm going outside for a ciggie.'

Grant changed the subject. 'I wondered if you'd seen any unusual activity around the port there in Algiers. Intelligence sharing at the moment is strongly focused on the possibility of either drugs or immigrants getting over the Mediterranean, but I wondered if anything different had reared its head?' Grant asked. He had the contents of what he'd found in the two flats in his mind – one in Paris and one in Lyon – and what his Signaller pal had told him about drones.

'Conversations here always revolve around what comes in and out of Africa. With twenty thousand miles of coastline to consider, it crops up a lot, but I've heard nothing specific directly. In fact, the border force at the port has been recently commended for the excellent job it's doing working with Europe to control its entry and exit points,' Levi said.

'And the border with Morocco?'

'Watertight. No one in their right mind would chance the land mines, bandits and guards charged with making the crossing utterly impossible.'

'And if you had enough money, and you couldn't go by sea or air?' Grant asked.

Levi exhaled. Grant knew that Levi was impressively familiar with North Africa. Not only did he take an interest in the country where he worked, but he'd also travelled there extensively as a student before meeting his wife. That was back in the day before the war, when the border was open and the Sahara had been a safer place. They'd both been drawn in by the dangerous allure of the continent. It was something they discussed over Singapore slings when Grant was in town.

'If you can't fly – and I can't imagine why, if you have enough money – and you can't take the ferry to Spain because you can't enter Europe, then the only other way is via Mauritania and Mali, which is crazy, as it'd take four or five days.'

'Assuming one couldn't fly because then they'd have to declare the goods on board,' Grant added.

'Goods?' Levi asked. The penny dropped. 'You want me to take a look at AlGaz's shipping lanes?'

Grant didn't answer straight away. And when he did, he changed the subject.

'Do you know anyone in the military attaché's office in Paris?' he asked.

'Of course, Colonel Palmer is the current defence attaché, and a friend of a friend works in his office. In fact my wife wants me to transfer there so I can take her to tea in the sodding garden.'

'Christ, Palmer? How the hell did he get promoted so quickly? How is he a colonel now?' Grant remembered Palmer's oily face and slippery fat hands as he tried to charm Helen, as many fellow officers did.

'Yes. The slippery pole is easier to climb if you can cling on for long enough,' Levi said.

'Can you ask your contact in his office to see how Helen Scott ended up working for Interpol?' Grant asked.

'I already know the answer to that question, mate,' he said. 'She was sent to Paris to conduct a security review of the embassy for the NATO summit at Versailles. So, I guess she was conveniently available when Interpol requested a close-protection specialist. Sir Conrad sent her to Lyon.'

Grant couldn't help himself swell with pride: she was doing well.

'One more thing,' Grant said.

'Go for it,' Levi replied.

'If I email you a close-up of a man, can you try to identify him for me? I suspect he's on some database somewhere,' Grant said.

'Send it over, mate,' Levi said.

'Thanks. How's Algiers?' Grant asked. 'I miss happy hour.'

'I'm sitting outside on the balcony now.'

'You avoiding going home?' Grant asked.

Levi sighed and puffed on his cigarette. 'Yup. You did the right thing, never marrying, mate.'

'Speak soon,' Grant said, and they hung up.

Chapter 36

The man was in his late sixties, with grey hair covering his head. His fingers worked meticulously and rhythmically. He had tiny glasses perched on the end of his nose, and his body was hunched over his computer, turning to the side and wheeling himself over to the other corner of the desk, after checking something. He scanned documents and checked measurements, before picking up a small circuit board and tweaking it with tiny tweezers. His spectacles magnified everything and, occasionally, he'd forget that they were on his face and had to remove them to see ordinary items around the room, like his teacup.

He sipped the hot liquid and placed the cup down on any available space on the work surface, which was minimal. The tables near him were covered in gadgetry, circuits, nuts, bolts, antennae, mini-propellers and brightly coloured wires. He was testing different configurations and worked quietly.

A woman came into the room and brought him more tea, and he thanked her in French. Marseilles had been their home for almost fifty years. She was his childhood sweetheart, but they'd been forbidden to marry because she was of lower class. They left Marrakech as teenagers and he hid her under tarpaulin in the back of a lorry bound for Tangier. He'd spent every penny he had on taking her to Europe with him. Passage back then, in the seventies, was much easier. The lack of technology, fewer predators looking to make a profit, lax border controls and little communication between border forces meant that migration from Africa was not as controlled. Europe was glad of the labour then; not like now, where gangs of immigrants and asylum seekers terrorised the imagination of delicate white sensitivities. Yes, they were useful back then, when France and Britain wanted foreign workers to clean their toilets and drive their buses. But now they made a difference in elections and brought their own sense of culture to the forefront of modern politics, they were seen as a threat: the biggest threat to Western civilisation since Hitler one newspaper had said. It made him chuckle. To think that his people had the politicians shaking in their boots.

They'd settled in an immigrant neighbourhood upon reaching France and had never left. They felt more comfortable among their own people. They were looked down upon by pure French and spoken about on TV as if they were carrion or some type of inferior beast. It still pained him after all these years.

His wife, no doubt about to admonish him for hunching over, came to him, resting a hand on his shoulder blade.

'Mustafa, what are you thinking about? You look perturbed, like you do when you lose money on horses at le hippodrome,' she said. He stopped what he was doing and looked at her over his glasses, thanking her for the tea and placing it among the plethora of equipment. She tutted and collected cups in various stages of abandonment. She counted eight.

'When was the last time you tidied this desk?' she asked. It was the same conversation they had most days when she came into his workshop.

His first job in France was at the docks in Marseilles. France's second largest city had always been sneered at because of its uncomfortable proximity to Africa and its working-class population. That was what kept Mustafa and Fatima there. They refused to climb upwards socially as a result of his success. Instead, they stayed where they had grown a family. They still heard on TV the familiar but ancient joke: 'What is the first Arab port the Paris–Dakar passes through?' Answer: 'Marseilles'. Of course, the Paris-Dakar Rally never passed through Marseilles, and had now been transferred to South America anyway, but the derogatory assumption was that Marseilles was more African than Africa itself.

'You know me too well, my love. I tried that strap you ordered for my back, but I'm afraid it's too old and bent now for it to work.' He referred to his spine not the contraption she'd bought to rectify his terrible kyphosis. She rubbed his back where it hurt, and he groaned with appreciation. His work involved him hunching over his inventions like this for hours without rest or move-ment, and ergonomics was a relatively new innovation (he wished he'd patented it). But they wanted for nothing. Despite the humble location of their apartment, it was lavishly decorated, and a brand new Mercedes sat in the garage underneath the building. His engineering degree and his aptitude for vision saw him quickly become sought after as one of France's most eminent structural designers. And the man who'd made all of it possible by paying for his education in the first place was also an innovator of great reputation.

Mustafa's gratitude was infinite, and that was why this job wasn't one that he would be charging for. It was extra to his other work, which was winding down now. He no longer needed the money, just enough work to keep him alert. He mostly gave lectures and advice to industry specialists. He could charge five thousand euros for an appearance at a dinner, where he would speak to the glitterati of the design world in Europe. It was very dull and Fatima never accompanied him, which is why he rarely went now: nights away from the family weren't worth it.

She smiled at him and continued to rub. 'It's so bad, Mustafa, look, you need to put this on!' She put the cups down and grabbed his harness and attached it to his back. It made him sit upright, but the pain was so unbearable after an hour at his desk that he knew he'd give up. He smiled at her and thanked her for her tenderness.

'What are you up to now?'

'A hobby,' he said. 'Fawaz asked me.'

'Fawaz? You spoke to him? How is he?'

They both still felt the loss of Rafik keenly. Fawaz bin Nabil had first come into their lives when Mustafa was still odd-jobbing at the port. A shipping company employed him to labour fourteen-hour days. One day, he'd been lugging a heavy carton of goods up a staircase, to be delivered to another level because the forklift wasn't working properly when he'd overheard two men talking about the quayside. Mustafa had stopped and listened. One of the men had begun to scold him for laziness and demanded that he return to work. Mustafa had pointed out that the design theory that the men were discussing, about expanding the quayside, could be immeasurably improved – and done much cheaper – if they used a new material resin, as well as digitalising all loading and unloading. In the early nineties, the concept of stand-ardising anything on such a massive scale in the shipping industry was bold indeed. The man who turned to him and asked his name was the CEO of Nabil Tradings: Fawaz bin Nabil himself. From there, he'd been sent to the Aix-Marseilles University and gained double honours and a distinction. Fawaz employed him straight away. Talk of his employer dealing in illegal this and that never fazed Mustafa, and besides, he never believed a word of it. When Fawaz decided to permanently settle back home in Morocco, rather than commute back and forth, it was a sad day indeed. However, Fawaz had flown Mustafa and his family over there for reunions sometimes. Mustafa hadn't seen him for the past five years, and so when he called, asking for his help, Mustafa couldn't thank him enough for getting in touch. He would do anything for the man who'd given them this beautiful life.

Of course he could build drones. He didn't ask their use and assumed it was some new innovation for delivery and communication. In fact, he spoke to Fawaz only this afternoon, telling him of the potential to transport heavier goods further than the current parameters forums and groups dedicated to such technology were stating. The trouble with engineers is that they're not artists, he would often say. Fawaz agreed. He asked him to test how far, how low and at what weight they could function.

Mustafa was in his final stages of prototype: it was time to build the real thing. The first model was a triumph, and he was adding the finishing touches to the on-board computer (which he'd designed himself). Once he was happy with the data and had tested the real thing, the drone would be replicated and transported to a factory in

Lyon and his work would be done. He felt, this way, he could repay at least some of the debt that he owed Fawaz: there was no price on improving someone's life. Mustafa sat back and admired his work.

'He's well, my love, and sends his love to you, as always.'

'What is that?' asked Fatima, lingering with the dirty teacups hanging once more off her fingers.

'It's a drone.'

'What's a drone?' she asked.

'It's an unmanned mini-plane that can fly anywhere, transport goods, deliver things, remotely report back information, monitor the weather, the night sky... anything you want. It is the future.'

'Is it safe?' she asked.

'What do you mean? Of course it's safe! I built it – it's not going to explode!'

'No, I mean, who is in charge of it if no one is flying it? What if it hits someone?'

Mustafa laughed. 'It's like a remote-control car but in the air – it's controlled by a human. It's so safe, I would deliver you chocolate in it!'

She laughed. 'Yes please! And what's that?' She pointed to his screen, where photos of people filled the monitor, to one side, next to the diagrams of equations and modules. 'Who are they?'

'They're the customers. Their profiles get uploaded into the computer. It's another safety feature. These machines are destined for very wealthy clients who want secure drones to deliver information, or that's how I understand it.'

'Like a fingerprint?' she asked.

'Exactly. Look.' He tapped his keyboard, and a face appeared on screen. He showed her how he divided the face into almost ten thousand parts and took each one, entering data for each section until a three-dimensional profile was created. He tapped some more and an identical face popped up next to the photo, showing how it had been replicated.

'This one's ready – see how it recognised the face?' he said.

She patted him gently on his shoulder with a cup. 'You are so clever, my love. Keep that on,' she told him, pointing to his harness. She walked away with all eight teacups jangling in her hands and closed the door. Mustafa went back to work, only slightly uncomfortable that one of the photos he'd been working on looked exactly like a man he'd seen on TV. He noticed him because his Afghan dress was so like his native attire of Morocco. The last thing Mustafa was doing when Fatima brought him more tea was looking at another photo of the man on his iPhone – he'd googled him out of curiosity. Sure enough, he was high up in the new Afghan government in Kabul.

Mustafa was no expert, but he didn't think an Afghan warlord would need a drone to get secure Amazon deliveries.

But that was none of his business.

Chapter 37

Helen ran along the river. It had been quite a week and tomorrow was Saturday, but she didn't expect a day off. The early-morning sky shone blue and pink over the city, and she tried to imagine what six days of captivity looked like for a young man of only twenty-one. The profile given to them by his family was one of strength and resourcefulness. Hakim's university had similar praise to give; his *chef de la faculté* said that he was a top-grade student, who was diligent, talented and popular. A gregarious man, as well as an intelligent one, would find imprisonment challenging; not that it wasn't hard enough for anyone, but an alert brain, used to absorbing and processing information, might be his saving or his undoing.

Lots of studies had been done into the minds of captors and their hostages. It wasn't rocket science, and Helen knew that Khalil had sent his eldest son on courses to learn about just those scenarios. At first, she'd thought it odd, though impressive, but then, when she'd thought about Khalil's wealth, exposure and vulnerability, it made sense. Celebrities stalked by nutters did it all the time. As she ran, Helen went over in her head the content of the programmes that Hakim had followed. He'd been well instructed as far as she could tell. He would have been trying to find ways into his jailers' hearts with human contact methods, patience and obedience. This only worked, of course, if one had a warder who cared, and, by its very nature, the business of keeping fellow human beings in degrading, difficult and terrifying isolation attracted a certain kind of person, normally without grace, compassion or capacity to feel much at all.

She shuddered. The image of Hakim's face she'd seen in numerous photographs burned into her head: his deep brown eyes, his soft skin and his open smile. How was he doing? Was he even still alive? She briefly tried to imagine his mother's pain, when her mobile phone jolted her out of that agonising spectre. She stopped running and answered it, taking it hastily out of its pouch attached to her arm. The bridge was empty – the summer tourists weren't awake yet. The number was from Interpol. A flutter of excitement made her rush to speak.

The junior finishing her night shift gave her the news that the lab had come back as promised and the report was ready for Major Scott.

'Can you open it, please?' Helen asked, short of breath. 'I'm looking for confirmation of DNA found at the address at the top of the report and if any of it matched our victim: Hakim ibn Khalil Said Dalmani. It should say his name on the report too.' She waited and paced up and down, as her heart raced from exertion. A young man and woman could be seen in the distance pushing a pram. She looked away.

'Right, I'm in the document now,' said the junior officer. Helen looked across the river at the huge building that was Interpol Headquarters and willed the woman to scan carefully.

'There's a match.'

'What?' Helen almost didn't believe what she was hearing. She stared at the river beneath her.

'There's a match. Hakim Dalmani was in that flat.'

'Christ,' Helen said. 'I'll be in the office in an hour.' She hung up and sprinted towards her apartment building. She dashed past the couple with the pram, forcing herself to look away from the vision of domestic normality. The couple looked at her as if she was a madwoman. And that's what she felt like: a madwoman on a mission to finally catch up with Hakim's abductors. They were getting closer, but it tasted bittersweet. What if they were too late? When had he been moved and was he still in Lyon? She felt her hope wither away as her feet pelted the pavement.

Her pace never faltered all the way back to her street, and when she reached the entrance, she bent over and held her knees, thinking she might throw up. It took her back to her training, when they'd march with heavy weights up near-vertical hills, past cadets bringing up their breakfasts in what was affectionately known as the tactical chunder. Her body shook, but she managed to gather herself together and take the lift to her floor. She raced into the apartment and stripped off her running gear as she walked to the bathroom, turning on the shower and ripping the last of her underwear off. The hot water soothed her, and she washed quickly, hoping that her body would cool down quick enough from her run to allow her to dress straight away and catch a cab to Interpol HQ.

Once she was dry and dressed, she applied some make-up and ordered an Uber. In the taxi, she opened the document in her emails and read carefully, scouring for the details. The DNA had been matched to that discovered on both the bed and the excreta inside the bucket. He'd been held there for sure. He was alive. She could feel it. She read on that Hakim's stool was hard and lumpy, indicative of constipation, which might be caused by stress. It also confirmed that he was in all probability, dehydrated. A high presence of prealbumin also suggested protein-calorie malnutrition. She was always taken by how quickly this could happen. It took about three days for the human body to shift its metabolism to emergency mode, once depleted of energy-giving glycogen. It meant that Hakim was being starved.

The cab pulled up, and she got out, slamming the door and heading to the entrance, where she'd have to clear security, like she did every morning.

Upstairs, Sylvia's office was quiet and Helen examined the case file before her, spread out on a board set up for all notices actively being worked at Interpol. There were so many of them it was too depressing if one dwelled upon it. Lately, they'd got wind of a child sex ring, set up in Germany, and fifty-seven children under yellow notices had been found in an apartment block just outside Berlin. It should have been a triumph, but it was a worst nightmare for the children and their parents. Yes, they'd been found, but some of them had been missing for years. What they'd suffered wasn't something Helen could bring herself to think about. It wasn't her department. Catching terrorists, assassins and snipers was cleaner, safer and morally more palatable. She wouldn't work sex cases for all the money in the world. No wonder Sylvia took a keen interest in what she was doing: it was a welcome break.

Helen moved to her desk and tapped her fingers on the table top, deciding whether she needed a coffee. She went to the De'Longhi machine outside her office and watched as it created a wonderful aroma of freshly ground beans. It was a far cry from what the MOD in Whitehall offered.

Her mobile phone buzzed, and she checked her notifications. It was an email from Lyon–Saint Exupéry Airport. Helen already knew that Khalil was in the city, though she hadn't been able to arrange to meet him at the InterContinental due to business clashes. He was remaining suspiciously unavailable. Ricard, who was running surveillance at the Ritz in Paris, hadn't anything to report back to her. There'd been no irregular conversations picked up from Taziri Dalmani either, who still resided in the hotel suite in Paris. Khalil had extensive trading links in Europe and she appreciated he was busy, but he was supposed to be showing an active interest in looking for his son.

What she read in the email frustrated her further. It was another passenger list, but this time from Lyon to Marseilles, by private jet. But it was Khalil's travelling companion that made her stop dead. Grant Tennyson was on the flight, which landed in Marseilles last night. Grant wasn't stupid. He knew she'd have this kind of information to hand. He knew.

Jesus. It had been years since she'd seen him, and now he was jumping back into her life as the spectre sitting behind a major case: one that she had to see through to the end. The coffee tasted bitter now. She threw it away and went back to her desk. Her computer was open on her emails and she went to close the page, not wanting to even look at Grant's name.

But what overshadowed her anxiety at bumping into an old flame – drowned it out completely, really – was the now indisputable fact that she needed to go to Marseilles.

The information from Angelo now made sense. And if that's where Grant and Khalil had gone, then that's where she needed to go too.

Chapter 38

Grant left Khalil at his private apartments overlooking the vast old port of Marseilles. He was amazed by the collection of residences, rented and owned, that Khalil used abroad. Everything was prepared: laundry, linen, attending staff and timings. He was always expected and ushered through seamlessly. Grant afforded himself the luxury of a quick shower and change in his own room, two floors below, as well as a couple of hours of sleep.

He wanted Khalil as far away as possible from the unloading ship once it docked and cleared customs. He argued that the goods coming into the country would be met with somebody representing Fawaz, who was already responsible for taking his son. What was to stop him taking Khalil too?

'He wouldn't dare – he has too much to lose. If he takes me or harms me, he makes himself a target and makes it obvious who's responsible,' Khalil argued.

'You've got a point, but I don't trust a man who captures somebody's child to get what they want,' Grant argued.

Finally Khalil backed down and Grant had made his way to the port alone, carrying two illegal firearms. Technically, the bodyguard of a high-profile VIP could carry a weapon in France, but only when in active service for that end. Grant wasn't protecting anyone tonight, only himself. He carried a Glock 9mm pistol and a Heckler & Koch MP5, a nice compact semi-automatic that could be hidden inside his jacket. Both weapons were perfect for confined spaces, should he find himself in a pickle.

He'd organised another vehicle for himself that was anonymous, unregistered and common. Grant left the luxurious waterfront apartment where Khalil would base himself for a few days and attend countless business meetings, trying to take his mind off why they were really there. He took the lift down to the underground private garage in the basement and found a Fiat 500 waiting for him. He drove to the port and headed to Quay 91, where Khalil's shipment from Algiers was due to dock at seven p.m.

The Grand Port Maritime de Marseilles saw traffic of almost one hundred thousand tonnes go through it in a single year. It was vast. It was the main seaport for the whole of France and pivotal to European trade going back over two thousand years.

Grant drove through the ancient port, which was now a gentrified tourist hub with fancy seafood restaurants, lavish hotels and apartments. Expensive yachts docked there and he could see hundreds of vessels twinkling and bobbing in the early-evening light. He headed north to the working port, a huge expanse of terminals, quays and warehouses: the beating heart of the city. It smelled functional and his open windows took in the aroma of the sea mixed with the fumes of colossal vessels arriving from all over the Mediterranean. Cargo from Algeria docked in the Quai de la Joliette area. The landing stages along the quay were separated from the street by white metal barriers, and to get inside, Grant had to enter through Gate 7 and show his ID, arranged by Khalil. He turned into the gate and waited at the barrier, showing the guard his photo card. He was ushered through and told that he could use the carpark to the right. After leaving his car, he headed to the dockside and waited inside a cafe frequented by dock workers and security guards. It served onion soup, terrines, croque-monsieurs and casseroles. Grant took a table at the window and ordered an espresso.

He watched the towering concrete structures overlooking the quayside and looked for anyone entering Quay 91. Vehicles of all shapes and sizes came and went from the carpark and he looked at his watch. It was half past six, and he gazed towards the entrance to the mighty port in the distance, seeing if any vessels were making their way to the terminal. Several working ships were either approaching or leaving the dock, and others were sat idle or being loaded or unloaded. He heard shouts, horns and announcements as he sipped his sweetened coffee.

The door opened, and a woman walked in and looked around.

Grant froze. She spotted him and smiled. She walked to the counter and ordered something and pointed to Grant's table. Then she walked towards him and sat opposite him. Her hair was free and her face was open and friendly. She hadn't changed. He felt his pulse elevate: she was gorgeous.

'Hi Grant,' she said.

'Hi Helen,' he replied.

Chapter 39

In the small cafe, on Quai de la Joliette, Grant stared at Helen.

Neither knew what to say.

The ambience of the place could have filled in the gaps for them, should they have wished, but Helen spoke first.

'You look well, Grant. Congratulations on the job. You deserve it,' she said.

He held out his hands, with upturned palms. It was more than a gesture: it was an offering of solace, want, need, apology and something else, guilt?

'It's good to see you,' he said.

She leant on the plastic tablecloth, coming closer to him, and put her hands in his. They locked eyes and seconds passed as each ex-lover read the other, deeply and fluently, like forgotten favourite stories.

'Are you following me?' he asked.

'Of course,' she replied.

'I'm sorry I didn't get in touch to tell you,' he offered.

'About what?' she asked.

'The job, how close I am to Khalil. I didn't know you were the lead investigator until a few days ago,' he said.

'Hakim has only been missing since Sunday,' she admonished him. She slipped her hands out of his.

'So, is that your brief? Missing person?' he asked.

'You know I can't tell you that,' she said. She sat back.

'What's it like?' she asked.

He looked at her.

'I mean, working for him?' she added.

'He's a good man. Hard, but authentic. He loves his son more than anything in the world. What's happened, it's cut deep.'

'Losing a child always cuts deep.' It was out before she could stop herself. 'Sorry, I didn't mean...'

'It's all right, Helen, you can talk about it any way you like.' He put his hands in his pockets and looked around. 'What about you? I heard you are working for the ambassador in Paris. How did that happen?'

'Well, strictly speaking, I'm not working for him, he just recommended me to Interpol. I report to Colonel Palmer.'

'Palmer? Jesus, how the hell can you stomach that?'

'It's bearable, just. He knows not to cross the line with me, but he's still an arsehole. Besides, I'm a pretty free agent back in Lyon. I don't have much to report at the moment, and Palmer hasn't asked. He did insult me, though, before I left Paris for Lyon.'

'What?' Grant bristled.

'He implied that the ambassador's faith in me was misplaced.'

'So you've got to prove him wrong?' he asked.

She smiled in answer to the question. He knew her well.

'He's a proper bellend,' Grant added.

'Why? Because he stuck his tongue down my throat and tried to cop a feel?'

Grant knew all about the incident, because he'd been there. He'd wanted to punch him in the face at the time and rip his balls off, but Helen had argued that it would end his career, and Palmer would still be a cock anyway, whatever he did.

'You look beautiful, Helen.'

She shifted uncomfortably, uneasy with the compliment, and he continued to stare at her.

'Come and work for me – you're wasted on these buffoons,' Grant said.

'Tempting, but I couldn't take your orders,' she replied.

'I'd work for you,' he said.

'No you wouldn't,' she replied before she changed the subject to why she had come all the way from Lyon to find him. 'Why is Khalil being so obtuse? He won't meet me.'

'He's distracted, his son's missing.'

'I hadn't noticed. Don't be vague with me, Grant. You're both hiding something.' She paused. 'Why are you packing metal?' She knew from the way he was sitting that he carried at least one weapon.

'I'm a private bodyguard.'

'But your principal isn't here.'

They looked at one another. Their eyes never drifted, and she carried on her questioning as he took his time to study her, drinking her in after all this time apart.

'I'm surmising that you're here waiting for a shipment arriving in one of Khalil's containers from Algiers at seven p.m., docking in Quay 91. It should be carrying rugs, canned goods, leather, fertilisers and citrus fruit, but I doubt that it is. What might really be in it do you think?' she asked.

No answer. She held his gaze.

'Why the secrecy from Khalil? Why send his new head of security, and the man tasked with finding his son, to meet a random container ship? Or are you here sight-seeing?' she asked.

Grant tapped his fingers on the table.

'We're working for the same side,' she said.

'No we're not,' he said.

'What? That's the first I've heard. Khalil has launched his own investigation, thanks to you, and we both want the same thing, so why don't we work together?' she said.

Grant continued tapping his fingers on the plastic.

'Quid pro quo?' she asked.

'What can you give me?' Grant asked.

Helen opened her mouth in shock. 'You want me to go first? You're no further along than I am, are you?' she asked.

He broke first. 'All right, let's stop this game. I still love you, Helen. I've been trying to forget you and when I heard your name I've been trying to put you to the back of my mind. That's what's on my mind right now, not what's in the fucking container?'

They both sat forward again.

She offered information first. 'A scumbag, known to Interpol, started working for Jean-Luc Bisset inside Khalil's security detail last month. He's called Ahmad Azzine, and he's been linked to Fawaz for decades.'

She watched him closely.

'You didn't know that, did you?' she said. She'd looked into his eyes so many times that she knew that she was correct. 'Quid pro quo.'

Grant retrieved a photo from his jacket, the one he'd emailed Levi, and showed it to her. 'This man?' he said.

'Where did you get that?'

'The nightclub where Hakim took his girlfriend last month before he went home.'

260

'Amélie Laurent? You were the Englishman who inter-viewed her. Of course you were,' she said. 'His code name is Sand Cat. Are you hoping he'll show up here?'

'That was my best guess,' he replied.

'He's already here in France. It's pretty certain that he was one of the drivers who originally took Hakim to Lyon.'

'You are positive Hakim's in Lyon?' Grant asked.

Helen saw the earnestness behind his eyes and realised that he cared about the young man. It touched her. She nodded.

'He's been moved at least once. Quid pro quo, Grant – what have you got for me?'

He took a deep breath and looked around the cafe.

'Fawaz contacted Khalil before we left Algeria.'

She fell back in her chair. 'For fuck's sake, Grant.'

'His son's life is on the line! He knows what this guy is capable of.'

'We could have been working together on this the whole time.'

'How did I know it'd be you leading the case? Khalil doesn't trust the authorities in Europe to find a kid of African descent, no matter how rich his father.'

'That's a serious accusation.'

'Oh, come on, Helen, don't pretend to be naïve. Your turn.'

'We found Hakim's DNA in a flat in Lyon.'

'What? And you haven't told his father?'

'Maybe if he accepted my calls and looked as though he was helping, then I might have had that conversation with him. Quid pro quo.'

'I found equipment in a flat in Paris, and the same type of equipment in a flat in Lyon. In Le Croix-Rousse. The address of the Lyon flat was on a phone I retrieved from the Paris address. It was a tip-off from an oil worker from Morocco,' he said.

'And the equipment is relevant because?' she asked.

'It could make drones.'

Helen absorbed this.

'Azzine was the driver of a black Range Rover that transported Hakim from Le Bourget airport. It was burned out near Lille. Where's Madame Bisset?' she asked.

'Safe,' he said.

'In one piece?'

'No missing digits,' he confirmed.

They heard the continuous, piercing honk of a ship's horn and both turned towards the window. A large ship was approaching Quay 91, and they looked at one another. Grant grabbed her arm as she went to get up. She stared at him.

'Helen, if Fawaz finds out that Interpol is on to him – I mean seriously on to him from what you've told me – Hakim will die.'

Chapter 40

The bundle underneath the blanket groaned and rolled over. The lump was a man, and he'd urinated again. It drained from his body and soaked through the blanket. The smell was rancid, and the heat attracted flies to dance upon his motionless mass. The windows remained closed, as instructed. Despite the heat, wallpaper peeled away from the walls and the air was laden with misery.

'Do you think he's sick?' one of the two sentries asked his colleague. He caressed his AK-47, which never left his side, unless he was out in the open; then he took a pistol off the flimsy temporary table and fingered it, shoving it into his pants. The weapons were integral to his make-up. Like a precious child in swaddling clothes strapped to his chest, they provided a reason to live. And a reason to die.

They'd come here in the middle of the night. It was an empty, anonymous dwelling, like the others, with the same smells: vegetables, chicken fat and tobacco. Their captive lay on his side and hadn't moved, but they could see that he breathed. They weren't given specific instructions on how to look after him, just to watch him. Were they supposed to buy him food? Were they supposed to make him comfortable? They hadn't been given money for such things, only to buy their own cigarettes and the odd pizza, and that was barely enough. What they did know, however, was that if their ward got away, the punishment for such incompetence would be slow and painful.

It had all happened so quickly since the other two members of the cell had been arrested and detained by the police. There were several two-men units on standby dotted around the city. They rarely communicated, but the raid on the flat had been called in by one such squad, and it had rippled through the others. They were called to action by burner phones, and spent the interim waiting in flats, smoking, playing cards and existing, until a Nokia ringtone alerted them otherwise.

The pair who now watched Hakim had been planted in France for eighteen months and this was their first major call to arms. Recruits didn't just come from the homeland; they were second- and third-generation descendants from migrant families, born here in France, and drilled for several years before being relied upon to see a mission through, whatever that might be.

They didn't care for their ward: they were indifferent to him and thus given to neglect. He was a commodity, and, as such a valuable asset to safeguard. But this didn't mean keeping him pampered. The gossip around the streets of Le Croix-Rousse was of the 'tifl ghaniun' rich kid. But they were safe here, for now. They were surrounded by neighbourhoods not given to colluding with authorities. The smarter areas of the district went about their business oblivious to the network of nocturnal soldiers ready to mobilise. Anyone who was caught was feeble and deserved to be cut off like a traitor. There was no room for error.

But, as the clock ticked slowly, punishing them with its taunting that time was slipping by, boredom took over, and the men became restless.

'Maybe we should get him some water?' the other replied.

'You go,' said Fudail.

'It's your turn,' replied Nizam.

Both were nervous about leaving the flat during daylight hours, and they were many, thanks to the summer sun. But they felt brave enough to venture out for food and water, and cigarettes, like now, when it was dark.

They'd moved three times in all, and so they'd used different shops. Le tabac on the street corner seemed quiet enough. Fudail shrugged and got up to leave. The TV was on constantly, and they watched it mindlessly, waiting for the next phone call. Fudail fondled his weapon as he laid it lovingly on the single table in the room. He took a pistol and checked its barrel. Two more automatic weapons leant against the table leg, loaded and ready. They'd fired arms since they were twelve years old, going into the desert to practise with older cousins, having been flown there by Air France. They shot Barbary sheep, jackals and the odd vulture, even a viper once. The metal felt homely to them, like perhaps a wallet or a newspaper might to a well-to-do Frenchman who worked in a government department. Fudail didn't want to leave his trusty firearm, and he touched it once more, as if saying farewell to a wife. He handled the pistol like a professional soldier, checking the sight and pointing it at Nizam, who waved his arm generally in the direction of his partner.

'Go fuck yourself,' he said in Arabic.

Fudail smiled and left, pulling up his hood and popping on a pair of fake glasses. He'd stolen them from a market selling prescription lenses. His beard was full and he wore a cap. He left the flat and walked down the stairwell, skipping a few steps at a time. The street was quiet and he entered the store. The shopkeeper was of North African descent and so Fudail thought him unlikely to betray a brother. Both he and Nizam knew their way around the neighbourhood well; they'd lived amongst it, watching and learning for this moment. They fed information back to Morocco, when required to do so, about the best locations to set up cells and both agreed on the places they selected. They also agreed that if a nosy old hag got in their way, they'd solve the problem with a bullet and a bag of stones to weight the body down in the Rhône. The woman who was suspected of informing the authorities, leading to the arrests, wouldn't survive should Fudail get hold of her, and he was ready and alert.

Neither man had expected such a high-profile mission as the boy, but their job wasn't to reason with those who made the decisions, it was simply to do their duty. When they'd accepted the transfer of the goods, they'd known instantly who he was. The abduction of the rich kid was all over the news, but it didn't feel as though they were doing anything wrong. How could their work be seen as a transgression when they were helping their families and friends? Funds had been sent home every week for the past eighteen months and Fudail's brother had been sent to school.

He chose some large bottles of water, some packets of crackers and biscuits, a pie and a bottle of Coke. He also bought more cigarettes. The man behind the counter spoke to him in Arabic. It was a short exchange and Fudail thanked him and left.

Back in the flat, he found Nizam in a panicked state. Fudail put down his shopping and told Nizam to calm the fuck down.

'He's supposed to be well – they're coming to check! I poked him and he whined like a diseased pig.'

'Who's coming?' asked Fudail.

'I don't know. I got a call on this.' He waved the mobile phone around. 'He's due to be transferred and he's to be seen by a doctor.'

'What? A doctor? When?' Fudail asked. He was irked by Nizam, who was proving to be twitchy and weak of character.

'Tonight. The ship docked. He's being let go.'

'Let's clean him up,' Fudail said. The function of their task was straightforward and nothing to get jumpy about. The boy was frail because of his cosseted nature, not because of anything they'd done.

They picked up their weapons and Fudail took a large bottle of water with him. They approached the body and blocked their nostrils from the smell of faeces.

Fudail cursed. 'Hayawan qadhar.' Filthy animal. Their predecessors should have taken better care of him. Fudail poked the lump. He still looked strong and moneyed.

'He can handle it.'

They'd inherited him in this shit state. Besides, they'd been warned that the boy might try to form bonds with them, as he had apparently done with an old man who'd fed him. An old man who had outlived his uses.

'What should we do?' Nizam asked. His agitation was verging on hysteria, and Fudail threw him a threatening look.

'We give him a shower,' he said.

Fudail poked Hakim again, and he stirred a little.

'Get up, you need a shower. We have water and some new clothes.'

Hakim's eyes flickered open, but they were stuck half-shut with mucus, oil and skin cells, accumulated due to the lack of care. He lifted his hand to shade his eyes from the light coming in from a lamp. Fudail strode across the room and flicked it off. He cocked his weapon towards the boy.

Hakim strained his eyes and lifted his head. Fudail instructed Nizam to offer him water. He baulked but did so, cautiously.

The boy gulped greedily and spilt much of it, attracting curses from the men. Hakim stared at them with fresh strength, and Nizam panicked.

'Calm the fuck down,' Fudail told him.

Fudail knew that Hakim sensed the inequality between his captors and he was incensed further. He felt like bashing his rifle butt into his head, but talked himself out of it. That wasn't the brief. Oh, how he wished it was though.

'Thank you,' Hakim said. Fudail tightened his grip on his weapon. The lad knew what he was doing, and Nizam fell for it by nodding his acknowledgement of the sentiment.

They watched as their hostage gulped and coughed through another drink. Nizam took the bottle away and offered him a bar of chocolate. He cooperated and took a bite. Fudail watched closely as the sugary treat rushed through his blood vessels and alerted his senses further. Chewing was clearly hard work. It was repulsive watching him masticate.

The boy was able to sit up.

'Come on, you need to wash,' Nizam said.

'Your name is Fudail,' Hakim looked at the man who seemed the more in charge of the two.

'No, it's Princess Leia. Shut the fuck up and stand up so you can take a shower,' Fudail said. Nizam helped him, but gagged at the smell as the blankets were pulled aside.

Finally, he was up, and they both had to help him walk to the bathroom in the next room. Hakim was given a bar of soap and told to wash himself. Fudail pulled a curtain around him, but made it clear that the door was to remain open.

Long minutes passed as the two men stood in the doorway.

They heard prayer.

Fudail banged angrily on the open door and told Hakim that his time was up. Nizam brought fresh clothes from a bag in the other room and threw them on the floor, alongside a towel. Minutes later, Hakim emerged from the bathroom, clean and semi-human.

'Could I have more of the chocolate bar, please? I feel as though I might fall down.'

Fudail nodded and instructed Nizam to get the chocolate, but the boy's manner wasn't lost on him: he was trying to provoke empathy.

'Go and wash the floor and get rid of the bed,' Fudail said to Nizam, never taking his eyes off Hakim.

'Where do I put it?' asked Nizam.

'I don't care. Be imaginative,' Fudail answered. He motioned for Hakim to go back to the living area. Fudail slung his AK-47 over his shoulder and followed him. He found new blankets and gave Hakim a fresh bottle of water. Nizam tutted as he rolled up the soiled bedding and gagged as he put it into bags. A thin mattress was laid down and Hakim instructed to sit. He did so.

'You fought, and we struggled,' said Fudail, his face not moving.

'What?' Hakim replied, puzzled.

But before he was able to say any more, the rifle butt was rammed into the side of his head and he fell sideways.

Chapter 41

'What's on that ship?' Helen asked Grant. She stood still, with his arm remaining on hers. His grip was tight enough to hold her there if that's what he wanted, but Helen could have pulled away if she wanted to.

She didn't.

'I have no idea, and neither does Khalil,' he replied.

A few people looked their way. Dock workers weren't the type of people to allow the rough handling of a woman on their watch.

'We're causing a scene,' she whispered. Helen gestured to onlookers that she was all right and leant over the table. Their faces almost touched.

'I have to call the port authority to get the ship seized,' she said.

'Don't be fucking stupid, Helen. That boy will die, I guarantee it.' He looked into her eyes, and they lingered there, motionless. Finally she sat back down. He held on to her wrist and she laid her hand flat on the plastic top. His touch turned to a caress, his hand on hers.

'I'm begging you. Give me time. Let's find out what's in it together. The minute you bring the authorities descending down on something imported by Fawaz Nabil, the boy dies. Think about it, Helen.'

'And what if the cargo of that ship is to make drones? Armed drones? How many people might die then?'

She looked into his eyes and recognised the familiar manner of his face when he was thinking about a solution. He was a problem solver and that had been part of their break-up: he always wanted to fix everything. But some things couldn't be fixed.

'So, let's follow the cargo and find out where the target is,' he said.

His eyes beguiled her. It was too much and she looked away. She acquiesced.

The labourers went back to their conversations.

'Let's get some air,' she said. Grant agreed and went to settle the bill.

When they were outside, they walked towards the quay slowly, and they talked about Sir Conrad.

'I tried to phone his private line this afternoon on my way here, you know, just to brief him on me coming here, and why, and I got diverted to Ben Palmer's office. He told me that I need to run everything through him, but I'm not comfortable doing that. It was Sir Conrad who generated this post for me,' Helen said.

'Does Sir Conrad know that Palmer is interjecting?' Grant asked.

'I don't know because I can't bloody get through to him,' she replied.

'Did you tell him anything?' Grant asked.

'Only that I wanted to speak to the ambassador to tell him I was travelling to Marseilles.'

'Did you mention me?'

'No. No one knows my connection to you, or indeed the significance of you working for Khalil,' she said.

'Which is what?'

'Oh, come on, Grant, an ex-army officer in charge of the security of a North African billionaire, currently a person of considerable interest in an Interpol case, not to mention an ex-close associate to Fawaz Nabil.'

'His son is missing – why is he a person of interest?' Grant asked.

'It's basic investigative statistical knowledge that ninety per cent of the time, family members are usually found to be the culprit of harming a close relative.'

'Don't throw statistics at me, Helen. You know he didn't plan this,' he said.

She nodded. 'Which is why I wanted to speak to you first. But I have so many questions for him.'

'They'll be answered, but my priority is finding Hakim.'

'Listen.' They stopped to face one another. The lights of a vehicle approached, and they receded into a corner in the shadows, away from sight. He reached his arm around her and she let him hold her. She could smell him, and memories of his naked body flooded her mind.

He turned to her, and she thought he might kiss her. Part of her wanted him to, part of her didn't.

'Can you give me twenty-four hours?' he asked.

She didn't reply immediately, instead watching the blood vessels near his temple. He touched her hand, but she withdrew it, putting it into her pocket. Grant spoke softly.

'I never wanted to leave. After Luke...'

She felt the warmth of his body next to hers.

'Don't mention Luke.' Her voice was a whisper. Why did he have to do this now? Luke was their son who'd lived for three hours. He was born prematurely, and his death was due to anencephaly, a rare neural defect. Helen and Grant simply fell apart afterwards.

'I'm sorry,' he said. He held her hand again, and this time she let him.

'I can still see his face,' she said. She fought with all her will to hold back her emotion, but seeing Grant had opened a gateway to her pain.

'Me too,' he said.

A pit of dread formed in her stomach as it dawned on her that the compulsion she'd had to throw herself into work after Luke was merging with the need to face this moment. One relied upon the other; in her quest to forget, she'd unwittingly set herself up to fail in her goal. Of course she couldn't forget; not as long as this man in front of her was breathing her air.

The parting had been messy, unclean, and left a gaping wound, which she'd tried to fill with the wrong things.

Her emotions muddied her thoughts, and Grant stepped away slightly. Damn, why did he know her so well.

'All right,' she said. 'Twenty-four hours, and then I go to Interpol.'

He smiled. They peered towards the quay and reckoned the ship would dock soon. He turned back to her.

'Can I ask you something?' he said.

'More?' she said.

'Are you happy about the security for the summit in Paris next week?'

'How do you know about that?' she asked.

'Remember Levi? We still speak.'

'Of course you do. The FBI is in charge and they've got everything covered, as far as I can see,' she said. 'The Afghans have been invited to discuss their national security progress. Sir Conrad is representing the UK at a special round of meetings after the big guns have gone home. Our PM and the president of the USA are flying in for three days.'

'That has to be it,' he said.

'What? A hit on NATO? Come on, I've already been down that hole and it's too far-fetched. Five Eyes would have been on to it by now – it's too big and Fawaz too well known,' she said.

'Does our intelligence know he's here?'

'Who?'

'Fawaz.'

'Here, as in France?' she asked, shocked.

'Europe, for sure. When Khalil has called him back on two separate occasions, it's a European dialling tone.'

'Holy shit, are you sure?'

'Dead sure.'

'But all the intelligence on Fawaz says that although he travelled recently to Madrid a few times and raised eyebrows – hence Sir Conrad getting jumpy – he's now back in Morocco at his pad.'

'He's not in Morocco.'

'If he's here and planning something big, then it's personal,' she said.

'I know that look,' he said. 'You know something, I can see the cogs of your brain whirring round,' he said. 'Come on, I've told you everything I know,' he added.

'Really?'

'Yes!' he said.

'His son,' she said.

'Whose son?'

'Fawaz's son, Rafik. He was arrested in the UK and deported back to Morocco, where he died in custody, probably tortured. The body was never released to the family. I've read the file.'

Peter Knowles had been as good as his word and had sent the Home Office file to her this afternoon. She'd read it on the train.

'And?'

'The then Home Secretary is our very own current prime minister,' she said.

He nodded again.

'The senior civil servant who signed the extradition papers was Sir Conrad Temple-Cray.'

Chapter 42

The remotely piloted RQ-4 Global Hawk flew at one hundred thousand feet above the Sahara Desert. The Rolls-Royce engines were silent, but it wouldn't matter anyway, given the altitude. It was equipped with high-resolution synthetic-aperture radar and long-range electro-optical/infrared and could survey an area of forty thousand square miles per day – about the size of South Korea. On-board data was sent via text message to control centres on the ground and processed by the US Airforce. With over thirty hours' flight time, it could send a steady stream of reconnaissance data, delivering a comprehensive picture of either a large area or a prime target. As well as conducting its usual task of searching the desert for alleged training camps for terrorist cells, the aircraft had been tasked with a flight over Morocco to confirm the where-abouts of Fawaz bin Nabil. Aerial photographs confirmed that he was present at his residence seven days ago. The check-up was routine for any persons of interest who had changed their habits lately, and Fawaz had. It was how Five Eyes had come across the anomaly in the first place. The US intelligence was the shared within the Five Eyes nations, and agents on the ground confirmed the data, with Fawaz's palatial mansion coming under further scrutiny. It had been noticed that activity at the riad had tapered off over the last couple of days, and so Secret

Service operators active in Marrakech were tasked with getting close to the property to observe and report back. The ground personnel in Marrakech submersed themselves in the culture of their target for years on end, and they knew the best ways to access routes by road and sea. Inland, they used Toyota Land Cruisers, perfect for the choking Saharan sand.

Fawaz bin Nabil was long suspected of being behind the biggest movement of hashish from Africa to Europe in the history of record-keeping. Morocco supplied one million kilos of hashish per year, most of it going to Europe, where it was worth around eight billion euros. Operation Lionfish had failed to link the transactions to Nabil Trading, but the surveillance continued at the cost of one member state with interest in where all the money was going – the USA. The superpower had been torn for decades by two divergent imperatives: the need to protect enduring American interests on the one hand – oil – and the desire to stay clear of the incumbent entanglements of the region. As a result, the American foreign policy budget sunk billions into Middle East and North Africa. The Global Hawk's contribution was a tiny part of the overall investment.

Photographs from the Global Hawk were sent in real time to an airbase near Bedford County, Virginia. From there, they were assessed and processed by specially trained military personnel, who forwarded them to the relevant department at the Pentagon. The photos showed zero activity at the riad for over thirty-six hours.

The operator, sat in an airbase near Washington DC, deftly sent commands to the lone vehicle and dictated the limitations of the search. Only last week, the same aircraft had searched for a missing vessel off the coast of Nigeria that had been hijacked. The mission was a success, but half the crew died in the rescue operation.

The Land Cruiser on the ground was picked up by the aircraft and visual confirmed by the operator in Bedford County. The two men stopped the truck away from the road and used night-vision binoculars to assess the lack of activity. They'd been there for four hours. Their communication with each other was infrequent and usually took the form of banter about the Super Bowl, women, what they missed about home. But for the most part, they concentrated on the task at hand.

Darkness shrouded them and they felt sure that they were alone. They'd done it enough times. They knew the usual suspects who ran North Africa, and they had names for them. This one they called Bin Bin.

'Door opening, twelve o'clock,' one said.

'Got it.' The other confirmed sight.

Even at a hundred thousand feet, the thermal warmth given off by the human body was picked up on the Global Hawk, and the operator sat at a desk in Virginia watching and listening to the whole manoeuvre.

'He's on his own.' The observation came from the agent on the ground. 'Why has he no guards? He's outdoors smoking a cigarette with no one else around.'

'Is it Bin Bin?' his partner asked.

'It can't be.' Their range was three hundred metres, easily manageable for the L3Harris night-vision goggles.

'Nope, it's his body double.' The special agent was sure. 'Nabil is never seen carrying a phone, let alone scrolling through it and interacting.'

The operator in Virginia requested authority to enter the property. It was granted. The two men moved quickly and silently, like the Barbary lion sometimes spotted in the dunes. They closed in on the only two entrances/exits and split up. The man they'd seen flicked his cigarette away, got into a vehicle, on his own, and drove away from the residence.

'Confirm, it's not Bin Bin.'

'Affirmative.'

They moved towards the entrances separately and approached the security fences that threatened enough voltage to kill ten lions. A quick test confirmed that it was switched off. They climbed over and worked quickly, searching each room of the luxurious residence. After ten minutes, they'd confirmed that no one was home. No security, no maids and no caretakers. The place was abandoned.

They had no record of Fawaz leaving the property and not even the US budget could spread to watching one man's back every day for a week at the cost of ten million dollars per flight.

The fact was that Fawaz bin Nabil, or Bin Bin, was gone, and it begged the question why he'd left his body double – well known to the Secret Service duo – swinging his dick in the breeze for all to see, and his mansion in the desert unguarded. The only explanation was that Fawaz bin Nabil no longer cared.

Chapter 43

Thirty miles southwest of Lyon in the city of Saint-Étienne, Fawaz peered out of the window of a stone townhouse, once owned by a mining family, across the dark Loire river to the cathedral, which was lit brightly in the night sky. The journey through France had gone without incident after the episode with the cyclists. He was quite confident that he looked pedestrian enough to be forgettable: just a Basque gentleman making his way to his farm in the mountains. His French was excellent and, after all, he'd likely saved the man's life. The poor cyclist's memory of the gentleman in the truck would be a positive one that would not conjure anything sinister in the men's minds to make them suspicious, even when Fawaz's profile was inevitably spread across the European media. And if it was, it would be too late.

'How is the boy?' asked the guest.

Fawaz turned to him, beckoning him to sit and eat. They'd get around to specifics in good time. The luxury of a clean bed, a shower and fine French food had been a shock to his system at first. He'd become used to the grime and dirt of the road. The table was laden with simple peasant fare: local cheese, artisan bread, charcuterie, pâté and jams and chutneys made from local Anjou pears and greengages. The butter was pale and salty, and Fawaz felt at home, in a way. He found the French at once the most despicable invaders, but also the most civilised and cultured nation on Earth and their gastronomy was testament to that.

'Let's eat. Pour some wine,' Fawaz said.

They sat and filled their plates.

'He's unharmed.' Fawaz finally answered the question. 'Mustafa has delivered the merchandise we need,' he added.

'Can you trust him?'

'Who, Mustafa? Of course.' Fawaz laughed. 'You are jumpy, my friend. You don't trust anyone, do you?'

'Why should I?'

'Good question. No, you shouldn't, except for me. Your father trusted everyone and look what happened to him.'

Fawaz noticed Jean-Luc wince at the mention of his baba. Fawaz knew that it was a painful subject. Jean-Luc's father had grafted all of his adult life, after fighting for the city of Algiers in 1957, which had ended with thousands disappearing to be executed or tortured and never seen again. Basem had been lucky to survive but independence would take another five years. Two million Algerians fled the country, but those who chose to stay won their freedom and set about rebuilding their homes, and their lives. That was what his own father had done, along with Khalil Dalmani's.

In little more than two decades, the Dalmani family rose to prominence in government, commerce and law. And all of this on the back of people like Jean-Luc's father.

'Your father should have been respected more,' Fawaz said.

'He would have been had he worked for your family and not the Dalmanis,' Jean-Luc said.

'He made his choice in good faith,' Fawaz said. 'You've proven your loyalty and everything is arranged for you to leave.'

'And my mother?' Jean-Luc asked.

'We still don't know where she is. Relax, she'll be unharmed, you'll see. To my knowledge, she was interviewed by the police and they had her under house arrest, but she isn't there now. This was released yesterday.' Fawaz showed Jean-Luc the appeal for the public by Interpol to report the whereabouts of Marie Bisset to authorities.

'If they don't know where she is, and she hasn't contacted me, then where is she?' Jean-Luc was becoming irritable and his emotions bubbled to the surface.

'Calm, now. There is only one explanation. This Englishman, who Khalil so trusts, you think he would be the obvious choice for your job?'

Jean-Luc nodded. The mention of Grant Tennyson, a foreigner, heightened his anxiety. The fact that Khalil bestowed such honour on him was shameful and only strengthened his resolve that his betrayal was justified.

'I have knowledge of his history,' Fawaz said. 'He's ex-military and there's only one reason that Khalil would employ somebody with such a background: to pretend that he is clever enough to outsmart me. He'll have your mother, but he's playing a desperate game. He thinks he's being shrewd, to get leverage for his son, but the opposite is true. I will tell him to release your mother, or his son dies.' Fawaz popped a large chunk of crusty bread topped with cheese into his mouth.

Jean-Luc looked away.

'Don't be weak, Jean-Luc. Hakim was your ward and nothing more. A spoilt brat who took you for granted. My son died at the hands of the enemy and so will Khalil's.'

Jean-Luc nodded and half-heartedly spread pâté onto a slice of bread.

'I can't leave without her,' Jean-Luc said.

'Ridiculous. You leave tomorrow. Your mother didn't raise you to be weak. You can't be found in France when things get ugly. You've done your job, and now it's time for you to start a new life, the one you deserve. You'll go by road to the Bay of Biscay, then by boat, from La Rochelle, to one of my ships off the coast of Spain. It will dock in Tangier in a week. Arrangements have been made to meet you and to transport you to your new home.'

Fawaz finished his food and sipped red wine. He stood again, taking his glass, and went to the window once more. The sight, smell and noise of water soothed him and he wondered why he hadn't settled near the coast. But when Rafik died, all thoughts of his own pleasure were lost. It had taken him three years to find out who'd interrogated him in Marrakech. Every man present in that cell had met with a terrible accident since and expired prematurely. Then it had taken another year to find out who signed the extradition order in the UK. He was tired. His body was drained from self-abuse, and his mind was primed for the end.

'Don't worry, my friend, you'll see your mother again. She never really loved France, did she? She'll be happier in Morocco. How forward-thinking of her to bless you with a French name – it'll make the transition easier. You need to go and pack. Here's your new passport should anything go wrong, which it won't. Don't worry, it's just a precaution. The beard suits you.'

Jean-Luc took the document and smiled. He left the room and Fawaz watched him. Jean-Luc would never make it to Morocco. He'd served his purpose. He was just like his father: a dead weight.

He ran his fingers through his hair, which had grown shaggy. He didn't mind: his physical appearance meant nothing to him now. When once, his prowess as a man of power – and the women that attracted – had been important to him, now, all he cared about was revenge.

Chapter 44

Grant pulled a camera from his pocket and began to take photographs. They remained on the quay, in the shadows, but had moved up a metal stairwell to a better vantage point above the docking area. From there, they could see the unloading of the vessel clearly. The flurry of movement was a combination of an end to a long journey and the desire to unload quickly. Men shouted and swore. Containers were lowered from decks and rolled away. Forklifts were on hand to manoeuvre tricky objects, and foremen appeared from nowhere, asserting their authority over junior labourers.

Helen had put the nagging unease that she could be seen as going rogue to the back of her mind. Peter and Sylvia both approved her trip to Marseilles, but she hadn't been entirely transparent with them. Instead of introducing herself to the port authority, her priority had been to find Grant. It was Friday evening, and she knew that both Sylvia and Peter had gone home for the weekend. She told herself that she'd check in with them at her earliest opportunity. She had enough evidence to suggest that Fawaz bin Nabil was using the ship before them to transport goods illegally into Europe, using the containers of AlGaz. She should be calling the port authority now, but she'd made a promise to Grant. If Sir Conrad turned round, when this was all over, and questioned her choices, then she could easily say, in all sincerity, that she'd tried to contact him, but Palmer blocked her calls.

The truth was, she trusted the judgement and capability of Grant Tennyson more than any of them. Her gut tugged at her conscience, knowing that she was doing the right thing. But sometimes the right thing is not the best thing. Sometimes, the best thing is to save one's career, to toe the line, to adhere by red tape and protocol, but right now she couldn't help but feel that she'd have a better chance of finding Hakim with this man than a hundred Interpol officers who had no idea that Fawaz Nabil was the orchestrator of the plot. But why? She still hadn't worked out his motives.

Was it to target the summit? More specifically, the British? It must be. There was no other explanation. She'd agreed to give Grant more time before she blew the whistle on the threat to the summit, but would it then be too late? She figured that whatever was in those containers was heading to Paris. Her brain raced: what if it was chemical or biological warfare? A missile loaded with a deadly virus, if exploded by drone over the city, could cause a global pandemic, or worse. What if Fawaz's intentions were merely to make more money, and he was a pawn of the Russians or Iranians? Anything was possible with a man who had zero compassion or care for his fellow human beings. Money and power were always behind the actions of those hell-bent on hurting others. Otherwise, what's the point? Only psychopaths kill for fun; clever people kill for money and power. But the elephant in the room, which was growing bigger as she got closer to the truth, was that Fawaz was plotting revenge against the system responsible for his son's death.

Grant distracted her.

'Look, who's this?' he asked.

She followed his direction and they watched as a smart vehicle pulled up along the quayside.

'Ship-hands and foremen don't generally drive Mercedes SUVs,' He added.

Helen agreed. 'And certainly not clean ones, anyway.' They watched a tall, well-dressed man, who appeared to be greeting the shipment, step out of a spotless silver Mercedes. Neither Grant nor Helen recognised him. He shook hands with an official in a high-visibility vest. A docket of some kind was exchanged and the official in the hard hat nodded and pointed to a hangar. Helen and Grant decided to head to where he'd pointed. They slipped down the staircase and walked in the shadows across the loading area. The hangar was brightly lit but there were plenty of places to hide.

'Wait,' she said. They'd walked past an open door, and inside, Helen had spotted a couple of spare hard hats and high-vis jackets. They stopped and went inside, slipping them on. They made themselves appear busy by talking about some stacked cartons to the back of the space. There, they noticed an elevated walkway above and headed up some metal stairs. From the higher position, they could see the cartons arriving from the ship at the entrance, and the man who'd arrived in the Mercedes was surveying the load. He spoke to several dockhands, and it appeared that he was arranging for where they should be sent. A medium-sized lorry arrived at the hangar door and Mercedes man pointed to it. The dockhands seemed to show their frustration at what looked like extra work. There was a short altercation, but they acquiesced and began unloading some of the cartons. Several boxes were unpacked and loaded onto the lorry. Helen took the number plate.

'Let's go – we can follow it if we move now,' she said. Grant agreed, after taking a few more photos. They slipped through a side door unnoticed and doubled back around the quay to the carpark where Grant's Fiat was parked. Helen had arrived by cab. From the car, they could see that any traffic leaving the quayside had to exit via the roundabout, near the carpark. Grant pulled away and waited in a lay-by. In his rear-view mirror, he could see various lorries, trucks and cars exiting the dock for the night. Workers were going home, officials were knocking off shift and cafe employees were closing up.

'There,' Helen said, spotting the lorry. Grant nodded. He kept his lights off for now and waited until it had passed. Behind it, the sparkling Mercedes drove close by. Grant pulled out and flicked on his lights. There was a queue to get out, but it didn't take long and the lorry took a right south along Quai de la Joliette. Traffic grew busier as they left the port area and headed away from the Old Port.

'Where are they going?' Grant asked.

Helen looked at the street names. 'Rue de la République, Boulevard de Dunkerque…' They stopped at traffic lights and lost sight of the lorry only once as it made better headway through the city.

'There!' Helen pointed.

'They're leaving the city,' she said. 'There's a sign up ahead. So, we're heading for the turning for Aix-en-Provence and Lyon.'

They made some distance up on the autoroute and Grant skilfully changed lanes and changed speed to fit in with the surrounding drivers. As far as they were aware, they hadn't been spotted. The driver of the lorry and the Mercedes weren't showing any signs of nervousness or making any rash decisions.

'The Merc is turning off,' Helen said.

'Let's stay with the lorry – we need to know where it's going and what's inside,' Grant suggested.

Helen agreed. After another twenty minutes, they came to another sign, and the lorry signalled to turn off for the A7 to Lyon.

Grant settled in, anticipating the three-hour drive ahead. They travelled in silence and Helen fidgeted in her seat. It was already eleven o'clock at night. She checked her emails and Angelo had updated her on Nabil Tradings. He'd also sent her the maritime manifest and the entry summary declaration for the ship that just docked in Marseilles. She read both documents and unsurprisingly, the cargo was logged as citrus fruit, canned goods, textiles, chemicals, seafood, pottery, fertiliser and argan oil as expected. Every item was registered as the product of AlGaz. Of course, the ship belonged to the oil giant, so it made complete sense. The question was, which of his imports had Khalil sacrificed to make room for Fawaz's contraband?

'Your boss must know which of the containers were handed over to Fawaz,' she said.

'You're awake then?' he replied.

She bent her head over towards his seat.

'You look beautiful,' he said. Lights flashed past them and the air had cooled since leaving Marseilles, and inside the car, the air-con wasn't top notch anyway, so they opened the windows. Her hair blew slightly.

'You always said that to me when you were trying to avoid something,' she said.

He laughed. 'Tell me you missed me and that you thought about me every night when you were alone.'

'Actually, now you mention it.' She smiled. But her humour was short-lived. 'We were both in a bad place. I couldn't move on. Not for a long time. Seeing him so perfect and then knowing that his skull hadn't formed properly.' She looked ahead. 'I don't blame you, Grant,' she added.

She knew that this was their Achilles' heel. He hurt too. That was what she knew he wanted to say, but couldn't, because he didn't think he had the right. It had been her body that carried Luke for five months and her labour that brought him into the world. Tiny, but perfect. Army men weren't very good at showing their emotions, but she knew Grant felt pain. She read his face like a favourite old book, well-thumbed and given pride of place on the bookcase. Being in the same space as him after so long, she felt at ease; as if she was home. Not that she'd ever had a home in the army, because home to her was inside, and this is how it felt. She swallowed hard. What made them so fractured that they couldn't weather the storm together? Couples do it all the time, survive the death of a child, but they'd failed.

'Fawaz didn't tell Khalil which container was used, it was simply provided and loaded with all the others.' Grant changed the subject, but Helen knew that he only did it because he, like her, couldn't allow himself to lose focus right now. But the feelings she was experiencing nagged at her. She always thought that he was a part of her past and she'd moved on. Now, she wasn't so sure.

'But surely he knew which container because it had to come from somewhere at his instruction,' she said. 'And it would have a manifest. I've got one here, and it's all the usual imports from North Africa that you'd expect. If I knew which container it was, I could work out where the goods were headed and prove that they never arrived.'

'Isn't it more important to follow the actual goods rather than the paperwork?' he asked, nodding towards the truck in front.

'Yes, right now it is.' She looked ahead at the lorry. It was nearing one o'clock in the morning, but she knew that there would be a night shift at Interpol HQ who could trace the registration plate. She made the call and asked for it to be run through their databases as well as the plate for the Merc. 'I take it Khalil knows who he's dealing with? Is he clean?'

'Who, Khalil?'

'Yes.'

'As far as I can tell. I looked into the company before I started to work for them, Levi rooted around for me too, and I found out that Fawaz and Khalil used to trade together until Fawaz followed the dope and Khalil wanted nothing to do with it,' Grant explained. 'Levi confirmed it.'

'Why can't Interpol pin anything on him?' she asked.

'These guys go to extraordinary lengths to protect their empires. No doubt there'll be a money trail that no one has ever found. I reckon it's always a simple case of following the money.'

'That's what I'm trying to do, and I've found a company registered to an address in Mayfair, London, called Rafik Mining and Minerals.'

'His son.'

'Yes.' Helen sighed. 'It's so obvious, it's laughable. But very well hidden.'

'How are you going to handle Sir Conrad?' he asked.

'I don't have to. I've been mulling it over in my head. I'm seconded to Interpol right now. Sir Conrad might have personally asked me to keep him briefed, and I can prove that I tried to call him several times, only to be blocked by Palmer. But, at the moment my line manager is Sylvia Drogan. Actually, I don't have to involve you at all. When the time's right, I'll involve the head of Counter Terrorism, Peter Knowles. I actually don't know why I've been so concerned about what Sir Conrad thinks of me.'

'It's because Palmer is in his ear, bad-mouthing you. It's got under your skin,' he said. He smiled.

She turned away and read the rest of Angelo's email, trying to absorb the figures and company names, but she didn't need to because Angelo had drawn her a diagram, predicting her bemusement.

'Holy shit,' she said.

'What? Are you all right?' Grant panicked.

'No, no, I'm fine. This intern has been working all day on that money trail. He's found out that a single transaction of ten million dollars was wired via Rafik Mining and Minerals to a phosphate mineral company in Morocco.'

'So? He's in mining, isn't he?'

'Yes, but the goods came from Mali.'

'Ten million dollars' worth of phosphate minerals from Mali?' he asked.

'Exactly – it stinks,' she said.

'You know what's worth ten million dollars to someone like Fawaz that the Malian government might have lying around from their civil war, funded by the French?' he asked.

'C4,' she said.

Chapter 45

Helen stood in Sylvia's office, bolstered with coffee, reflecting on the previous evening. She and Grant had travelled through the night, arriving back in Lyon around two a.m. They'd gone back to her apartment and chewed over their theory about C4, the mouldable plastic explosive that had more complete destructive power than TNT. She had no choice but to move on it.

'I promised you twelve hours at seven p.m.,' she'd told him when they woke. They'd fallen fitfully asleep on adjacent sofas and when the dawn light peeked through her curtains, she'd rubbed her eyes in disbelief at the man who slept opposite her.

At seven a.m., she'd called Peter and Sylvia. It was Saturday morning, but they both agreed to meet her in Peter's office.

She hadn't mentioned Grant by name – yet, and she still hoped she wouldn't have to.

Everything she'd learned about Fawaz's operation, the shipment and Rafik was laid out before them. Sylvia stood against the vast window, tapping a pen on her teeth. Peter strode up and down the office. Helen had made her case for delicacy regarding a hard pursuit of Fawaz and the potentially fatal outcome for Hakim.

'I'll have to involve the NSCT in Washington,' Peter said finally.

The National Strategy for Counter Terrorism dealt with all threats to US citizens. Helen had to concede that what she'd uncovered transcended any incidental or localised threat levels and now involved every member of the summit. The timing was too pertinent to ignore. But the biggest and most concerning unknown was Fawaz's whereabouts.

'It's unlikely this will remain our investigation,' Peter said. 'Everything needs to be shared from now on. I'm awaiting direction from the FBI and CIA, as well as MI6.'

Helen felt flat. Peter spotted her deflation.

'It doesn't mean we won't be involved, Helen. You're the one who did all the work on this. The Americans want to meet us in Paris ASAP. I hope you don't mind me observing that I think you're wasted in the army. Maybe you should transfer to us permanently?' Peter said. She looked at him.

'What, you mean join the civilian police and transfer?' she asked.

'Not necessarily. We employ all kinds of experts. We'd have to get it signed off by the MOD, but we can be very persuasive.'

'You'd do that?' she asked.

'I would. I believe in you. What you've uncovered is the most important intel we've had this year. But we've got lots to do.' He went to his laptop and tapped some keys; a plan was projected onto his white wall behind them. Helen let what he'd just said sink in as he carried on.

'Surveillance is on the warehouse where the lorry arrived. All European ports, air and sea, are on high alert. Internet notices have been put on social media. By the way, we had intel from Five Eyes via the US Airforce this morning that Fawaz has been confirmed as absent from his property for four days. It came from a Global Hawk surveying the Sahara. I admire your balls for insisting that we don't go busting in and lose the chance to find Hakim Dalmani, which is still our mission priority as part of Interpol yellow notice. What it does mean, though, as I'm sure you're acutely aware, is that the price on Hakim's head is even bigger now and will grow out of control if Fawaz gets a whiff we're on to him. I should imagine that Washington will have it on their radar for the president's visit – if they get in before us, Hakim, I'm afraid, might be put down as collateral damage.'

'If only we could find him,' Helen said.

'That's exactly what we're going to do,' he said.

'Let's get cracking then,' Sylvia said in her Irish lilt. 'We're calling it Operation Tradewind. Fraud is drawing up a case against Nabil Tradings, and their accounts have been frozen. We've made sure that the company has been informed and hope the information filters through to Fawaz, wherever he may be. Fingers crossed, it will act as a smokescreen, and he'll think it's yet another poke around in his business affairs. In the meantime, we need to find Hakim Dalmani. We've been given extra time to hold the two suspects arrested on Thursday, and they've been transferred here to our cells.'

'Well done, Sylvia,' Peter said.

'Helen, you have interrogation experience, I believe?' Sylvia said.

Helen nodded. She'd taken the Special Investigations Branch qualifications for the job in Afghanistan and had used them countless times. There was a fine line between what was legal under the Geneva Convention, but changes to counter terrorism laws in recent years meant that certain exceptions applied, and here in France, they were more fluid than in the UK.

'We'll go in together and squeeze them both,' Sylvia said.

'What about the goods at the warehouse?' Helen asked. She and Grant had followed the lorry all the way from Marseilles to Lyon, and she was desperate to know what was inside.

'We can't wait any longer to go ahead and raid it. It needs to be done today. Surveillance has reported little activity there. It doesn't appear to have been moved or unloaded,' said Sylvia.

'And the Mercedes?' Helen asked.

'Nothing yet. Helen, you said armed drones? What damage can they do?' Sylvia asked.

'I've got to say, they've developed at lightning speed over the last couple of years and I'm not up to date,' Peter said.

But Helen was, thanks to an interesting conversation with Grant, in the car from Marseilles. 'As far as I'm aware, even a lightweight drone of five kilos can carry a payload of double that. My guess is explosives, but if the target is Versailles, then I can't think how they'd get them anywhere close. There's no way drones could be flown undetected from outside the grounds. Security round the estate is tighter than ever after last year's train bomb in Madrid. The airspace is closed for three miles and they have armed snipers on the roofs. The only way a drone can be effectively stopped is by deploying nets. Gunfire simply won't work – the target is too small and mobile. The best snipers in the world would be hard pushed to successfully bring one down. We've got to assume that the objective is to take out a major head of state. I have to throw in my opinion here. Peter, it could be the UK prime minister, as well as his ambassador in Paris.'

'Sir Conrad?'

She nodded. 'The motive being the death of Fawaz's son, Rafik, while being interrogated in Morocco. The current prime minister signed the order as the then Home Secretary. Sir Conrad signed the extradition paper, essentially condemning the young man to death.'

'You've spoken to him about this?' Peter asked.

Helen shook her head. 'I've got a technical issue, Peter. My line manager in Paris is being obstructive. He doesn't like me, plainly put. I haven't been able to access Sir Conrad's office.'

'Why doesn't he like you, the arse?' Peter asked. Sylvia snorted.

'I seem to remember spurning his affections,' Helen replied. She could see Sylvia out of the corner of her eye.

Peter tutted. 'Military men,' he said. His phone rang. It was a brief, tense conversation and he hung up with a sigh.

'That was Special Agent Roy White, in charge of security around Versailles for the summit.'

'I met him,' Helen said. 'The ambassador sent me to liaise with him and report back to him confidentially about the measures in place. I did so, they're excellent.'

'But without the knowledge of a possible drone strike. This changes everything for them,' Peter said. 'He's demanding a report to be discussed this afternoon so he can brief the FBI chief, who reports to the president.'

'It's time to bring in Khalil Dalmani and his head of security,' Peter said. This is what Helen had been expecting, and she'd left Grant in her flat, cooking eggs, awaiting such a call.

'Khalil is the only one who has been contacted by Fawaz – we need all of his cell phones, not just a handful of numbers, and addresses of warehouses and any information he gave to him,' Peter said.

'I've already explained that to his head of security. He needs reassurance from us that this will be handled well. He's under no illusion that if we fail to find Hakim before Fawaz realises that he's compromised, then it's all over. However, Khalil has been convinced by his head of security that this is the only way forward. They've done a sterling job under their own steam, but they need our help, and we theirs. The appeal for Fawaz has already had some results – I've been sent four possibles that appear interesting and plausible,' Helen said.

'Right, let's get on with it,' Peter said. 'Sylvia?' He handed over to her.

She introduced a plan for a three-pronged attack.

'Our priority is finding Hakim, let's all be clear about that,' she said. 'There'll be a sweep of the Le Croix-Rousse area this morning, involving two hundred officers. We'll concentrate on addresses unregistered to real people with a formal identity footprint, as well as around the addresses we've searched so far. We're no further towards finding out where Madame Bisset went, and we can only assume that Fawaz got to her via Jean-Luc somehow.'

Helen tensed. She didn't think Peter or Sylvia noticed. Grant had confirmed to her that he had indeed been the six-foot Caucasian to move her. Helen kept this information to herself for now. Grant had shared his assessment of the old woman, and if she could be as calculating as he described, then making her a priority could jeopardise their efforts prematurely by her getting a message to Fawaz

299

somehow; she was better off under the watchful eye of Grant's pal.

Sylvia moved on. 'Peter will fly to Paris,' she said. 'There, he'll hold talks with Special Agent White.'

'Sir, do I have your permission to handle Khalil's head of security on our behalf? I'll take care of it. I know him, he's ex-military,' Helen asked.

'Do it,' he said.

'Get what we need. You'll also be coordinating the hunt for Hakim here in Lyon. You've got twelve hours, then you'll be expected in Paris,' Sylvia finished.

Helen felt Sylvia's eyes bore into her. Their conversation about Grant Tennyson was not lost on either of them.

'Good,' Peter said.

Helen knew that to be trusted on both counts was a massive responsibility, as well as an opportunity to prove herself to everyone involved. Peter busied himself with gathering his notes, and Helen checked her notifications on her phone.

Sylvia came towards her and lowered her head, so Peter couldn't hear. 'Just don't make it personal,' Sylvia said. Helen stared back at her. 'I've got your back, for now,' she added.

Helen turned back to her phone and pretended to read intently, but a genuine report from a member of the public caught her eye. The mighty engine of the internet had kicked in and particulars of tips from the general public from Spain to Russia had begun to trickle in. 90 per cent of such leads turn out to be insignificant, but they all needed checking for that one tiny piece of information that could turn out to be crucial. This one caught her attention.

'Listen to this,' she said. Peter and Sylvia stopped what they were doing.

'A group of cyclists say they saw a man of Fawaz's description crossing the Pyrenees three days ago. One of them fell off his bike, and they said the man stopped his truck to help them. He was face to face with him and said he'll never forget the man who saved his life,' Helen said.

Peter stopped what he was doing. 'Check it out,' he said. 'By the time I arrive in Paris, I want to know if it was him.'

Chapter 46

'Shall we?' Sylvia asked. Helen nodded and got her bag. The two suspects arrested on Thursday had been transferred to Interpol HQ and were waiting for follow-up interviews downstairs. They'd been granted custody for both suspects for up to twenty-eight days by the Cour de Cassation, the highest court in France. A ton of work had gone into finding out as much about their backgrounds as they could, and Helen had read the information through several times. She needed a way in, and both she and Sylvia desperately needed the suspects to crack. This time, they'd go in hard. Without them being persuaded to give up information, the authorities faced a futile search of *les traboules*, which would essentially be like going down a foxhole.

Grant agreed that the chances of Hakim still being in Lyon were great. There was no point moving him; it would be too much of a risk getting caught now, when he was nearing the end of his usefulness.

The two men had been continuously disturbed during their two nights in custody. They'd be tired, confused and disorientated. They decided that Sylvia would go in hard with the Reid technique, which was to go in all guns blazing, telling the accused with determined certainty that they did commit the crime. Helen was to use a softer emotional approach to render the suspect disarmed and vulnerable, by concentrating on facts about their lives. She'd read that the one called Farid had lost his little sister under tragic circumstances. At the age of six, she'd been playing in a field near her home and had been talked in to going with two young men. Helen read the file and her stomach knotted. The girl had been subjected to hours of sexual abuse before her body gave in. The two men were hunted down and killed vigilante style, but even such swift justice wasn't enough for the family, and her brother was left haunted.

Helen and Sylvia took the elevator and chatted about the case.

'This source of yours, how did you talk him round?' Sylvia referred to Grant.

'Like I said, he's an old army colleague, I noticed his name on the flight manifest when Khalil flew to Marseilles. I presumed that he was Khalil's head of security.'

'And you were right. He's put a lot of trust in you – did you serve together?' Sylvia asked.

Helen nodded, but said no more, as Sylvia's gaze burned into her cheek.

'I presume you know where he is now?' Sylvia asked.

'At my flat,' Helen said.

'Marvellous, always keep a man either near your kitchen or your bed,' she said, winking. Helen returned the scrutinised stare but said nothing.

'Easy to gather the intel from his boss, then?' Sylvia asked.

'Yup,' Helen replied. Sylvia was telling her that as long as she got the job done, she wasn't going to examine her methods too closely.

They parted company and entered the two suites.

Helen smiled broadly to the man slumped over in the chair. The lawyer next to him read his documents and appeared bored. She'd had a brief telephone conversation with him where he'd confirmed that his client was close to caving in to the pressure of incarceration. The sleep disruption was doing its work. It could be a cleaner's hoover outside the door, a faulty light going on at two a.m., a barking police dog or a new bottle of water delivered at three a.m.: they were all common tactics.

Helen sat down and he raised his head. Farid looked exhausted. She took a can of Coke and a pain au chocolat out of her bag and put them down on the table. He stared at the items and Helen smiled again.

'How are you doing, Farid?' she asked.

He looked confused.

'Here, I thought you could do with the sugar.' She spoke in French as she pushed the Coke and pain au chocolat over to him.

The lawyer glanced at her and blinked his acknowledgement of what she was doing. He settled back to watch the show. They both knew it was a slam dunk, anyway; his client was guilty as hell, and the quicker he confessed, the quicker they could all get on with other things. Farid looked at his lawyer, who nodded his approval that he could take what was being offered. His cuffed hands shook as he struggled with the can's lid.

'Let me help,' said Helen. Farid let his hands drop, and Helen could see that his eyes were full of emotion. Poor bastard. It was young men like this who were groomed and radicalised all over the world, and easily so because they usually felt they had nothing to live for. Images of his little sister screaming for her mother, no doubt, brutalised and in agony at the penetration, must haunt his every waking moment. He ate the *pain au chocolat* greedily and Helen watched as the sugar made him feel slightly human. He sat up and glugged the Coke.

'Better?' she asked. He nodded.

'Farid, I absolutely respect your loyalty. There's no question of that. My priority, and all I care about, is getting a young man, about your age, back to his little brothers.'

Farid swallowed hard.

She placed a photograph of Hakim on the table. In it, he was flanked by two boys, each beaming into the camera. His arms were flung around them in protection and sheer love.

'This is Hakim, isn't it? The man you were holding? These are his brothers. They're devastated. I want you to try to imagine their pain. For whatever reason you chose to follow your orders – and I do believe they were orders – all I want you to do is understand the damage and trauma caused by a son, a brother or an uncle going missing, potentially harmed, and as time goes on, perhaps never coming home.'

He stared at her and to his lawyer, who whispered into his ear. Farid looked back at Helen.

'This one's called Farid, can you believe it?' She pointed at one of Hakim's brother's. 'It means "unique", doesn't it? It's a beautiful name. Was it your father who named you?' Helen had also read in his notes that another family tragedy had befallen this man. His father had been killed in a mining accident, which was how he'd come to be taken under Fawaz's wing.

Farid looked down and nodded. The tears came suddenly, and Helen handed him tissues. He let go a groan and bits of pain au chocolat flew out of his mouth.

'It's okay, I understand. You've done something because someone else asked you, and you felt loyal to them. It's not you we're after for this, Farid. We know that you work for Fawaz bin Nabil.'

Farid looked up and stopped crying.

'He's on the run in Europe and planning to hurt many, many people, just like Hakim is being hurt and many more families will be too. Can you imagine the pain those boys will go through if we don't find him in time?'

Farid nodded and buried his head in his cuffed hands. His shoulders shook.

'Drink some more Coke, Farid. This can all be over if you want it to be. If you choose to save that young man's life, then we can look after you. Fawaz has got what he wanted. He's managed to bribe someone very powerful into giving him what he wants: container ships. That journey is over for Fawaz, but don't you think it's time Hakim went home to his family? There is no longer a need for him.'

Farid took another gulp of Coke and looked at his lawyer. More whispers followed and more nods from the lawyer. Helen guessed that he was checking if he was being tricked.

'We have very specific boundaries when we interview people in this country, Farid. We can't interrogate you, we can't hurt you and we can't lie to you.'

This in itself was a little white lie, because in the pursuit of justice, a certain type of deception was legal. The lawyer shifted in his seat. However, Helen was relying upon the common distaste amongst lawyers for representing potential terrorists. It wasn't worth risking his good name for. He let it go.

Farid rubbed his temples, and Helen saw that his wrists were raw under the cuffs.

'If you could talk to your father right now, what do you think he would tell you to do? Have you got brothers and sisters, Farid? Like Hakim has?'

He buried his head again. He whispered under his breath and Helen realised that he was praying.

'Is it comforting?' she asked. He stopped and nodded.

'Did Hakim pray in captivity?'

A nod.

She was in.

'Did you talk to him?'

A nod.

'Do you think he's still alive?'

Another nod.

'Do you want his little brother to see him again?'

A nod. A tear spilt down his cheek. His eyes were droopy, and they lacked any kind of sparkle or love.

'Fawaz has what he wants, thanks to you, now let Hakim go home,' she said.

'I don't know where he is,' Farid spoke, in French, for the first time directly to her.

'But you know where he might be?'

'*Oui.*'

Helen passed him a piece of paper, knowing from his education history that he couldn't read or write.

'Can you write it down for me?'

'I'll do it,' the lawyer said. He took a pen and the piece of paper. Farid looked at him and took a deep breath.

Helen watched as Farid gave four addresses to his lawyer. Her whole body wanted to jump up and down, but she had to control herself. All four addresses were in

Le Croix-Rousse. The lawyer passed her the paper, and she took it.

'I'll make sure you get some sleep, Farid,' she said. She felt a pang of guilt, knowing that he'd probably spend a good stretch of time in prison for his role in the abduction and incarceration of Hakim.

'One more thing, can you identify this man?' she asked.

He stared at the photograph held up by Helen. 'Is this Sand Cat?' she asked.

He stared at her, swallowed and nodded.

'Ahmad Azzine?' she asked.

Another nod.

'Who was in charge of the arrangements? Was it Ahmad Azzine or Jean-Luc?' she asked, not expecting anything else out of him.

'Both. They're cousins.'

Chapter 47

Ahmad Azzine pulled in to a garage close to Gare du Nord, Paris. The journey from Marseilles had been long, but he was quite happy that the goods were now on their way here. At the port last night, he'd witnessed the unpacking of the cartons himself and, as instructed by Fawaz, the first pallets had been unpacked and loaded onto a decoy lorry. He'd watched it leave, followed by their driver. The lorry contained rugs and oranges, bound for Lyon. It was just another safety measure in case anyone had been tipped off to greet them. The pallets containing the C4 were successfully loaded onto another lorry and he'd followed it all the way to Paris. It was parked in the warehouse mere metres away.

The building was overly warm, but he didn't mind; he was used to more heat than a Paris summer threatened. He greeted the three men working quietly at desks. The final design was ready to fly, and there was an excited charge to the atmosphere. Ahmad approached the desk of the man who was adjusting some final touches to a quad-copter unmanned aerial vehicle (UAV). It was the size of a football and weighed three kilos. It had four arms, each with three tiny rotor blades. The technology had been in wide circulation for years, but it had been ISIS that first used them as weapons in Syria, to attack Russian forces successfully. Russia, in return, was scrambling to create their own force of armed UAVs to tackle the growing threat. All it involved was taking a small UAV that any hobbyist could order from the internet, and arming it. However, this quadcopter went one step further.

Mustafa, who hadn't been invited to the warehouse, had invented facial recognition software to be incorporated into the little machines via an on-board computer. It had taken two years for the designs to become a reality, and finally, they'd get to see one fly and perform. They were using Ahmad's facial features to fire up the final demonstration, and the men poked fun at him, asking if he was ready to be a guinea pig.

'As long as it isn't armed,' he joked. He picked up the contraption to admire it. He couldn't believe how light it was and asked if they were sure it could do the job. The men, who each had a specific skill set, acted offended and gathered around to show Ahmad their pride and joy, pointing to the kit fitted to the device that they'd each contributed.

'This is a DJI Mavic 2 Pro – only the best! It has a thirty-five-millimetre lens – they sell for fifteen hundred dollars.'

'I think they're worth a bit more now,' said Ahmad. The men laughed.

'How does it avoid things we don't want it to bump into?' Ahmad asked.

'Here, these are the sensors. It can detect shrubbery, birds, power cables and other drones. It's highly sensitive – let's fly it.'

Ahmad stood with his hands on his hips. The quadcopter was placed in the middle of the floor and one of the men held a remote control.

'What's the range of that thing?' Ahmad asked.

'This is a handset, but it can be controlled via computer, and, like mobile phones, it has unlimited range when it finds a satellite.'

Ahmad raised his eyebrows and whistled. He wanted to see it in action for himself before he filmed it to send to Fawaz and his cousin.

'Come on, then.'

The copter rose off the ground gently, and the blades made no sound at all. The tiny landing gear retracted, and it flew up to the ceiling but stopped suddenly.

'Was that you?' Ahmad asked.

'No, it registered the ceiling.'

It flew around easily, and Ahmad gazed in wonder at the grace of it. There was a mixture of expressions and gestures, all appropriate and expected from a group of men playing with a toy, except this plaything happened to be deadly.

'I'm activating the facial recognition now,' the controller said. It was a solemn announcement, and everybody hushed. Ahmad looked at the flying device and waited. There was a pause as the aircraft hovered in the air. Its movement caught them by surprise and it made its way around the room over their heads. Within seconds it had moved towards Ahmad, and he stepped back. It kept coming and stopped about a foot from his face. He felt the wind whip from the propellers and smiled. Only now could he hear a slight rumbling buzz from the motor. A red light appeared on the front of its main body.

'It's armed.'

'What happens now?' asked Ahmad.

'It will be programmed to explode when the red light goes on after facial recognition is confirmed.'

'How much explosive is needed and can it carry it?' Ahmad asked.

'About the size of half a pack of butter and we're loading nails in there too.'

'Excellent. Do it again, I want to film it,' Ahmad ordered.

Chapter 48

Twenty armed police surrounded the entrance to the garage. Three went up to the roof to secure any escape routes as Helen and Sylvia watched on their screens. Several raids were happening simultaneously. This one, on the garage where the lorry had pulled in after its long journey from Marseilles, and others on the addresses supplied by Farid to Helen. They'd moved to a control room downstairs that could handle the volume of simultaneous material. Six screens filled the wall and each had live footage of the progress of the Gendarmerie Nationale armed response units.

'What's the latest?' Helen asked Sylvia.

'There's been no activity around the property since surveillance was set up,' Sylvia said.

'Shit, do you think we missed them somehow?' Helen asked.

Last night, she and Grant had waited in the shadows, watching the lorry pull into the garage and the doors close behind it. It couldn't have gone anywhere else. It was while they were sat outside the building that she'd brought him around to the idea that they needed to join forces on this. Khalil could be talked round. The fact was that neither of them knew where his son was, but with shared effort and cooperation, they had a better chance of finding him alive. They had to work together to find

Hakim, as they only had the precious little time until Peter Knowles and his team had no option but to move in and take Fawaz down, even if Hakim still hadn't been found.

Of course, they both knew that Interpol would go ahead regardless of having Khalil on board or not. They didn't need his blessing to do their jobs, but they'd much rather he was on their side and not trying to deal with Fawaz alone.

Helen and Grant were creatures cut from the same cloth: their powers of persuasion were what defined them. With Khalil on board, surveillance had been set up quickly but had there been a gap between when Helen and Grant left and what the surveillance teams witnessed? Had the lorry in fact left or, more importantly, had the goods inside been somehow unloaded and taken out of the garage, for example, through the roof or via the rear?

Helen couldn't sit still and she stood with her hands on her hips. Sylvia sat before the control centre that linked them to all six screens. All she had to do was flick a switch to denote which feed she wanted access to. She checked in with each of the teams preparing to enter the addresses around the Le Croix-Rousse, but Helen kept her sight on the warehouse.

The operation downtown was trickier because of the nature of the urbanisation. Houses had been built on the hill since the sixteenth century and it showed. The crooked arrangement of tenements, stone houses and apartments looked, in places, as though it might fall down. The tiny passageways, so useful to the resistance fighters during the war, were any gendarme's nightmare. However, the officers were in place, as far as they could be, and the first mission of Operation Tradewind was about to begin.

Local residents had been told to stay indoors. The streets thrummed with activity as the gendarme gently requested people go inside and await further instruction. Some complained, but, by and large, they did as they were told. The personnel of the Police Gendarmerie Nationale had a fitness level suited to clambering upon garages and roofs joined together with washing lines and terraces. They were also heavily armed. Residents poked their heads out of windows to watch the unfolding drama. Sylvia and Helen could see clearly from body cameras that they were in position and ready to go.

Meanwhile, Sylvia flicked her mic back to the warehouse and gave the signal to advance on the storage facility, and Helen watched keenly, listening for any orders or events that might give them the answers they so wanted. After all, it was she and Grant who'd led them there. They heard bangs and foot stomping. The camera on screen with the best view was the chef d'escadron himself who had been tasked with running the mission.

They were inside. The lorry was there, but reports came in simultaneously from all over the building that no persons were present. Helen didn't like it.

'Check for explosive devices,' she said.

They watched as a careful sweep of the garage and the lorry itself was performed. Officers were trained to spot improvised explosive devices in wheel arches, engine parts, door handles and other parts of the vehicle. They used long-armed mirrors, fingertip searches as well as handheld vapour and molecular detectors.

'Clear.'

The lorry was opened, and Sylvia and Helen could see that there were intact boxes loaded into it. Had the guardians of the precious load been spooked and left their cargo?

Sylvia gave the command to open the boxes, one by one.

Sylvia pushed herself away from the table.

'Let's go back to the city,' Helen said. She couldn't bear to wait around doing nothing as the boxes were unpacked.

In Le Croix-Rousse, in the heart of *les traboules*, five separate teams were in position and ready to enter the addresses, by force if necessary. Sylvia and Helen watched as some doors were opened by terrified occupants, but others had to be smashed in. They listened carefully to all the commands and reports, staying on top of each search. At the top of each screen, an address reel allowed them to follow along. For a moment, the noise of simultaneous raids took over, and to a bystander, it might look like chaos, but Helen and Sylvia knew exactly which addresses were yielding results, and which ones weren't. Rooms were cleared, suspects found inside were lined up on the floor and cuffed, and arrests were made. All five properties were to be made secure and forensic teams sent in. Body-cam images were streamed back to the office, and Helen and Sylvia both stood now, leaning over the desk, adrenalin rushing through their bodies, making them unable to be still. Sylvia tapped her foot and Helen grabbed the desk harder. They were looking for familiar faces.

'Wait!' Helen said. 'There.'

'Which screen?' Sylvia asked.

'Five. I want to see the two suspects on the ground, on the blue carpet… that one!' she pointed. Sylvia communicated this to the capitaine leading the raid on that particular property. Helen looked at the notes in front of them and linked the screen to an address overlooking the

Rhône, high up on the hill. The capitaine went back to the suspects lying on the ground and made the two men face the camera. Helen tried to concentrate on managing the barrage of reports coming in to her audio, but couldn't take her eyes off the men.

'We've found two automatic weapons and four pistols,' said the capitaine.

'Any sign of the target?' Helen asked, as she surveyed the room from the vantage point of the capitaine's chest camera. It was sparse, vacant almost, and the men were putting up no resistance.

'We're still searching.'

'Check balcony exits, underfloor hatches, loft spaces and chimneys – the bath panel if they have one. He's most likely gagged.'

Helen stared at the two men, in particular the one looking directly into the chest camera of the capitaine, as if he could see her, and he said something in Arabic. The capitaine swiped him over his head and Helen silently thanked him. The suspect had called her 'beyra'.

Helen's tiny hairs on her arms stood up. The Arabic word was used to describe barren land that no one wanted because it couldn't be farmed. But it was also used to shame women who weren't married as washed up and undesirable. Helen had heard it plenty of times in Afghanistan, where she'd studied the language. It was highly offensive, but what Helen couldn't understand was how he knew that the person running the operation, and thus watching the cam footage, was a woman, and she was indeed unmarried.

'I want those two brought here,' Helen said.

'Agreed,' Sylvia said.

'What are your names?' the capitaine bellowed into the faces of the two men. He handled them roughly and Helen waited, used to witnessing forceful apprehension techniques in her time. Eventually, one of them had his head banged on the floor and decided to reply.

'Fudail,' he said.

'I can't hear you,' the capitaine said, bellowing in his ear and holding his neck at an awkward angle. The man looked into his body cam and repeated his name.

Helen seethed and forced herself to look away to the warehouse search. It was a coincidence, she told herself. Unless Khalil... No, that was absurd.

'Look,' said Sylvia, bringing her out of her pondering.

Inside the garage, all the boxes had been opened and photographed. They contained oranges and rugs.

Chapter 49

Three catering lorries and four minibuses carrying the staff entered the back gates of the Palace of Versailles. It would be a long security check-in and the catering company had factored this in to their employees' shifts. A tightening of perimeter surveillance and defence had been ordered by Special Agent Roy White, and seven French gendarmes took responsibility for this particular entrance to the west of the Grand Canal. The convoy had to pull over into specially designed bays provided for the purpose of the summit, and the staff climbed out while checks were done.

The gendarmes had in their possession a whole armoury of gadgetry: thermal imagers, extender mirrors for checking under vehicles, infrared cameras, carbon dioxide sensors, as well as good old-fashioned canines. Four German shepherds, considered the best breed for olfactory prowess, barked and pulled against their leashes and the catering staff huddled away from them.

A gendarme apologised: they weren't here, after all, to scare anyone, and if they had nothing to hide, then they'd be on their way very soon. Once well away from the jaws of the animals, several of the staff lit cigarettes and chatted amicably about their excitement at catering, serving, and – for some of them – cooking, at the great palace. The entrance was surrounded by trees and hedges, so they couldn't see the grand building yet, but it had been a large contract for the company to land so the excitement was palpable. Versailles didn't keep its own standing kitchen staff any more; those days were long gone. They'd been given maps, equipment lists, timings and dietary requirements months in advance, and each knew their job. Cooking for the president of the United States at a NATO summit would look good on any CV, and it was a chance to stand out.

Maybe the president was already there, inside the palace? Maybe he was even staying there? They gossiped and smoked as the checks were carried out inside the vehicles. Boxes were opened, the spaces under chairs were searched, inside the engine and side panels were photographed and imaged, and the gendarmes took notes and nodded. A few of the cooks gazed nervously at the officers, worried that some of their cold storage might be compromised.

Finally, one of the gendarmes walked over to them and handed one of the drivers a piece of paper. They were free to carry on towards the great kitchens, where, they apologised, further personal checks would be made. They'd been instructed to bring their passports, a staffing list, spare photographs and one other form of ID. It was worth the extra hassle, and they piled back into the minibuses. They were given directions and were escorted by a gendarme on a motorbike. The buzz of being so close to something on the world stage pushed exhilaration around their bodies, and they peered out of the windows, trying to get the first glimpse of the palace itself.

There were slight logistical problems – as there often are when catering in large stately homes – but the Palace of Versailles was a whole other ball game. It was colossal.

Luckily, the main kitchen was only two storeys underneath the Hall of Mirrors, where the welcome banquet was being held. The staff had to get five courses for sixty people up five different dumb-waiter systems. There was so much that could go wrong. What to serve? It needed to travel, stay warm – or cold – present perfectly upon arrival and be tidied away with the same efficiency. The executive chef had worked for six months on the details.

Suddenly, they were in the open, travelling next to a beautiful gully of water, which was crystal clear and surrounded by flowers of all shapes and colours.

'That's the Grand Canal!' one shouted.

As they neared the centre, white marble statues adorned the treeline, and they spotted the golden sculptures in the middle of the water. Animals, nymphs, cupids and virgins frolicked in the water and stared as the catering trucks rounded the fountain. They'd had no idea that they'd be allowed to drive around it. They'd wholly expected to be sent on circuitous access routes and service roads, but, they supposed, with no one around – the palace being shut until next week to the public – it was the quickest way.

The motorbike stopped in front and the gendarme turned back and smiled, he pointed in the distance and, as each truck rounded the fountain, they knew why. Up on the higher ground to the south east, framed by perfect blue sky, sitting as regally as she had for centuries, was the palace. Box bushes, preened to the ultimate precision, lined the route to the house, which sat white and resplendent. No one talked.

The small cavalcade carried on, not directly to the house, as the gravel walkway wouldn't allow, but over the crossroads and round past the Grande Trianon. No further such view was available as they made their way around the back of the great house and reached their destination, but they didn't need it; they'd seen everything they'd wanted and more.

Chapter 50

The flat where the man called Fudail had been arrested this morning had been searched, but there was no sign of Hakim. The fact that he'd looked into the body cam of a gendarme and said 'beyra' haunted Helen. Was it mere coincidence that she was a woman and unmarried? But she came back to the fact that the man had looked into the body-cam lens while being apprehended by a man. There were plenty of insults he could have hurled against the male gender, but he hadn't.

Or was she simply paranoid? They were closing in on suspects and her mind whirred. She tried to concentrate on her phone call to the forensic officer at the scene of the flat where the same man had been arrested.

'What exactly was searched?' Helen asked him. 'Bath panels? Loft spaces, floorboards? Cupboards? Have we sent in dogs or carbon-dioxide sensors?' She fired questions off, partly to escape the thoughts of Hakim, and what shape he might be in after a week of captivity. If, indeed, he was still alive. It was a sweltering day and the forensic officer was no doubt kitted from head to toe in plastic. Helen knew it was a shitty job, but she needed answers. She grabbed her bag and headed out of the door.

'The two men are in custody,' Sylvia told her. The other had finally given his name as Nizam; Fudail's accomplice.

'He knows something – I'm convinced Hakim is in that flat or somewhere nearby. I'm going over to Le Croix-Rousse to work with the forensic team. Keep in touch,' Helen said.

Sylvia nodded. 'I'm going to interview that one first,' she said, pointing at the still copied from the body cam of the man calling himself Fudail. 'He's not on any of our databases, by name, but he'll have DNA and fingerprints extracted as soon as he's booked in,' Sheila said. 'Good work with the young man earlier – the transcript was genius to read,' Sheila added.

'Thank you,' Helen said. She didn't hang around for compliments and left, charging an Interpol driver to shoot her across town.

The journey was frustrating but she knew that she needed to be close to where she believed Hakim had been, and perhaps – if they were lucky – still was. The door-to-door was still ongoing in Le Croix-Rousse, taking longer than normal because of the alleyways and hidden corners of *les traboules*, but the Police Nationale was admirably diligent, and updates pinged up on their inquiry notice-board as more and more residents were accounted for. She peered at her iPad in the back of the car and fiddled with her clothing. Her shirt felt uncomfortable and her hair hot. She tied it back and checked her mascara in a tiny mirror she pulled from her bag. Smudged make-up wasn't a great look, but it was sometimes a hazard of the job. She was thrilled when she'd found a super-waterproof brand in Paris, and it seemed to be holding up so far. Her phone rang and her cheeks flushed when she saw it was Grant. She answered the call.

'I've got Khalil on board, and I've gathered everything you wanted. He's had another phone call. You know I said Fawaz alluded to a woman he wanted released?'

'Yes,' Helen replied.

'He confirmed to Khalil that it's Madame Bisset. He said if she wasn't released into his custody this afternoon, Hakim will die. It's our last chance. Khalil is on the verge of breaking – we haven't got much time,' he added.

This was their first solid lead linking Fawaz to the abduction, Jean-Luc and to Europe. It solidified her position and gave her the conviction she needed to proceed.

'Grant?'

'Yes?'

'Has Khalil at any point told Fawaz that a woman is in charge of the Interpol inquiry into Hakim's disappearance?'

'I don't know, why?'

'Oh, nothing.'

She hung up and communicated the information to Peter, who informed her that he'd contacted Sir Conrad to update him. He was awaiting his flight at the airport.

'I think it's safe to say your line manager is in shit alley,' he said. Helen couldn't help but smile at the thought of Ben Palmer crawling out of this one.

They hung up and, as if on cue, her mobile rang again and it was Sir Conrad himself. Not his secretary or military attaché lackey, no. Now he wanted to speak. Well, he could fuck right off. She ignored it and instead called Grant back.

'I'm heading to *les traboules*, if you happen to be over that way,' she said.

Grant laughed gently.

'You're already on your way there?' she said.

'I can't sit and do nothing, and we know that if he's anywhere, it's in that neighbourhood. When's your ETA?'

'Three minutes.'

They hung up. She got the car to drive her up the hill and stop next to the building that was being searched and showed her ID tag. The street was quiet, as many people were abiding by the wishes of the gendarmerie and staying indoors. It didn't stop people peering over balconies and from behind shutters, but that was fine. She spotted Grant and met him on a stairwell overhanging with bougainvillea. The deep purple flowers reminded her of Cyprus, which is where her body had laboured to bring Luke into the world. The hospital at RAF Akrotiri had provided excellent care, talking her through every step of her spontaneous abortion. She hated the term, but that's exactly what it was: her body was giving birth because her child was dying.

Nature is so clever, she'd mused at the time, as if in some manically warped daze. It was her mental protection mechanism, she knew now: it prevented utter overload of pain, grief and bereavement.

Her senses returned to the stone wall, painted yellow, hot in the sun, and the man smiling at her.

'You look as though you never drove through the night and have had zero sleep,' she said.

'You know I'm not the best sleeper,' he replied. It was true, she never knew him go more than five hours in one stretch. She guessed some people didn't need it. His mind was hard-wired to whatever was coming next.

'Is it up here?' he asked. 'I guessed because of the number of police.'

'How did you get in?' she asked.

'I know some of them,' he replied.

She shook her head. Of course he did. 'Come on, it's up here. You'll have to suit up,' she said.

'I don't think I've ever been inside an active crime scene before,' he said.

'First time for everything. The dogs are due any minute, so I hope you haven't been handling firearms this morning,' she said and winked.

Sniffer dogs used for bodies were different breeds to those used for firearms or bomb detection and disposal. He feigned a smile and nodded to the back of her pants, where he knew she carried a Glock. She tapped it and led the way up the stairwell.

A forensic officer checked Helen's ID and gave them both masks, plastic over-suits, shoe covers and gloves. They both turned at the sound of dogs barking and went inside to make room for the newcomers. Inside, the flat was almost completely stripped, if ever it had been furnished at all. Helen had already read the inventory, and it was sparse. The weapons had been taken to a special military facility outside Lyon for forensic firearms testing. DNA swabs were circled in blue, numbered evidence cards were laid out on the floor and counter surfaces and plastic-covered areas like the toilet, kitchen sink and TV were all items well used. She didn't envy those lab workers who dealt with bodily fluids all day long, but whatever floated your boat, she thought.

She approached the forensic officer in charge and spoke through her mask. He'd ordered thermal imaging cameras and a carbon-dioxide sensory kit, which should be here soon, he confirmed. Helen walked around, aware that Grant was close behind her. She tapped the walls, feeling for cavities, and went to the bathroom, realising that both the shower panel attached to the wall, the airing cupboard

327

door, as well as a tiny door to a cupboard at floor height had been removed. She bent down and shone her miniature torch into the cupboard. She crawled inside and sat in the tiny space. It was large enough for perhaps two people and Grant hovered at the gap, on his knees.

'Shhh,' she told him, putting her fingers to her lips. He sat silently and watched her. Her eyes grew accustomed to the darkness, and she looked around. Wooden panelling was roughly hammered onto the walls and a few rugs were scattered on the floor, numbered with markers for evidence, which she avoided carefully. She began tapping the wooden panels.

The sound of dogs panting took her attention away, and she and Grant listened as they came to the bathroom. 'In here,' she said. Grant got up and allowed the officer handling the dog to enter the tiny space. The dog seemed excited and went straight to Helen. She sat still, not wanting to distract it. It began to bark and Helen jumped, startled by the volume. The handler let it go, and it disappeared behind her, Helen spun around and the officer peered inside. The dog barked continuously now. It headed for one of the wooden panels and sat down.

Helen crawled towards it. 'Boy or girl?' she asked the handler.

'Girl, she's called Keekoo.'

'Good girl, Keekoo! What have you found? Grant, get me something to get through wood, but carefully,' she asked.

'A wrench?' he asked.

'Smart arse,' she replied. She waited, her ears deafened by Keekoo's bark. The handler had crept in also, and knelt beside the dog, praising her and giving her treats.

'What does it mean?' Helen asked.

'She's trained to sit still and bark when she finds a match,' he said.

'A match as in the body was here or is here?' Helen asked.

'Either.' The handler was calm and stroked Keekoo, who looked pleased with herself. Helen always believed that dogs were capable of smiling. Compare the picture of a miserable one to one that is loved, and it's obvious. Keekoo was loved. She panted and her tongue lolled as the corners of her mouth curled up. Helen petted her.

Grant returned with a wrench and she took it, rolling her eyes at him. It was about the only part of her body he could see.

'Thanks.'

She crawled behind Keekoo, who nosed her hand towards the panel.

'Good girl,' Helen soothed.

She used the heel jaw to grab a nail and closed the nut. She yanked it out and went on to another, and another, until the whole thing came off. Dust flew everywhere and Keekoo went crazy, charging into the space.

'Grant, get a medic up here now!' she shouted from the tiny space. He hesitated for a moment, but she communicated her urgency to him silently and he got it. He left. She turned her attention back to where Keekoo had disappeared. The dog had stopped barking and Helen heard what could only be described as a whimper. Helen hoped the dog wasn't hurt, there must be all manner of broken wood and old rusty nails in there. She called to her gently, squinting in the darkness. There was no doubt they'd found some kind of sealed-off eaves, but the whole flat must be surrounded by botch jobs covering old roof space, as the buildings grew exponentially on top of one another. It was like a hidden cave.

She could see Keekoo now, sitting; panting, and whining ever so gently. Helen crawled towards her in the dark. She could hear the concerns of the handler behind her: there was only room for one. Helen concentrated on getting to Keekoo. Out of the darkness, next to the dog, Helen spotted a lump. She inched closer, on all fours, carefully moving obstacles in her path. Her eyes adjusted to the dark, and she saw that the lump was a body, and the body had a face.

It was Hakim.

Chapter 51

Grant came back, followed by a medic. He wore the familiar navy-blue shirt and trousers of the SAMU emergency medical responders, and he peered into the hole and shouted at her from beneath his red helmet. Other voices penetrated the gloom, but Helen was absorbed by the plight of the young man bundled into a blanket. She couldn't tell if he was breathing.

'Wait, I need to come back out to make room,' Helen advised the auxiliaire paramédical. She could see his heavy black boots, into which his trousers were neatly tucked. She'd begun to sweat, and wiped her eyes with the back of her hand as she crawled towards him. Breathless, she made it to the opening and allowed him through. He carried a standard responder's bag, which was slung over his chest as he got down on his knees and swapped places with her.

'I tried to find a pulse,' she said after him.

She remained on the floor, peering into the bleakness and felt an arm on hers.

She turned around, and Grant helped her up.

'It's him. It's Hakim,' she said.

'Is he alive?' he asked frantically.

'I don't know,' she replied.

A second medic rushed up the stairs and past Helen and Grant to the hole in the wall with a medical bag and a collapsible stretcher and rushed in.

'It's tight in there,' Helen said in French. He entered anyway and Helen was amazed that he made room.

She looked at Grant who, she could tell, felt as helpless as her.

'He was put in here to rot,' he said, spitting his words. 'Bastards.'

Helen remembered the face of the man called Fudail, who'd been arrested here in this apartment. He knew what was in these walls, and he'd left him there to die.

They heard sirens, but they both knew that it would take vital minutes for a fully equipped team to get up here and then into the tiny space, to provide any emergency care that Hakim might need. If he was still alive. They'd both seen active service and what happened when medevacs were minutes, or seconds, too late.

'Des nouvelles?' she shouted into the airless hollow.

'Il est vivant!' a medic exclaimed. Grant closed his eyes and Helen bent over, holding her knees with her hands, feeling as though she might vomit. 'Thank God.'

They both stood back and watched as a medic backed out of the space, carrying a stretcher. Neither Helen nor Grant knew how they manoeuvred their bodies into such contortions, but they got him out, and the first medic brought up the rear. They backed up against the wall and allowed the professionals to do their jobs. They both watched Hakim's face, which was ashen and unmoving, tubes stuck out of him, and the rear medic carried a saline bag. They disappeared down the stairwell, handling the stretcher deftly. Helen touched Grant's arm. Who knew what Hakim had endured, and indeed if he'd survive?

'He's going to be all right,' she said gently, hoping it would be true. 'Do you want to inform his father?' Grant nodded. They both walked down the stairs, following the stretcher. Downstairs, they stripped off their forensic covers and went outside. They watched the stretcher being loaded into the waiting ambulance, which sped off, sirens blazing. Helen took the name of the hospital destination and called Sylvia. As she did so, she saw Grant make a call and figured it would be bittersweet. Khalil might still lose his son.

The dog handler followed them outside into the sunlight, petting Keekoo, and Helen put out her hand as they passed. Keekoo nuzzled her and looked up.

'Good girl,' Helen said. She watched them leave and walked down the steps.

Sylvia answered her phone and Helen briefed her.

'Fecking fine job!' Sylvia exclaimed, and Helen imagined her doing a celebratory dance in the office. They'd achieved their number one priority: finding Hakim. Now they could go after Fawaz. He'd lost his chief bargaining chip. The gloves were off.

'But I have less exciting news,' Sylvia continued.

'Go on.' Helen said.

'The Mercedes SUV you followed out of Marseilles, when it split from the lorry, travelled north to Paris, but it disappeared between two péages halfway up the E15 between the Orléans junction and the merging of the A77. There's absolutely no way it could have exited on that stretch of road – a helicopter is searching now. However, what we do have is the appearance of another vehicle, not filmed before the Mercedes disappeared.'

'Our lorry was a dummy,' Helen said.

'Exactly. I reckon we'll find the Mercedes abandoned and empty,' Sylvia said.

'So, do we have an ongoing trail on the other vehicle? What is it?' Helen asked.

'We've got the registration and we've traced it entering Paris. A notice is out to apprehend. It's a Ford Transit, navy blue, darkened windows, we think driven by two men,' Sylvia said.

'So no ID?'

'The camera footage wasn't close enough, I'm afraid.'

'And where is it now? Do we know?' Helen asked.

'It entered the Gare du Nord district and travelled east. We lost it on an industrial estate that has three exits, we now know that the CCTV cameras around that area were vandalised recently,' Sylvia said. 'It could have gone in any direction if it left the estate,' she added.

'Or maybe it's still there,' Helen said.

'That's what we're looking into. I'll take care of booking your flight to Paris. Now we have Hakim, you're free to get your ass up there. Peter left strict instructions that should you find Hakim, then he wanted you on the first flight. Do you need to go home and grab some kit from your apartment?'

'Yep, I'll take a driver from here and be quick,' Helen replied. 'Good luck with that Transit,' she said. Her original brief was to investigate any potential breaches of security at the summit regarding Fawaz bin Nabil. Sylvia was right: she was now free to chase the bastard. They hung up.

'I'm going back to Paris,' she said to Grant, who'd be been waiting while she took the call from Sylvia. 'Interpol will arrange for Khalil to be allowed into the hospital, but he might not be able to see Hakim straight away.'

Grant nodded.

'Tell me where Marie Bisset is, and I'll have her arrested. She's no longer leverage,' Helen said. The bitch could roast in hell as far as Helen was concerned, and when finally in her custody, she was tempted to hand her over to Fawaz to give herself enough rope to hang. But, alas, that wouldn't be the case. He gave her the address.

'Give me an hour to warn my man to get out of there,' he asked.

She nodded. 'Come on,' she said to Grant. 'I'll give you a lift.'

They walked towards the car and got into the back seat. She gave the driver the address of her apartment. They didn't speak. The physical effects of the adrenalin rush of the last twenty minutes were draining and they were weary. On route, Colonel Palmer called her, but she ignored it. The last thing she needed right now was a smarmy colonel fawning over her and backtracking to save his skin. An overwhelming sense of peace came over her: she'd achieved her mission to find the boy. But – and there was a big but – now she had to find Fawaz and make sure the summit was safe. She'd had to choose one over the other, and she hoped that time would prove her choice justified.

The car pulled up outside her address and she told the driver to wait. Grant followed her up to her flat. Inside, she grabbed a bag and threw clothes in, as well as toiletries, which she always kept packed and ready. She left her weapon in the safe: she'd be re-issued in good time. Grant lingered in the doorway.

Helen turned to him. 'What will you do?' she asked. They'd spent less than twenty-four hours together, but it felt like days. Her dread that ever seeing him again would turn her world upside down hadn't happened. In fact, the opposite. She didn't want this to be goodbye.

'I'll go and see Hakim in hospital and ask Khalil for some time off. I won't head back to North Africa just yet.

I'll go back to London and do normal stuff like sit by the Serpentine and read a paper.'

'Well, you've earned it,' she said. 'Interpol will still need to interview both of you,' she said.

She was packed and ready to leave. She walked towards him and stopped a foot away. He closed the gap until their bodies were touching. He reached over and kissed her forehead. She didn't pull away, but leant on his body and closed her eyes.

'I want you to come with me,' she said.

'I can't,' he replied.

'I know,' she said. She looked up. He put his arms around her and bent his head, and she opened her lips. His hands ran underneath her hair and held her gently as they kissed. Moments later they parted and Grant let his hands fall.

'You need to go. I'll have time between connections in Paris if you want to see me before I go back to the UK. I'll head there tonight,' he said.

'I do,' she replied.

They left her flat and locked the door, and they got into the waiting car. She gave the address of the hospital to the driver and they travelled in silence. Only once did Grant reach over his hand to touch hers, and she let him.

Chapter 52

The car drove on to Lyon–Saint Exupéry Airport and dropped Helen by the private entrance reserved for security and first-class celebs. She was escorted straight through security and onto a waiting plane that had been delayed twenty-five minutes for her. She took her seat in first class and ignored the irate stares of the few privileged passengers around her who clearly didn't approve of being held up.

As the plane took off, Helen watched the city below getting smaller and smaller as they banked north and then east, west and then north again. Only clouds could be seen down below as they climbed even further.

The flight took a mere hour, and it was as if they'd reached cruising altitude only to begin their descent into Charles de Gaulle. Within twenty minutes, they were on the ground and she heard the scream of the reverse thrusters.

She was escorted off the plane before any of the passengers were allowed to unfasten their belts, and a car waited on the tarmac to take her to the US embassy in the city centre where she was to brief Special Agent White. She made contact with Peter to see if she'd missed anything while travelling. She had. The Transit van had been picked up again, driving around the same industrial estate, in an area of Gare du Nord. It had been stopped and a secure perimeter was in place on the estate. The drivers of the van were in custody and the search was about to begin.

'I'm on my way,' Helen told him.

The Paris traffic was more forgiving in July and it didn't take the driver long to negotiate his way south through the ninth arrondissement to Avenue Gabriel and the graceful white stone building of the US embassy. Cordons were in place all around the perimeter, something that the Americans did year round as a matter of course, and guards looked solemn and proficient.

The car sped through two gates, manned with pristine-looking US soldiers in full uniform. She was taken to a back entrance, and her door opened for her. The driver carried her bag and after entering a corridor, he handed it to another soldier, who escorted her to a flight of stairs. She followed him two flights up to a lavish landing carpeted in red, white and blue. He knocked on a double door, which was closed. It was the first time he spoke.

'I'll take care of your bag, ma'am.' His voice was formal and direct. She reckoned he was from Texas or somewhere nearby.

'Thank you.' She smiled at him and heard the door open. Peter greeted her warmly. She entered the room and scanned it quickly. There were several high-ranking officers from the US military, all male, as well as some suits, sat at a large table, over which was positioned a huge screen. Special Agent Roy White strode over to her and extended his hand, but she saw no sign of Sir Conrad. The arrogant idiot, she thought. Better for her, though.

Peter introduced her, and she sat down opposite the uniformed officers and suits, including Peter and Roy.

'Major Scott has been piecing together the facts from the very beginning,' Peter said, 'and we now have solid evidence that an attack will take place directly on the members of the summit, notably the UK prime minister and the British ambassador here in Paris.'

'Where is he?' Roy White asked.

'The ambassador is busy making final arrangements for the prime minister's arrival early tomorrow morning,' Peter answered.

Helen took a deep breath and ran over the facts in her head. The room went silent, and all eyes were on her.

'This morning, before I left Lyon, I was part of a team that recovered Hakim Dalmani from an address in Le Croix-Rousse, an area in which we long suspected he was held by associates of Fawaz bin Nabil.' She took a breath. 'Hakim's stable.' Sylvia had texted her while she was in the air to say so. 'We have four men currently in custody and have raided over fifteen addresses so far. There is strong evidence to suggest that bin Nabil is planning an armed drone strike here in Paris. He is now confirmed as inside Europe – something that slipped past us all.

'We did think that we'd apprehended contraband shipped by Fawaz on Sunday evening, but it turned out to be a dummy, and once again, we're reminded of how complex this operation is. We have been told by Khalil Dalmani that Fawaz Nabil used his son as a pawn to leverage shipping vehicles to import contraband to Europe. We don't know for sure, but we think it's C4 bought in Mali, off the government, for ten million dollars.'

She waited while this information sunk in.

'C4? God damn! How in the hell did a douchebag like Fawaz get hold of ten million dollars' worth of C4?' a three-star general butted in, but she'd expected it.

'Were there any Global Hawks up in the air over southern Morocco and Mali in the last week?' she asked. The three-star had so many medals, it was hard to see past his chest. He looked to the man to his left, who ruffled through some notes. He nodded. 'Yes, there were several fly-bys over the new pipeline being built in southern Morocco.'

'Right, we need to search that footage for vehicles crossing the Moroccan border along the border with Mauritania and down to North Mali. Maybe a convoy, but surely busy traffic for those parts. They'll have headed to Algiers after that. A shipment came in to Marseilles yesterday evening carrying Fawaz's contraband, and we hope we've traced it to a warehouse here in Paris, close to the Gare du Nord district.'

'Wait a minute, what about motive? Fawaz has never been political or a zealous nut,' another general interjected.

Peter nodded to her.

'The transaction for the C4—' Helen began, but was interrupted.

'What you think is C4,' said the general.

'What we think is C4,' she conceded. 'The transaction went through a company registered in London called Rafik Mining and Minerals. Rafik was Fawaz Nabil's eldest son. He was picked up in London five years ago on terror charges, and extradited back to Morocco, where, we believe, he was tortured to death. Sir Conrad Temple-Cray signed the order, and it came out of the then Home Secretary's office.'

'Who is that?'

'Our current prime minister,' Helen said.

The two generals whistled.

'We know he's making drones – we now think they're going to be armed with C4,' she added.

'You'll never get close to Versailles with drones,' Roy White stated.

'I would have agreed with you but I did some digging. If the drones aren't assembled until they're on site, there's no reason why any sniffer dogs, cardon-dioxide sensors, thermal imaging or any such technology would pick up the components.'

The three-star laughed. 'There's no one on the planet who can assemble drones that fast, ready to set off at the summit tomorrow.'

'Actually, we think there is,' Helen said. Peter pushed some buttons, and a photograph came up on their huge screen. They studied the man's face; he looked amenable, gentle and harmless, like anyone's grandad.

'This is Mustafa ibn Tafila. He's been Nabil Tradings' structural engineer since he was in his late twenties, when Fawaz put him through college. The man's a genius. We've put a tail on him, and we're raiding his workshop at his home in Marseilles, where he's semi-retired, in about ten minutes.'

She had maintained their interest and now they were taking her seriously. Peter nodded to her.

'We understand that the president won't change his plans. The same goes for our PM. I'm taking charge of his close protection, but can I borrow some of your guys?'

Roy White nodded and made some notes.

'We've got less than twenty-four hours before sixty VIPs sit down to the welcoming dinner in the Hall of Mirrors tomorrow evening,' Roy White said. 'I want the place turned upside down. I haven't even got any nets covering the airspace,' he added.

'Shoot them down,' suggested the three-star.

Roy White looked at Helen.

'With respect' – Helen smiled – 'drones can't be shot down – they're too quick and small. Only nets deployed from aircraft or launchers can be effectively used, and then you need to see them coming.'

'But if they're being built on site, surely we'll know?'

'Let's make sure of it,' Roy White said.

'How much damage can a small mechanical drone really cause?'

Roy White looked at her again.

'With a cigarette-packet size of C4 in it, plenty,' Helen replied. 'The question is, who will arm them and from where.'

Chapter 53

Helen hadn't slept. The ambassador had arranged for her to have a room at the embassy, usually reserved for visiting civil servants or advisers. It was basic but had everything she needed for a short stay. She hadn't heard from Grant, but she'd heard from the hospital that Hakim was growing stronger and that his mother and father had both spent all night there. She imagined the emotional reunion and pictured their embraces. He was going to pull through.

Her restlessness was down to the adrenalin running through her veins, anticipating the events of the days ahead. Her rapprochement with the ambassador had been brief and functional. Nothing was mentioned about Colonel Palmer blocking her access to Sir Conrad, and he didn't give any impression that he was anything less than delighted with her work. He'd asked her questions about the agenda at Versailles and how much faith she had in Special Agent White, and she'd reassured him. He'd been briefed separately by the Foreign Secretary, but she'd never know what conversations went on inside Downing Street about the engagement itinerary.

She didn't need to. Her job now was to work with Peter Knowles and Roy White in order to make sure the summit went ahead without incident. As she went to leave the embassy to make her way to the Palace of Versailles, she was issued two firearms, plus ammo, by the ambassador's armed guard, one for close quarter and the other for longer range. She signed them out and checked their weight and barrels, as well as how they handled in her grip. Later today, she'd meet the prime minister, who would arrive at Versailles with Sir Conrad.

Her mood was sombre. She'd been away from Paris all week, and it felt different somehow. She had a damn sight more answers than what she'd left with, but now, the mission had turned into something international, with her remit and boundaries unclear. It reminded her of a multinational collaboration, which she was familiar with, but with a twist of glaring uncertainty. She couldn't remember ever having been involved in a direct threat to so many world leaders gathering at a summit before.

She was nervous.

It was en route that she found out that, at around two a.m. this morning, a man meeting the description of Jean-Luc Bisset had been reported speaking to some boat owners in La Rochelle, on France's western coastal region of the Bay of Biscay. The sighting had been reported by a member of the public who recognised him from newspaper articles, read keenly as the gentleman followed the story of the abducted young man; he was himself of Algerian descent and took a personal interest. A quick-thinking local gendarme had called Interpol HQ, and the man had been arrested. Helen looked at the mugshot, taken inside a processing room near La Rochelle. It was him.

She'd previously briefed the ambassador's head of security about the coming days, and it had gone smoothly. She'd worked closely with him during the Embassy security review two weeks ago. Was it only two weeks? It felt like six months. It was crazy, now she thought about it: she'd taken the Eurostar from St Pancras and read the log of the ambassador's private security team during the time it took to get to Paris. Now she was hunting an international crook and facing responsibility for the life of the Prime Minister. And she'd seen Grant.

She needed a stiff gin.

She tried to relax and keep a clear head. She faced nothing she wasn't professionally prepared for. The consensus so far between Peter Knowles and Roy White was that if the summit was to be hit, the best opportunity was travelling to and from the venue, and so everybody's itinerary had been changed. All VIPs were to arrive separately with sizeable gaps between them. Also, each route had been altered and would be further changed mid-journey. Only Helen, Peter and Roy knew this for now.

It would take time and might cause inconvenience, but they could take no chances, and each government had approved the changes to the arrangements. Each entourage would be led by gendarmes on motorbikes and would be given live updates on which route to take. Only the two men on motorcycles would hear the instructions. Each pair of gendarmes had been handpicked by the office of the director general of the Police Nationale, with the approval of the French president's personal-protection team. The highest security clearance vetting had been supplied on the gendarmes by the director general's office to Roy White, who'd briefed the US president by video link as he crossed the Atlantic on Air Force One.

The hours before such an event, especially knowing that an incident was very likely to occur, was like waiting for the green light to deploy on an operation to lift a high-value target. The jumpiness in the pit of the stomach, the sweaty palms, the constricted throat, and the bare, naked, unmistakeable dazzling flashes of fear.

No one knew where Fawaz was. None of the intelligence services from any of the attendee countries had a clue where he'd gone to ground. Yes, they thought he was in France, but, according to what they'd revealed so far, this was a complex plot with many moving parts and many players. After the sighting by the cyclists, there'd been nothing. Rien.

Mustafa ibn Tafila was in custody in Marseilles. The raid on his workshop revealed kit perfect to make drones, but also capable of making a coffee machine or a model dog. The guy was obsessed with invention, like Maurice in Beauty and the Beast or Geppetto in Pinocchio. His workshop was a chaotic mess of stuff. So far, his interrogation had garnered a few titbits about what engineering projects he'd worked on with Fawaz over the years, but he did not admit to making drones.

Helen watched some of the interview footage via email as her driver neared the outskirts of Paris. She leant forward and studied the man who'd been loyal to Fawaz for over forty years. She wondered who else had displayed such allegiance and faith: Jean-Luc? According to Grant, Marie Bisset had said her son came to her disorientated, scared for his life and confused, and had staggered off to go into hiding. It was an unlikely story, but all they had. Only his interrogation, due to start any minute in La Rochelle, would give them the answers they needed, but they might not have time to wait. Mustafa was turning out to be a wily old foot soldier, unwilling to give anything away. She had no idea what sort of interviewee Jean-Luc would turn out to be.

She rewound footage of Mustafa being asked directly about drones and watched his body language. Over and over again, he remained true to his lines, but his body told a different story. Basic deception causes disruption in the brain, which displays as discomfort in the body. End of. Mustafa looked awkward when he answered certain questions about what he thought Fawaz was building, if he'd been asked to help and where he thought the goods were being used. Mustafa was clearly no liar: the more distress lying caused a person, the more honest they were. In other words, the more relaxed a person was with lying, the more likely it was that they'd learned to become expert liars as children.

Mustafa was a decent man. And that's why he was struggling.

She turned to the inventory of his workshop and shook her head. It was like reading ancient Greek. She'd never understood science that much at school, and the equations, gadgetry, circuits and scribbled numbers on bits of paper frazzled her brain. But one thing caught her eye. It was a newspaper. A French newspaper dated yesterday and it was open on a page which ran an article on the upcoming summit. Three colour photographs adorned the article: three beaming statesmen, wearing similar suits, sporting thinning hairstyles and identical paunches. The president of France, the president of the United States and the UK prime minister. To a forensic officer not familiar with the intricacies of the case, it was another item to be bagged and tagged and sent to Interpol. To Helen, it struck her as interesting, especially when she zoomed in and spotted the doodles.

But they weren't doodles, they were dots. Dots arranged in a pattern.

Chapter 54

She found Roy and Peter poring over the electronic map of the estate in the control room. They both stopped what they were doing and greeted her.

'Look,' she said. She showed them the photograph of the newspaper, taken by forensics inside the workshop of Mustafa ibn Tafila.

'Facial recognition,' she said.

'Blow me,' Peter said. Roy looked at him curiously. Helen didn't bother explaining the nuances between American and British English.

'He won't break – I'm telling you that now,' she added.

'Tafila?' Peter asked.

She nodded. 'We need to work on Jean-Luc. I was curious as to why he was so easily caught leaving the country. Clumsy? Stupid, or double-crossed perhaps. Either way, he knows where Fawaz is,' she said. 'It wouldn't surprise me if his ticket out of here was Jean-Luc's reward for his part in the abduction of Hakim, which enabled Fawaz to ship the C4 here in the first place.'

'If it's C4,' Peter reminded her.

'Sir, I think the lady's right. If you're going to arm a facial-recognition-enabled drone, arming it with anything other than C4 would be stupid and inefficient. That's what I'd do,' Roy said.

'But where is it?' he asked. Peter explained that the industrial estate where the van had been stopped was being searched thoroughly, but nothing had been found yet. There were twenty-two depots to search, and the place had to be emptied first due to the threat to life, should explosives be used in any capacity against them.

Helen received a text and looked at her phone.

I'm in Paris, it read. It was from Grant.

> JL arrested. La Rochelle. B of Biscay.

> Interviewed?

> Not yet. You hanging around?

> Prince de Galles Hotel – *perks of the job.*

They'd stayed there together for an anniversary.

> Room 525.

She looked up as the debate between Peter and Roy raged on about how possible it was to fly drones into the estate of Versailles.

'I still can't fathom how anyone could get drones close to the palace,' Roy said.

'Unless they're already here,' Helen said. It was a theory she'd flagged up yesterday at the US embassy, and one that had garnered cynicism from the military men present.

They walked to the window as information came through to Peter that the first VIPs were entering the estate. Helen looked at her watch: the dinner was in eight hours. The heads of state would assemble in the Hall of Mirrors and the US president, the president of France and the UK prime minister would arrive last.

'Do we have exit routes secured?' Helen asked.

Roy nodded his head and read through the plans submitted by each member state.

'Final walk-through?' Peter suggested.

The next couple of hours were pivotal in affecting potential outcome. They had time for one more run-through of their systems. An unmanned aerial vehicle was checking the perimeter for abandoned or parked vehicles near the boundary. Final checks were to be done on the backgrounds of auxiliary staff such as drivers, catering staff and bodyguards. ETAs of VIPs were to be finalised and entrance points double-checked. Sniper positions and any reports of unusual activity on the surrounding horizon were expected every fifteen minutes. The VPNs of all vehicles expected to enter the estate were checked and double-checked.

Anxiety affected all three of them, regardless of their combined experience. Roy White had served the US president's office directly for ten years; Helen had given fourteen years to her country; and Peter Knowles had racked up twenty-two, most of that in Counter Terrorism.

They'd each drunk three coffees, and counting.

'ETA of the US president?' Peter asked Roy.

'Two p.m. sharp.'

'Right, let's get moving. The UK PM is having lunch with Sir Conrad, and they will travel here together. Helen, you take a walk through the catering facilities. I'll stay here with Roy and collate information from the perimeter,' Peter said.

'Has anyone explained to Sir Conrad and the PM about the link to Rafik Nabil? I mentioned his name regarding Nabil Tradings when I updated him, and he reacted oddly,' she said.

Peter answered. 'Roy didn't think it wise,' he said.

'A direct link to two attendees?' she asked again, puzzled.

'It's much more likely that Fawaz will take out as many high-profile names as possible, otherwise, why choose the summit?' Roy asked.

It was clear to Helen that they'd discussed this without her.

She left, putting a call through to the ambassador's driving team, as she did so. Hunch, jitters, vacillation or scepticism: it didn't matter the rationale behind it, but she put in a request for a driver familiar with J-turning an automatic vehicle. Evasive driving was something that all ambassadorial drivers were skilled in, but complacency and lack of practice was always a possibility. She spoke to the ambassador's driver in person. He assured her that he was fully competent with the manoeuvre, which, executed perfectly, thrust a vehicle one hundred and eighty degrees in the opposite direction with the engine still running.

She was connected to Peter and Roy via radio and she could feel their apprehension. She listened as they confirmed checks on all the finer points of their last opportunity to check security. Voices checked in from all over the estate. One more inspection of the guest list would be done, including all entourages. It was a mammoth task, but they were used to it. Peter's department could do this sort of thing with their eyes closed. She wondered what sort of action Roy White had seen to reach such a senior position of trust at a relatively young age, and how he'd got the scar on his face.

She was taken by Polaris Ranger to the main house, and a short walk across the gravel brought her to a rear entrance. The kitchen was two storeys below. She met with the security team overseeing the catering and sat on the edge of a table, in an adjacent room to the main kitchen, and listened to their brief. They showed her photographs of every vehicle registered as arriving and leaving, which one had delivered what, along with their inventories and the vetting updates on the staff.

She took her time and checked each name against the security information. It took her two hours to plough through, by which time her stomach was telling her to eat, but she didn't know if she could face a morsel.

'This team here – the sous chefs accompanying the head chef,' she said.

A security agent checked what she was looking at. 'Yes, Ma'am,' he said.

'They've been added last week. Why weren't they cleared before that?' she asked.

'I'll find out, ma'am,' he said, and left the room.

She heard a final update from Peter across the radio.

All they could do now was wait.

Chapter 55

Helen visited the kitchens and accepted a sandwich from a chef. The smells coming out of the various stations were incredible and all tension at the thought of eating dissipated. She quizzed the young helpers about their jobs and residential statuses, without attracting any animosity at her prying. She made it sound the most natural thing in the world. She'd memorised the files of most of them and checked minor details with them, ticking them off in her head. She peered in cupboards and looked under tablecloths. A few ancillary helpers looked at her oddly, but most were gracious and patient with her questions.

She moved upstairs to the main hall, where she could see Roy White in place behind the Hall of Mirrors, coordinating the security measures covering the whole estate, which is where he'd remain. The perimeter had been closed and all VIPs were in place inside the great hall, which was most famous for the signing of the Treaty of Versailles in 1919. Where Clemenceau strutted and demanded Germany's blood, and where hundreds of presidents and prime ministers had graced the ornate stateroom since. Actually, it was garish and pretentious, and the light reflecting off the mirrors from the huge windows overlooking the Grand Canal hurt Helen's head. She'd come to the kitchen to snoop around and have a break. She was no good to the prime minister and the ambassador if she was lacking in energy. Her nerves were holding and the journey times and routes, chosen by Roy and communicated to the gendarmes via the Police Nationale, had been a huge success. She heard the guffaws of politicians and statesmen and women vibrate through the long serving halls of the palace, together with regular updates from Peter and Roy about sniper positions and perimeter policing. Shortly, the guests would be asked to be seated for dinner. The sun still shone brightly and the west-facing Hall of Mirrors welcomed the brilliant rays through the huge glass windows. Crystal reflected across the room as Helen watched from the door as the arrival of the US president was announced. She eyed the personal security of each head of state, and watched as they spoke in earpieces, communicating with each other via updates from Special Agent White. It was a familiar sight and one that Helen felt comfortable with. The suits, fancy dresses and glittering accessories mingled into a blur, and she drowned them out. Sir Conrad entered the room, and she watched him as he was submerged in flattery and pomp. The room was full and noisy now.

She fiddled with her earpiece and made her way back to Roy. She was happy with the personal bodyguards standing behind the VIPs at all times, packing enough metal to put a dent in the Titanic. The photo opportunities outside in front of the magnificent building had run smoothly and the world's media was happy. The best-case scenario was that they had it all wrong, and could all go back to their hotels after dinner was over.

Canapés circulated and waiters worked tirelessly to make sure no one was empty-handed. Roy gave her the thumbs-up, and she went back into the hall. She saw that the prime minister was never more than a few feet away from his guard, and the same was true for the ambassador. Sir Conrad had greeted her cordially earlier when he'd spared a moment to check up on things, gushingly almost, and congratulated her on her work at Interpol. He was back to his official self; busy and far more important than she'd ever be. It was a curious context, given the work she'd done in the last week for him. It made her feel like an outsider, but that was common and not unexpected. She didn't do her job for thanks.

Everything changed in a second. An ear-splitting cracking sound made the crowd of people duck and scream. Two of the vast windows of the Hall of Mirrors shattered into a thousand pieces onto the floor as Helen watched and screamed into her earpiece.

She could hear Roy White shouting, and it rang in her head. She saw him run into the Hall of Mirrors, pointing his weapon skywards and waving his free hand, dashing for the American president. But he couldn't get through. The president's bodyguards were manhandling him away from the room. But he didn't want to be bundled like a child and began to object. Women screamed, caterers dropped their trays and people charged for the doors.

Behind her, a second crash of glass made everyone turn towards the windows, except the close-protection teams, who were trained to do the opposite. Air rushed in with the flying glass and Helen watched as shards stuck into bodies and people fell down.

'Cover your faces!' she screamed. She found a table and stood on it, flailing her arms about and taking the safety off her weapon, bellowing her words out. A queer hush fell upon the chaos and people began to realise that, one by one, a stream of mini helicopters had entered through the windows. Five, six and then seven flew in through the gaping frames.

For a second it was like a scene out of the War of the Worlds, where no one quite believed what they were seeing. Helen jumped onto a table and bawled. 'Cover your faces!' She drew her other pistol and aimed both at one of the drones as two lights turned red in the front. She'd said herself that to bring a drone down with gunfire was impossible, but she had to try. She fired both weapons, emptying the barrels, and hit it, and watched as it dropped like a stone on to the floor. More people surged forward and toppled her table but she managed to remain on it as it steadied.

Another drone stopped in front of a man frozen in fear. Helen recognised him as the Canadian prime minister, who was being dragged by his security detail, but they were struggling to move him as they were pressed up against the crowd. She reloaded, took aim and got four shots off, bringing it down.

Suddenly, she was thrown from the table by an explosion behind her. Her ears rang, and she saw people on the floor and a space where the epicentre had been. She spotted a severed foot with nails in it, bastards. People were now running in all directions.

Panic had gripped them. Scores of bodies were on the ground, cowering behind suit jackets, tablecloths and napkins: anything to cover their faces. But others were stunned into inaction and another explosion caused more windows to shatter as well as centuries-old mirrors that fell apart with the blast. The noise of broken crystal, accompanied by the spectrum of reflective colours on the glass all around them, was mesmerising, but Helen didn't stop moving. She spotted the British prime minister and saw him bundled out of the room, on his hands and knees. Then she saw Sir Conrad frozen to the spot. She ran to him and grabbed his arm, throwing her jacket over his head.

'It's programmed to read your face,' she hissed breathlessly. He was easy to drag away in his state of fear, and she managed to get him out of the room before they heard a third explosion.

Then silence and three thuds, which she later found out were the unexploded drones dropping to the floor, as they failed to identify their targets. Two had been successful, and she'd taken the other two out.

The British prime minister's face was ashen.

'Car!' screamed Helen, cocking her weapons upwards, looking for more drones. Where the fuck had they come from? Her mind raced.

'How did they get past the snipers?' she hissed at Roy in her ear. 'Haven't they got sights on their weapons?'

He confirmed his position and informed her that he was taking the US president to Marine One, which was waiting on the lawn. She replied that she was accompanying the British prime minister and the ambassador back to the British embassy. The prime minister's primary armoured vehicle pulled up – a four-tonner – but she refused and instead directed them to the ambassador's driver who she'd spoken to earlier. His saloon was less-heavily armoured, but still effective under fire. She ordered them in while she jumped in the front.

The PM's personal bodyguard climbed in beside him and they set off, followed by four cars carrying the other members of the prime minister's security team. Helen leant over into the back seat, surveying the sky, expecting another attack. Sir Conrad huddled with the prime minister and his bodyguard, being knocked from side to side, having not bothered with seat belts.

'Put on your belts and get down!' she ordered them.

'What happened?' The prime minister was shaking.

'Sir, just sit tight and we'll get you to the embassy. It was a facial-recognition-drone strike, sir. You're okay now.'

'But the explosions?'

'There were casualties,' she said. Helen looked at her shirt where it felt wet and realised that she had human matter on her clothes. She ignored it. Sir Conrad handed her a napkin with shaky hands and she wiped at her shirt, scrunching the napkin up and placing it in a side pocket of the door. She checked her weapons and chose the Sig Sauer P320, cocking it towards the window.

'Stay down,' she ordered the others, except the body-guard who had his weapon cocked on the opposite side. They spoke without words and fell into a dual pairing as they would if they were clearing a room together.

'What route are you taking?' she asked the driver, facing the front.

'A13.'

She nodded and kept looking around. They saw Marine One take off, and the decoy full of Secret Service agents flanked it. They'd never know which one carried the president. She radioed ahead to the gate, and it was flung open as they sped out towards the autoroute.

As they reached the quiet of the main road, Helen's body didn't relax.

'Keep all windows and doors locked,' she said.

'Did you see them coming?' she asked the guard. He shook his head. Like everyone, he'd just heard the windows smash.

'Are you alright?' she asked him, noticing two nails sticking out of his hand.

'It's nothing,' he replied.

She was now out of range to hear Roy, and he'd have switched to a different channel anyway as all his efforts were to keep the president safe. Soon, they'd have the PM back in the confines of the embassy, which had already been told to prepare for the highest alert scenario. No one else in and no one out.

'I need to call my wife,' the prime minister said. Helen thought he might vomit and looked around for a bag. The driver indicated the glove compartment, and she handed him a sick bag. He spoke briefly to his wife and placed his mobile back in his pocket.

'What a major balls-up,' he said. Helen remained looking forward as she prepared to be blamed for everything that had just unfolded.

'My guess, sir, is that they were built on site.'

She'd flagged the scenario several times, but it had still happened under their noses, and she had no idea how. The question was who were the assemblers and how had they got the necessary equipment past the dogs. Particularly the explosive. Helen knew better than to postulate and trusted everything would become clear as the inevitable inquiry was rolled out. She wondered if Fawaz had been on site.

'ETA at the embassy is seven minutes, sir,' she said, looking at the satnav.

'Put the radio on,' the prime minister ordered. The driver did so. 'It's in damn French,' he said.

Helen translated. The news had hit the media and Versailles was in lockdown.

'Seven dead, thirteen injured. The French president and the German chancellor are unhurt.'

'That's a shame,' The Prime Minister's acerbic humour was legendary. Helen watched as two of the security vehicles pulled in front of the armoured car and two remained behind. The PM's personal bodyguard communicated to the other cars and they agreed a dummy route. Pedestrians stood and stared at the spectacle.

'Who did the final check of the undercarriage of this vehicle?' she asked.

'No one's been near it since it left the embassy this morning,' the driver confirmed.

She was worried about tracking devices but trusted the prime minister's team to do a thorough job. She dialled Peter's number and checked in. He'd been in the room behind the Hall of Mirrors when the shit hit the fan and watched them leave. He remained back at Versailles to help the emergency services.

'It's carnage. The Americans are working on one of the failed drones already. They're trying to trace the signal it used before it cut out due, they think, to not identifying its facial target in the time allotted to it. I've seen one of them – C4 ready to go, all still intact – it's like nothing I've ever seen.'

'Manufacture?' she asked.

'Parts any Joe can order online from Amazon.'

'My money is on them originating in Mustafa ibn Tafila's workshop,' she said. 'ETA is six minutes, I'll call you when we're inside the Embassy.' She hung up.

The atmosphere was eerily quiet as they drove in a cavalcade of five towards the Bois de Boulogne. She swallowed hard and needed water, but she ignored her thirst.

The park was busy as always and people stared at the entourage, some, no doubt, having heard the news about the attack on Versailles. The ancient seat of kingship, turned into an iconic trophy of the end of all wars, now turned into a bloodbath by a very different enemy.

Her hands still grasped her weapon tightly, and she wasn't happy to flick the safety on until they were inside the embassy compound. She was reminded of Afghanistan, where she'd been travelling behind a Warrior IFV when it ran over an IED and exploded, throwing its two cannon operators twenty feet in the air like dolls. The men inside were toasted alive.

They neared the Jardin d'Acclimatation, and soon they'd be on the Champs-Élysées.

The vehicle in front leapt five feet off the ground and an ear-piercing bang made the driver swerve. Helen knew straight away that it had driven over an IED. Their vehicle stopped, and she side-glanced at the driver, who was reaching inside his jacket. She raised her weapon with seconds unfolding before her as her rules of engagement flashed before her. She was unaware of the prime minster or Sir Conrad screaming, only that this man was reaching for a weapon. Disbelief made her hesitate, but his face said it all: he was reaching to aim at her. His face crumpled in determination and he failed to respond to her demands to communicate with her. She made a split-second decision.

She shot him between the eyes and blood spurted onto the car ceiling. She turned to the prime minister and Sir Conrad who stared at her horrified.

'Get down!' The bodyguard shielded both of them with his physical presence and nodded to her, oblivious to his injuries. The cavalcade had stopped dead and Special Forces were spilling out of cars, pointing weapons, taking cover behind car doors and crawling along the ground. She grabbed the body of the dead driver and reached over to open his door, shoving him outside with her feet and as much power as she could muster. The bodyguard helped.

'Belts on! And that's not a request!' she screamed.

She settled in the driver's seat and rammed the car into reverse, checking behind her for an escape route. She floored the accelerator and got to around fifty kilometres an hour. She plunged the gearbox into neutral and waited for the engine to smooth over, then, without warning, she turned the steering wheel from left to right. The car turned one hundred and eighty degrees, screeching on the tarmac, and Helen heard panting from the back.

'Bravo,' the PM's bodyguard complimented her. She ramped the gearbox into drive and accelerated away the way they'd come.

But it wasn't over.

Two men emerged from behind the treeline. Park visitors screamed and ran away, grabbing children from picnic rugs and diving for cover. Gunfire rattled over the bonnet and they all took cover inside the vehicle. They slammed into a tree.

The impact wasn't serious and Helen was barely winded. She scanned the faces of the two shooters. They both carried short-barrelled automatics with an extra AK-47 slung over their shoulders for good measure. One of them was Fawaz bin Nabil. She realised in horror that the attack on Versailles was a diversionary ruse: his true target was Sir Conrad and the PM, and she'd driven them right to him. Here in the early-evening sunshine, in the middle of families enjoying picnics, he planned to gun down those responsible for his son's death.

'I need you,' she told the bodyguard. They sank down and cowered in the foot well.

'Keep down,' she screamed at the two men in the back.

'I'll take left, you, right,' she said. Two vehicles in the PM's entourage had driven towards them, under fire. Helen peered above the window level and saw Fawaz walking calmly towards the car as the other unidentified shooter was taken out. Fawaz kept walking. Helen could tell by his face that he knew that Sir Conrad and the prime minister were with her in this car. She cocked and fired, but missed because her aim was out at the last minute: a woman ran behind Fawaz and Helen knew she'd have killed her if she'd been on aim. She took cover again. The bodyguard got off a few rounds.

Fawaz returned fire and sprayed all around him for good measure with the AK-47.

'Give me a fucking MP5,' she said, gutted that she'd only been issued a few pistols. They were good at short range but not accurate at the distance Fawaz was currently. They'd expected close combat. She needed something destructive. The bodyguard crawled to the back seat, making sure the VIPs were keeping low, and produced two pristine Heckler & Koch submachine guns. She snatched one, ducking from bullets pinging off the body armour.

'Drive!' she shouted. The bodyguard crawled into the driver's seat. Fawaz kept coming. Why wasn't he dead? He was so close now; he fired again and again, and a shot from behind sliced through his arm. More rounds split his shoulder and hand on his left side. There was hush in between rounds as, no doubt, the PM's bodyguards checked crossfire.

They were trapped by the other vehicles now, and Helen opened her door and got out, crouching behind the door. She brought the automatic up and took aim. She squeezed her left eye shut and aimed for his head, gently pressing the trigger, landing her first burst of ammunition. He went down, and she lowered her weapon.

But it wasn't over. They created a barricade of armed guards around the principal's car and waited. Distant screams and calls for help could be heard, as well as birds singing and an aeroplane up above.

Were there more attackers?

She wiped her brow as she waited, crouched behind the door of a support vehicle. The PM's car remained static, gas seeping from the hood, with all the windows and doors locked, as she'd told them. She caught the bodyguard's eye, and he nodded to her: they were okay.

It wasn't for her to judge who was in the right. Sir Conrad could have made the connection way before she did, but he probably didn't even remember signing the extradition form of an incidental Moroccan who he'd sent home to be electrocuted, beaten and probably sexually humiliated in some way.

She heard the familiar sirens of the gendarmes and emergency vehicles but kept watching the treeline, expecting more followers to emerge holding automatic weapons.

A helicopter buzzed overhead, and she looked up: it was the damn media. Ah well, if they got a close-up at least Grant would know she was alive. She heard a car door open and turned around angrily. It was Sir Conrad.

'Shouldn't you come back inside here?' he asked. She smiled weakly.

'Thank you, sir, but I think I prefer to be outside.' She turned away and heard the door slam. Later, as the emergency services arrived and the park was made secure,

Helen walked up to the body of Fawaz bin Nabil. She leant over and studied his face, realising that a photograph had fallen out his shirt pocket. It was of his son, Rafik.

Chapter 56

L'Aiguille du Midi cable car ascended through the clouds on its way to Mont Blanc. The sky seemed to shine a crisper blue up here at almost four thousand metres. They looked out of the window and seemed suspended above sheer rock as it scaled the peak up to the highest point reachable by transport. From there, one had to climb the final thousand metres to the glorious summit, but climbing wasn't on the agenda today. They'd both done it before and they watched as climbers and walkers, eager to tackle Europe's highest peak, gathered their thoughts excitedly and nervously at the same time. Mont Blanc wasn't a hill walk, though many had died thinking it might be.

The hairiest part of the cable-car journey was the final push, hanging underneath ancient rock, expecting it to fall down over one's head, bringing the tiny module with it. At the top, the clunking grew louder: enough to put anyone off trusting the rusty machinery that was covered in snow for half the year, and they filed out, thankful to have survived. There was a platform where tourists took photos that everyone flocked to: it was a cube of glass, suspended over the cliff edge high above Chamonix, and Helen had never done it. She supposed it was her army roots demanding control: Grant wouldn't do it either. They had to be in charge of their destinies, and standing on a pane of glass over a four-thousand-foot drop didn't cut it for either of them. Maybe why that's why they'd fallen apart over Luke's death.

They'd stayed in the Prince de Galle for three days after the events of the summit. After that, they'd both returned to London, agreeing to take a trip here, in the place where they'd skied as lovers and kept going back to. France had been the place they planned to settle once they were parents.

Grant soon returned to Algiers to sort out Khalil's security, and Helen had attended her parents' ruby wedding anniversary as guest of honour. Her parents' friends had bombarded her with questions about the attack on Versailles, despite the fact Helen had specifically asked her parents not to divulge her involvement. Fat chance. She told Grant the stories of how she'd had to sit with an audience of oldies listening to her describe how she'd saved the prime minister.

'Did he say thank you?'

'Are you getting a damehood?'

'Will you meet the Queen?'

'Are you going to retire now?'

And so it went.

Grant told her about Hakim and his recovery. About the reaction of Farid and Samir when they saw their big brother. Helen had watched the funerals of the seven people who died at Versailles, on a TV in a London bar. The footage of her pointing her weapon at the treeline as Sir Conrad opened the car door to ask her to come in, had gone viral, but no one recognised her. She ate a club sandwich and walked along the river.

The seven fatalities were three Afghan interpreters, when one of the drones fixed on the face of the new president of Afghanistan, there to discuss his country's future; and four security operators from Germany, who'd been checking last-minute details when the other drone detonated, when it successfully digitalised the face of the German chancellor, who'd had a suit jacket shoved over her head as she was forced to the ground in the moments of the carnage: that bodyguard died.

The news saw a seismic shift in counter terrorism, but Helen and Grant knew that it was just another piece in the hate puzzle. Attacks like it wouldn't stop because someone was horrified and people died. Would Sir Conrad have sought vengeance if his son had died the same way as Rafik did?

But they weren't here to weigh up political rights and wrongs.

They wore shorts and thin layers and applied plenty of sunscreen to combat the deceiving wind. Helen used a headband to keep her hair off her face. They wore sunglasses and strode away to the beginning of a rare walk on Mont Blanc that was relatively quiet. Few people knew about it. They were only made aware of it on an adventure training exercise they'd shared. The instructors scaled the peaks around here like mountain goats, but they also passed on their extraordinary knowledge.

No one would follow them where they were going.

Fawaz had had been pronounced dead at the scene in the Bois de Boulogne. Nabil Tradings was seized in name and assets by Operation Lionfish and the investigation was ongoing. Jean-Luc was rotting in a French prison somewhere near Calais, awaiting trial, and his mother was incarcerated in a female prison on the Swiss border. Ahmad Azzine had been shot by combined French and US security forces in the grounds of Versailles, along with six others, posing as caterers. The drones were constructed at night, in the great kitchen where she'd grabbed a sandwich. The catering company was fake and created by Nabil Tradings four years previously. Sniffer dogs hadn't picked up the scent of C4 explosives because the material was stable for days as it sat inside boxes of dried spices. New training methods were now being tested on bomb-detecting dogs for scenarios when filaments of explosive are not directly released into the air.

Mustafa cooperated with Interpol and was spared prison for his information on how the drones were armed with facial-recognition technology, which was already being developed into weapons by the US military. He and his wife entered the witness-protection programme over there and were given a new life in LA.

Sir Conrad Temple-Cray retired and was replaced by a woman. Colonel Palmer moved to a desk job at the MOD. Helen had been asked to join a new mission at Interpol, and Whitehall was considering it. Sylvia Drogan was promoted to chief commissioner back home in Ireland, and Peter Knowles accepted the post of head of SO15, Counter Terrorism Command, in London.

The vetting of the driver of the prime minister's car flagged up glaring anomalies: he'd been groomed by a cell on an estate in Wandsworth, then funded through college by money traced back to Morocco. He'd been the prime minister's driver for four years: the amount of time investigators reckoned Fawaz had taken to plot the attack. During the autopsy, the driver was found to have a tracking device in his rectum.

After two hours of walking, they stopped to listen to the wind and eat chocolate bars.

'Ready?' Grant asked her. She nodded. She opened her bag and took out a box. They'd been asked to donate Luke's body to medical science, but the thought of some scientist poking around their baby was too much, and they'd declined. The guilt was keen, but not as much as the pain. Their baby could have given valuable insight into one of the rarest diseases in foetuses, but they couldn't bring themselves to do it. Instead, they'd had a private service for him in the hospital chapel, which only she and Grant attended, and he'd been cremated. Now it was time to let go.

They stood as close to the cliff edge as they dared and opened the box together.

They looked out across the valley below and a carpet of cloud covered their view. The sun shone above them and glinted off the glass of the cable car descending beneath them. It disappeared and then the clouds parted, revealing blue sky to the north. They turned to one another and held the box between them, tipping it slightly, then more and more, until the contents caught the wind and floated away.

They held the box tightly and moved closer together. Helen turned to him and closed the box gently. She put her hand up to his face and wiped away his tears.

Acknowledgements

I'd like to thank two people in particular whose input was invaluable for me in inspiring this book. Firstly, Andrew Fleming for his incredible knowledge and vast experience. Secondly, to Vickie Long for her expertise and for sharing her fascinating background with me, despite being crazy busy.

I'd also like to thank Samantha Clynchard for her unfailing encouragement and support, especially over a small beer. I want to pay special honour to the military community, of which I was proudly part for sixteen years. It remains a unique inspiration for me and I value your continued friendship and approval.

Thanks to the whole Canelo team, especially my editors Louise and Siân, who push me to do my best. Also my agent Peter Buckman for his faith and tenacity. To my husband Mike for his tireless commitment to what I do, and my amazing children, Tilly and Freddie for making me so proud.

CANELO CRIME

Do you love crime fiction and are always on the lookout for brilliant authors?

Canelo Crime is home to some of the most exciting novels around. Thousands of readers are already enjoying our compulsive stories. Are you ready to find your new favourite writer?

Find out more and sign up to our newsletter at canelocrime.com